1
2
3
4
5
6
4-6
7
8
9
10
11
12
13

BY SAMANTHA SOTTO YAMBAO

Before Ever After

Love and Gravity

A Dream of Trees

The Beginning of Always

Water Moon

WATER

MOON

ウォータームーン

WATER MOON

A Novel

SAMANTHA SOTTO YAMBAO

DEL REY
NEW YORK

Water Moon is a work of fiction. Names, characters, places, and incidents either are products of the author's imagination or are used fictitiously. Any resemblance to actual events, locales, or persons, living or dead, is entirely coincidental.

Published in the United States by Del Rey, an imprint of Random House, a division of Penguin Random House LLC, New York.

DEL REY and the CIRCLE colophon are registered trademarks of Penguin Random House LLC.

Library of Congress Cataloging-in-Publication Data
Names: Sotto, Samantha, author.
Title: Water moon: a novel / Samantha Sotto Yambao.
Description: First edition. | New York: Del Rey, 2025.
Identifiers: LCCN 2024029832 (print) |
LCCN 2024029833 (ebook) | ISBN 9780593724996
(hardcover; acid-free paper) | ISBN 9780593725009 (ebook)
Subjects: LCGFT: Fantasy fiction. | Novels.
Classification: LCC PR9550.9.S68 W38 2025 (print) |
LCC PR9550.9.S68 (ebook) | DDC [FIC]—dc23
LC record available at https://lccn.loc.gov/2024029832
LC ebook record available at
https://lccn.loc.gov/2024029833

International ISBN 978-0-593-97408-7

Printed in the United States of America
on acid-free paper

randomhousebooks.com

1 3 5 7 9 8 6 4 2

First Edition

Endpaper illustrations by Haylee Morice
Origami design and instructions by nickorigami.com
Book design by Fritz Metsch

For everyone in search of new beginnings

落花枝に帰らず破鏡再び照らさず

PART ONE

The fallen blossom
cannot return to the branch.
A broken mirror cannot
be made to shine.

CHAPTER ONE

The Pawnshop of Almosts and Ifs

Time has no borders except those people make. On this particularly cold autumn day, Ishikawa Hana fashioned that border out of the thinnest layer of skin. Eyelids were useful that way. Because as long as she kept her eyelids shut, she could keep the two halves of her life apart: the twenty-one years she had lived before she opened her eyes, and all that was going to happen next.

She pulled her blanket over her head and pretended that her hungover first morning as the pawnshop's new owner had yet to begin. It didn't matter that she was now wide awake, that the last of a tangled string of dreams she could not remember had unraveled more than an hour ago. Her head felt heavier and her mouth drier than usual, but she figured that this was less on account of the alcohol she'd had the night before than on what awaited her.

In a few moments, her father, Toshio, was going to knock on her door to start their day.

Hana insisted on clinging to the tiny hope that the unwise amount of sake they had celebrated his retirement with was going to keep him in bed a little longer. This hope—if it indeed could be called hope given its size—was smaller than a mossy river pebble and just as slippery.

In all the years that the pawnshop had been in Toshio's charge, there were only two occasions when it had not opened on time. On both those days, it had not opened at all. But Hana and her father didn't talk about those two days. Ever.

If their pawnshop were like other ordinary pawnshops that traded in diamonds, silver, and gold, the Ishikawa family, who had run the pawnshop for generations, might have had the luxury of sick days and weekends. But Toshio had trained Hana to appraise far more valuable treasure.

They found their best clients when summer ended and the nights grew colder and longer. Melancholy was good for business. It didn't matter that their little shop, tucked along a quiet alley of Tokyo's Asakusa district, didn't have a name. Those who required its services always managed to find it. But, if anyone was curious enough to ask Hana what she thought the pawnshop should be called, she had a ready answer. Ikigai. There was no other word that suited it more.

Hana was a little more than a year old when she learned to walk on the shop's dark wooden floors, and every step she had taken since then had been toward taking over the shop when her father retired. He was a widower, and she was his only heir. The pawnshop was her life's path, her singular purpose. Her ikigai. But not once, in all the time that she had played as a toddler at her father's feet or worked by his side as a young woman, had any of their clients bothered to inquire what the pawnshop's name was. They had far more urgent questions darting behind their eyes when Toshio welcomed them with a polite bow. The first was almost always about where they were, and the second about how they had gotten there.

After all, no one expected to find a pawnshop behind a ramen restaurant's door.

Anyone who stood in line outside the long-standing popular restaurant would tell you that its shoyu ramen was the best in the Taitō prefecture. For some, the wafting scent of steaming bowls of chijirimen noodles and perfectly braised slices of pork belly swimming in a dark and rich bone broth made waiting easier. For others, it made their time in the snaking queue feel twice as long. Still, they all drew deep breaths, taking their fill of the air's savory promise until it was their turn to enter the cramped dining room that might have been considered modern two decades ago. Yellowed walls plastered with autographed photos of the restaurant's celebrity clientele welcomed them as they weaved their way to empty seats. But, despite stepping through its door, some of the hungry did not make it into the restaurant's dining room. Instead, they were greeted by a pawnshop's dimly lit front office and the tinkling of a little copper door chime.

The memory of that chime rang in Hana's head as she curled beneath her blanket. It commanded her to rise and accept the inevitable. She clamped her palms over her ears and fought a losing battle to keep her mind from getting out of bed ahead of her. Some of her thoughts were already almost dressed, fastening the last buttons of the pawnshop's crisp black suit uniform. Others were already at the office beneath her room, imagining how her father was going to spend the first day of his retirement: hovering close, double-checking everything she did.

He would not say anything if he caught a mistake. He never did. The slightest twitch of his right eyebrow sufficed. Toshio preferred silence to words, reserving his energy and breath for his clients. Hana had become rather adept at interpreting his quiet breathing, half smiles, and glances. Her only memory of him losing his temper was of the stormy afternoon when she was ten and had misplaced a pawned antique watch. His eyes had grown darker than the clouds churning above their home's courtyard garden, and when he gripped her by her thin shoulders and lowered his mouth to her ear, her heart dropped to her toes. His voice was as quiet as the breeze, but his words howled inside Hana louder than any typhoon.

Find it.

Now.

Hana did not know what would have happened if she had not found the watch later that day behind a stack of books in the back room. All she was certain of was that she never wanted to hear her father speak to her that way again.

Hana drew a ragged breath, reeling her thoughts back to the present. An invisible weight pushed down on her chest. She had expected her future to feel heavier, or at least heavier than a well-fed cat, but instead the pile of days teetering on top of her chest felt as light as a mountain made of mere husks, each hollowed out and spent before it began. She knew every second of the days that lay ahead of her by heart. After all, she'd spent her life watching her father live them. And now her father's life was hers, and from here on, nothing was ever going to be new.

She rolled to her side. The edge of a yellowed photograph peeked from under her pillow. Hana pulled the faded photo out and squinted at it beneath her blanket. The eyes of a young woman who could have been her twin gazed back at her. "Good morning, Okaa-san," Hana greeted the mother she never knew and tucked the only picture she had of her back into its hiding place. She pulled her blanket off and peeped through her dark lashes. A sliver of sunlight pierced her irises. She squeezed her eyes shut and pushed herself out of bed. She didn't need to see to navigate her bedroom. This room and the pawnshop beneath it made up her entire world, and today, that world felt even smaller.

And quiet.

Hana cocked her head, straining to hear the familiar clinking of cups and bowls from the kitchen downstairs. But only silence seeped through her door. She bit her bottom lip.

Retirement, she was certain, would not be enough to keep a man like Toshio from his rituals. Though the small shrine her father kept in their home honored the spirits, the god her father really worshiped was routine. The steaming cup of roasted green tea he had every morning was sacred, no matter how much sake or whiskey swam inside him from the night before.

Hana pressed her ear to her door. There were only two possible reasons the pawnshop was this quiet, and neither of them was good.

CHAPTER TWO

Ishikawa Toshio's Last Client

❀ *The day before*

Autumn had come early, and since its arrival, the number of the pawnshop's customers had doubled.

Toshio shifted his weight, relieving the bunion on his left foot. His stomach growled twice through his black suit. He ignored it and adjusted his tie. This was not the first day he had been too busy to have lunch, but it was going to be his last. When they closed shop in less than an hour, he was going to be officially retired and would never have to work through lunch again. He had expected the thought to make him smile, but the corners of his mouth refused to be persuaded to curl the slightest angle upward. A copper bell tinkled, heralding the arrival of his last customer.

"Irasshaimase." Toshio bowed with a practiced smile, his voice smooth like warmed sake.

Hana peeked out from the back room with this month's record book tucked under her arm. Toshio waved her back inside and turned his attention to the elegant woman who had just walked through their door. "How may I help you?"

The woman met Toshio's smile with a bewildered look. Though her porcelain features made her appear to be younger than Toshio, her hair, tied in a loose knot at her nape, shared the color of the single strand of white freshwater pearls she wore around her neck. "I'm so sorry. I made a mistake. I thought that the line outside was for the ramen restaurant."

"It is," Toshio said.

The woman glanced around the room. "This is the restaurant?"

"No. This is my pawnshop."

"Is the restaurant upstairs?"

Toshio shook his head. "It is not."

A wrinkle deepened across the woman's handsome forehead.

"You must be tired from standing in line this whole time. Perhaps you'd like to sit for a while?" Toshio gestured to a low table surrounded by a set of silk floor cushions in a corner of the room.

The woman tilted her chin and touched her thin lips. "I . . . I could have sworn that this was the restaurant. I watched the man in line in front of me walk through its door. I saw tables and chairs and . . ." She dipped her head in a small bow. "I am sorry for bothering you."

"There is no need to apologize. May I offer you something to drink? Some tea?"

"Thank you, but I—"

"Please, I insist. It is no trouble at all." Toshio walked out from behind the counter and called over his shoulder, "Hana? Will you bring out some tea? We have a guest."

Hana shut the record book and stood up from a desk that had once belonged to her mother. She knew her cue as well as she knew the single thought presently rolling around the woman's mind.

Tea. At this point in their conversation with her father, all clients pondered the same thing. It was a simple thought, small and as light as air, without any sharp edges they could cut themselves on. They had all drunk tea before and remembered how it washed over their tongues, slipped down their throats, and warmed their souls. No harm had ever come from a cup of tea, and they could not think of a single reason to refuse the pawnshop owner's kind offer. If anything, it would be impolite to say no, seeing as they had been the ones who had mistakenly wandered into his shop. They tried to remember where they had been headed in the first place, but the most they could recall was feeling a cold emptiness in their stomachs. Tea could soothe that. Perhaps it was tea that they had been standing in line for all along. Hana filled a kettle with water and set it on the stove.

"Tea would be nice." The woman nodded with a smile.

"Wonderful. My name is Ishikawa Toshio." He gestured to a floor cushion. "Please, have a seat."

"Thank you." The woman settled onto a cushion that was the same shade of gray as the day outside. "I am Takeda Izumi."

"Thank you for choosing to visit us today, Takeda-sama. I am certain that you will find that we make very fair, if not generous, offers at this pawnshop."

"But I'm not here to . . ." Izumi rolled a pearl from her necklace between her forefinger and thumb, her brow furrowed as though she were rummaging through drawers inside her head, trying to find what she had meant to say next.

Hana carried over their tea on a black lacquer tray.

"Hana, this is Takeda-sama," Toshio said.

Hana bowed. "Welcome to our pawnshop. Please enjoy your tea," she said, setting the tray on the table.

Izumi turned to Toshio as Hana took her leave. "You have a lovely daughter, Ishikawa-san."

"Thank you. She takes after her . . ." Toshio banished his next words with a stiff smile.

He anchored his eyes on their tea and poured it into small clay bowls. The bowls were the color of the calmest sea, but cracks of varying sizes crawled over their glaze. If not for the kintsugi technique used to repair them, they would have fallen apart. Gold dust and lacquer filled the cracks, streaking over the bowls like lightning.

"Those are exquisite," Izumi said, admiring the bowls.

"Thank you. I was rather upset with myself for tripping and dropping them, but in this instance, I will admit that I am grateful for my clumsiness." Toshio handed Izumi her tea. "Broken things have a unique kind of beauty, don't you think?"

Izumi traced the bowl's delicate gold joinery with the tip of a perfectly manicured finger. "Some things wear their damage better than others," she said softly, so softly it was as if she were worried that her voice might shatter the bowl.

"I have found beauty in all manner of broken things. Chairs. Buildings. People."

Izumi looked up from her tea. "People?"

"Especially people. They shatter in the most fascinating ways. Every dent, scratch, and crack tells a story. Invisible scars hide the deepest wounds and are the most interesting."

Izumi twisted one of her two large diamond rings around her finger, pulling on her skin. "That is a very unique point of view, Ishikawa-san."

"Oh, it is more than a point of view. It is the very reason I run this business. This is a different kind of pawnshop, Takeda-sama. We are not in the business of trading trinkets. Diamond rings and pearl necklaces have no value here."

* * *

Hana listened in on Izumi and her father from the back room. She had heard the same conversation carried on over tea more times than she could count.

But no matter how many times he said those words, her father always sounded sincere. For the most part, he told their clients the truth, regardless of how hard the truth was for them to believe. While what he shared with the clients, in her opinion, was not by any means a staggering revelation, it always took them a few moments to wrestle their eyebrows down. This was understandable. On the other side of the ramen restaurant's door, up was up, down was down, and pawnshops such as this one did not exist. Her father's special skill, as Takeda Izumi was about to learn, was to, in the time it took her to finish her tea, convince her to let go of everything she was brought up to believe and allow her mind to grasp what her hands could not.

Hana strode back to her desk and picked up a book from the pile on top of it. It was a dog-eared paperback whose pages clung to its spine by sheer will. A client named Ito Daisuke had pawned it that morning. She checked the item against the list in her record book and put a little tick mark when she confirmed that everything was in order. It was her favorite among the items that had found their way into the pawnshop that day.

Hana pulled out her mother's old gold-rimmed glasses from a desk drawer. She put the glasses on, adjusted them over her nose, and, through its lenses, saw the book for what it really was: a choice that had changed the course of Ito Daisuke's life.

Its true form was much prettier than that of a book. It had traded its pages for feathers made of wisps of light, transforming into a glowing songbird. It perched on Hana's finger, its colors constantly shifting between blue and gold.

Once, this bird had sung brightly inside Daisuke while he

worked on writing a mystery novel every night for five years, after his shift as a convenience store clerk. When he had abandoned it and deleted all his unfinished drafts two years ago, the bird dimmed, grew silent, and turned as black as coal. It pecked at his gut whenever he thought about the series of fictional Harajuku murders he was never going to solve. But now Daisuke had pawned his choice, and he was free. There were going to be times when he would feel a cold emptiness where the choice had once lived, but these would pass. He was not going to remember this choice, or this pawnshop, or the man who had persuaded him to part with a battered mystery novel. Peace of mind, Toshio had told him, was worth the price of never knowing what happened after page 254.

Hana took the glasses off and made room for Daisuke's book on a shelf next to a set of house keys and a plane ticket torn in two. That evening, when the pawnshop closed, her father would take all the items from the shelf and store them in the vault, together with the rest of the day's acquisitions.

Takeda Izumi blinked, trying to comprehend the words that hung in the air over two cracked bowls of tea. "That doesn't make any sense. How can people pawn choices?"

" 'Sense' is relative," Toshio said. "There are things that make sense in your world that are ridiculous in mine. I have never been able to understand the purpose of televisions or telephones."

"What do you mean by 'your world'?"

"You come from the world outside that door. My daughter and I are from the world inside it. Whenever anyone from your side finds their way to our pawnshop, there is always a good reason for it. Our clients have choices that have become too burdensome to carry. We take these choices off their hands so that they may return to their world lighter. Content."

"Is this a joke?"

"I would not make jokes about such things. We do important work here."

Izumi grabbed her bag. "I do not know what kind of game this is, but it is not amusing."

"It is not a game, and it is not meant to be amusing. I cannot force you to stay, but I do know that no one finds the pawnshop by accident. If you had no need for our services, you would have opened that door and walked into the ramen restaurant just like all the other customers waiting in line outside."

Izumi pulled her shoulders back and lifted her chin. "Assuming that what you are saying is true, which it is not, I still would not require your services. I do not have any regrets."

"I apologize if I have offended you, Takeda-sama." Toshio bowed his head. "But I have been doing this job for a very long time. I can tell when people are happy and when they are not, regardless of how well they are dressed or how bright their smile is. Happiness has little to do with what you have, and everything to do with what you do not."

Izumi tightened her grip on her bag. "You do not know anything about me."

"Perhaps. But what I do know is what I have learned from the collective experience of the generations of my family who have run this pawnshop. Every client who has passed through our door has insisted that they stumbled into our little establishment because they were lost. And they were right. Losing your way is oftentimes the only way to find something you did not know you were looking for."

"I know perfectly well what I was looking for today. Ramen."

"There are many good ramen restaurants in the city. Why were you looking for this restaurant in particular?"

"I used to live in this neighborhood when I was younger. I ate at this restaurant all the time."

"But surely you must have had better ramen since then?"

"Yes, of course, but—"

"And I am certain that a woman such as yourself could easily afford an establishment with better ambience."

Izumi twirled her pearls around her neck, her eyes fixed on her tea.

"But this restaurant isn't like just any other restaurant, is it?" Toshio said.

Izumi looked away.

"Do not worry, Takeda-sama. I have no intentions of prying. I do not need to. I already know why you decided to visit the restaurant today."

Izumi's thin brows shot up.

"You said that you used to frequent this restaurant when you were younger." Toshio clasped his hands over the table. "People revisit the past to relive pleasant memories, chase away bad ones, or both."

"Since you seem to think that you know me so well and are unwilling to accept my simple desire to eat ramen as my only explanation for being here, would you care to share which of these reasons you believe is mine?" Izumi said.

"You came to the restaurant to dine with a ghost."

"That's . . ." Izumi's voice caught in her throat. "That's nonsense."

"So you were joining a friend for a meal, then?"

"Well . . . I . . . no. I was going to eat alone. I like coming here by myself. I visit at least once every autumn."

"But no one ever really dines alone, do they?" Toshio said. "Our thoughts share our meals with us. They keep us company whether we invite them to or not and are especially noisy when they are the only ones at our table. They chatter about all the things we cannot say aloud. In your case, I would guess that they like to reminisce about a time when you were not the woman you are today, a time, perhaps, when you liked to share your table at the ramen restaurant with someone else."

"Stop."

"You argue with your thoughts and insist that they are wrong, but they keep on going until your ramen turns cold. But that does not stop you from coming back whenever you have the chance, because a cold bowl of ramen still tastes better than any hot meal in your home."

"Stop." Tears welled in Izumi's eyes and streamed down her pale cheeks. "Please, stop."

"I'm sorry. You asked me a question and I answered it. There are many things that I wish I did not know, but after spending a lifetime at this pawnshop, I can read the stories of my clients as though they were written on their faces."

Izumi dried her eyes. "I am not your client."

"You are correct." Toshio laced his fingers. "I have not yet decided if what you wish to exchange is of any value."

"Enough. I'm tired of your games." Fresh tears filled her eyes. "Who are you?"

"I am simply a man who offers a unique service to those who require it, a man who can tell that you are crying not because you are sad, but because you are angry. But not at me. You wish you were, but you are not. You were furious even before you set foot inside this pawnshop."

Izumi glared at him, color rising over her neck. "Of course

I'm angry. I hate that I have every reason to be happy and yet all I feel are the cracks spreading inside me each time I force myself to smile. Is that what you wanted me to say? Is this what you want me to pawn? A broken smile patched with gold like one of your tea bowls? Because if you will take it, I will give it to you right now."

"So you believe what I have told you about the pawnshop?"

"Prove it. Make me believe."

"Very well. Show me your choice and I will tell you what it is worth."

"Show you? How? A choice isn't something you keep in your pocket or purse."

"You carry around all the decisions you have ever made in your life, Takeda-sama. This choice is no different," Toshio said. "And I think that you already know exactly where to find it."

CHAPTER THREE

Bus Fare

A compact mirror. A gold tube of matte lipstick. House keys. Takeda Izumi found that, as a rule, you had to shove aside at least three things in your handbag before finding what you were looking for.

She pushed her keys away. A red leather coin purse hid behind a packet of unscented hand wipes. She pulled it out, just as she had done each time she needed to pay for her favorite sweets at the konbini on the ground floor of her apartment building. She didn't trust herself to keep a supply at home and preferred to treat herself whenever she had collected enough loose change. It had been easier to keep her figure when she was younger, but now even the most furtive glance at the imagawayaki stall she passed by on her way to the flower shop she owned made her gain weight. Still, there were days when the scent of freshly made stuffed pancakes proved too hard to resist. The ones filled with a sweet red bean paste were her favorite. She skipped dinner on those days. Fortunately, her husband didn't mind eating alone. Sometimes, he even seemed to prefer it.

It would have been different if they had had children. Izumi imagined that they would have meals together at the same time every night, their son politely answering questions about his day. Their daughter, the chattier of the two, would giggle softly when she shared stories about her friends. Her husband would eat without speaking, nodding occasionally when he thought that someone said something interesting. Izumi tried to picture him talking more, but after almost three decades of marriage, her thoughts were not as malleable as they used to be. She didn't mind. Only people who still had dreams required a good imagination.

Living without a dream made things simpler. Routine was a good substitute for anything life lacked. If you planned it well enough, it could whisk you from the moment you opened your eyes in the morning to the second right before you drifted off to sleep without leaving any room for daydreams, yellowed wishes, or dusty thoughts. Izumi almost enjoyed her daily schedule of running her little flower shop, heading home in time to make dinner for Yoshi, and stopping by the konbini to replenish the little stash of sweets in her handbag.

But today, she pulled out her coin purse from her bag for an entirely different purpose. A strange pawnbroker had asked to see a choice she had made a lifetime ago, and for a reason she was never going to be able to put into words, she knew that it was tucked inside her coin purse, jingling with her change.

Izumi unzipped the purse and made a quick mental calculation. She rummaged through her coins and plucked an amount equivalent to the bus fare she'd needed to get from her childhood home to the ramen restaurant. She laid the coins on the table.

It was not enough coins to pay for the same trip today, but years ago, she would have been able to buy a bus ticket and still have enough change left over to buy a couple of her favorite sweets. And back then, she didn't have to worry about gaining weight. Because, unlike her husband, Junichiro loved her, whatever shape she was. It was Junichiro, after all, who was directly responsible for her dresses fitting more snugly, ever since they had started meeting twice a week at the ramen shop where he worked.

It was a long time ago now that Junichiro had left the ramen shop, but all these years later, Izumi still visited it when the trees turned a reddish gold and the ramen's savory steam mingled with the chill in the air. She liked to draw the scent as deep as she could into her lungs, warming herself with old memories of easy smiles and easier conversations. Today had been one such autumn day, but this time, a pawnshop had taken the restaurant's place.

"May I?" Toshio gestured to the coins Izumi had laid on the table between them. He picked them up and felt their weight. "They are heavier than they look. Most choices are. I need to examine them more closely to give you a fair price." Toshio plucked an old pair of glasses from his shirt pocket and set them on his nose. They were identical to his wife's, except that his were rimmed in silver, hers in gold. His made him look like an owl.

"I do not care about the price. Just take it."

"I am afraid it does not work that way. If I did not give you something in return, you would forever wonder what it was you left behind." Toshio examined each coin and nodded slowly. "I understand," he said, shifting to a tone that was softer and gentler.

"What do you understand?"

"Why you did not take the bus all those years ago and meet Junichiro at the ramen restaurant as you had agreed to."

Izumi lowered her eyes. "I . . . did not have a choice."

"And yet, here it is." Toshio arranged the coins in a straight line on the table.

"I was—"

"You do not need to explain. I have examined your coins. I know the choice you made and why you made it."

"You must think that I am a horrible person."

"I think that you are a client who needs our services. I am sure that you are tired of carrying this choice around."

"My husband is a good, loyal man. He deserves a wife who does not live in the past."

"Do you love him?"

Izumi stared at her hands.

"Does he love you?"

"Love is something that people are taught to want. But all we really need is to not be alone when we come home and to have someone to wave goodbye to us at the door when we leave."

"And that is more than what many people have." A smile that made Toshio look older and tired found his lips. "I think that you will be very pleased with the value of your choice. I can take it off your hands right now and you will never crave ramen in the fall again."

Hana wrapped a small wooden box in a silk cloth that looked like spring. She had painted the flowers on the silk herself, striving to make each wrapped box look unique even if their contents were exactly the same. Her father never varied what he offered in exchange for his clients' choices, no matter their worth. Each box contained the same amount of green tea.

When she was younger, her father made a game of hiding the tea boxes around their home, leaving all manner of clues for her to find. Riddles tucked inside empty sake bottles. Math puzzles folded into origami foxes. A chipped vase that was out of place. Nothing could be overlooked. His little scavenger hunts kept her happily occupied while he was busy doing inventory or attending to clients. She often caught him trying to bite down a smile when his clues tricked her into going left instead of right. In time, she got better at solving his puzzles even if, at first glance, they didn't seem like clues at all. Toshio took particular pride in the clues he hid in plain sight.

These clues were Hana's first lesson in the art of dealing with clients. Just like looking for her father's clues, with practice and a good eye you could always find the truth a client tried to hide as clearly as any feature on their face. But Hana had never thought of her little treasure hunts as lessons. Instead, she liked to pretend that the boxes she found were presents from her late mother, and each clue a secret code for *I love you, I miss you,* and *I will see you again.*

Hana had chosen one of her favorite wrapping cloth designs for Takeda Izumi. Izumi appeared to be the age her mother would have been were she still alive. Based on the sole photograph Hana had of her mother, Izumi and her mother shared the same face shape and thin lips. Their eyes were different, but that was okay. Hana knotted the silk twice, placed the tea box on a lacquer tray, and headed to the front office where Takeda Izumi was waiting.

Izumi admired the garden painted over the silk wrapping. A smile spread over her lips even if she still had no idea what was inside it.

"Please open it," Toshio said.

Izumi untied the silk knot, letting the cloth puddle around a simple wooden box. She lifted its lid. A fresh, green scent, blended into the sweet fragrance of candied fruit, wafted out of it. Izumi's smile brightened at the smell and the sight of the dark green leaves it came from. Gyokuro. It was the highest grade of tea, carefully grown in shaded plantations. Brewing it required as much care, but Izumi looked forward to every meticulous step. Taking the time to coax its flavors out was worth the luxury of escaping into them.

"I hope it is to your liking," Toshio said. "This is the standard exchange for all the items brought to the pawnshop."

"Standard? Then why did you have to examine my choice?"

"To check if it was worth this tea."

"I could have just bought this tea myself."

"You could have, and it would probably taste wonderful. But it would not be this tea that I am offering you now. It would not be the tea that you are taking in exchange for a choice that broke your life in two. It would not be the tea that you will finally be able to enjoy without your mind drifting back to a ramen shop and the memory of the man who waits inside it. I may send all my clients home with this tea, but it will no longer be the same tea once they sip it from their cups."

"What do you mean?"

"No two people unshackle themselves from the same choice. Each person has his own idea of what freedom tastes like. For you, it might be soothing and warm like the joy of staring out the window on a rainy day, not wanting to be anywhere else. For my next client, it might taste like courage, intoxicating and darkly sweet."

Izumi closed the box.

"Do you agree to this exchange?" Toshio said.

"This pain is all I have left of Junichiro. I have lived with it for so long that I do not think I will be able to recognize myself without it."

"Then consider this your opportunity to find out."

"But what if I change my mind? What if I want my choice back?"

"This is a pawnshop, not a store. If you wish to retrieve your choice, all you have to do is pay me back."

Izumi exhaled, relaxing her shoulders. "Good."

"With interest."

"What kind of interest do you pay on tea?"

"We can talk about that if you change your mind, but if you did, you would be the first."

"None of your clients have ever come back to claim their choice?"

"Not one," Toshio said. "And if choices are left unclaimed at the end of the week, the pawnshop keeps them."

Izumi chewed on her lower lip. "That does not seem like a very long time."

"How long does it take you to decide whether or not you feel like smiling? I am not forcing you to make this exchange, Takeda-sama. If you are having any doubts, you are free to take your choice and make your way back to the ramen restaurant."

"Will I be able to find you again?"

"I have no power over who walks through the pawnshop's door."

"So this may be my last chance to leave this choice behind."

"Yes."

"Then I will take your tea."

"Are you certain?"

"Certain?" A dry laugh escaped her lips. "I do not think I know what that word means anymore. Not since I opened a ramen restaurant's door and walked into this pawnshop. I am not even sure if any of this is real or if all of this is just a strange dream. The only thing I do know is that I cannot carry around another regret. If this is real, then I am not here by chance. I was meant to meet you and make this trade."

"Then it is done. The tea is yours. Enjoy it in good health."

"What? Just like that?"

"Yes. Just like that. We keep things simple here. There is nothing left for you to do." Toshio collected Izumi's coins from the table.

"I do not feel any different."

"The change will happen when you return to your world."

"What if it does not work?"

"You did not purchase a radio or a clock, Takeda-sama. You made a simple exchange. There are no moving parts that will get stuck or fall apart."

Izumi carefully tucked the box of tea into her bag. "Thank you."

Toshio bowed with a smile.

Izumi walked to the door and closed her hand around its worn brass knob. She twisted it and pulled, opening the door by a crack. She paused and turned to face Toshio. "Ishikawa-san?"

"Yes?"

"I was so preoccupied thinking about getting rid of my choice that I never bothered to ask why you wanted it. Why do you collect choices? Of what possible use could they be to you?"

CHAPTER FOUR

Sake and Silence

A hint of honeydew lingered over her tongue as Hana drained her third cup of sake. She held her alcohol better than most, a skill that her father took full credit for.

If her mother had been alive or if Toshio had any friends to go out drinking with, their nightly routine might have been different. Instead, Toshio seemed perfectly content to simply have Hana sit quietly across from him at the table, keeping him company while they drank sake until his eyelids grew too heavy to keep open. Their evenings were filled with more silent sips than conversation, but Hana still thought it was a fair exchange. Waiting made the night feel longer, and she was grateful for anything that kept the morning away.

But on the eve of her father's retirement, not even the longest pauses or slowest sips did anything to lengthen the hour.

"Hana," Toshio said, setting a wrapped box on the table. "This is for you."

"For me?" Hana stared at the box. She recognized the wrapping cloth as one she had recently painted.

"A small token to celebrate the next chapter of your life."

"Thank you, Otou-san." Her father was a practical man, and so it did not surprise Hana that he had gifted her a box of tea from the stock meant for their clients. The memory it conjured of the treasure hunts of her childhood made up for any creativity the gift lacked. Her father did not have to say anything for Hana to know his intent. His eyes, slightly misty with tears, said everything.

"Do you remember what I tell our clients about tea?"

"It tastes different for every person."

"That rule applies to you too. You have known this tea all your life, but tomorrow, when you sip your first cup as the new owner of this pawnshop, you might be surprised at how many things will change, even if, on the surface, they look exactly the same. Do you think you are ready for it?"

"Tonight is not about me, Otou-san. It is your retirement that we are celebrating."

"Endings and beginnings are the same point in time. Tonight is as significant to you as it is to me," he said. "Perhaps even more. I can tell that you have a lot on your mind."

Hana wrapped her fingers around the tea box, trying to find some comfort in the cool folds of its silk. "Did it . . ." Hana looked away, deciding to keep her thoughts to herself.

"Go on."

"Did it make you happy?"

"Did what?"

"This pawnshop."

"I see." Toshio nodded slowly, pouring sake into his cup. "Tomorrow, the pawnshop will be your responsibility, and you wonder if it will make you feel as miserable as you believe it made me."

"No . . . no . . . Otou-san, that is not what I meant." Heat flared in Hana's cheeks. "I did not say that."

"Since when did we need words to tell each other exactly how we feel? I would not be passing the pawnshop on to you if you had failed to learn that lesson. We would lose half of our business if we could not hear all the words clients did not say out loud.

"You have a gift for reading our clients, Hana. You can read them almost as well as you read me. My work here has never been about trying to be happy. We both know what the pawnshop is really for, what service we actually provide."

Hana stared at her reflection in the window. "Do you ever envy them, Otou-san?"

"Envy who?"

"Our clients. I know that I should not, but sometimes I—"

Toshio slammed his sake cup on the table. "Do I need to remind you about what happened to your mother?"

Hana lowered her head, swallowing hard. "She stole a choice from the vault."

Toshio lifted Hana's chin, forcing her to meet his eyes. "And?"

"And paid for her crime with her life."

Toshio set his hands on the table and exhaled a sigh that echoed in his chest. When he spoke again, his tone shifted to the gentle one he reserved for more anxious clients. "I know that you do not want this life. You never have. It is the cruelest of duties, but it is also the most important one."

"I know, Otou-san. I know."

"I was not the husband your mother deserved, and neither have I been the best father to you. But I have run this pawnshop as well as I could and have tried to train you to do the same. It is all I know and all I can give you. I failed your mother in the worst possible way, but I hope that I have taught you better.

"Tomorrow, this pawnshop will be yours, and with it, all its rules and consequences. I will not always be around to protect you, Hana. Promise me that you will not repeat your mother's mistake. You can forget every lesson I ever taught you, but you must never forget that the only choice we are allowed to make in this world is between death or—"

"Fate." Hana bowed her head. "I will not forget."

Hana stumbled into bed, her head spinning. She couldn't tell if it was the sake or her father's words that made her dizzy. It was difficult to decide whether what he said sounded like a warning or a goodbye. Hana was more familiar with the former than most people. Her mother's ghost lived in every room of their home, reminding Hana about what happened to those who broke the pawnshop's most important rule: *Forget.*

Toshio had taught Hana to say the word before any other, making her repeat it like a prayer when they opened the pawnshop for business in the morning and locked up at night. Once the pawned choices were inside their vault, Hana had to push them completely from her mind. It didn't matter how bright, beautiful, or fascinating they were.

The new owners, who came every new moon to collect the choices of the shop's clients, did not like to share these precious finds. This, Hana thought, was the real reason why her father kept the vault hidden behind a bookshelf in the pawnshop's back room. Wandering thoughts were the stealthiest of thieves, and Hana was never allowed to forget the consequences of dwelling on choices that could never be hers. But while warnings were nothing new to her, she did not have much experience with farewells. Her father was as constant as the moon, except for that one silent morning when he was not.

It had been eight months since Hana had found Toshio lying

motionless at the bottom of the stairs after his heart attack. The image remained etched behind her eyelids. It was the last thing she saw before she sank into sleep and the first thing that greeted her when her dreams ended. Toshio's heart had never fully recovered. Neither had Hana's. Her chest tightened whenever he looked tired or short of breath. So when Hana awoke to nothing but the sound of her thoughts on the first day of his retirement, she imagined the worst. She hurried to his bedroom, not bothering to wear her slippers.

The door was ajar.

"Otou-san?" Hana peeked inside.

An empty bed stared back at her. Hana rushed to the stairs, holding her breath.

The stairway and landing were empty. Hana exhaled. Her father, she told herself, had probably been just as anxious about her first day in charge of their family business as she was and had gone downstairs to the pawnshop early. Hana took her time going down the steps, conjuring images of Toshio reviewing her record books and checking their inventory of tea.

This was a far more pleasant explanation for their home's silence than the second possibility Hana was struggling to shove out of her mind. She was too young to remember that particular quiet morning when her mother had died, but when she was old enough to understand, Toshio described to her the day of her mother's execution for the first and last time.

Hana reached the bottom of the steps and stubbed her toe on something small and hard. A lidless wooden tea box skittered over the floor and crashed into her father's overturned desk. A pale stream of sunlight revealed the rest of the chaos at her feet. Record books strewn everywhere. Chairs knocked over. Glass shelves shattered. Hana staggered back and tripped over the stairs. White heat exploded in her tailbone.

Hana bit down a yelp and scrambled to stand. Her eyes flew around the ransacked pawnshop and fell on the trail of sunlight that led over the floorboards, across the room, and out a wide-open front door.

CHAPTER FIVE

The Vault

No one in line on the other side of the dark-stained hardwood front door had any idea what was asked of it. While other doors were tasked to keep in and out apart, this door that stood between a hungry crowd and a pawnshop most of them would never see bore a far greater responsibility.

The door was, to Hana's knowledge, the only door in the whole history of doors that had been built to keep an entire world safe. And now it was open, allowing another world's dawn to trespass into Hana's home.

Hana sprinted toward the door, not caring about the toppled shelves and glass shards in her way. She slammed the door shut and leaned against it, blood thundering in her ears. She crumpled to the floor and hugged her knees to her chest.

A glint of gold next to the doorway caught her eye. She inhaled sharply and reached for it. Her fingers instantly recognized the object's weight and shape.

Hana held up her mother's old glasses, checking for any damage. It was almost a miracle how possibly the most fragile thing in the entire pawnshop had made it all the way from her locked desk drawer to the front door unscathed. Hana could only hope to find her father in a similar condition.

The only thing worse than thinking about how a stranger had broken into and ransacked their pawnshop was imagining what could have happened when Toshio stumbled in on him. As desperately as she tried, she could not convince herself that her father knew the difference between being brave and being foolish. Hana pushed herself off the floor and ran to the one place in the pawnshop that could have kept him safe.

The trees of the tsubo-niwa rustled in the breeze behind the pawnshop's back door. The small courtyard garden was Hana's favorite part of their home, a place where, when the night was clear, the moon swam in their small koi pond.

But the moon was still a full day away from rising, and Hana's destination was not the tsubo-niwa, but the bookcase that stood next to the pawnshop's back door. She ran her fingers along the side of the bookcase and grazed a notch in the wood. She pushed the notch and stepped back. The bookcase swung open, revealing a wall of solid stone. Hana hooked her mother's glasses over her ears. A thick timber door appeared in front of her. A muffled chorus of birdsong trickled from behind it, beckoning Hana inside.

The vault was not a place Hana frequented. Her father took on the sole responsibility of storing their acquisitions in it. If he had been in any danger, the vault, Hana guessed, was where he would have sought refuge.

The vault could be seen only through Toshio's or her mother's glasses and expanded and contracted as required. Three autumns ago, it had grown three times as large as the pawnshop. One slow summer, it was smaller than her room. Here, pawned choices perched inside rows of tagged hanging wooden cages, singing the same, unchanging song. When she was a little girl, she thought that it was the most beautiful song in the world. Later, she came to realize that it was the saddest. It was a song of farewell to the owners who had left them behind, and now, as Hana stepped inside the vault to search for Toshio, she could not shake the feeling that they were singing for him too.

The glow of more than a hundred birds surrounded her, brightening and dimming to the rhythm of their song. Hana did not pause to listen. She sprinted between the rows of cages as shadows danced over her face. "Otou-san?"

Frenzied chirping drowned out her voice. The birds' feathers grew brighter, illuminating the breadth and length of the vault. Hana's eyes darted around the room. Toshio was not inside it. Strength drained from Hana's legs. She dropped to her knees. Wood dug into her shin. Hana glanced down. Pieces of a shattered birdcage littered the floor, the choice it had once held gone. A hand-painted playing card and the cage's crumpled tag lay next to a broken perch. Hana snatched them up.

The card was from Toshio's Hanafuda deck and depicted the full moon in red and black paint. Hana frowned, wondering how it had gotten inside the vault. She set the card down and smoothed out the birdcage's paper tag. Her father's elegant calligraphy spelled out the name of the missing choice's previous owner.

CHAPTER SIX

Takeda Izumi's Choice

❁ *The night before*

The songbird perched on Toshio's finger and stretched out its glowing wings. Toshio brought the bird closer to his face, admiring it through his glasses. "This kind of choice does not come along very often, Hana. Have a look."

Hana pushed the birdcage she had been preparing aside and slipped on her mother's glasses. Takeda Izumi's coins shimmered into the shape of a bird made of the brightest blue light. In the night sky, it would have put the stars to shame. "I . . . I have never seen anything like it."

"I have."

"When?"

"Once. Before you were born. I did not think that I would ever see something shine like that again."

Hana squinted at the bird. "Why is it so bright?"

Toshio carefully put the bird in its cage. "Choices radiate the light from all the possibilities they contain. Most choices cause a few ripples at best. But this choice, had it not been abandoned, would have sent the strongest and tallest waves surging in every direction."

"I wonder if Takeda-sama had any idea about all that could have been." Hana handed Toshio a blank tag.

"Our clients often fail to see anything more than what is

right in front of them. And some are even blind to that." Toshio dipped a brush into a small paint pot and painted Takeda Izumi's name on the tag with swift, sure strokes.

"Perhaps it is better that way." Hana threaded a piece of red string through a hole in the tag and tied it to the cage.

The bird screeched and frantically flew around its new home.

"Hush. Hush." Hana reached for the latch on the cage's door.

"Don't." Toshio grabbed her wrist.

"But none of the birds have ever behaved this way. Is it hurt? Maybe I can try to calm—"

"No."

The bird furiously pecked at the cage, rattling its bars.

"Never take a bird from its cage. You know this."

"I will be careful. It won't escape."

Toshio shook his head. "That is what I said before a bird flew out of my hands when I was a boy."

"You . . ." Hana's mouth went dry. "You lost a bird?"

"My father caught it before it reached the door. If he hadn't—" He closed his eyes, his bottom lip trembling.

"What would have happened, Otou-san?" Hana leaned closer, lowering her voice.

"It would have flown back to the moment it was made."

"Flown back?" Hana's eyes grew large. "To the past?"

Toshio nodded. "A bird that has tasted freedom would do anything to keep from ever being trapped again. It would reset time itself to change its fate."

"But that would mean that . . ."

"Everything on the other side of the door would change. Small things. Big things. Forgotten stories would be written, lost lovers found. The path not taken and all its branching roads would lead the choice's owner to a whole other life."

"Would it be better or worse than the life they had before?" Hana asked.

Toshio glared at her. "Does it matter? Have I not taught you anything? If you lose a bird, what kind of life your client leads is the least of your worries." He looked away, shaking his head. "Go. Take the cage to the vault."

"Me?" Hana jerked her head back.

"Tomorrow, this pawnshop will be your responsibility. You may as well start now."

Hana nodded and carried the cage over to the bookcase that hid the entrance to the vault. She reached for the notch at its side.

"Hana?"

Hana turned. "Yes, Otou-san?"

"The new moon is in three days." Toshio lowered his voice. "All must be in order when the Shiikuin come to collect the birds."

Hana's fingers froze around the edge of the bookcase. Shiikuin was not a name either of them often said out loud. And though her father had barely whispered it, it was enough to corrupt the air with the memory of rot that filled their house whenever the Shiikuin came by. The layers of their kimonos and their pale white Noh masks did not conceal the stench of rusting metal and decaying flesh from their patchwork bodies. Hana clamped her mouth, trying not to retch.

"Are you all right?" Toshio asked.

Hana nodded, vomit and a realization rising up her throat. It fell to her, as the pawnshop's new owner, to oversee the turnover of the pawned choices to the Shiikuin. She had grown up watching their silent visits from the top of the stairs, never daring to come any closer. Once, she had made the mistake of allowing her gaze to linger over a Shiikuin's mask a second too long. It had stared back at her with a hard, carved smile. Wells of darkness where there might have once been eyes swallowed her whole. "I . . . I will have everything ready. The records, the tags, the cages—"

"Yourself." Toshio squeezed her shoulder.

"Yes, Otou-san." Hana bowed and stepped aside as the bookcase swung open. The saddest of songs invited her in. Hana navigated her way through the rows of cages, searching for an empty hook from which to hang Takeda Izumi's choice.

CHAPTER SEVEN

Rule Number Two

Hana stood in front of the pawnshop's door, her fingers wrapped around its tarnished brass knob. The metal chilled her skin. She had watched countless clients walk in and out of their pawnshop, but not once had she dared to follow them outside. Her clients were not bound by the same rules as she was, and this particular rule did not require an enforcer.

What Hana had been told about the world outside the front door was something out of a tale mothers would tell their children to make them behave. She had heard that there was a time when it might have been difficult to tell the two worlds apart, but now they could not be more different. Her clients' world was a twisting maze of blind corners and dark paths of regret. Hana had not met a single client who was not lost. Raised in a world where detours were forbidden and one's entire life was mapped, she could not imagine a more terrifying place. To be sent to the other world was called "exile," though Hana knew that it was just a kinder word for the truth. To linger in the world beyond the door was to be erased, until not a strand of hair, an inch of skin, or a fragment of bone remained.

Hana's father told her that being erased wasn't painful, but the look in his eyes told Hana that it was simply what he chose to believe. She did too. Hana did not like to think that her mother had suffered when the Shiikuin had sentenced her to exile, dragged her outside the door, and left her to die.

Hana tightened her grip on the doorknob, wondering how much time she had on the other side before she faded away. Takeda Izumi's choice and her father were missing, and it had become very clear where they had both gone—out the front door. Whether the choice had been stolen or had escaped did not matter. The consequences of not retrieving it were the same. The Shiikuin's greatest pleasure was to be cruel.

Hana imagined her father chasing after the missing choice, casting every rule aside. And now she was about to do the same. She steeled her jaw and pulled the door open. A dark shape towered over her. Hana jumped back and screamed.

"I . . . I'm sorry," said a voice as smooth and smoky as the whiskey her father saved for special occasions.

Hana ripped off her mother's glasses and squinted, trying to make out the figure standing against the sunlight. The man was tall and lean, his perfect posture cutting a sharp line. "Who are you?"

"I'm sorry I startled you. I was just about to knock. My name is Minatozaki Keishin."

Hana studied his face, attempting to reconcile his accent with his features. Though there was no fault in his choice of words, the way he spoke them gave away that he was from a place far from Tokyo. Her gaze traced his sharp jawline and the elegant symmetry of his nose and lips, but the warmth of the pools behind his dark lashes kept her from straying from his eyes for too long. Hana blinked to keep from falling into them. "What do you want?"

"A cure for jet lag." Keishin flashed a lopsided smile. "But I'll settle for a bowl of ramen. This restaurant was highly recommended by a colleague at work. I haven't been able to sleep since my flight got in last night and so I figured I would just take my chances and check if you were open for breakfast."

"This is not the restaurant." Hana spoke slowly, trying to keep her voice steady.

"But the sign outside said—"

"This is my pawnshop." *My pawnshop.* The words cut Hana's tongue.

"Oh. My mistake. Sorry for bothering you." He made a small bow and froze midway, his eyes stopping at Hana's bare feet. "You're bleeding."

Hana glanced down. Blood pooled beneath her left heel. She winced, noticing the pain for the first time.

"That looks like a pretty deep cut."

"It is nothing." Hana gripped the edge of the door and took the weight off her bleeding foot.

Keishin caught a glimpse of the chaos behind her. *"Holy shit,"* he said, cursing in a language Hana did not understand. He dug into his pocket and pulled out his phone. "I'm going to call the police."

"No." Hana clutched his wrist. The warmth of his skin rippled through her fingers. Her breath caught in her throat. This was the first time she had touched anyone from the other side of the door.

Hana had taken great care to keep her clients at a distance, regardless of how much they wept or silently longed to be held. She had imagined they would feel cold and stiff, like the tags she wrote their names on. Transactions, her father often reminded her, were not meant to be warm. She pulled Keishin inside the pawnshop and shoved the door shut. She let go of his arm and stuffed her hands deep into her pockets, keenly aware of the lingering heat over her skin. "There is no need for the police."

Keishin ran a finger over the spot where Hana had held him, seemingly undecided if he was startled or bemused. Hana wondered if she felt warm to him too. He glanced around the pawnshop, his brows wrinkling into a frown. "What happened here?"

"There was . . . an accident."

Keishin narrowed his eyes. "What kind of accident?"

The cut in her foot throbbed. Hana bit down the pain.

"We should take a look at that cut. Do you have anything we can use to clean it?"

"I do, but—"

"Good. Hopefully, it isn't too deep and you won't need stitches."

"Thank you, but I do not—"

"Don't worry. I'm a doctor."

CHAPTER EIGHT

Lies

Keishin was not in the habit of lying, but today, half kneeling in the back room of a strange little pawnshop, in the company of its wounded owner, he made an exception. The woman whose bleeding foot was now resting on his knee would not have accepted his help otherwise. He steadied his hand, hovering a tweezer over the shard of glass stuck in her heel. "I'm going to pull it out now. Try not to move, okay?"

The woman nodded, her back stiff against the chair. "Thank you."

"I haven't done anything yet."

She looked up at him. "You stayed."

"I thought you didn't want me here."

"I don't. What one wants and needs are two very different things."

Keishin quirked a brow and wrestled it down. In a morning filled with the unusual, this woman was the most extraordinary of it all. There was a calmness in the way she spoke, a steadiness he did not expect from a person in her circumstances. Her large brown eyes mirrored her quiet composure, filled with something he had long desired for himself.

An absolute certainty of purpose.

He did not know as of yet what this purpose might be, only

that this question would gnaw at him until he found the answer to it.

"Hold still." He pulled the piece of glass out in one smooth motion. "Got it."

The woman exhaled.

Keishin dabbed at the wound with a clean cloth soaked in alcohol and bandaged it. "How does it feel?"

"Much better. Thank you." The woman stood up and packed away the medicine kit into a small basket. She paused, her eyes fixed on a gap between two amber bottles. Her forehead creased.

"Is something wrong?"

"No." She smoothed her brow before meeting his eyes. "Thank you for your help."

"It was the least I could do. You wouldn't have stepped on glass if I hadn't startled you. Are you sure that you don't want to call the police?"

"Yes."

"Why not?"

"They . . . cannot help me."

Keishin glanced around the room and lowered his voice. "Are you in some kind of trouble?"

"I am grateful for your concern and for helping me with my foot, Minatozaki-san, but—"

"Please, call me Kei."

"Kei . . ." The woman said his name quietly and slowly as though buying time to consider what she was going to say next. "You should not be here. It is not safe."

"Not safe? Then you shouldn't be here either. Is there somewhere I can take you? Do you have family you can stay with? Friends?"

"Please just go."

"You can't expect me to just walk out and leave you here, do you? Were you robbed? Do you know who did this?"

"I know that you mean well, but if you insist on getting answers . . ." The woman folded her arms over her chest. "I will be forced to lie to you."

"Look, whatever you say won't change what I can see right in front of me. I know that something terrible happened here," Keishin said. "But go ahead and lie if you want to. It's only fair."

"Fair?"

"Because I lied to you too."

The woman backed away from him. "About what?"

"Who I really am."

CHAPTER NINE

Heads

One month ago

Summer was officially over, but no one had bothered to inform the sun. The city was an armpit and Keishin was wading through its sweat. If he had not committed to being a guest lecturer that afternoon, he would have happily spent the rest of the day sitting in front of his refrigerator. Keishin would have refused the invitation if it had come from any person other than Ramesh Kashyap.

The walk to lecture hall B was enough to soak Keishin's collar in sweat. He might have been concerned if he had wanted to make a good impression, but the latest batch of freshmen were not high on his list of people who mattered. Half of them were going to be gone before the semester was over. The other half had yet to prove they were interesting enough for him to bother remembering their names.

Ramesh liked to torture him this way. Sitting back while Keishin welcomed the latest batch of physics majors with a lecture that obliterated any fantasy they might have had of breezing through college almost made Ramesh smile, and an Almost Smile from him was nearly as rare as finding a neutrino. Keishin let Ramesh have his little joys. And as the lecture hall's central air-conditioning cooled him down to a more agreeable temperature, Keishin even admitted to himself that he was grateful for his mentor's invitation, even if, technically, it was to the second law of thermodynamics that he owed his relief.

This was what Keishin appreciated the most about physics. It was predictable and reliable. Unlike the weather. For as long as he could remember, the latter had never been on his side.

Keishin watched the students file out of the auditorium at the end of the lecture, furrows of varying depths wedged between their brows. It was usually the ones with the deepest dents who fared the best. They had the most questions. Curiosity was fuel, and if you didn't have enough, you would sputter, stall, and eventually decide that you were better off graduating with a degree in something practical like computer science.

"You looked exactly like them when you were a freshman, Kei." Ramesh's tone was flat as always, but those who knew him caught the little twitch just beneath his left eye that told you if he was serious, happy, annoyed, or sad. Catching when he was telling a joke was harder. Ramesh's jokes were never funny no matter how much his eye twitched. "Just ten times more miserable."

"Liar," Keishin said. "You didn't even know my name until I was a sophomore."

Ramesh pushed his thick glasses up the slight bump on his beak-like nose. With his slicked-back silver hair and narrow-set eyes, he looked like an eagle about to swoop down on its prey. "I knew exactly who you were the minute you walked into my lecture hall. I just pretended I didn't. I didn't want you to get any cockier than you already were. You were the new wonder boy on campus. How could I not know your name?"

Keishin gathered his notes from the podium, trying to remember the exact point at which his relationship with Ramesh had shifted from mentor to friend. "You deserve an Oscar. You had me convinced that as far as you were concerned back then, I was invisible."

"The most interesting things are invisible." Ramesh shrugged. "Speaking of which, have you responded to Takahiro's email yet about joining him in Japan?"

"Not yet."

"What are you waiting for? Working at the Super-K detector is an amazing opportunity. You may just beat me to that Nobel Prize."

"Then why aren't you going? Takahiro invited you, not me. I'm his second choice."

"I don't like sushi."

"Another lie," Keishin said. "You should stop that, you know. You're not very good at it."

An Almost Smile. Ramesh leaned on his walking stick, taking his weight off his bad leg. "The truth is, if I had gotten this opportunity twenty years ago, I would have been on the first plane to Tokyo before you could say 'neutrinos.' But I've grown to like my old leather chair and my quiet walks around campus. I like that the little coffee shop at the corner knows exactly what I'm going to order as soon as I step through the door. I've finally earned the right to be old and boring. You haven't. Besides, haven't you been wanting to go back to where you were born?"

"I have, but—"

"But what?"

"I've carried around this idea of Japan in my head for so long, a place in my mind I could return to whenever I—" Keishin shook his head. "Forget it. I feel like I'm back in high school, stewing in my pubescent angst about not fitting in."

"You're afraid the real thing won't match up to your memories of it," Ramesh said. "And you're absolutely right. That place stopped existing the moment you left. Maybe it didn't even exist at all. Memory has a way of smoothing and polishing edges. I've known you for a long time, Kei. I don't think you've ever really fit in anywhere."

"Wow. Thanks, Ramesh. Just what I needed to hear. All my 'only-Asian-at-my-school' and 'mommy-abandonment' childhood issues confirmed."

"I didn't mean that in a bad way. It was a compliment. Your drive, all your achievements—you wouldn't have them if you 'fit in.' Unlike people who quickly find their place in their little corner of life's puzzle, you need to see and understand the puzzle in its entirety."

Keishin ran his hand through his hair, combing through a streak at his left temple that had prematurely turned silver. He let out a heavy sigh. "A puzzle that doesn't even seem to have any borders."

"And perhaps that is where you will find your place, at the ever-expanding edge. Who knows? Maybe you'll find it in Japan."

"I wish it were that simple."

"It is that simple, Kei. There is only one question that requires an answer. It's all the other questions spinning around it that make it look more complicated than it is." Ramesh dug into his pocket and pulled out a coin. He pressed it into Keishin's palm. "Here. You know what to do."

Eight years ago

Keishin's father liked to say that he was in a rush even before he was born. He broke his mother's water one and a half months early and forced her to give birth on a restaurant's floor. He started talking at six months and had taught himself to read by the time he turned two. Keishin entered college at fifteen only because his father insisted that he defer his enrollment by a year. *Why are you in such a hurry to grow up?* he asked. Keishin would have given him an answer if he thought he would understand. Slowing down wasn't a choice. The questions that chased him were too fast. They were going to bury him alive if he stopped. Until he met Ramesh Kashyap, Keishin did not believe that it was possible to find another person who was just as terrified of standing still.

"The first thing you need to accept is that most if not all of your questions will outlive you." Ramesh looked out from the rooftop of the university's physics building and took a long drag of his cigarette.

"That dirty habit of yours isn't going to help," Keishin said. "You should quit."

"And you should start."

"You're my mentor and I take most of your advice, but I think I'm going to have to draw the line at knowingly reducing my life span. You do remember that I told you my father died of lung cancer, right?"

Ramesh shrugged. "Of course I don't. You've known me long enough to know that I'm not good at that sort of thing. The point is, you need to find something to do, at least a few minutes each day, that doesn't involve trying to figure out how the universe works. I hate slowing down as much as you do, but if you want to stay sane long enough to have at least one of your theories be proven true, you'll listen to me. Smoke. Watch funny dog videos. Knit, for all I care. Just go somewhere quiet and slow down. But not here. This is my place. Go find your own rooftop. Try the economics building. It has a nice view."

Keishin folded his arms over his chest. "And if I don't?"

"It's basically a choice between jumping out of a plane with a parachute or without one. Terminal velocity. You're a physics major. Figure it out."

Keishin never took up smoking or learned how to knit. But he did find a little space he could call his own. Ramesh had been right about the economics building. Keishin came to an arrangement with the maintenance guy to leave the door to the rooftop unlocked at night. The rooftop was best when it was dark. It was harder to see where the edge of the roof ended and the long fall to the campus's courtyard began.

Keishin liked spinning coins on the ledge, holding his breath, wondering if they were going to drop off the building or come to a stop. If he had been braver, he might have taken to walking along the ledge himself. But he had never been that kind of man. He was content to have pennies as his proxy. He lost half of the coins he spun, but it was a small price to pay for a moment of quiet. His mind was at its most still when resting on the third side of a coin. As the coin teetered on the edge of the roof, Keishin could think of nothing else but its fate. There was no fraction of time before or after it that mattered more. Ramesh had taught him that the best way to tackle his questions was to leave them behind. When the coin stopped, the answers he was looking for were usually waiting for him, twiddling their thumbs and wondering where he had been.

One month ago

The coin slipped off the ledge, abandoning Keishin on the economics building's wet rooftop. A downpour that had stopped as suddenly as it began had left puddles on the roof and Keishin soaked. He wasn't surprised. The weather took every opportunity to show its disdain for him.

He pushed his wet hair off his face and sat on the roof's slick ledge, no closer to coming to a decision about whether to accept the position in Japan at the world's largest neutrino detector. He stared up at the night sky, searching for the constellations through the clouds. As a boy, he'd taken pride in knowing all of their names. He later came to realize that the names were just another of man's early attempts to impose an order to things he didn't understand. Generations had looked to the stars for meaning, but tonight, Keishin needed to decide if he was willing to uproot his life and search for answers deep in the ground.

The Super-Kamiokande detector was located one thousand meters beneath Mount Ikeno in Japan's Gifu prefecture, silently keeping watch for dying stars and the neutrinos their explosions sent the earth's way. These invisible, elusive particles were the rarest of breadcrumbs, a trail of clues to how the universe began. Without mass or electrical charge, they were little more than ghosts. Ramesh liked to joke that to study neutrinos was to search for nothing to figure out everything. Keishin pretended to laugh even if he didn't find it funny. To work at the detector was essentially a commitment to wait for something that might never come, and Keishin did not have any illusions of being a patient man.

He spun another coin and watched it twirl toward the edge. He lunged forward and scooped it up. He squeezed his fist around it, digging his nails into his palm. In a debate with himself, there was never going to be a winner. He could spend the night thinking of as many reasons to go as to stay. He stepped back from the ledge and into a puddle, rippling the moon floating inside it. "Kyouka suigetsu," Keishin whispered to himself. *Mirror flower, water moon.*

It was a phrase he had learned from his stepmother. She enjoyed painting on Sunday afternoons, and reflections were her favorite subject. She made chrysanthemums bloom inside shimmering glass and poured the sky into the sea. She also painted Keishin's father, capturing his smile in a mirror, frozen in a time before he had gotten sick.

When Keishin asked her why she liked painting reflections, she told him that it was because the most desirable things were the ones that you could see, but never touch. Keishin crouched by the small moon floating in the puddle and wondered if it longed for the sky. His reflection stared back at him from the water, looking more trapped than content.

Keishin got to his feet and looked at the coin in his hand. He tossed logic and the coin into the air and, for the first time, surrendered one of the most important choices of his life to fate.

"Heads."

CHAPTER TEN

Tails and Tea Boxes

On their own, one man's eyes were not more memorable than another's. It was how they looked at you that made you remember them. Hana understood, in the moment that Minatozaki Keishin had told her about his lie, that his were going to be impossible to forget. No person's eyes had ever invited her in. Her father's had always been guarded, their clients' more so. But Keishin's eyes were an open door that drew her inside, offering her a seat and hot green tea.

"I'm sorry for misleading you. I really just wanted to help," Keishin said. "As you now know, I am a doctor, just not the kind that's qualified to stitch up wounds."

"I see," Hana said.

"And you were absolutely right when you said that I shouldn't be here. Not if I followed logic. Tossing a coin isn't any way to make a decision. I suppose that doesn't speak well of me as a scientist, but, as I told you earlier, I chose heads, and here I am. I could have opened another door and could be eating a bowl of steaming ramen right now, but I didn't. Instead I opened your door and found you, your bleeding foot, and a pawnshop that's been turned upside down."

"The door is not locked. You can turn around and leave anytime you want."

"I could, but my father taught me better than to abandon someone simply because it's easier to walk away."

"You don't even know me."

"We could change that. You could start by telling me your name."

"I—" Hana's eyes fell to his lips. Her name in his mouth was a dangerous thing. She imagined how his lips might shape its syllables and how his voice might turn them into a stream of honey wine. Sweet drinks were the worst traitors. You drowned in them with a smile. "I can't."

"I'll make you a deal. Since you already know my name, I'll throw in a little secret about myself in good faith. It might make you believe that I'm even stranger than you think I am now, but it's a risk I'm willing to take. Does that sound fair? Your name in exchange for something no one else in the entire world knows?"

"I grew up working in this pawnshop," Hana said. "You may want to reconsider trying to win any negotiation with me."

"I don't care about winning. I want to help. That's all."

"And just like that, you have lost," Hana said. "You've shown me your hand."

"You might have the advantage in negotiation skills, but all the years I've spent in a lab may have taught me a thing or two about observation."

Hana narrowed her eyes at him. "And what have you observed about me?"

"That you haven't decided what to do with me yet. If you really wanted to get rid of me, you would have pushed me out the door by now. Instead, I'm standing here while you try to figure out whether or not my secret is worth it."

"You should not be so carefree with your secrets."

"You're right," Keishin said. "But I trust you."

Hana looked away. Had Keishin been a client, she would have been elated. Instead, the Shiikuin's shrieks tore through her mind. She had allowed Keishin to step into a world whose dangers he could not even begin to comprehend. To give him her name was to let him take another step closer to her. And all the secrets her door hid. "Perhaps you shouldn't."

Keishin shrugged. "It's only my credibility and my entire reputation as a scientist at stake. No big deal."

"You are making a mis—"

"Whenever I'm stuck on a problem, I conjure up my mentor, Ramesh, to help me work it out at an imaginary Indonesian restaurant that serves the best nasi goreng and pecel lele. Sometimes we have beer. And dessert. They have the most amazing—"

"Hana." She sighed and closed her eyes. "My name is Hana."

"Hana . . . 'flower,'" he said, translating her name into a language Hana did not understand. "I hope that I pronounced it correctly. My Japanese is a bit rusty. I'm sorry."

Hana nodded. She had never heard her name spoken with greater care.

"So will you let me help you, Hana?"

Hana pulled her shoulders back and lifted her chin. "Heads."

"Sorry?"

"I choose heads."

"Heads?"

"I can tell that you are a stubborn person because I am one too," Hana said. "You will keep on insisting on helping me, and I will keep on refusing you. This is like the debate you had with yourself on that rooftop before coming here. As you said, you cannot win an argument with yourself. You have less chance of winning one with me. So let a coin be our judge. You trusted a coin to take you across the world. Why not trust it to decide whether you should stay or go? Heads, you leave right now."

"Tails, you tell me what happened here."

Hana nodded. "Agreed."

Keishin fished a coin from his pocket. He flicked it with his thumb and sent it into the air.

Hana watched it fall. She did not understand Keishin's world of subatomic particles and underground neutrino detectors, but she understood fate. Her father had made sure of it. *Death or fate. The only choice anyone in their world could ever make.* She caught the coin midair. She flipped the coin over the back of her other hand and lifted her palm, revealing the coin's decision.

Keishin looked up from the coin. "Tails."

Hana drew a heavy breath.

"I win," Keishin said.

"My father is missing," Hana said, allowing the words to slip from her tongue before she could change her mind.

"What?"

"I thought that he might have heard the intruder and chased him outside. But now . . ." She squeezed the coin. "I think that I was mistaken."

"Mistaken? How?"

Hana fixed her eyes on the gold-rimmed glasses and the hand-painted playing card on the table. "I suspect that my father set all of this up to look like a theft."

"You think that your father did this on purpose?" Keishin's eyes flew around the room. "Why?"

"Because of these." Hana picked up her mother's glasses and

Toshio's playing card. "And a childhood spent searching for tea boxes."

Eleven years ago, when Hana turned ten, the tea boxes her father hid became harder to find. She had spent the morning searching for one but had nothing to show for it except the sweat dripping down her neck. Toshio's clues had sent her up and down the stairs, in and out of her bedroom, and through the kitchen thrice. The latest led her to their dining table. She scanned the deck of playing cards laid on it.

Her father's Hanafuda deck was a set of forty-eight hand-painted cards that were divided into the twelve months of the year. Each month was a four-card suit that featured a unique flower in its design. When arranged in a row and in the right order, the four cards formed a panoramic scene. Her father seldom played with the cards, using them instead to teach Hana sleight of hand. He made cards disappear from his hand and reappear behind Hana's ear or in her pockets. The tricks, he said, honed two of the most important skills of a pawnbroker: misdirection and manipulation.

Hana carefully looked through each row of cards. January was a crane among pines, February a nightingale in the midst of plum trees. March. April. May. June. July. August. September. October. November. December. Every month appeared as it was supposed to be. She looked through the cards again and stopped at August. Hana closed her eyes, trying to recall what the scene was supposed to look like. Susuki ni tsuki—kari. *Moon over Pampas Grass—Wild Geese.* Hana stared at the cards and caught the mistake. The geese card that was meant to come after the moon now appeared before it. Hana smirked, creasing a dimple on her left cheek. This was her father's favorite type of clue, subtle and small. If only she knew what it meant. She picked up the two cards and held them in front of her.

Hana studied the cards, making two lists in her mind: what she knew and what she didn't. August, she thought, was the month of falling leaves and changing seasons. In the traditional calendar, it was also the month for Tsukimi, the festival for viewing the autumn moon. Hana ran her thumb over the full moon on the first card and checked the time. It was only a few hours until sunset, and she doubted her father would let the treasure hunt run for so long. Dinner to him was as sacred as the sake he drank before bed. But she also knew that the cards' misplacement in the row was not an accident. Toshio had wanted her to notice the moon for a reason, and Hana could think of only one place he intended the clue to direct her to. With a well-rehearsed flick of her wrist and a grin, she made the cards vanish up her sleeve.

At this time of day, the pond in the middle of their courtyard garden reflected the blue sky. On cloudless nights, it revealed its true purpose. Hana made her way to the pond, thinking about how generations of her family had followed the same pebbled path. She stood at the edge of the pond and watched the sun sparkle inside it. Though pretty, it was not half as beautiful as the visitor who swam in its water at night. The pond existed to catch the moon, and when the moon was full it filled the pond to its brim.

Hana pulled out the moon and geese cards from her sleeve, wondering what she was supposed to do next. On the table, the geese had been on the left side of the moon, but now Hana held them in their proper place on the right. She walked over to the right of the pond and knelt on the grass. The corner of a wooden box stuck out from behind a bush. Hana grabbed it, grinning wide. She pulled off the box's lid and looked inside. It was empty. Her father usually packed the box with different kinds of sweets, and this was the first time he had not put anything inside it. She wondered if he had simply forgotten to fill it or if it was another clue.

Toshio walked up from behind her. "Have you found it?"

"Yes, Otou-san. But it is . . ."

"Empty? You found the wrong box." Toshio strode to the left of the pond and retrieved a box from behind a rock. He opened it, revealing little wrapped bars of yōkan, sweet red bean–flavored jellies Hana loved having with her tea. "This is the correct one."

"But the geese card is supposed to be on the right side of the moon."

"Not in this pond." He took the cards from Hana and held them over the pond.

Hana looked at the reflection and saw where she had gone wrong. In the water, right was left, and left was right. She sighed, dropping her shoulders.

Toshio held out the box of sweets to her. "Here."

"But I failed. I did not find it."

Toshio smiled and unwrapped a sweet for Hana. "This time, it found you."

"Thank you, Otou-san." Hana took the sweet and popped it into her mouth. A fat raindrop splattered on her forehead.

Toshio looked up at the darkening sky. A flash of lightning broke through a gray cloud. Toshio's smile slipped from his face. "Hurry inside, Hana. It is about to rain."

CHAPTER ELEVEN

The God on the Shelf

Droplets condensed on the dark brown bottle of ice-cold beer. Keishin wiped them away with his thumb before tipping the bottle into his glass. The golden liquid burbled and the sound blended into the restaurant's hum. Conversation, punctuated by bursts of laughter, added to the melody of clinking plates and silverware inside the cramped Indonesian restaurant. Keishin sipped his beer, determined to enjoy it even if it wasn't real: The imaginary Ramesh who lived in the back of his mind always chose this restaurant for their conversations.

A server in an intricate batik vest expertly weaved through a maze of square tables carrying a large tray of colorful dishes. The heady scent of coconut, lemongrass, and coriander trailed him. He stopped at Keishin and Ramesh's table and set a bowl of steamed rice and an array of small plates on the steel food warmers in front of them. An ironwork lamp cast a yellow-orange glow over the small feast. Keishin's eyes flitted over the appetizer portions of satay, marinated vegetables, curries, fried bananas, egg rolls, nuts, and fruit compote, and just the sight of them made him feel full. "You always order too much," he said, looking up at Ramesh.

Ramesh shrugged and scooped a mound of steaming fragrant rice onto his plate. "I never know how long our little chats are going to take. I don't want to get hungry. What's on your mind? Having second thoughts about working at Super-K?"

Keishin shook his head and sipped his imaginary beer. "No."

"What would you like to talk about, then?" Ramesh closed his eyes, savoring his food.

"A puzzle."

"A puzzle?" Ramesh set his spoon down and grinned. "You have my attention."

"I met a woman. Her name is Hana."

Ramesh held up his hand. "I'm going to stop you right there. I don't give advice about women—in your imagination or in real life. Remember? My wife will be the first to agree that women fall far beyond my expertise."

"Hana isn't the puzzle," Keishin said, even though he wasn't sure that he meant it. There was something about Hana and her odd stories about tea boxes and treasure hunts that piqued his curiosity, which was something that, outside his lab, had not happened in a very long time. He had met his share of beautiful women, but it was not Hana's quiet, delicate beauty that made a part of him glad that he had stumbled into her pawnshop by mistake. Just behind the calmness in her eyes lurked the shadows of secrets, peeking out one moment and darting away the next, as though daring him to give chase. And there was nothing Keishin enjoyed more than a good puzzle. "Her pawnshop is."

"Pawnshop?"

"It was robbed and ransacked. She believes that her father is behind it."

"And what do you think?"

"To be honest, I don't know what to think. I tried to convince her to call the police, but she refuses to."

"Ah, a stubborn soul." Ramesh eyed Keishin over his bottle of beer. "Sounds a lot like someone I know."

Keishin rolled his eyes. "Anyway, the point is, I want to help her, but I can't."

"Why do you want to help her so badly?"

"You know why."

"It's not something I like to think about."

"No one helped you, Ramesh. They all just stood there and watched that man attack you like you were invisible. But they did see you. They just chose not to care."

"You did. You took me to the hospital."

"I just wish that I had gotten there sooner. Maybe you'd—"

"Be more than just a figment of your imagination? Wishing for such things is useless. We can theorize all we want about bending space-time, but we cannot change the past."

"And that's exactly why I want to help Hana. I know what happens when people pretend not to see you. I will never know for sure if I would have been like those people who chose to look the other way when you were assaulted. Finding out if you are a coward isn't something any hypothetical scenario can answer. I refuse to be the kind of person who looks away." Keishin struggled to push the image of Ramesh bleeding on the sidewalk from his mind. He drew a deep breath. "I need to be better than that, but . . ."

"But what?"

"I'm not a detective. I'm a scientist."

"Then be a scientist," Ramesh said. "Don't sell yourself short. Physicists have solved some of the universe's greatest mysteries. Remember the case of the missing solar neutrinos?"

"What do solar neutrinos have to do with anything?"

"For years, we were confounded by the fact that, compared

to the predictions of our models, fewer neutrinos made their way to Earth after being emitted by the sun. It made us conclude that either our models were wrong or something happened to the neutrinos along their journey."

Keishin nodded. "But eventually, the mystery was solved when the physicists discovered that the neutrinos everyone thought had gone missing were not missing at all."

"Yes," Ramesh said. "They had shifted from one type of neutrino to another, a kind that just happened to be so much harder to find. It was all a . . ."

"A masquerade." Keishin smirked. "Of course. Thanks, Ramesh."

"Good luck with your puzzle."

"Thanks."

"And the woman you're pretending very hard not to be intrigued by."

Keishin looked up from the hand-painted playing card and gold-rimmed eyeglasses Hana held out. The pawnshop morphed around him. It was no longer the space he had walked into, even if everything looked exactly as it did when he had first arrived. Like the neutrinos, the changes were intangible and invisible, but a masquerade just the same. Desks were still overturned, glass was still shattered, papers were still strewn every which way, but now Keishin began to see the design disguising itself as disarray. Chairs had not simply been haphazardly flung, and shelves had not been carelessly toppled. The scattered furniture was scratch- and dent-free, carefully laid on their sides, almost artfully arranged. As with the universe, this chaos had an author. "I think that you might be right about this being staged," Keishin said. "But what makes you think that it was your father who set this up?"

"My father left that very same card as a clue for me once," Hana said. "It cannot be a coincidence that I found it in the vault."

"But what about the glasses? Why do you think they're a clue? The intruder may just have dropped them at the door on his way out."

"Then that would make them the luckiest pair of glasses in the world." Hana shook her head. "They were placed by the door, in the exact place where they could be noticed, but conveniently out of harm's way."

"That still doesn't mean your father is behind all of this."

"You are right. It does not," Hana said. "But the missing bottle from the medicine kit makes me believe otherwise. It contained my father's sleeping medicine. It has been bothering me how I could have possibly slept through all of this. Now I know why. My father must have slipped his medicine into my sake last night."

"You think that he *drugged* you? Why would he do that?"

"That is not important now. I just need to find him before—" Hana bit her lip.

"Before what?"

"Nothing." Hana shook her head. "Nothing. All that matters is finding him soon."

"Then call the police. They'll be able to comb the city faster than anyone."

"My father is not in Tokyo."

Keishin frowned. "How do you know that?"

"Because that is what the glasses were supposed to make

anyone who saw them by the door think. They were placed there to create the impression that my father had chased an intruder into the city's streets." She held up the moon card. "But this card told me the truth, the same way it did in that treasure hunt when I was a little girl. It told me to go left when I thought I was meant to go right."

"So . . ." Keishin rubbed his jaw. A ransacked pawnshop, its missing owner, and a woman determined to follow a trail of strange clues were not things he had expected to encounter on his first morning in Tokyo. But somewhere between walking into the pawnshop and seeing the conviction in Hana's eyes, Hana's questions had become his. Those questions now clung to him just as fiercely as he refused to let them go. "Where is 'left'?"

"That is a question for the god on the shelf."

The kamidana altar was set against the hallway wall across from Hana's bedroom. Keishin's father had kept a similar one in the spare room in the attic, at the highest point of their home. When he was a boy and his friends asked him about the kamidana, he simply told them what it was. A god shelf. They didn't ask him any questions after that. The wooden household altar looked like a miniature Shinto shrine and was built to house a chosen deity. His father would light two tiny candles on either side of the altar, make offerings of rice and salt, and pray to their god on a shelf each day. Keishin went through the motions of bowing and clapping thrice, but he could never think of anything to say. "Are you . . . um . . . going to pray?"

"My prayers would be useless," Hana said.

"Then why are we here?"

"Because my father's may not be. He always visited the

kamidana before going to bed. He might have mentioned something in his prayers that could explain what he did to the pawnshop and why he disappeared."

"Did he write down his prayers somewhere? Did he keep a journal?"

"No."

"Did he make recordings on his phone?"

Hana shook her head. "Not on his phone."

"Then where did he keep his prayers?"

"Kei . . ." Hana drew a deep breath. "There are things I will tell you that will be hard for you to believe. You are free to change your mind about helping me and to leave anytime you wish."

"I think you might be underestimating my curiosity. I love puzzles probably as much as you do. Maybe more."

Hana caught a glimpse of the fire that had ignited behind Keishin's irises. "I can see that."

Keishin shrugged. "It's pretty much a job requirement."

"But this mystery has little to do with your science. It may even be beyond everything you know." Hana was aware that her words were kindling to Keishin's flame, but she warned him just thc samc.

"I chase invisible things for a living. I don't scare off that easily."

Hana took one of the candles from the kamidana. "Even if I ask you to listen to smoke?"

CHAPTER TWELVE

The Easiest of Experiments

Hana stood over the pond, listening to the thunder crackle above her. Today was supposed to be her first day as the pawnshop's owner, but as she stared at her rippling reflection, she struggled to push away the icy feeling that it was also going to be her last. She was about to break more rules than she cared to think about, but her father had left her no choice. A gust of wind chilled her nape. She bundled her coat tighter, feeling the bulge of the kamidana's small candle in her pocket. She looked at Keishin. "I do not understand why you are still here."

"Why wouldn't I be?"

"Because I told you that we need to take the candle to the place where all prayers go and that jumping into this pond is the only way to get there. I did not expect you to believe me."

"I don't."

"Oh." Hana folded her arms over her chest, surprised that a part of her felt disappointed. A gust of wind whipped her hair over her face. "Then why stay?"

"Because I . . ." Keishin's eyes softened as he reached out to push a wayward strand of hair from Hana's cheek. He bit his lip, pulling his hand back before his fingertips grazed her skin.

"I'm staying because this is probably one of the simplest experiments I've ever had to conduct in my life."

"Experiment?"

"Compared to all the hours of work I need to do in a lab just to prove a hypothesis, jumping into a pond is a relatively easy way to get answers. If you're telling the truth, then I will be whisked away on the greatest adventure of my life. If you're not, we'll be soaking wet." He looked up at the dark sky. "With my luck with the weather, I'd be soaked to the bone by the time I got back to my hotel anyway."

"Or I could lend you an umbrella and you could return to your hotel warm and dry."

"But then I wouldn't be able to find out if this was all just an elaborate lie."

"And what are you hoping for? To prove that I am a liar, or to leap into a truth you might drown in?"

"I've always found it best not to root for one hypothesis over another. I only care about facts and proof."

"Both of which you will have soon." Hana extended her hand to him. "Hold on to me."

Keishin laced his fingers through hers.

Tiny bolts of lightning struck wherever Hana's skin touched Keishin's and sent a current through her veins. She had cradled countless bright, glowing choices and carefully set them inside their cages, but this was the first time she had held anything that felt so free. Keishin could go anywhere he wished, say anything he wanted, and chase after whatever he desired. He was the wind and the rain, unshackled and unpredictable, a storm swirling in her palm.

"Hana? Is something wrong?"

"What? No . . . no. I . . . was just thinking about my father."

Keishin gave her hand a gentle squeeze. "I'm ready to jump whenever you are."

"Do not let go," Hana said, her eyes on Keishin's shimmering reflection. "And remember . . ."

"Yes?"

"That this was your choice."

CHAPTER THIRTEEN

Whispers and Wax

Tokyo had been a stopover on his way to his new job at the Super-Kamiokande detector in Gifu. His new home was a two-hour shinkansen ride away from Tokyo and then another thirty-minute ride on a local train. Keishin wasn't expected at the research facility until Monday, and he had pictured spending the weekend rediscovering his old city.

He was eight when he and his father packed up their lives and moved across the Pacific. Keishin had not returned since. There had been no reason to. He no longer had any family in Japan, and all his childhood friends had long faded away. Still, Keishin held the hope that somewhere along the city's streets, he would stumble upon a lost memory to welcome him home. There was one other thing that he hoped to find, but that was something he was never going to say out loud.

Keishin knew that his chances of finding fragments of his past were less than slim, but they were enough to draw him from under the covers of his hotel room's warm bed to brave the early hours of an autumn morning. The sooner he got his nostalgia out of the way, the sooner the questions buzzing between his ears were going to quiet down and move on to more important things. Miyazaki Hayao's Studio Ghibli was at the top of his to-do list, as it was unthinkable to leave Tokyo without making a pilgrimage to the home of one of his favorite animes, *My Neighbor Totoro.* The film's Catbus character, a grinning, hollow, twelve-legged cat with windows and fluffy, furry seats, had made every car, bus, train, and plane ride Keishin had taken since watching the movie painfully mundane. But the pond in the pawnshop's backyard put Catbus to shame. Traveling by pond trumped any mode of transportation, including ones covered in fur.

Finding words to describe how he had fallen through water and emerged completely dry on the other end was not a problem that had ever crossed Keishin's mind. Today, it became one of two challenges that were going to haunt him for the rest of his life. The second was explaining how, when only moments before he had been standing over a pond in Tokyo, he had come to find himself in the middle of a seemingly endless sea of pampas grass. He turned to Hana, not realizing that he was still clutching her hand.

"You can let go now," Hana said.

"Oh . . . uh . . . sorry." Keishin dropped her hand, heat rising beneath his collar despite the chill in the air. "Where are we? How did we get here?"

"We jumped into a pond, remember?"

"Yes, but . . ." Keishin closed his eyes and rubbed his forehead, unable to decide whether his experiment had succeeded or failed. To accept that a mossy pond had somehow teleported them was to call into question more scientific laws than he cared to enumerate. "That's not possible."

"And yet here we are."

Keishin shook his head. "Ponds can't—" He snapped his mouth shut, his eyes growing large. "Unless . . ."

"Unless?"

"It wasn't a pond."

Hana lifted a brow. "I was not aware that there was another name for the pool of water one watches the moon swim in."

"There isn't," Keishin said. "But there *is* a word for things that connect two different points in space-time. An Einstein-Rosen Bridge. A wormhole. A wormhole, Hana! In your backyard! Do you have any idea what this means? My god. This could change everything."

"It changes nothing."

"Of course it does." Keishin paced over the grass. "This is the discovery of the century! The applications are—"

"My father is still missing."

Keishin stopped mid-step, sending a jumble of plans and possibilities crashing into the front of his skull. He winced. "Hana . . . I . . . I'm sorry. I didn't mean to—"

"I understand," Hana said, her voice flat. She turned away from him and pointed at an empty field. "That is the Whispering Temple."

Keishin scanned the swaths of grass swaying in the breeze. "There's nothing there."

"Things are not always as plain to see in my world as they are in yours."

"*Your world?* What's that supposed to mean?"

"The place where I am from and you are not. Does your science have a name for it too? I shall call it whatever you prefer, even though I still do not understand why you would rather call a pond a hole for worms."

"I . . ." Keishin searched for a neat little label printed in bold, fifteen-point black font that he could stamp over the ground he stood on. Debating the existence of a multiverse was something he indulged Ramesh in, but only on Fridays after a few rounds of twelve-year-old Scotch.

Though Keishin was more than well-versed in every hypothesis and counterargument about parallel dimensions, he failed to find anything that could adequately describe the rustle of the grass around him, the sunlight warming his cheeks, and the patient gaze of the woman waiting for his answer. How her eyes were both impenetrable and inviting was a greater mystery than the impossible world a pond had whisked him to. "No, it doesn't."

"We do not have a name for it either. There has never been a need for one. We only have one world, and this is it," Hana said. "But if you feel that you must call it something, then you may call it Isekai."

Other world. Keishin translated the word in his head, convinced that his Japanese was rustier than he thought. "This is a dream," he said, more to himself than to Hana. "It has to be."

"If choosing to believe that this is a dream makes it easier to accept where you are, then I will not stop you. But if you wish to see the truth . . ." Hana handed him her mother's glasses. "Wear these."

Hana had first visited the Whispering Temple when she was seven years old. Her grandmother had asked Toshio to let Hana spend the weekend with her, and they had stopped by the temple on the way to her grandmother's home.

Hana climbed out of a small puddle in the middle of the grassy field and stood up. "Where is the temple, Sobo?"

Oshima Asami smiled down at her granddaughter. She took her glasses off and offered them to Hana. "Look again."

Hana put the glasses on. A towering, ornate building of red wax rose in front of her. A perfectly aligned row of more than a hundred red-and-black torii gates led up to imposing carved wax doors. The shape of the painted wooden gates reminded her of the kamidana her father kept at home. The building, however, was unlike anything she had ever seen. Spires reached for the sky from a large domed roof, and winged wax creatures with monstrous faces perched on arched buttresses. Some columns writhed and twisted like trees. It was as though the building had been melded from different places and times and left to grow as it pleased. Hana gasped. "It is beautiful."

"It is."

"Why are we here?" Hana said, unable to tear her eyes from the temple.

"I come here whenever I miss your mother." Asami stroked Hana's cheek. "You look so much like her."

"Was she pretty?"

Asami nodded. "Your father fell in love with her as soon as she stepped into the temple on their wedding day. He could not hide how happy he was. Before that meeting, they had not even seen pictures of each other, and I imagine that he was very pleasantly surprised when he finally saw the face of the girl he was meant to marry."

"Why do you come here when you miss her? Is this where my parents got married?"

"No. This is a different kind of temple. This is where all our prayers go."

"How do prayers come here?"

"They are carried by smoke." Asami dug through the woven bag slung across her chest and pulled out a small candle that had nearly burned to a stub. "This candle is near its end. This will probably be the last chance I get to light it. I wanted you to be able to hear your mother's voice before it burns out."

* * *

Keishin stepped inside the Whispering Temple, his sharp jaw slack. As large as the temple was on the outside, it was nothing compared to the cavernous hall that opened up within. Countless votive candles, cupped by tiny brass hands mounted along the wax walls, made the entire hall glow. A soft wind kissed Keishin's cheek. In spite of the flames, the air inside the temple was pleasantly cool and swirled around the hall as it would in a meadow. Candles flickered in the breeze.

Hana walked up from behind him. "You do not need the glasses once you are inside."

Keishin took the glasses off, bracing himself. Every second he spent with Hana ripped a stitch from the fabric of all he knew. It was not going to take much more to leave him utterly undone. "How is this real?"

"I sometimes find myself asking the same question when I see the things our clients bring from your world."

"Clients?"

"The people who walk through a ramen restaurant's door and find our pawnshop instead. They have the strangest things. Tiny buttons that play music in your ears, shiny—"

"Hold on." His head pounded with every impossible thing he had crammed inside it since meeting Hana. "What are you saying? I was looking for the ramen restaurant when I found the pawnshop. Does that make me one of your clients?"

"I will explain everything later. But now we have to listen to my father's prayer. We do not have much time. If the Shiikuin find out that he and the choice are missing—" Hana clamped her lips.

"The Shiikuin?" Keishin tried to remember the meaning of the word. "The Keepers? Like the caretakers of a zoo?"

"Later. I promise." Hana set the candle she had taken from

the kamidana on a pair of empty brass hands. A tiny flame flared up from the candle's wick as though lit by an invisible match. Loud murmuring echoed through the hall.

"What is that?" Keishin strained to hear what the voices were saying. They talked over one another, making it impossible to tell where one word ended and another began.

"Every prayer every single person throughout history has made. When one candle whispers, the rest like to join in." Hana brought her ear next to her father's candle. "You need to listen closely if you want to hear what the candle has to say."

Keishin leaned toward the candle, his face inches from Hana's cheek. The candle's flame danced to the rhythm of their breath.

Help me find her. Please.

Keishin inhaled sharply. "Did you hear that?"

"Yes, but . . ." Hana frowned. "That cannot be right."

"Who is your father looking for?"

Hana leaned as close as she could to the candle's flame without burning her skin. She closed her eyes, listening intently.

"Hana?"

Hana straightened, looking dazed. "I . . . do not understand."

"*Help me find her.* Your father's prayer seems straightforward to me. It looks like your hunch was right. Your father isn't missing. He's gone off to look for someone. A woman."

Hana stared into the candle's flame. "There is only one woman my father has lost."

"Who?"

"My mother."

"Okay. Good. We have a lead then. Do you have any idea where she is?"

Hana blew the candle out with a trembling breath. "I thought I did."

"What do you mean?"

"My mother is dead. She died on your side of the door. That is what my father told me. Now it seems that either this prayer is a lie or my entire life is."

"Hana . . ."

"There is one way to learn the truth." Hana took the candle from the wall. "I am sorry."

"Sorry? For what?"

"For what must happen next. I am afraid that you are not going to like it."

CHAPTER FOURTEEN

Skin and Ink

Second times were almost always more enjoyable than firsts. Kisses. Sex. Lab experiments. As far as Keishin was concerned, first times were created for the sole purpose of getting failure out of the way. Jumping into puddles was an exception. At the pawnshop's pond, he had jumped to pull Hana out of what he believed to be a delusion. But when he dove into that puddle and landed in a field of pampas grass, he also dove into a cold new truth: Science was a lie.

In the span of a morning, he had discovered that smoke carried prayers and that candles could speak. And when Hana finally made good on her promise to tell him the truth about the pawnshop, he learned that discarded dreams and lost choices could be traded for peace. Though he did not believe in regrets, Keishin was almost willing to make one up to pawn for a quiet room in his head. Bent rules and broken scientific laws clattered inside him, crashing into everything he had seen behind the ramen restaurant's door. And now Hana was going to show him more.

I must warn you. The next place will look . . . different. Whatever you see, do not panic.

Keishin repeated Hana's words as he disappeared beneath the water. He imagined that he might emerge in darkness, even if he knew that there was no such thing. Many people feared the dark, but not him. Not since he was a boy and discovered the truth in one of the stacks of books he brought home every week from the local library. This had been the best thing about learning English. Books didn't tire from answering his questions. They taught him that darkness was a human limitation, our eyes' failure to see the entire spectrum of light. Had we been engineered better, we would have been able to see all the flickering remnants of the Big Bang that lit up the night.

Keishin broke through the surface of the puddle and clambered out. His heart pounded against his ribs. He had been wrong about emerging in darkness. The dark was something he understood. This place was not.

A stone-paved street lined with traditional machiya, narrow merchant houses made of wood, and dotted with weeping cherry blossom trees stretched out before him. Canals filled with clear water and schools of koi flowed along both sides of the road. The town reminded Keishin of the preserved historic Japanese villages he had wanted to visit, but with one difference that made every hair on his neck stand on end: The entire town was a scene in black and white, painted against a canvas of paper that stretched up to the sky. The sun. The clouds. The stones beneath his feet. Hana. She was drawn with expert strokes in black ink, with the greatest care taken in sketching the bow of her lips.

"Everything inside the scroll looks like this," Hana said. "Even you."

Keishin held up his hands in front of him. His fingers were outlined in black ink and shaded in with the subtlest brushstrokes. He forced his voice from his throat. "Where are we? What is this place?"

"A story. You read them in your world. We walk inside them."

Keishin watched a sketch of a fallen leaf tumble in the breeze. "I'm beginning to think that nothing will ever make sense again."

"Things don't have to make sense for them to be real." She took his hand and pressed it over her chest.

Keishin felt Hana's heartbeat through his palm. Though she looked like a drawing, Hana was still soft and warm to the touch. She was solid. Real. "There aren't enough questions in the universe to make me fully grasp any of this. I still don't even know what happened to your mother."

"The Shiikuin executed her for stealing a choice from our vault."

"What? Why?"

"Because all the choices we collect in the pawnshop belong to them. Stealing from the Shiikuin is the highest of crimes. I was a baby when they came for her, and all I know about that day is what my father told me."

"But now you believe that she may be alive."

"I . . ." Her voice cracked. She turned away and hurriedly dabbed at a tear. "I do not know what to think."

"Hana . . ."

"I told you that I could handle this on my own. Go home, Keishin. One jump will take you back."

"Back to what? To the ramen restaurant? To my hotel? To my job at Super-Kamiokande? All the years I obsessed about the mysteries of the universe, trying to explain how everything began, was a complete waste of time. That 'everything' turned out to be only one side of a very strange coin. How can I pretend that any of that matters when I'm standing inside a scroll?"

"Of course it matters," Hana said.

"Does it?"

"It matters to you. Is that not enough?"

"It used to be." Keishin sighed, shaking his head. "Look, we're here to find out the truth about your mother. I'm not leaving until we do."

Hana looked down the street. "I am hoping that the Horishi will have some answers."

"A tattoo artist?"

"*The* tattoo artist. There is only one Horishi in our world."

"And this person will be able to tell us if your mother is alive?"

"The Horishi's ink will." Thunder rumbled over Hana's voice.

Keishin looked up at the paper sky. He took some comfort in knowing that even in this strange world, one rule remained true. The weather still didn't like him. Fat drops of rain burst from the sky and splattered over his face. "Then we should find this Horishi and his ink before we get soaked and—" Keishin gasped, staggering back.

Rain ran down Hana's cheeks and snaked down her neck. "What is it? What's wrong?"

"Hana . . ." Her name caught in Keishin's throat. "You're glowing."

As was the custom, Hana's father took her to the Horishi when she was a month old. She remembered nothing of the visit, but whenever it rained, a souvenir from that trip glowed on her skin. Pictures and words appeared in bright blue ink wherever raindrops touched her, narrating the story of the life she was fated to live. No crossroads. No detours. Just a single path in a map of blue over almost every inch of her body.

When she was younger, Hana liked to stick her arm outside

the window and watch the scenes the Horishi had etched onto her skin come to life. Wisps of steam curled up from tattooed teacups. A tiny moon swam in a little pond. Caged birds sang a silent song. On her wrist, an empty cage's door opened and closed in time with her pulse. But with every shining bird she locked away, it grew more difficult to tell which side of the ink bars she was standing on. When her father's retirement drew near, Hana found herself soaking longer in steaming baths, trying to scrub herself clean.

"Do not look at me." Hana pulled her collar closer around her neck. "I'm hideous."

"What? No. No. I was just surprised. That's all. I swear. There's nothing you need to hide. You're still . . ." Heat rose up Keishin's neck. "Beautiful."

"Be careful." Hana tightened her grip on her clothes. "Lying is becoming a habit for you."

"I'm not lying."

"Then you are blind." Hana's knuckles paled around her collar. Tiny glowing origami cranes flew in an unchanging path around her wet fingers.

"Nothing could be less true. I'm seeing more now than I ever saw when I spent my days viewing the world through telescopes and blinking screens."

"And what do you see, Kei? Another experiment like the pond? An oddity you might find some use for in your world? Or perhaps a monster covered in wretched blue scars?"

"You're not a monster."

"The countless clients who have walked through the pawnshop's door would disagree with you. They have all wanted one thing. To be clean. Unblemished. Generations of my family have done nothing but mend, buff, and polish our clients' stains, dents, and cracks away." A blue kite circled Hana's forearm. Hana gritted her teeth. "Porcelain perfection."

"Scars don't make you any less than what you are. They are simply stories, just like this scroll. You may not see mine, but I have my fair share."

"Not like these." Hana turned her cheek, exposing blue lotus flowers blossoming behind her ear. "Your scars tell you where you've been. Mine tell me where I am going. All children are brought to the Horishi to learn their path. The rain reminds us that what is fated can never be washed away." Hana tugged her collar to the side. The rain fell onto her chest, revealing the glowing vault door that stood guard over her heart. Unlike her other tattoos that coiled and fluttered, the door remained locked. "Can you tell me that you do not see this grotesque map of skin and ink?"

"What I see is *you,* Hana. I see your courage. Your determination . . ."

"Determination?" A dry laugh cut her lips. "Do you mean stubbornness?"

"Well, that too." Keishin smiled. "And there is nothing ugly or revolting about what I see that would make me want to look away. I'm still here. Standing in a scroll. In the rain. Not lying to you."

A driverless rickshaw came to a stop in front of them. Hana hurriedly adjusted her collar and climbed aboard. "Come. This will take us to the Horishi."

"I should be surprised, but somehow in a town painted over a scroll, a driverless rickshaw almost makes perfect sense." Keishin settled next to Hana and realized how narrow the seat was. No matter which way he shifted, there was no way to keep their bodies apart. "It's a tight squeeze. I'm sorry."

"It's all right. It is a short ride to the Horishi's house. Nothing inside a scroll is far away."

Keishin pulled off his coat and held it over Hana's head, shielding her from the rain. The map on her skin faded away. A smile, tentative at first, settled over her lips. "Thank you."

Keishin let the rain drip over his lashes. He should have felt cold, but Hana's body warmed him through his clothes. That and her smile. Though it was fleeting, Keishin was aware that it had been the first to touch her lips since they met. It invited him to meander over the rest of her face, to explore it as one would study a star-filled sky. Her features were as carefully curated and assembled as any constellation, but more fascinating. Stars were interesting but did not hold his attention. In life, as in science, he was more drawn to the unseen. And he had never met a person with more secrets than Hana. He didn't mind that she kept them. He was used to it. The universe was like that too. It hid its most compelling secrets behind clouds of nothing and noise.

Keishin adjusted his coat over Hana's head, making sure that she stayed dry. He didn't know if Hana believed what he said about seeing through her scars. He was about to ask her when she relaxed against his ribs and he realized that he didn't need an answer. Hana fit next to him perfectly, a complement of angles and curves. Had he believed in destiny, Keishin might have allowed himself to think that their bodies had been carved exactly for this moment, for this one rickshaw ride in the rain. But as he did not, Keishin kept his eyes forward, away from Hana's face and the memory of her smile.

The Horishi's house was located in the center of the town, indistinct from the narrow wooden townhouses Keishin had seen along the way. He stepped off the rickshaw and offered Hana his hand.

Hana took it and climbed down. She glanced up at him, thanked him with a small smile, and let go.

"It . . . uh . . . must be difficult for you to be back here after what the Horishi did to you," Keishin said, finding it hard to form words with the warmth from Hana's small hand still lingering in his palm.

"It was the Horishi's duty. We all have our roles to play."

A wooden gate swung open, inviting them in. They followed a paved path shaded by a cherry tree waiting to bloom. A breeze blew through its painted branches, rattling the empty birdcages hanging from them.

"Where are all the birds?" Keishin asked.

Hana paused beneath an empty cage. "Kei, listen to me. Do not concern yourself with anything except for what I am about to tell you. When we meet the Horishi, you must remain absolutely quiet. Do not make a sound. Do not utter a single word. Do you understand?"

"Why?"

"The Horishi only speaks when spoken to, and there may be things you do not wish to hear."

"Like what?"

"Your future."

Keishin had lost count of the number of fusuma that had slid open and closed as they made their way through the Horishi's house. The silk-covered sliding screens moved on their own, ushering them through what felt like endless rooms. If he paused to think, Keishin would have questioned how the maze could have possibly fit into a townhouse of that size.

But Keishin had time to entertain only one thought. That thought grew with every step he took, rolling around in his head and tumbling over everything else. He had never been the sort of person who spent time pondering what his future would be. It was an unknowable thing and a waste of his time. But now he stood under the same roof as someone who might tell him if, at the end of his lifelong hunt to find the missing puzzle pieces of the universe, he would finally find his place in the world. All he had to do was ask.

"This is the Horishi's room," Hana said.

Keishin looked up from the floor. A burst of color filled his irises. He shielded his face with his hands. Inside a black-and-white scroll, four panels of a brightly painted fusuma were blinding. Keishin squinted, waiting for his sketched eyes to adjust.

A moonlit lake, surrounded by mountains half-covered by fog, stretched across the fusuma. A small boat moved slowly across the water, leaving a trail of ripples in its wake. It stopped beneath the full moon. Keishin leaned closer, trying to see if its occupants had paused to look at him too, but the two panels in the middle of the painting slid open, breaking the little boat in half.

A blindfolded girl, no older than twelve, sat behind a low wooden table in the center of the room. Keishin shot a glance at Hana. "She's a child."

"The eldest of the Horishi's children takes over when the Horishi passes, no matter how old they are," Hana whispered. "Remember, once we step inside, you must not speak."

Keishin nodded.

Hana greeted the seated girl with a low bow. "Horishi-san."

"Ishikawa Hana," the girl said as though she were able to see Hana through her blindfold. "Welcome."

Keishin followed Hana inside and bowed, but kept silent as Hana had instructed.

The girl turned toward him, tilted her head slightly, then shifted her attention back to Hana.

"Horishi-san," Hana said. "I have a question that I was hoping you could provide an answer to."

The Horishi nodded. "Please sit."

Keishin sat down on the tatami mat, folding his knees beneath him. His eyes swept over the tattooing instruments on the table. Nomi of varying sizes were arranged in a row. From afar they looked like long, slim paintbrushes with bamboo handles. Upon closer inspection, Keishin saw that the tips were not soft bristles, but tiny needles fastened to the bamboo with silk string. Next to the nomi was an ink stone. Keishin had watched a documentary on traditional tattoo techniques and knew that the stone was used for grinding charcoal blocks into black ink. The blocks arranged next to the Horishi's ink stone, however, were not black, but a bright, shimmering blue.

"What do you wish to know that is not already written over your skin?" the Horishi said, sounding far older than her years.

"Death," Hana said.

"The one thing that neither I nor your skin can tell you. Death ends your story as it pleases."

"Not my death. My mother's."

"Your mother's fate is known by all. She was a thief and was executed for her crime."

"Yes."

"And yet you have doubts. You think that there is a chance she may still be alive."

Hana nodded.

"In the years since my father passed, I have learned that most people do not wish to hear the answers they seek. Know that once I speak it, I cannot take the truth back."

"I understand."

"Show me your right arm."

Hana rolled up her sleeve and held out her arm.

The young girl rinsed her hands in a silver bowl and patted them dry. She ran her fingers over Hana's skin and stopped at a spot just above her elbow. "A chrysanthemum," she said, admiring an invisible patch of ink. "My father took great care in crafting your mother's symbol." The girl chose a nomi and poised it over the spot she had selected on Hana's arm. "This will hurt. Stay still."

"I am ready."

The Horishi pressed the nomi into Hana's skin, jabbing the needles along the lines of a design only she could see. Little droplets of blood formed along the nomi's path. Keishin watched Hana take slow, measured breaths without flinching. Hana, he thought, was used to hiding pain.

The Horishi straightened, lifting the nomi from Hana's arm. "The ink from your mother's symbol will tell us what has become of her. Blue means she is alive. If it is black, then she is . . ."

"Dead," Hana said. "I understand."

The young girl rested the point of the nomi over the empty ink stone as though she were dipping its needles in ink. Ink flowed from the tips of the needles, filling the ink stone's shallow well. It glowed bright blue.

"She's *alive.*" Hana gasped. "Do you know where she is, Horishi-san?"

"The ink does."

"Tell me, please."

The Horishi shook her head. "Your mother played her part when she birthed you. Beyond that, she has no place in your story. You cannot stray from what has been written."

"Please." Hana prostrated herself by the Horishi's feet. "I beg you."

"I am sorry. That knowledge is not meant for your eyes or ears."

"How about mine?" Keishin blurted. The sight of Hana crumpled over the floor twisted like a knife between his ribs.

The Horishi tilted her head his way, and though she was blindfolded, Keishin felt her gaze bore into him.

"Ah. You speak. I wondered what your voice might sound like."

"Can you tell me where Hana's mother is?"

Hana sat up and urgently mouthed a silent word. *Stop.*

"I can," the Horishi said. "*If* she is in your path. Minatozaki Keishin, would you like to know your story?"

"Thank you for your help, Horishi-san." Hana grabbed Keishin's arm. "We should go."

"My story?" Keishin said, his eyes fixed on the Horishi.

"The road to all that must happen next. People learn their path before they can walk or talk. You are older." She tilted her head, touching her chin. "But also very new. Your map is unlike anything I have seen before."

"What do you mean by 'new'?"

"Kei." Hana gripped his hand. "Don't."

"We can't leave," Keishin said. "She knows where your mother is."

"But one thing cannot be revealed without unveiling all that is linked to it," the Horishi said. "Your beginning, middle, and end. You will see your entire path stretched before you as clearly as you see me."

"Then tell me everything."

"You misunderstand. The ink will speak. Your skin will listen." She picked up a nomi. "Do you consent?"

Keishin stared at the nomi, thinking how such a small thing could soon silence every question that woke him up at night. Everything from this day forward could be certain. Set in skin. He would never again have to wonder if his life was going to mean something more than just a byline in another research paper, or if he was massless and invisible, a waste of time and space.

All he had to do was say yes.

CHAPTER FIFTEEN

Consent

Hana's eyes watered, but she didn't dare to blink. She feared her thoughts would wander from the full moon quivering in the fusuma's painted lake and escape. She knew exactly where they would go. The second they slipped from her, they would dart away and find Keishin behind the sliding cloth panel, lying on the Horishi's table, making a cruel trade so that she could find her mother.

Hot tears stung her eyes. Hana blinked. A small boat drifted over the lake and scattered the moon's reflection, leaving Hana with nothing to stare at except the truth: Though it was the Horishi's hand that gripped the nomi, it was she who was stabbing it into Keishin's skin. She cursed under her breath and pushed the fusuma open. "Stop!"

"Hana!" Keishin sat up from the table, his clothes in a pile on the floor.

"I cannot let you do this." Hana's eyes darted over his bare skin. The Horishi's map revealed itself only when touched by the rain, leaving Hana to wonder if she was too late.

"I want to, Hana." Keishin stood up.

"He has given his consent." The Horishi set a nomi down, its tip tinted with blue ink. "He cannot take it back."

"But I can." Hana grabbed Keishin's clothes from the floor and knocked the silver water bowl from the table. A puddle pooled by Keishin's feet. She shoved Keishin into it and jumped in after him.

Hana climbed out of her courtyard's pond and found Keishin standing in front of her.

"Why, Hana?" Keishin's throat tightened around his voice. "Why did you stop her? The Horishi would have told us where to find your mother."

Hana averted her eyes from his nakedness. Keishin had stripped himself of more than just clothes. The sacrifice he had been about to make for her bared his soul. She did not need her father's or mother's glasses to see that he was blinding. She held out his crumpled bundle of clothes.

"Get dressed and leave." Her words trembled as much as her hands. She had never meant anything more. Or less. She wanted him to stay as desperately as she needed him to go. Though the map of her skin was not visible, she knew every inked detail on her tattooed map by heart. Keishin was not in it.

"Hana . . ."

"Go home, Kei." She dropped his clothes on the ground. "While you can."

PART TWO

目は口ほどに物を言い

The eyes speak as much as the mouth.

CHAPTER SIXTEEN

Payment

Keishin stood at the pawnshop's door, his hand around its brass knob. It was ironic, he thought, that the only regret he would have wanted to pawn was going to be the moment he stepped back into his world and shut the door behind him. He looked back over his shoulder at Hana. "Tell me why you stopped the Horishi."

"The price was too high."

"I was willing to pay it." He let go of the knob and turned to face her. "It wasn't your place to decide for me. It was my choice."

"And it would have been the last real choice you made. Did you think that the Horishi was going to give you your future for free? The same fee is paid by everyone whose path is mapped out on their skin. Freedom. Knowing your future would have stripped you of every choice, every chance you could have turned left instead of right. You would lose the ability to dream and hope, to wish for an outcome other than what is written. Is that a price you would be willing to pay to help a stranger?"

"It would be a lot simpler for me to walk away if that was true. But you aren't exactly a stranger anymore."

"You do not know me."

"I know enough. I know what it's like to have a parent vanish like smoke and leave you with nothing but questions and pain.

My mother abandoned us when I was a young boy. We left Japan because of it. Breathing the same air she used to breathe was like breathing broken glass."

"I'm sorry . . ." Hana said. "But this is different. My father did not abandon me."

"Didn't he? The doubt gnawing inside you is the very reason you're trying so desperately to find him. You want to prove yourself wrong. You want to find him and hear him tell you that this is all a misunderstanding. I haven't seen my mother since she kissed me on the cheek and tucked me in bed the night before she left us. And yet today I found myself walking around Tokyo at dawn hoping that I would run into her and finally be able to ask her why she didn't love me enough to stay."

"I . . ." Tears crept into Hana's voice. "I'm sorry. I didn't know."

"I want you to be right, Hana. I want you to find your father and not spend your life searching for answers that will never come."

Hana shook her head. "Just go. Forget that any of this happened."

"How?"

"In time, you will be able to live your life just as our clients do. Everything you have seen and heard here will feel like a dream. I should have never allowed you to come with me."

"You didn't force me to do anything."

"I took advantage of your curiosity and kindness. I can read people. It is what I have spent my whole life training to do. I dangled the strange and impossible in front of you because I knew you would not be able to resist trying to figure out whether what I told you was true."

"You and I both know that isn't what happened. A coin decided for us."

"Did it?"

"What are you saying?"

Hana held out her fist and opened her fingers. Keishin's coin sat in the middle of her palm. "I needed your help even if I did not want to admit it."

Keishin stared at the coin. "You cheated at the coin toss?"

"I did my job. Misdirection and manipulation. That is what pawnbrokers do to win at every negotiation."

"Why bother with tossing the coin then? I told you that I wanted to help you. All you had to do was say yes."

"Fate, even the perception of it, seals deals better than any word could."

"Why are you telling me all of this now?"

"Because I made a mistake. I was selfish and desperate. I was wrong."

"And this is how you're making things right? By asking me to leave? Because you feel guilty about showing me a world I never imagined existed? If that's the case, then I'm sorry to tell you that you aren't as good at reading people as you believe. You didn't appeal to my curiosity or my kindness, Hana. You appealed to my greed." Keishin waved his hand around the pawnshop. "This place . . . your world . . . it's what I've been looking for my entire life."

"Another mystery to solve?"

"Not a mystery. *More.* Something beyond the known, beyond reach. The flower in the mirror. The moon in the pond. I thought science and the stars would help me find it, but here it was, all this time, behind this door. If you truly believe that you've wronged me, then make things right the *right* way."

Keishin walked up to Hana. "Pay me. If you won't accept my help because you think it's from a misplaced sense of empathy, then pay me. Pay me by letting me stay, at least until we find out what happened to your parents."

"You will have no memory of any of this once you leave. None of this will matter."

"I'll have now. For the first time in my life, I won't have to spin a coin on a ledge to keep my mind anchored on what's right in front of me. Don't take this from me. Not yet."

"Even if you stayed, we still do not know which way to go next. We have reached a dead end."

"Good."

"What?"

"Because if we don't hit walls, we can't break through them. Every significant scientific discovery ever made was because someone hit a blank wall and decided to push further."

Hana shook her head. "This is not one of your experiments."

"But it's a puzzle just the same. Maybe we can't find answers because we're not asking the right questions."

"What question is there left to ask? Where is my father? Why did he do this? He had every chance to say something to me about his plans. Anything. But all he did was—" Hana froze.

"Hana?"

"My father . . . he . . ."

Keishin watched a thousand thoughts dart across Hana's eyes like cars speeding down a highway, but much faster. Her brow furrowed, slowing them down. Keishin held his breath, convinced that the rest of his life depended entirely on what she was going to say next. "What did your father do?"

"He gave me a box of tea."

CHAPTER SEVENTEEN

The Gift

The box of tea patiently sat on the table next to Hana's bed, waiting for someone to notice it. It was wrapped in a silk cloth Hana had painted the week before. Though it was distorted by knots and folds, Hana recognized her design. A water lily bobbed over the cloth, floating along the edges of a calm pond. Hana untied the silk and let it pool over the table.

"What's so special about this tea?" Keishin said.

"Absolutely nothing." Hana had not asked Keishin to stay. Nor had she pushed him out the door. But she found herself drawing steadier breaths when he stood by her side, as though his voice made the air easier to breathe. "It is the same tea that we give to our clients in exchange for their choices. I thought that my father did not have the time or imagination to get me anything else. Now I think that there may be another reason. When he gave me the tea, he told me that it would taste different today because it was my first day as the pawnshop's owner. He said that things would change even if they looked the same. This tea could be another clue."

Hana poured out the tea into a broken bowl mended with gold. The tea looked and smelled exactly as it always did, roasted and slightly sweet. Doubt filled her gut as she inhaled its fragrant steam. It felt foolish to entertain the notion that her father had left a message for her in the tea when it was growing clearer by the second that he did not wish to be found. She filled a second bowl.

"If you're right about it being a clue, then it probably contains a message that is intended only for you," Keishin said. "I can wait in the front office while you drink it."

"You can stay."

"Are you sure?"

"I do not think that I am certain of anything anymore." She handed him his tea.

"Believe me when I tell you that I know exactly how you feel."

"We should drink to that."

"To what?"

"Uncertainty." Until today, the word was a stranger to Hana's mouth. It coated her tongue with the taste of metal. "The one thing we can share."

Keishin looked up from his cracked bowl. "Is it?"

"What more can two people from different worlds have? A ride in the rain? A trip through a puddle? Tea?"

Keishin reached across the table and rested his palm over Hana's. "A hand to hold."

"The tea is getting cold." Hana retreated from his touch. She brought the bowl to her lips, hoping the tea would wash away the truth Keishin's hand had left on her skin. Warmth felt the same no matter which side of the door you were from. Kindness did too. Her father's voice in her head reminded her that she could not allow herself to know either. The pawnshop's rules applied outside its walls. Empathy lost deals.

The tea tasted like it always did. A knot formed in Hana's throat. Another dead end. And then there it was. A forgotten, deep sweetness rose like a wave from the back of her tongue. It swept Hana to a warmly lit room, across the table from a smiling, wrinkled face. She drew a sharp breath. "Sobo?"

Hana? Keishin called to her from far away. *Are you all right?*

Hana ignored him, her eyes fixed on her grandmother. The older woman sat across from her, sipping tea from a glazed clay cup. She smiled at Hana, seemingly undisturbed by her sudden appearance in her home.

"Do you know where my mother is, Sobo?" Hana said.

"Please have some more, Hana. You are too thin," her grandmother said, offering her a plate of little cakes made from mochi and red bean paste.

"Did you hear what I said, Sobo?" Hana gripped the edges of the table.

"Time goes by so fast," her grandmother said. "I cannot believe you are ten now. Your mother looked exactly like you at your age."

"Ten?" Hana frowned. "Sobo, please listen to me. I—" The ground shook, rattling the cups on the table. Her grandmother smiled at her and sipped her tea, oblivious to the rumbling. Hana jumped from her seat and grabbed her grandmother's hand. Her fingers closed around thin air. "No!"

"Hana!" Keishin's voice exploded in her ears.

Hana snapped her eyes open and found Keishin shaking her by the shoulders, her teacup broken at her feet.

"Are you okay?" Keishin clutched her shoulders.

Hana blinked. "What happened?"

"You were in some sort of trance. You didn't move or say anything for almost half an hour."

"What? It was barely a few minutes for me."

"What did you see?"

"I think it was a memory."

"Of what?"

"Of the first time I tasted this tea. I was wrong, Kei. This is not the tea my father offers our clients. It is what my grandmother serves hers. I think the memory in the tea means that I need to see her."

"You don't have to do this alone, Hana. You said it yourself, none of this will matter when I return to my world. When all of this is over, I'll forget everything about this place. What harm will it do if you let me stay and help you a little longer?"

Hana ran her eyes over the invisible map on her arms. Every moment she spent with Keishin was uncharted and pulled her further from her fate. Her mother was a constant reminder of what the Shiikuin did to people who strayed. "You are not a part of my path."

"Of course I am," Keishin said. "I'm your client. You told me that everyone who walks through your door is a client. That means that I can't leave. Not until our business is concluded. You're not breaking any rules, Hana. By letting me stay, you're following them."

Hana could not argue with the truth. She shook her head and laid her hands on her lap with a heavy sigh. "My grandmother's teahouse. That is where we need to go. But we need to wait until midnight."

"Why?"

"Because that's the only hour of the day that her teahouse exists."

CHAPTER EIGHTEEN

The Truth Well Told

The pawnshop was almost pristine if you didn't look too closely. Only the missing glass panels on some cabinet doors hinted at its earlier state of disarray. Hana and Keishin had spent the day putting the place back together. They hardly spoke as they worked, and when they did, it was mainly Keishin asking where something went and Hana giving him the shortest answer possible. Hana felt that it was safer this way. Talking inevitably led to telling the truth, and there were secrets that she needed to hold close to her chest.

Keishin wiped the sweat from his brow with the back of his hand, leaving a streak of dust on his left temple. "It looks like we're finally done."

"You missed a spot," Hana said.

"Oh?" Keishin surveyed the room. "Where?"

Hana wiped away the smudge on his face with a fresh cleaning cloth. "There. Now we are done."

"Thanks." Keishin blushed. "So, what next? We still have a few more hours before midnight."

"Dinner. I just realized that we have not eaten anything all day. You must be starving. I am sorry."

"I didn't notice." Keishin's stomach grumbled.

"Your stomach disagrees with—"

Sharp knocking cut her off. Hana shot a glance at the back door. She motioned for Keishin to be quiet.

The knocking grew louder.

"Upstairs," Hana whispered. "Hurry."

Keishin crept up the stairs, careful not to make a sound. A step creaked. He glanced back at Hana, swallowing hard.

Hana whispered a plea. *"Hide."*

Keishin disappeared into the hall.

Hana made her way to the back door, her heart pounding louder than the knocking. She steadied herself with a breath and pulled the door open. A shadow fell over her.

A slim figure dressed in a white kimono stood at the doorway. A Noh mask, carved from cypress and painted in a hue that matched the moon, covered its face. The slits from where the figure's eyes looked out were small, revealing only two bottomless pools of black.

"Shiikuin-san." Hana bowed deeply. "I did not expect you to come so early. The new moon is not yet in the sky."

"We have not come to collect the birds." A chorus of at least ten hollow voices, ancient and young, spoke from the Shiikuin's mouth. The last word was spoken by a young child, but with no less gravity than the oldest in the choir.

Hana nodded. "Please come in."

The Shiikuin entered, gliding over the floorboards as though floating on air.

"May I offer you some tea?" Hana said.

The Shiikuin slowly tilted its head, allowing the curves and angles of its mask to catch the light. Shadows morphed the wooden face, shifting its expression until it settled into the illusion of a dark, joyless smile. "We have come to ask you a question."

"I am happy to provide anything you wish to know."

The mask's painted lips tightened into a thin line. "Where is your father?"

Hana's spine turned to stone.

"And if you lie . . ." The Shiikuin outstretched its arm, a foul melding of iron and rot. It opened its hand, extending black talons where there should have been fingers. "We will know."

Hana nodded, not trusting her voice. She slowly placed her wrist in the Shiikuin's grasp, using every ounce of strength and will to keep from shaking.

"Ishikawa Hana." The Shiikuin's talons closed around her arm, digging into a vein and her pulse. "Tell us where your father is."

"He is not here."

"We sensed his absence." The Shiikuin pushed a black talon deeper into Hana's wrist. A drop of blood dribbled from her arm.

Hana clenched her jaw, ignoring the pain.

"Where has he gone?" a chorus of voices demanded.

"I do not know."

The Shiikuin leaned closer, peering at Hana through its mask's hollow eyes. "Tell us where he is."

"The last time I saw him was before I went to bed yesterday evening." Cold sweat beaded on Hana's nape. "He was gone when I woke up. I do not know where he is. I swear it."

The Shiikuin tightened its grip, drawing more blood. "Tell us what you do know."

She sucked in a deep breath and exhaled it slowly through her teeth. "This morning, I discovered that the pawnshop was ransacked and that a bird was missing from the vault. My father was missing too. It appeared as though the thief escaped into the world beyond the door and that my father gave chase. He has not returned."

"Ishikawa Hana." The Shiikuin brought its mask to within a breath of Hana's face. It wrung her wrist, cutting her skin deeper. Shadows turned the Shiikuin's smile into a sneer.

"Yes, Shiikuin-san?" Blood spattered onto Hana's foot.

The Shiikuin released her. "You speak the truth."

Hana clutched her arm to her chest. It trembled against her pounding heart. "Thank you, Shiikuin-san."

"We will come to collect the birds in two days."

Hana bowed. "Yes, Shiikuin-san."

"*All* the birds."

Hana paled. "But—"

The Shiikuin tilted Hana's chin up with a black talon, nicking her skin. "You have your mother's eyes. You might find reading your clients' faces and examining their choices more difficult without them. The new moon is in two days."

CHAPTER NINETEEN

The Teahouse at Midnight

Keishin listened in on the conversation between the masked creature and Hana from the top of the stairs. The Shiikuin's chorus of voices sent ice through his veins. He crouched, just out of sight, clutching a kitchen knife in his right fist. He had never stabbed anyone before, but this day was a day of firsts.

When the Shiikuin demanded the truth from Hana about what had happened to her father, he gripped the knife tighter. But as Hana calmly gave her answers, Keishin found himself loosening his grip, understanding in that moment the reason for her father's ruse. He had ransacked the pawnshop and staged a theft so that Hana would have a truthful story to tell. He had lied so that she would not have to.

"You can come down now." Hana stared at the door, her arms wrapped around her stomach.

Keishin rushed down the steps, dropping the kitchen knife. He pulled her into his arms. "Are you okay?"

"No." Hana crumbled against his chest.

"That creature . . ." He held her tight. "That was the Shiikuin?"

"One of many. They want the missing choice."

"I heard that part. And their threat."

"That was not a threat." Hana stepped out from the circle of his arms. "That was a promise."

"Then we have to find the choice. Fast. Your father must have taken the choice with him. If we find him, we'll find the choice." Keishin checked his watch. "It's just a few more hours until midnight. We'll have answers soon."

"*We?* You still want to do this? Even after seeing the Shiikuin?"

"That thing will be back in two days. I'm not about to abandon you now."

"Kei . . . there's something I need to tell you."

"Hana, there's nothing you can say that will make me change my mind." Keishin affixed what he hoped looked like a convincing smile onto his face. "Besides, I'm getting used to jumping into puddles."

"Puddles cannot take us to my grandmother's teahouse."

"How do we get there?"

"We need to share a bed."

They lay next to each other on Hana's futon, their bodies close enough to feel the other's warmth. Keishin stared up at the ceiling, trying to summon the most boring lecture he could think of. He imagined himself back in high school, sitting in the back of his history classroom, making up math problems in his head to keep his eyes open. It wasn't that he found the Renaissance uninteresting, it was just that Mr. Whitecotton's idea of teaching was to read from their textbook until the bell rang. But not even the memory of his old teacher's nasal droning could weigh his eyelids down this evening. The Shiikuin's voices echoed over Elizabeth's Golden Age, denying him sleep. Keishin sat up and groaned. "This is impossible. I can't sleep."

"Lie down." Hana gently drew him back next to her. "And try not to think about anything. Sleep will come."

Keishin rested his head on a pillow and sighed. "Are you sure we can't just dive into a pond or a puddle?"

"I have never met a man like you." Hana turned to face him. "You are unlike anyone who has stepped through the pawnshop's door."

A lock of silver hair slipped over Keishin's eyes. Hana ran her fingers through his hair, pushing it from his face. Keishin stiffened, inhaling sharply. Hana met his startled gaze. A smile crinkled his eyes and softened them. Keishin took Hana's hand, gently pressing it to his cheek. "In what way?" he whispered, the corner of his lips grazing her palm.

"I . . . uh . . . I'm sorry." She stared and blinked at him, withdrawing her hand. "What did you say?"

A dimple dug into Keishin's cheek. "In what way am I different from your other clients?"

Hana blushed. She did not bother to hide it. "All our clients, even if they do not know it, come looking for help. You are the first one to ever offer it. You jump into the unknown without thinking twice and do not hesitate to take my word when I tell you that the way to find my grandmother is through a dream. You are a good man, Kei." She laced her fingers over her stomach. "Perhaps too good."

"I didn't realize that wanting to do the decent thing was a character flaw." Keishin propped himself on his elbow.

"It is not a flaw. It is a weakness. It makes it easier for people to hurt you."

"The only motives and actions I am responsible for are my own. How people choose to respond to that is their problem."

"It becomes your problem when they cause you pain. I have seen enough tears in the pawnshop to know that this is true in both our worlds."

"Do those tears include your own?"

She turned her back to him. "We should try to sleep."

"Hana . . ."

"It is almost midnight."

Keishin lay down. "You wouldn't happen to have a spare bottle of your father's sleeping medication lying around, would you?"

"Close your eyes and listen to my voice. I will tell you a story."

"A bedtime story? Are you serious?"

"Trust me."

Keishin lowered his eyelids. "Fine."

"A long time ago, there was a fisherman named Urashima Taro. He was fishing when he saw some children torturing a turtle. Taro saved the turtle and set it free in the sea. The following morning, an old turtle swam up to him and told him that the turtle he had saved was the daughter of Ryūjin, the Emperor of the Sea. Ryūjin asked the turtle to invite Taro to his kingdom to thank him. The turtle gave Taro gills and led Taro to Ryūjin's underwater palace. At the palace, Taro met Ryūjin and his daughter, Otohime, who had turned from a turtle into a beautiful princess."

Hana's voice soothed Keishin like a lullaby, bundling him up and rocking him. He followed Hana's words as though they were crumbs on a forest trail, each leading him closer to a dream of the sea.

"Taro stayed with Otohime for three days but found himself longing to see his elderly mother. Otohime regretfully agreed to let him go. Before he left, she gifted him with a mysterious box that would protect him as long as he did not open it. The old turtle took Taro back to the shore of his village."

Keishin struggled to stay awake, torn between exhaustion and curiosity. Hana turned on her side and rested her head on his chest. Keishin held her to him, no longer sure if he was dreaming or still awake.

"Hold on to me," Hana whispered over his heart. "I will lead you through the dream."

Keishin nodded, half asleep. "What happened to Taro?"

"When Taro returned to his village, he discovered that everything had changed. Three hundred years had passed. Everyone he knew was gone. Distraught, he opened the box from Otohime . . ."

Hana watched him sleep. She was going to join him soon, but for now, she let him dream. In a way, she felt like she had gone ahead of him and was already dreaming. Keishin was the stranger in her world, and yet since he had arrived, nothing around her was familiar anymore. Her room. Her bed. Even her own skin. All it took was the briefest of glances from Keishin to set it humming, tingling from the top of her head to her toes, the way it did when she had climbed the tallest tree along one of the mountain trails she enjoyed exploring as a child. Her father had told her not to, but still she climbed, higher and higher, away from the echo of his rules, above the walls of everything she had been told she could or could not do. Looking down at the world from her quivering perch, she was unable to tell if the current buzzing in her limbs made her feel alive or terrified. A gust of wind whipped the canopy beneath her into a blur of green and gray. Hana looked up in time to see an angry sky break open. She clung to a trembling branch.

Icy shards of rain struck her fists, awakening the glowing

paper cranes tattooed on her skin. The flock took flight across the back of her hand, oblivious to the wet lashing. Hana envied their wings. She loosened her fingers around the branch and considered letting go, if only to know, for the sliver of time before she lay broken on the rocks, what it was like to fly.

Curled on her mattress next to Keishin, her face near enough to feel the warmth of his breath on her lips, Hana dangled from a tree that towered over everything she knew. From this distance, the world below was tiny, and she was free from its grasp. Still, she had no wings. She nestled her cheek against Keishin's chest and closed her eyes, wondering if falling into him would hurt as much as crashing into the ground and shattering all her bones.

Gravel crunched by his ear. Keishin snapped his eyes open. He sat up and looked around. An arched bridge stretched out in front of him. A long line of people dressed in white sleeping robes made their way over the bridge from a gravel road, their pace unhurried.

"That is the Midnight Bridge. It connects night and morning." Hana stood up and brushed the dust and gravel from her clothes. "People cross over it in their dreams. My grandmother's teahouse is across the road."

"Where?" Keishin craned his neck to see over the people in line for the bridge. A large, fiery tree that reminded him of the maple trees in his old university's courtyard grew in a garden across the road.

"That is Sobo's teahouse."

"The tree?"

"It's called a kito tree. It means 'calm,' which I think is quite appropriate. My grandmother's teahouse offers refuge to those suffering from nightmares."

"Nightmares?" Keishin glanced at the people lining up for the bridge and noticed that their eyes were closed. "They're all asleep . . ."

"Yes. And so are we. The difference is that we know that we are dreaming. My grandmother taught me the way to her teahouse when I was a little girl. You turn left when you fall asleep and turn right at the end of your second dream."

Keishin watched Hana's breath turn into mist in the night air. In the middle of a dream, next to a bridge that led to morning, he took comfort in knowing that at least some laws of science still held true. Most people mistakenly believed that you saw your breath simply when the weather got cold. Humidity, however, played an equal part in turning one's breath into minuscule water droplets that floated in the air. "Dew point," Keishin murmured absently like it was a memorized prayer.

"Did you say something?"

"I . . . uh . . . was just saying that I was glad that we didn't wake up in the river."

"Yes. I have seen what happens when a person falls into it." Hana stared at the rushing water. "During one of my visits to my grandmother, I saw a Night Market vendor being chased down this road by a Shiikuin. Everyone on the road and the bridge froze in place. Only the vendor ran. The Shiikuin moved slowly, and sometimes it paused mid-stride, not moving at all."

"I thought that the Shiikuin was chasing the vendor?"

"It was, but time passes differently for a Shiikuin. My father said that while we may see them standing still, they could be racing through time, living several lifetimes in the blink of an eye. They never run because they know they don't have to. There is nowhere any of us can hide from them. They will always catch us in the end."

"Why was the Shiikuin chasing the vendor?"

"For the same and only reason they hunt down anyone from this world. The vendor failed in his duty. He fell asleep while tending his stall. I will never forget the terror on his face. The Shiikuin nodded at the people on the bridge and they began to move like puppets on a string. They grabbed at the vendor, ripping his clothes and tearing his skin. He screamed and tried to shove them out of the way, but they were too many. They blocked the end of the bridge, keeping him from reaching morning. He jumped into the river, choosing to drown rather than get caught."

Keishin watched the violent water sweep a fallen tree away. "It was a good thing it was only a dream."

"The vendor was in a dream, but the Shiikuin was real. The vendor never woke up. Anyone who falls into the river will never be able to cross over to the morning."

Keishin stared at the river and swallowed hard. "We should keep our distance from it then."

"Unfortunately, crossing the bridge is our only way back."

A manicured roji stood as a mossy border between the gravel road and the large kito tree. Keishin sensed a change in the air as soon as he entered the tea garden. The gentle breeze drifting over the serene landscape of sculpted evergreen bushes felt solemn and sweet, a silent signal that a tea ceremony had begun with his first step. Each stepping stone laid over the grass took him further from the mundane.

"The tsukubai is for purifying ourselves before entering the teahouse." Hana stopped by a stone washbasin surrounded by artfully arranged stones. She picked up a bamboo ladle and proceeded to wash her hands and rinse her mouth.

Keishin followed her lead. A pleasant, soothing tinkling, similar to the music made by a zither, echoed from the ground next to the basin. "Do you hear that?"

"That is the suikinkutsu. I helped my grandmother make it. We put a hole in a clay pot and buried it upside down. When water drips through the hole, it falls into a small pool of water and makes the pot sing."

Keishin did not remember most of his dreams, but he hoped to hold on to the suikinkutsu's song when he woke up. "It's magical."

"There is nothing magical about a buried pot." Hana walked over to a bamboo lattice gate by a hemlock hedge. "Do not be so quick to fall in love with things in this world, Kei. You will find that many things here are not as they seem."

"A beautiful song is a beautiful song." Keishin's eyes lingered over her face. "Whatever world it's from."

The gate swung open, inviting them into the teahouse's inner garden. Hana stepped through the gate without looking back. Keishin followed her into a more intimate, rustic scene. Shrubs were left to grow naturally in the shade of the kito. Keishin looked up at the tree's dense, sprawling canopy. Even in the moonlight, its leaves looked as though they were on fire. He ran his hand over the tree's trunk and felt it beat beneath his palm like a heart. "I still can't imagine how your grandmother's teahouse is inside this tree."

"It grew inside it when it was still a seed," Hana said.

"A seed?" Keishin's mind raced with possibility. "I don't suppose your grandmother would have some extra seeds I could take back with me? They could solve—" He wrinkled his nose, regretting his words. "Sorry. Forget I said anything. Bad habit."

"We could ask her, but I am not sure how well such a seed would grow in the ground. The mind is a thousand times more fertile than any kind of soil."

"Good point." Keishin chuckled. Lightning streaked across the night sky. The wind blew, carrying the scent of rain. Even in a dream, Keishin could not escape terrible weather.

"We should head inside." Hana rapped her knuckles against the tree's trunk.

A long branch reached over from the side of the tree and clasped a ridge in the trunk with fingerlike twigs. It pulled the bark open like a door. Another branch tapped Keishin on the shoulder. He jumped and twisted around. The branch nudged his chest.

Hana tried to hide a small smirk. "It is telling you to go in."

The branch continued to tap Keishin. "I'm going. I'm going," he said, removing his shoes. He left them on a flat stone by the entrance to the tree.

"Kei, wait."

"What is it?"

"I think it would be best if we do not mention anything about my mother being alive to my grandmother. We do not have any concrete proof, and it might upset her."

"I understand."

Though it had no windows, the empty teahouse was warmly lit by the glow of fireflies, flying freely across the shop's high ceiling. A sky filled with dancing stars. An old woman dressed in a simple kimono looked up from a wooden counter that grew from the shop's mossy floor. Behind her, knobby shelves displayed an assortment of tea stored in clay jars.

"Hana?" A smile spread over Asami's face, crinkling the lines around her eyes.

"Sobo." Hana ran to her grandmother and embraced her tightly.

Asami hugged her back. "What a nice surprise. Why didn't you tell me you were coming?" She glanced at Keishin. "And who is your friend?"

Keishin hesitated, unsure of how Asami would react to his presence.

Hana gave him a quick look, prodding him to answer.

"I'm . . . uh . . . Minatozaki Keishin." Keishin bowed to her.

"I thought I had met all of Hana's friends," Asami said, eyeing him.

"Keishin is . . ." Hana drew away from her grandmother's arms. "Not from here."

Keishin held his breath.

"Not from here?" Asami furrowed her brow.

"He is from the other world."

Asami's hand flew over her mouth. "What have you done, Hana? Why did you bring him here?"

"Keishin is helping me find my father."

The veins on Asami's neck tightened. "Your father? Why? What happened?"

"I woke up this morning and found the pawnshop ransacked and Otou-san . . . gone."

Color drained from Asami's lips. "Did the Shiikuin—"

"No." Hana clasped her grandmother's hands. "They are looking for him too. That is why I need to find him first. He left clues that led us here."

"We were hoping that you would have some answers," Keishin said.

Asami ignored him, fixing a sharp gaze on Hana. "This is about your mother, isn't it? Your father paid me the strangest visit two moons ago. He said the oddest things about her. I thought that he must have been overworked or drunk. I told him to go home and rest."

"What did he say?" Hana said.

"Foolishness." Asami shook her head. "It would shame me to repeat it."

Hana gripped her grandmother's hands tighter. "But it might help us find him."

Keishin bit his lip, resisting the urge to jump in and help Hana plead their case. It was clear that Asami did not want him there.

"Forget about all of this. Go home, Hana."

"I cannot. You know what the Shiikuin will do to him if they find him first. You must tell me what my father told you. We are not leaving here until you do."

"You are as stubborn as your mother. I will not lose you too."

"You won't. I promise."

"That is not a promise you can make. Only the Shiikuin can decide your fate. They will make you suffer as your mother did."

"Not if you help us," Keishin blurted.

Asami scowled at him. "This does not concern you."

"Hana is my concern." Keishin raised his voice louder than he had intended but did not regret it. The image of Hana being chased into a river by the Shiikuin filled his mind. "I'm begging you." He softened his tone. "Please tell us what you know. It might be the only way to keep Hana safe."

Asami glared at him then exhaled, deflating her tiny frame. "Toshio . . ." she said, lowering her voice. "He told me that he was going to retire soon and that he was finally going to be able to make things right."

"How?" Hana creased her brow.

"He said that he had a plan that would keep you safe while he . . ." Asami's eyes blurred with tears. "While he searched for your mother. I tried to tell him that she was gone, but he had a wild look in his eyes and insisted that she was alive. He said that as soon as you took over the pawnshop, he was going to look for her." She clenched her jaw. "As I said, utter foolishness."

"But what if . . ." Hana said, "he was not being foolish?"

"No one wants your mother to be alive more than I do, but that is not reality. The Shiikuin came to me after she died and gave me a kioku pearl containing her last day."

"A kioku pearl?" Keishin asked.

Asami looked at him pointedly. "You may look like one of us, but your ignorance reveals where you are really from. If you do not wish your presence to be discovered, then you must watch what you say when you leave here. There are many who would not hesitate to betray you. You will wish that the Shiikuin find you before I do if any harm befalls my granddaughter because of your carelessness."

"I'm sorry." Keishin bowed his head. "I will be more careful."

"A kioku pearl is a vessel for memories," Asami said. "The Shiikuin made one to contain Chiyo's trial to show me what happened that day. The Shiikuin wanted their warning to be clear. There is only one fate for those who fail their duty."

"You never told me that you had a kioku pearl from that morning," Hana said.

"I don't. I threw it away. Why would I keep such a cruel thing? All I have tried to do since I saw Chiyo's last moments was forget them. If I had been there, I would not have just stood by like . . ." Her words died on her tongue.

"Like my father did?" Hana said.

"It is in the past," Asami said with a heavy voice. "But your father convinced himself that the past was not as it seemed."

"What do you mean?"

"He was convinced of the impossible. He thought he could find Chiyo if he turned back time."

The queue of dreamers moved at a snail's pace toward the bridge, but none of those in line seemed to be in a hurry. Each was too preoccupied with navigating a dream to notice the gravel crunching beneath their feet. But Keishin was keenly aware of every pebble and every second that passed as he waited for his turn to cross over into morning. He rubbed the back of his neck. "Would it be so terrible to jump the line? Everyone here is asleep anyway. They'd never notice."

"Yes," Hana said. "It would."

"I wish I had half of your patience."

"When you spend your life dreading your future, you learn to welcome anything that makes you wait."

"Is it really that awful? Running the pawnshop? I mean, apart from the Shiikuin, not that they're easy to set aside. But the pawnshop itself helps a lot of people from my world. You do a lot of good."

Hana kept her eyes on the bridge.

"Hana? Did you hear what I said?"

"I cannot stop thinking about what my grandmother said about my father's plan to turn back time."

"I know that your world doesn't care about science or any of its rules, but even your grandmother said that time travel isn't possible," Keishin said. "We should find another lead. What about that pearl your grandmother mentioned? She said that it showed her what happened the day of your mother's trial. Is there a way we could get our hands on another one?"

"A kioku pearl of an event can only be made by those present during the occasion. I do not think that asking the Shiikuin if they have a spare one would be wise. Finding another pearl containing that same memory would be harder than traveling through time."

"So we're at a dead end. Again."

"Maybe not. I know that time travel is not possible, but my father is not the kind of person to throw around words he does not mean, no matter how drunk he is. It is when he is drunk that he is the most honest. Time must have some part in his plan to find my mother," Hana said. "What does your science say about time?"

"Nothing definitive. But we have our theories."

"What kind of theories?"

"Well, for example, we know that space can be bent by gravity. This means that space-time can be bent. In theory, that means that time can be bent too."

"*Bent* . . ." Hana gnawed the corner of her lips.

The people in line froze mid-step. Hana cursed.

"What is it?" Keishin asked. "What's wrong?"

"They are here."

Keishin twisted around. A masked figure stood at the end of the road, its dark eyes boring into him. "Shiikuin."

Hana grabbed his hand. "Run."

* * *

Hana bolted up from her futon, her clothes soaked in sweat. Dawn spilled through a slit between her bedroom curtains. She gripped her arm, remembering the cold, rotting hands that had tried to keep her from crossing the bridge. Their touch had turned her marrow to ice, extinguishing her warmth and courage. Keishin had pushed them back, using his body to shield her. They clawed at him, drawing blood. He had screamed for her to run, telling her that he was right behind her.

He was not.

CHAPTER TWENTY

Trips and Trains

There were nightmares you woke up from and there were nightmares you woke up to. Mornings were powerless to stop them. And so was Hana. She watched Keishin writhe in bed, blood dripping from wounds the Shiikuin left on his arms. His face twisted in pain. Sweat plastered a silver lock of hair to his face. She grabbed him by the shoulders and shook him hard even though she knew that she couldn't wake him. The only way he was going to wake up was if he made it to the other side of the bridge on his own.

Keishin sat up with a jolt, wrestling himself free from invisible hands. His eyes found Hana's face. "Hana . . ." he said, breathing hard.

"Kei!" She threw her arms around him. "You crossed."

Kcishin pantcd. "I almost didn't."

Hana jumped to her feet. "Get up. We need to go."

"How did they find us?"

"It could have been the Horishi, or maybe someone who saw us at the teahouse or the temple. It does not matter. The Shiikuin have caught your scent."

"My scent?"

"The Shiikuin can smell our secrets. That is how they track us down. Now that they know you are here, they will not stop looking for you."

"I'm not leaving you."

"I know. You have made it very clear that it's useless to argue with you. I am not asking you to go back to your world, but we cannot stay here."

"Where are we going?"

"Everywhere."

They emerged from a puddle next to the entrance of a sprawling redbrick building with a large slate dome roof. An old-fashioned circular clock beneath the dome told the hour. Three floors below the clock, people scurried in and out of the building's tall front doors.

"This is our Tokyo Station," Hana said. "Does it look similar to the one in your world?"

"I don't think I've ever been to the one on my side. If I have, I don't remember. My life in Tokyo is blurry at best. I hardly even remember my—"

"Your mother's face?"

Keishin's heart tightened. "How did you know?"

"I have the same look on my face whenever my father catches me staring at the only photograph he keeps of my mother. I have no memory of her, but I keep stealing that photo from his room, hoping that the next time I look at it, I will find some trace of her in my mind."

"I try not to think about my mother." Keishin looked up at the clock. "She doesn't deserve an ounce of my time or the smallest space in my head."

The sky turned dark.

"It's going to rain," Hana said. "We should go inside."

"Are we catching a train?"

"A part of us is."

* * *

A high octagonal coved ceiling made Hana feel small. Eight marble eagles perched around the ceiling, their eyes following the travelers beneath them rushing to catch their trains.

"Did that eagle just move?" Keishin said.

"Of course it did. It is a statue. They are supposed to move."

"You'll be very disappointed by statues in my world then." Keishin looked around the station. "Where do we buy our tickets?"

"The tickets have already been purchased." Hana glanced in the direction of a crowd making their way to the train lines. "By them."

Keishin stood in the middle of a crowd waiting on the train platform, kneading his temples. "Out of everything I've seen and heard in your world, this plan is by far the strangest."

"But it will work," Hana said.

"You actually want me to go up to complete strangers and tell them my deepest secret?" Keishin said with a pained look.

"Both of us will. The more people we tell, the harder it will be for the Shiikuin to find us. They are tracking us, latching on to our secrets. A secret's perfume is stronger and more distinct than any scent. No two people keep the same secret."

"And that's why we need to share it?"

"With as many people as we can. They'll take our secrets with them wherever they go. It will confuse the Shiikuin and hopefully buy us enough time to find answers."

Hana weaved through the platform, stopped behind a man checking the time on his watch, and whispered in his ear. Kei followed her lead, sharing his secrets with the crowd.

* * *

They stood on the platform and watched a train pull away from the station. "I'm glad that's over," Keishin said. "I don't think I've ever been more uncomfortable in my life. I felt like I was in one of those dreams where I was teaching one of my classes stark naked."

"In a way, I suppose you were. Honesty strips away everything that hides who we really are. It is easier to share secrets with people you will never see again." Hana buttoned up her coat. "It will take the Shiikuin a while before they discover that we have sent them after every train that has left the station in the past twenty minutes. We should not waste any of the time that we just bought."

"Where to next?" Keishin asked.

"The edge of the sea."

CHAPTER TWENTY-ONE

The Sky, the Sea, and a Song

Keishin had been to the beach only a handful of times in his life, and yet each time he strolled along the shore, a sense of familiarity washed over him and warmed him down to his toes. He rationalized the feeling as a result of man's primordial connection to the sea, a carryover from the time when life emerged from the planet's prebiotic soup. His toes were of a simpler school of thought, happy to simply accept that they liked the sea because they enjoyed the feel of the sand between them. Today they were bereft, taking it personally when Keishin denied them the pleasure of a stroll. This beach was unlike any he had ever visited. Here, where powder-fine sand ended, clouds lapped at the shore. Keishin crouched next to the puddle they had climbed out of and dipped his hand into the sky at his feet. Wisps of a cloud curled around his fingers. "Incredible . . ." he said, his voice more air than sound.

"You are lucky," Hana said.

"Lucky?" Keishin stood up and brushed the sand from his pants.

"I cannot remember the last time I saw something and felt a sense of wonder. Unless you count the time I—" Hana's eyes darted from Keishin to the clouds crashing into the sand like waves.

"Unless you count what?"

"Nothing."

"Come on. You've just shared your deepest secret with complete strangers at a train station. This can't be that bad. I can trade a secret for it if you want."

"There is no need for a trade."

"Good. I would hate to have to tell you all about the time I accidentally set fire to the lab. Go on then. When was the last time you saw something that left you in awe?"

"Not something. *Someone.*"

"Oh?"

"You."

"Me? Why?"

"Because you broke every rule I knew."

Keishin knitted his brows. "What rules?"

"Too many."

"Name one."

"Instead of pawning a choice, you offered me one. Until the day I die, I will never fully understand how you came to stand with me on this beach, helping me search for my parents."

"You were a mystery to me too." Kei took a step closer. They were running for their lives and searching for a dead woman, but all he saw was the halo of calm in Hana's eyes and his face staring back at him from her irises. He envied his reflection. It could go where he could not. He wondered how many of Hana's secrets it knew, a privilege he doubted he was ever going to share. No matter how close they stood, Hana was always a universe away. Without thinking, he reached out to touch her cheek, his oldest instincts compelling him to know the unknowable. It was softer than he'd imagined. "You still are."

Hana looked away, hiding the blush that had formed where Keishin's long fingers had grazed her skin. She pointed to a group of wooden structures standing on stilts in the distance. "That is where we will catch our next ride."

"Our ride. Right," Keishin said, tearing his thoughts from Hana's face. He shielded his eyes from the sun. "I don't see any boats."

"There aren't any. Boats cannot travel on the Sky Sea."

It was a village built on thick timber stilts, extending several houses from the shore. Weathered wooden planks connected one house to the next, forming a complex web of streets above the sea of clouds. Vendors hawked a universe of goods from colorful stalls along the streets, some items confounding Keishin with their possible use.

"Why is that man selling bottles of sand?" Keishin whispered in Hana's ear. "And why are people buying it from him? They can just scoop some up from the shore for free."

"That is not sand." Hana picked up a bottle and offered it to Keishin. "It's time. Not much, just a couple of minutes inside every bottle. Selling any more than that is forbidden. People like to take them along on trips in case their journey takes longer than expected and they run late."

"Time?" Keishin held up the bottle and examined the little grains tumbling inside it.

"You do not see vendors selling it very often. It is quite rare. But sometimes pieces of time wash up on the shore. The vendors gather them up and sell them."

"Wash up from where?"

"From people who are lost at sea." Hana took the bottle from Keishin and returned it to the vendor. "This sand is the time they never got to use."

"Oh," Keishin said quietly, walking away from the stall.

"Is something wrong?"

"Time is a subject that physicists love to debate. I have colleagues who can go on for hours arguing about whether or not it exists, or if it increases or decreases. And yet here it is, salvaged from the dead and sold in bottles to travelers who are worried about being late." Keishin sighed. "We spend all our lives studying the universe and what do we have to show for it? Do we really know anything at all?"

"You do," Hana said. "That is why we are here. Do you remember what you told me about time when we were on the bridge?"

"That it theoretically could be bent?"

"What if it was not just a theory? What if there was a person who could bend time for us and show us what really happened to my mother?"

Keishin's eyes widened. "You know someone who can bend time?"

"I might. He works at the Kyoiku Hakubutsukan."

"The Museum of Education?"

Hana nodded and stopped by a stall selling rice cakes. "Would you like some for the trip? We have not eaten anything all day."

Keishin pulled out his wallet. "I . . . er . . . only have dollars and yen. Is that okay?"

"This is a market. You do not need money here." Hana smiled and made her selection.

The vendor wrapped the rice cakes and handed them to her.

"What would you like for them in return?" Hana asked.

"A book," the vendor said. "Something I have not yet read. A thick one stitched with gold thread."

Hana dug into the woven bag slung across her chest. She

pulled out a book on the history of kite making that Keishin had seen on one of the shelves of the pawnshop. "Will this do?"

The vendor nodded and smiled, admiring the book. "Thank you. Have a safe journey."

Hana stowed the rice cakes in her bag and moved down the street.

Keishin caught up to her. "How did you just happen to have the exact book the vendor wanted in your bag? What else do you have in there?"

"Nothing." Hana slipped off the bag and gave it to Keishin.

Keishin looked inside it. "It's empty . . ."

"I thought the rice cakes might get crushed, and so I left them on the table in my kitchen. And I got the book from my father's shelves," Hana said. "It would be a pretty useless bag and would get very heavy if I had to carry around things inside it."

Keishin laughed.

"Is something amusing?"

"Yes. My world." Keishin's cheek creased into a lopsided smirk. "We've sent people into space and built massive underground detectors to study the universe, but somehow, we haven't discovered how a bag is really supposed to be used."

"Stop."

"Stop what?"

"What you're thinking."

"What am I thinking?"

"The same thought you've had since you discovered that we could travel through ponds. You've been trying to figure out how you could accomplish such things on your side of the door. But the ponds . . . this bag . . . they're not meant for your world. You'll only fail."

"What's wrong with failing?" Keishin tilted his head. "Or wanting to make things better? Just because things have been done a certain way doesn't mean that's how they should always be. And if I fail, so what? That just means I'm eliminating a wrong turn and getting closer to the right one. Science was built on the shoulders of great people—as much on their mistakes as on their accomplishments. The whole point of everything I do is to explore all that was, is, and—"

"Could be."

Keishin nodded. "Exactly."

"It must be nice . . ." Hana traced the invisible map over her hand. "To be able to want more."

Narrow docks splintered from the cluster of houses, each leading out into the clouds. Queues of travelers waited on the docks, but what it was they were waiting for, Keishin could not ascertain. There were no boats or ships in sight.

Hana pointed to a dock on their left. "That is our dock."

"Tell me again why we couldn't use a puddle to travel to the museum?" Keishin asked.

"You will understand when we get there." Hana walked over to the dock.

"The museum doesn't seem to be a popular destination," Keishin said. "There's only one person in line."

"She is not in line. She is one of the kashu."

"A singer?"

Hana nodded. "These docks belong to the kashu. Each kashu takes you to a different place."

The kashu stood at the end of the dock, dressed in a blue kimono and cradling a shamisen. The stringed instrument resembled a banjo with a long, slim, and fretless neck and a square, hollow body. The kashu bowed in greeting. Hana and Keishin bowed back.

"Welcome," the kashu said in a voice that reminded Hana of the pawnshop's brass door chime. "The wind carries my song east, crossing the Sky Sea and sending the last of its notes to the Kyoiku Hakubutsukan. It goes no farther and does not turn back."

"How much is the fare for two people to the museum?" Hana asked.

"I do not require any payment." The kashu eyed Keishin from head to toe and tilted her head as though considering a thought. "*If* your companion will share a song from his world. I have always been curious about the other world's music."

"How . . ." Keishin stiffened. "How did you know?"

Hana gripped the kashu's arm. "I beg you, please do not tell the Shiikuin that he is here."

"Why should I tell the Shiikuin anything? My duty is to ferry travelers. It is all that I am bound to. The rules you break are your concern, not mine." The kashu turned to Keishin. "And I know that you are not from here because I can hear your heart. Only half of it beats inside your chest. The other half is calling to it from far away, from a place beyond any that our songs can travel to. So, do you agree to the exchange? Another world's song to send you to your destination?"

"But I can't sing."

"There is no need to sing. All you must do is think of a song that carries you away."

"Away?"

"From here and now. From everything that holds you to the present. Our worlds cannot be that different. You must certainly have songs that you have called upon to cast your thoughts adrift?"

"Well . . ." Keishin said. "There is one song that I can think of."

"Good." Thunder clapped over the kashu's voice. "Share it and be on your way. The Kyoiku Hakubutsukan is quite a distance away, and you do not want to sail your song in a storm."

"How do I share it with you?"

"Close your eyes and fill your head with your song. Think of nothing else if you do not wish to get lost at sea," the kashu said. "And hold on tightly to each other."

Keishin took Hana's hand and shut his eyes, still uncertain about how a song was supposed to whisk them away. He drew a deep breath and let a familiar melody grow inside him.

The winds of the Sky Sea fell silent. A song took their place. A fire engine's siren wailed along with it. Keishin's eyelids flew open. The black-and-white painting of a caged bird he had bought at a flea market a year ago stared back at him, hanging from the brick wall of his loft apartment.

CHAPTER TWENTY-TWO

Rooms

There were afternoons at the pawnshop when business was slow and Hana would lean her elbows on the counter and imagine the world behind the door. She stitched together the snippets of their clients' lives, creating a patchwork world of gray office buildings filled with people wishing they were somewhere else, overcrowded trains that were not powered by dewdrops, and brightly colored rooms with rows of pachinko machines that ate money. Not once, in all her daydreams, had she conjured a place with ten-foot-tall windows and an assortment of black-and-white paintings displayed over redbrick walls. Or that she would be sharing it with a man such as Keishin. He had chosen, over and over again, to stay at her side, even when, through any lens, no one would have found fault if he had chosen to walk away. "What is this place?"

"Hana?" Keishin jumped. "You're here."

"Where else would I be? We are traveling to the Kyoiku Hakubutsukan, remember?"

"But this is my old apartment. I thought you said that we were going to travel to the museum by riding a song."

"We are. Listen." Music wafted from a record player beneath the painting of a caged bird. The player's needle shifted from side to side, finding a woman's rich and buttery voice in the depths and shallows of the vinyl record's grooves. The tale of a girl drifting at sea in the night filled the room. "This is your song. We are inside it. I am glad you chose it. It's beautiful."

Keishin kneaded the bridge of his nose, sinking into a worn tan leather couch. "I don't understand."

"Why I like your song?"

"I don't understand how we are traveling inside a song and why we are in my apartment."

"This music playing is the same song that you shared with the kashu, is it not?"

"It is."

"And this room is where you often listen to it? Perhaps from the exact spot you are sitting in now?"

"With a glass of wine or whiskey after work."

"Then that is the reason why we are here. This is where the song lives." Hana sat down on the other end of the couch. "But this is not your apartment. It just looks like it."

Keishin stood up and ran his hand along the brick wall. "This isn't real?"

"It is, but it is not your home. This room was created to ferry us to the museum. It is unique to you and your song. My father's room was very different."

"What was his room like?"

"It was the pawnshop's vault," Hana said. "He always used the birds' song when we traveled. The vault and all the choices we kept in it were on his mind wherever we went. Unfortunately, sitting in a vault for a whole evening is not very comfortable."

"The whole evening?"

"The museum is very far away." Hana fished out her pack of rice cakes from her bag. "Are you hungry?"

* * *

The rice cakes' empty wrappings lay over Keishin's dark wooden coffee table next to a miniature old-fashioned telescope made of brass.

"May I?" Hana gestured to the telescope.

Keishin nodded. "Sure."

Hana picked up the telescope and looked through it.

"I'm afraid it doesn't work," Keishin said. "It's just for décor."

"Nothing we keep around us is only for décor, is it? We select and surround ourselves with objects that speak to or for us, whether we are aware of it or not." Hana set the telescope down, leaving streaks of dust on her fingertips.

"And this telescope is clearly saying that it desperately needs to be cleaned. Sorry. I have some paper towels in the kitchen." He stood up and paused mid-step. "Um . . . do I have a kitchen? I'm not sure how this ferry thing works."

"You do not." Hana wiped her hands on the front of her coat. "You only get one room."

"Just one room? Good thing this isn't a date then." Keishin chuckled.

"What is a date?"

"Wait. You don't know what a date is?"

"Am I supposed to?"

"Well . . . uh . . . it's when two people try to get to know each other better. They go to dinner. Watch a movie or a show. And when things go well . . . they . . . uh . . ."

"They visit each other's homes?"

"Er . . . yes. They . . . um . . . visit."

"Like what we are doing now."

Keishin nodded. "Like what we are doing now."

"And?"

"And what?"

"What else do people do on these visits? Why is this room insufficient? What other rooms do they require?" She sank deeper into an oversized cushion, placing her hands on her lap. "This room is quite pleasant. I do not find it lacking in any way."

"You know what? You're right. This is a perfectly good room."

"It is."

A quiet settled over the living room like a layer of dust neither Hana nor Keishin seemed willing to disturb. Keishin shifted his weight on the couch, making the leather squeak.

"Have you taken many lovers home?" Hana asked as though she were asking something as mundane as the time.

Keishin coughed. "Lovers?"

"That is the purpose of a date, is it not? To find a match?"

"Well . . . I . . ."

"Marriage is different in my world. It is a duty just like everything else in our lives. All you need to know about your future spouse is their name." She ran a finger over her right hand, tracing the invisible path paper cranes flew over in the rain. "We have no use for dates."

Keishin stared at the bare skin on her arm, wondering if another man's name might be etched on it. He shoved the thought away. "Then . . . um . . . maybe this could be your first date. I mean . . . that is, if you want it to be."

Hana smiled, quirking a brow. "I thought that you needed to have dinner first and see a show?"

"Those are optional. Rice cakes and dusty telescopes are all you really need to make it official."

"Is that so?"

"Absolutely. We're just missing one more thing." He walked over to a tall window.

"And what would that be?"

"A view. Mr. Li's Chinese takeaway is across the street. They have the best chicken chow mein. It's why I chose this apartment." He tugged the curtains back. Black clouds swirled behind the glass, their outline illuminated by bolts of lightning streaking through the dark. Keishin jolted back.

"We are sailing over the Sky Sea," Hana said. "In quite a storm. I'm sorry."

"Sorry?" Keishin shut the curtains. "For what?"

"Bad weather follows me around."

"Really?" Keishin wrinkled his forehead. "The weather hates me too."

"You are making fun of me. But it is true. I am certain that you have noticed that wherever we go, the sky soon shows its disapproval."

"I have, but I assumed that it was because of—" The record skipped and stalled. The room shook beneath Keishin's feet, sending him staggering against a wall.

"Kei! Your song!" Hana yelled over the rumbling of wood and bricks.

Keishin clutched the windowsill to keep from stumbling.

"Sing it in your head. *Now.*"

Keishin squeezed his eyes shut, summoning the song's notes. The record resumed playing. The quake stopped.

"You got distracted," Hana said. "The song cannot stop. You must empty yourself of thoughts that might keep it from playing in the back of your mind."

"This is how people get lost at sea," Keishin said, swallowing the realization that had lodged in his throat like a rock.

"Yes. That is why no matter what happens, you must not let go of the song," Hana said. "Or me."

"I won't. I promise." Keishin sat next to her, wiping cold sweat from his brow. "I won't put you in any more danger than I already have. The Shiikuin wouldn't be chasing us if not for me."

"You may have chosen to stay, but I chose to let you. It was . . . the first real choice I made in my life."

"Is that a good or bad thing?"

"I . . . don't know yet."

Keishin rested his neck on the couch.

"And how about you? Are you regretting your decision?"

"I've been scared and confused more times than I would like, but I don't regret a single second of my time here."

"Why?"

"Because . . ." Keishin sat up, finding his smile.

"Because?"

"Because I get to take you on your first date."

"I do not recall agreeing to this being a date. Besides, you said that an official date required a view."

"I did say that, didn't I?" Keishin smirked, scratching his nape. "I really wish I could have taken you someplace other than this boring apartment. There are so many things and places you would enjoy seeing in my world."

"Like what?"

"I would have loved to take you around my university. The campus is especially lovely at this time of year. The maple trees in the courtyard know how to put on a good show."

Hana nodded, her gaze drifting to the window without a view. "There is something about autumn that makes things more beautiful. Out of all the seasons, it is the most honest about time. Summer and spring blind you to its passing with their colorful displays. Winter paints over everything in white.

But autumn is not shy about things coming to an end. It welcomes it, waving leafy flags of red, yellow, and gold. It celebrates its sadness."

"Not just sadness though, right?" Keishin said. "It's also a celebration of all that is waiting on the other side of it."

"Yes," Hana said, surprised by how quickly she agreed with him when, only a day ago, she thought the season meant only melancholy. Like his dimpled smile, Keishin's hope was contagious. "That too."

"So are you curious about what else we would do on this date?" Keishin said.

"We don't need to go anywhere. I am still enjoying the trees," Hana teased, staring up at imaginary leaves.

"I promise that you'll like the pumpkin spice cake at the coffee shop around the corner even more. It's just a short walk. You'll need to hold my hand though. I wouldn't want you to get lost." He offered his hand.

Hana clasped it. "Tell me more about this cake," she said, leaning against his shoulder.

"Where do I begin? Its cream cheese frosting? Its moist goodness? How it's perfect with coffee? It's basically everything I like about autumn baked into a perfect little treat. Cinnamon. Nutmeg. Cloves. All things cozy and warm." Keishin pressed Hana's palm against his cheek. "And sweet."

"That sounds delicious." Hana found herself running her thumb over his jaw, savoring its sharpness and heat. "I think . . . I like this date."

"Me too." Keishin brushed his lips against her wrist.

Hana's cheeks flushed. She pulled her hand away.

"I'm sorry. I shouldn't have—"

"There is no need to apologize. It was my fault. This world

is new to you, but not to me. I should know better. This place can make you feel things that are not real. This room. This couch. They trick your mind."

"And are you also a trick, Hana?"

"I—"

"Because if you are, then consider me willing to be fooled. The way you see things, speak about things . . . when I'm with you, you make things feel new. Even this dusty room."

"It's . . . um . . . not that dusty." Hana sneezed loudly.

"You were saying?" Keishin chuckled.

Hana laughed too because when Keishin laughed, he made her forget all the reasons she was not supposed to be happy.

"I made you laugh. I hope this means that our first date wasn't a complete disaster."

"No, it was not," Hana said, the last of her laughter still tingling on her lips. "Though I think that traveling inside that café would have been slightly more enjoyable than this room. I have always preferred cake to dust."

"I don't even know why the song chose this room for us to travel in," Keishin said. "Whenever I used to listen to it, my mind never stayed in this place."

"The song didn't create this room. You did. Perhaps even as much as you insist on wanting to explore my world, the kashu was right. A part of you is longing for home."

"If I'm responsible for creating this room, then I can certainly try to do better." Keishin closed his eyes and weaved his fingers through Hana's. "If this is my one chance to give you a glimpse of my world, I want to show you where this song really takes me."

* * *

Eleven thousand giant, unblinking glass eyes surrounded Hana as she floated on a small rubber boat. She drew a sharp breath through her teeth and squeezed Keishin's hand.

"It worked." Keishin blinked, looking around the enormous cylindrical stainless steel tank. "We're here."

"Where is here?" Hana said breathlessly.

"More than three thousand feet beneath the ground," Keishin said. "Do you remember the neutrinos I told you about?"

"The invisible particles that are like ghosts?"

"This is where we trap them. We're inside the Super-Kamiokande neutrino detector. The mountain we are under acts like a filter. Only neutrinos can pass through its layers of rock and soil." Keishin pointed to the large glass bulbs covering every inch of the detector's curved walls. "And those are PMTs, photomultiplier tubes. They detect the light that's created on the rare occasion that a neutrino passes through the mountain and strikes a water molecule. They're so sensitive that they can detect light from a candle lit on the moon. This tank is normally filled with water, but it's been partially drained for maintenance. Today, it's a small lake for two. Or the inside of the TARDIS."

"TARDIS?"

"Er, forget I said that. That might be harder to explain than neutrinos."

"So this is a memory from where you work?"

"A borrowed one. A colleague at the detector recorded a video of the tank during maintenance work and sent it to me. There was a chance that the maintenance would finish early and that the tank would be filled before I reported for my job at

Super-K, and he didn't want me to miss out on seeing this. Very few people get to see the tank this way. I thought that it was the most peaceful, otherworldly place I had ever seen. Of course, that was before I stumbled into your pawnshop," Keishin said. "And yes, I do see the irony in escaping to a place that is essentially an elaborate trap."

"A beautiful one," Hana said. "As the best traps should be. I'd hide away here too. I don't think I've ever been to a calmer place. Thank you for bringing me here." Hana studied her face in the water. A thousand bulbs shimmered around it like silver moons. She did not recognize herself. For the first time in her life, she looked almost content. She reached over the side of the rubber boat to touch her reflection.

Keishin grabbed her hand. "It's not the kind of water you want to touch. It's extremely pure water. It's corrosive. It sucks the minerals out of anything it comes in contact with. Someone accidentally dropped a metal hammer into the tank, and when they found it years later, all that was left of it was an eggshell-thin chrome shell. The water had hollowed it out."

"This water can eat flesh?"

"If you made the mistake of taking a leisurely soak in it."

"Then it is not just in my world that things are not always as they seem." Hana stretched out over the bottom of the boat. "Still, I'm glad we're here. It's best to get all the rest we can, while we can. The next part of our journey may not be as peaceful."

Keishin lay next to her, their fingers almost touching. "You never told me the end of the story."

"What story?"

"The story about Urashima Taro and the turtle. What happened to Taro after he opened the box?"

"Are you sure you want to know?"

"Of course. You can't tell someone a story and not tell them how it ends."

"But isn't that what life is like in your world? A story whose ending has yet to be written? I have often wondered what it would be like to live like that. To me, that would be the greatest of luxuries. I imagine that it is that very uncertainty that makes working in a place such as this worthwhile. The excitement of discovery. The prospect of learning something that could change the course of your world."

"You aren't wrong. But it is also a life that comes without the smallest guarantee. There are so many choices pulling you left one second, right the next. People stray from commitments and paths. It's easy to get lost."

"You would prefer that a map of your life be written on your skin?"

"I can't help but wonder if things would have turned out differently if my mother had a map. If her fate had been clear, then perhaps she wouldn't have been so restless; maybe she would have . . ."

"Stayed with you and your father?"

Keishin turned to face Hana. "The honest answer is I don't know. The answer I want to believe is yes."

"Duty isn't the same as love."

"Do reasons even matter if you can't tell the difference?"

"Close your eyes."

"Why?"

"Do you trust me?"

Keishin lowered his eyelids.

Hana pressed her lips against Keishin's mouth, rocking the boat beneath them.

"Hana?" Keishin jerked his head back.

Hana cupped his face, guiding his lips to hers. Keishin's shoulders tensed, but he did not break away. He folded her in his arms and deepened the kiss, melting into the warmth of her mouth. Hana pulled back and sat up.

Keishin stared at her, breathing hard. "What was that?"

"A kiss."

"I know that was a kiss. I want to know why you kissed me."

"I thought you said that reasons didn't matter."

"So it wasn't a kiss." Keishin's face grew somber. "And I thought that I was the only scientist here. It was an experiment to prove that I was wrong and you were right."

"Was I?"

Keishin lay back in the boat, casting his eyes over the bulbs above them. "Yes."

"You were right too."

"About what?"

"The kiss. The first one was an experiment."

"And the second one?"

"Was the second real choice I have ever made."

"And was it a good or bad thing?"

Unanswered questions were like boxes you never opened, their contents vanishing and reappearing, stretching and contracting, being nothing and everything all at once. Hana did not make a habit of hoarding them. In her world, it wasn't difficult. For every question that had ever crossed her mind, there was a black-and-white answer that stripped it of all mystery.

But tonight she sat on a rubber boat, a box containing Keishin's question balancing on her lap. The question knocked on the box's lid, trying to get her attention. Hana tried to ignore it. She kept her eyes on Keishin as he slept, watching his song dance behind his lids as he dreamed. The box rattled louder. Hana heaved a sigh. She leaned closer to the box and heard the whisper inside it. *Was it a good or bad thing?* Hana touched her lips, remembering the moist heat of Keishin's mouth.

His question was simple. Answering it was not. If she was going to find her parents and bring them home, it was not an answer she could ever say out loud. She tossed the box into the water, drowning it in the reflection of eleven thousand moons.

CHAPTER TWENTY-THREE

Sand

The most comfortable bed in the world was the one you needed to get out of before you were fully awake. In this instance, the bed wasn't a bed, but a rubber raft floating on extremely purified water. Keishin turned to his side and reached for a snooze button that wasn't there. He pressed it anyway. The last few minutes of sleep were always thicker, creamier, and more delicious than all the hours that came before them.

"Kei," Hana said. "You need to get up."

Sand whipped against Keishin's face. He spat grains out and pried his eyes open. Sunlight shimmered over golden dunes.

"We're here." Hana turned her collar up against the blowing sand.

Keishin scanned the desert. Every trace of the Super-Kamiokande detector had vanished, but the memory of Hana's lips on his remained. Understanding how he felt about the kiss was easy. Hana was an intelligent, beautiful woman, and Keishin did not deny being attracted to her. But finding words to describe what he felt about her was proving to be more difficult. She was the moon in the water, close enough to touch, yet beyond reach. "Where is 'here'?"

"The end of your song," Hana said.

"I can see why we couldn't use water to travel to this place. Please tell me that the museum isn't far."

"It isn't," Hana said. "This is the Kyoiku Hakubutsukan. We are standing on it. We need to purchase tickets so that we can go inside."

"Is this the part where you fish something out of that magical bag of yours?"

"I wish I could, but the only currency the museum accepts is time."

"And how exactly are we supposed to pay with time?"

"We spend and waste time every day. This is no different. The price of a ticket is little more than a few seconds, but they need to be precious ones."

"Precious? Does that mean that I have to give up a happy memory?"

"Not a happy one. A mistake. It will be stored in the museum's archives." Hana grabbed a fistful of sand. She straightened and unclenched her fingers, letting the wind snatch the grains from her palm. "As these are."

Keishin gaped at the endless ocean of sand. "All of this is time? Moments from other people's lives?"

Hana nodded.

"But what does the museum want with our mistakes?"

"This is the Museum of Education. How else are its visitors supposed to learn if not from other people's mistakes? Some lessons are bigger than others, but all are grains of wisdom."

"Should I be worried that what you're saying makes perfect sense to me?" Keishin said. "So how do we do this? How and where do we pay for our tickets?"

"The ticketing clerk should be here soon."

A swirling column of sand rose a few feet from where Keishin and Hana stood, twisting and morphing until it took a shape that resembled a woman's body. Arms. Legs. Tail. The face of a fox. It moved slowly and lithely toward them, dispersing and gathering, collecting more sand with each step it took. It stopped a foot from Hana, growing to twice her height. Hana and Keishin bowed to it. It bowed back.

"Greetings, Kitsune-san." Hana craned her neck. "We wish to purchase tickets to the museum."

"Are you aware of . . ." The sand fox scattered and collected itself. "The price?"

"A grain of time for each ticket we require," Hana said.

The fox nodded, its features of sand shifting in the wind. "Choose your payment well." It dispersed into nothing and re-formed. "And I will judge if it is worthy of a place in the archive."

Keishin shuffled through his mistakes, trying to find one that he wouldn't miss. Though each had caused him varying degrees of embarrassment, disappointment, and pain, it was difficult to select one that he could live without. What he once thought he would have easily and gratefully forgotten felt like hard-fought treasure, each mistake a precious, priceless scar. The kitsune had asked for only one grain of his life, but Keishin found himself wondering if it was that one grain upon which everything else was built.

"I will pay for both of us," Hana said.

"No," Keishin said. "I can pay my own way."

"You can, but you mustn't." Hana pulled him aside. "Losing time, no matter how small, changes you."

"Which is exactly why I need to pay for my ticket."

"But it will affect me less than it will affect you. My fate is set. Yours is not. No matter how much of my time I give up, my way will always be clear. Yours could swerve in ways you cannot even imagine."

"For a person who has lived her entire life without making any real choices, you seem to be very good at making them for other people."

"I am sorry, Kei, but you do not have the privilege of being stubborn, and I do not have the luxury of time to argue with you. I will not change my mind."

Keishin looked into Hana's eyes and saw that she was telling the truth. He threw up his hands. "Fine."

Hana walked up to the kitsune. "You may take your payment."

The kitsune's face took human form as its body shrank to Hana's size. It cradled Hana's face in its hands and gently pressed the briefest of kisses on her mouth. It stepped away, leaving its gaze on Hana's lips. Two specks of light, each no bigger than a grain of sand, drifted from Hana's half-parted lips and floated in the air. The kitsune took a deep breath, drawing the lights into its mouth. A warm glow pulsed in its chest and spread throughout every grain in its body. The kitsune nodded solemnly at Hana and, without uttering a word, scattered in every direction. Two gold keys appeared in its place.

Hana picked up the keys and handed one to Keishin.

"Did it hurt?" Keishin asked softly, taking a key from her. "Do you feel any different?"

"No," Hana said.

"Are you sure?"

"As certain as anyone who has no memory of what they gave up can be. The time I paid to the kitsune is gone, erased from my life and my mind. It is as if those moments never happened.

If I have changed, I would not be able to tell you what has changed or why."

Keishin planted his hands on his hips, lowered his head, and sighed.

"You are still upset with me," Hana said.

"I don't have any right to be."

"And yet you are still angry."

"No." Keishin shook his head, his shoulders heavy. "I'm not. It's just that I came on this trip to help you and all I seem to be doing is making this more difficult."

"You're not." The wind tousled Hana's hair. "But if you want to leave—"

Keishin tucked wayward strands of Hana's hair behind her ear. "I don't."

Keishin followed Hana's instructions and drew a door in the sand with his fingertip. He rolled his eyes and groaned at his crooked sketch. "I'm horrible at this. Can we compute the velocity of this desert's wind instead?"

"All that matters is that you fit through it." Hana stuck her key into her drawing. "Just do what I do," she said, twisting her key in the sand.

Keishin did the same.

Their doors shimmered. The wind picked up, stirring the sand.

Hana shielded her face with her coat. "Try not to breathe. Don't worry. This will be quick."

A gust of wind blew in their direction, carrying away the sand from their sketches. Sand stung Keishin's eyes. He held his breath and braced himself. The wind howled in his ears and, just as swiftly as it started, grew quiet.

Hana shook the sand from her hair. "The doors are open."

Keishin glanced down. Two bottomless holes, in the shape of the doors they had drawn, replaced their sketches. Keishin leaned over them and grimaced. "Let me guess. We're supposed to jump in, right?"

Hana smiled at him over her shoulder, leapt into the hole, and disappeared into the dark.

CHAPTER TWENTY-FOUR

The Museum of Education

A double helix crystal staircase spiraled from the center of a circular white hall, its top hidden by clouds. The clouds hovering inside the museum might have surprised Keishin had he not been distracted by the tiny folded paper cranes flying around and weaving between the stairs' floating steps. A crane the color of the sunset landed on his shoulder and playfully pecked at his ear. Keishin gently ushered the origami bird onto his finger. It settled on its new perch and preened its triangular wings. Keishin lifted the crane to examine it. "Is it alive?"

"As alive as a bird made of paper can be," Hana said. "It seems to like you. It can probably sense that you are from the same place."

"Same place?"

"This crane is from your world. All the cranes are."

"What?" Keishin said, startling the crane on his hand. It flew away and sought refuge in the clouds. "But I've never seen anything like them."

"In your world, they look quite different. No. Wait. That's wrong," Hana said. "In your world, they don't look like anything at all."

* * *

Wisps of mist swirled around Keishin as they ascended the spiral staircase. Cranes sailed in and out of the clouds. "This museum doesn't seem to be very popular."

"Why do you say that?" Hana said.

"I haven't seen any other visitors since we got here."

Hana smiled and pulled out her mother's glasses from her bag. "Look again."

Keishin put the glasses on and nearly tripped over a step. He pulled the glasses off, glanced around, and put them on again, blinking rapidly. People made their way over both staircases, some stopping to offer their arms as perches to the paper cranes. He took the glasses off and scanned the empty museum. "Where did they go?"

"They're still here." Hana took the glasses from him. "Just not at the exact time as we are. When the museum admits us through its doors, it shifts time for each of the visitors so that we're not all crowding around the same second. This way, we can all have the museum to ourselves."

Keishin clamped his hand over a gasp. "My god."

"Let me guess," Hana said. "You are currently trying to think of ways to do this in your world."

"I'm sorry. I can't help it. This is incredible. I can't wait to see the exhibits. Are the galleries upstairs?"

"This is the gallery. The cranes are the Kyoiku Hakubutsukan's prize exhibit. All of them are crafted by the museum's origami artist." Hana whistled and extended her hand. A crane swooped down and rested on her wrist. Hana examined it closely. "This one is from a ship called the *Titanic*. Do you know of it?"

"The *Titanic*? Yes, of course."

"This crane is fifteen seconds of the life of one of its crew masters. He was replaced at the last minute before the ship set sail. This is the exact fragment of time where, in his hurry to leave the ship, he neglected to turn over the keys to the locker where the ship's binoculars were stored. Because of this, the crew master who took his place failed to see the iceberg the *Titanic* collided into. Fifteen seconds cost one thousand five hundred people their lives."

The crane flew away. Hana whistled for another one. A second crane burst from the clouds and perched on her shoulder. Hana scooped it up and weighed it in her hand. "This is a lot heavier than the first one. Thirteen minutes. They belonged to a man named Georg Elser. He attempted to assassinate someone called . . ." Hana squinted at the crane as though trying to read something in small print. "Adolf Hitler. Have you heard of him?"

"I have," Keishin said stiffly.

"Elser planted a bomb at a beer hall where Hitler was speaking, but Hitler cut his speech short and left early. The bomb exploded thirteen minutes later, killing eight people and injuring sixty-two others."

"What kind of museum is this, Hana?" Keishin said, his jaw tight.

"The kind that collects the tiniest moments from your world, seconds and minutes that shifted the course of your history." Hana pointed to the clouds enveloping them. "These are part of the exhibit too. It saved one city and caused the destruction of another."

"How?"

"A bomb was supposed to be dropped on the city of Kokura on August ninth, 1945. But because of the heavy clouds over

Kokura, the plane carrying the bomb decided to drop it over the city of Nagasaki instead."

"Why . . ." Keishin's voice caught in his throat. "Why put such things on display?"

"The Shiikuin built this museum, and everything they have curated serves a single purpose: to show everyone what happens in a world that is free to chart its own course, and to remind us that the worst thing about choices is . . ." Hana bit her lip.

Keishin remembered the softness of her mouth. "Is what?"

"Is having to live with them."

The clouds thinned, revealing a thick bamboo grove at the top of the museum's steps. Tall green stalks swayed in the breeze and filled the silence between Keishin and Hana with the rustling of leaves. Keishin stared at a crane that had followed them up the stairs. He watched it fly into the grove without speaking.

"Bringing you here was a mistake," Hana said. "It has clearly upset you."

"I'll admit that it's unsettling, but I'm glad you took me here. It's one thing to read about these events in history books and quite another to come face-to-face with the very seconds that made them."

"I apologize. I neglected to consider how the museum might make you feel. In this world, this museum *is* a history book, a cautionary tale from a place that, for most of us, does not even feel real."

"It's not your fault. It's not even the Shiikuin's. Every single second on exhibit in this museum was spent, squandered, or forgotten by my world. It was our time, and we did with it as we pleased. I'm not angry that your world has a place like this. I'm saddened that my world does not." Keishin took Hana's hand in his. "I don't want to make the same mistake."

"What do you mean?"

"I don't want to waste another second of my time here hiding what I need to say."

"What are you talking about?"

"Come with me, Hana." He closed his hands around hers.

"What?"

"After we find your father and the missing choice . . . *come with me.* I know that my world isn't perfect, but you'd be free. You don't belong here, Hana. You can have a life. A real one."

"With you?" Hana said quietly.

"That would be your choice to make. All I am asking is that you leave this place."

Hana let go of Keishin's hands. "I cannot cross over to your world. None of us can. We will fade away. That is how my mother was sentenced to die, remember?"

"But she wasn't executed. She's still alive. I'm a scientist, Hana. I believe what I can prove. Do you know of anyone who has crossed into my world? Have you seen them fade away? What if the stories are just that? Myths made up by the Shiikuin to keep you afraid?"

"And if they aren't?"

"What if I could come up with a way to prove that it was safe? Would you come?"

A chorus of urgent whispers rose from the bamboo. Stalks shivered.

"What's going on?" Keishin said.

"They sense that somewhere in this grove, other stalks are being cut down to be turned into washi, the paper used for the cranes," Hana said. "We need to make our way to the orizuru maker before they get too upset."

"Why?"

"They may not let us pass if they do." Hana stroked a bamboo stalk until it grew still, and then whispered something to it Keishin couldn't hear. Rows of bamboo parted, giving way to a narrow gravel path. Hana bowed to the grove. "Thank you."

CHAPTER TWENTY-FIVE

Paper

A small house made of crisp white folded paper stood at the end of the gravel path at the edge of the bamboo grove. White origami cranes held together by long pieces of string hung from the origami house's doorway. Long fingers parted the paper curtain. A tall man emerged from the house, his features as strikingly beautiful as they were sharp. He wore his long white-blond hair in a messy bun, leaving stray wisps to soften his jawline and graze the shoulders of his kimono. A winter fox in the snow. The crane that had followed Keishin and Hana up the stairway flew past Hana and perched on the man's shoulder.

"Hana," the man said with a smile that could melt the frost from trees. "I did not believe Maro when he told me you were here." He glanced at the crane. "What a nice surprise."

"It is good to see you too, Haruto," Hana said. "This is my friend Keishin."

Keishin bowed.

Haruto paused, narrowed his gaze at him, and bowed back. "Any friend of Hana's is a friend of mine," he said with a smile that stopped short of his clear gray eyes.

"I am sorry that I was not able to let you know that we were coming," Hana said.

"You are always welcome here. You came at a good time. I

finished making today's cranes early," Haruto said. "Please, come inside."

Keishin followed Hana through the curtain of paper cranes. "I didn't realize you knew the orizuru maker personally," he said, lowering his voice.

"He is an old friend," Hana whispered back.

"Please make yourself comfortable." Haruto gestured to paper cushions around a low origami table. "May I offer you some tea?"

"I am sorry, but we cannot stay long. I do not mean to be rude, but we are here on a matter of some urgency. My father is missing."

Haruto's smile slipped from his face. "What happened?"

A cloud of silence, heavier than the cloud on display at the museum's staircase, hung over the group gathered at the table after Hana recounted the events that had led her to Haruto's origami studio. She had left out the part about where Keishin was from, refusing to make Haruto an accomplice in her crime. What she was about to ask of Haruto came with enough consequences of its own.

"This is my fault." Haruto hung his head low. "I am deeply sorry, Hana. I swear to you that I will make this right."

"What are you talking about? None of this is your fault."

"But it is. Entirely. I am certain that your father's disappearance is connected to his last visit."

"He was here?" Keishin said. "When?"

"A month ago," Haruto said.

"My father never mentioned coming here. We always visit you together," Hana said.

"He did not want you or anyone to know. He made me promise to keep it a secret. I am sorry. I should have never agreed to the favor he asked."

"What favor?" Hana leaned forward, struggling to keep her hands folded over her lap.

"The same one, I imagine, that you came to ask of me."

Hana's mouth grew dry. She swallowed hard but found no relief.

"And your face tells me that I am right." Haruto sighed, slumping his shoulders. "Your father looked at me the same way. I have known him since I was a boy, and in all those years, not once had he ever let any emotion hotter than tepid tea slip past his half-smiling lips. I believed that smile to be a permanent fixture, unchanging as the moon. The day of his unexpected visit, I learned that I was wrong. Your father's stoic smile guarded far more than I ever imagined."

"Please, Haruto. Tell me why my father was here."

Haruto stole a glance at the crane perched on the window's paper sill and lowered his voice. "It would be wiser to have this conversation in a place where we can be alone. Let me pack my things and we can continue this at my home."

"Thank you," Hana said.

"You may be less grateful after I tell you about the part I played in your father's disappearance." Haruto stood up and waved the crane on the windowsill away. He turned to Hana and Keishin. "Have either of you traveled through a paper door before?"

"Er . . . no," Keishin said.

"Neither have I," Hana said.

"Then I must warn you that it may feel a little different from walking through a wooden one," Haruto said.

"How different?" Keishin asked.

"It is difficult to find another thing to compare it to, unless, that is, you have experienced being pressed as thin as paper and folded in two. But it looks more painful than it feels." Haruto walked over to a folding paper screen at the back of the house. He moved the screen to the side and revealed a large sheet of paper lying on the floor. "This door will take you directly to my home. It is large enough for both of you. You can travel there together. Lie down, and I will take care of folding the door. I will follow as soon as I pack my tools."

Hana lay on the paper. Keishin stretched out next to her.

"Close your eyes and try to relax." Haruto tucked Hana's hair behind her ear, his fingertips brushing her cheek. Hana nodded with a small smile.

Keishin clenched his jaw and looked away.

Haruto held up the ends of the paper. "You will feel a little uncomfortable, but I will fold as fast as I can. I will need to focus and make every fold precise, so please stay quiet."

Hana closed her eyes, her heart pounding against her ribs. She could not imagine what it was like to be folded, and she did not have high hopes that it would be pleasant. She drew a deep breath, exhaling it slowly through her mouth.

"Are you ready?" Haruto asked.

Hana nodded.

"Then I will begin."

Hana felt the paper lay over the length of her body. She reached for Keishin's hand. He gently squeezed her fingers and sent a warmth through them that spread beneath her skin and up her arms, melting the tension from her shoulders. It was radiating down her spine when she felt pressure over her chest. It pushed harder, pinning her down. Paper rustled in her ears as her ribs collapsed, squeezing her lungs and leaving her without air to scream. But if being flattened had caused any pain, Hana could not feel it. Being paper-thin left no room for anything other than the sensation of repeatedly being folded over one's self, shifting in shape, and growing increasingly small. And when she was so small that she thought another fold would have made her disappear, she felt herself rapidly unfold. Her chest expanded, filling with muscle, blood, and bone. Hana opened her eyes, gasping for air. A sheet of paper lay over her. She pushed it away and sat up.

"Let's never do that again." Keishin stood up and offered Hana his hand. "Are you okay?"

"I think so." Hana pulled herself up. "I do not know how Haruto does that every day."

Keishin looked around the room, admiring the elaborate origami pieces displayed on its walls and shelves. "He seems to genuinely like being an origami artist."

"He does. He is very lucky," Hana said. "He found his passion in his duty. His mother was the museum's artist before him. Haruto once told me that she was not very happy."

"The two of you seem to be . . . um . . . close."

"We are. We have known each other since we were children."

Paper rustled behind her. Hana turned. "Haruto?"

The paper door on the floor swung open. Haruto emerged from it and gracefully stood up. A paper satchel was slung across his chest. "How was the trip? I hope that it didn't cause you too much discomfort."

"It was . . . uh . . . good," Hana said.

"You have always been a terrible liar, Hana." Haruto smirked. "It is one of the things that I like most about you. I spend my days distilling honesty from history. It is refreshing when I do not have to work so hard to see the truth."

"And it is the same thing that I have always appreciated in our friendship. You have always told me the truth. I am counting on your honesty today."

"As I am counting on yours." Haruto looked her in the eye, his tone turning serious. "Stop lying, Hana."

"Lying?" Hana tensed. "About what?"

"Before I tell you anything about your father, I need you to tell me who this man really is." He turned to Keishin. "And why he is with you."

Hana pulled her shoulders back. "I told you the truth. His name is Keishin, and he is—"

"A friend I have not seen or heard of . . ." Haruto walked up to Keishin, drawing himself to his full height. "Ever."

Hana stepped between them and gripped Haruto's arm. "Who he is isn't important right now."

"I think it is." Haruto drew his arm away. "How do you know you can trust him? What I know about your father puts us all in danger."

"You can trust me," Keishin said. "I promise. I'm only here to help."

" 'Only here to help' . . ." Haruto repeated Keishin's words slowly. "And where did you *come from* before you came *here*?"

Keishin shot a glance at Hana. "I—"

"I think you already know where Keishin's from," Hana said. "He's risking his life to help me. Do you think anyone from our world would do the same?"

Haruto lowered his head, shaking it. "I would," he said softly.

She cupped his face and looked into his eyes. "Then trust me. And him. Tell us what my father wanted from you."

Haruto walked to the window and gripped its sill, his nails digging into the paper it was made of.

"Please, Haruto," Hana said.

Haruto sighed and turned to face her. "He wanted an answer to a question that had been haunting him for a very long time. He wanted to know if your mother was alive, and he believed that the only way he could do that was to see what really happened the day the Shiikuin came for her."

"My father wanted you to turn back time," Hana said.

"No, Hana." Haruto sat at a table and pulled a small sheet of paper from one of the colorful stacks laid on top of it. "He wanted me to fold it."

CHAPTER TWENTY-SIX

The Favor

❁ *One month ago*

Haruto emptied a paper kettle into two origami cups that cradled the steaming tea as well as any cup or bowl made from clay. He looked up from the cups and smiled at Toshio. "I wish you had told me that you were coming. I could have brought some of the rice cakes my mother sent me."

"I am sorry to have dropped in unannounced," Toshio said. "I didn't realize that I was going to push through with this until I found myself standing outside your studio. If you had not stepped out from the bamboo grove when you did, I would be on my way home."

"Why? You know that you are always welcome here. You are like a father to me."

"I wish that was not the case."

Haruto frowned. "Why?"

"Because a true father would never ask what I am about to ask of you now."

"I don't understand. Are you in trouble? Do you need help?"

"What happened to my wife, Hana's mother, is not a secret."

"Every child is told her story. The Shiikuin made sure that no one would ever forget the punishment for her crime."

Toshio stood up and walked over to the window. He leaned out and checked in both directions.

"What are you doing?" Haruto asked.

"I need to make sure that we are alone."

"The museum's visitors never come up here. Only the cranes keep me company while I work."

"Then we need to talk elsewhere, because what I am about to say is only for your ears."

"Will you tell me what this is all about?" Haruto asked as soon as he stepped out of the paper door and into his home. "I assure you that we are completely alone."

Toshio drew a deep breath. "I believe that my wife is alive."

"What?"

"I saw her in a dream, just before I crossed the bridge into morning. I heard someone call my name and I opened my eyes. When I looked back, I saw her on the other side."

Haruto shook his head. "That is impossible. The dead are not allowed at the Midnight Bridge. You must have been mistaken. It was probably just someone who looked like her."

"That is what I told myself too," Toshio said. "Until I saw her again the following night. And the night after that. On both nights, she called to me just as I stepped into the dawn."

"But the dead do not dream."

"Which is why I believe that she must be alive," Toshio said. "I think that the Shiikuin lied to me about her death."

"Why would they lie?"

"I don't know. All I know is that there is only one way to know the whole truth. I must see what really happened on the day they came to the pawnshop and took her from me." Toshio's voice cracked. "And from Hana."

"Does Hana know you are here?"

"I do not want to involve her in any of this. It is too dangerous."

"But you want to involve me," Haruto said. "Because I am not really your son."

"You know that is not true. You are family, Haruto. I would not ask for your help if there was another way. But there isn't. I am trusting you with this secret because you are not like Hana. She is too much like her mother. Impulsive. Questioning. Free. She tries to fight her nature for my sake, but it is in her blood. If she believed that her mother was alive, she would defy every Shiikuin to find her, no matter the cost," Toshio said. "You would not."

"You are asking me to lie to her."

"To keep her safe."

"And you do not care for your own safety?"

"I thought about my safety when I let the Shiikuin take my wife without a fight," Toshio said. "Not anymore."

"You were thinking about your newborn daughter."

"I told myself that I was, but now I am not so sure. I was a coward. I said nothing, did nothing. I just stood there and watched them take my wife away," Toshio said. "But I did not see everything that happened. That is why I need your help."

"What possible help can I give you?"

"You have a gift, Haruto. Each day, your hands create cranes from the seconds and minutes of the other world."

"I fold paper."

"You fold time," Toshio said. "And I believe that you can fold time back to the morning my wife was taken."

"Belief and reality are two different things. You know as well as I do where the time we collect from the museum comes from and what we must do to take it. The years you wish me to fold are different. They belong to this world, and everything in this world belongs to the Shiikuin. I cannot fold time without becoming a thief."

Toshio pulled out a corked bottle from his satchel. A bright blue light glowed inside it. "Which is why I have already stolen what is required for you."

Haruto stared at the bottle, his mouth agape. "What have you done?"

Toshio uncorked the bottle and poured its contents into a small glazed bowl. Three glowing grains sat at the bottom of the bowl, and Toshio made sure to count them twice. A Shiikuin's bones were nearly impossible to find, their whereabouts all but lost in a maze of rumors and lies. Toshio had caught whispers of the ground-up bones at the Night Market years ago but did not have any cause to pursue them. Until he dreamt of his dead wife.

The versions of the stories of how and where the bones were hidden far outnumbered the fragments to be had. The early whispers said that the bones could fill a sake cup to its brim. As the rumors faded, Toshio heard that all but a few grains remained. He wasn't surprised. A Shiikuin's bones were precious enough to make even the most dutiful become daring. Or foolish. Toshio had no illusions that he was anything but the latter.

"How did you get these?" Haruto asked.

"You would be surprised how many people believe that it is in their best interest to do a pawnbroker a favor."

"And they would be correct. Everyone in this world owes you a great debt," Haruto said. "And I owe you more than most."

Toshio held out the bowl. "Then help me. Please. Do you think these are enough? They were all I could find."

Haruto took the bowl from him and examined the bones. "I don't know. I have no experience making paper out of anything other than bamboo pulp and the other world's time. What do three fragments of a Shiikuin's bone even mean? Do these bones hold the story of one life? Ten?"

"A Shiikuin's bones contain the memories of all the Shiikuin that came before and after them, everything they have witnessed, every word they have spoken and heard," Toshio said. "But no one really knows how powerful they are and what they can do."

Haruto stared at the bowl. "Because the only stories you hear about those who attempt to use the bones are about those who fail."

CHAPTER TWENTY-SEVEN

Duty and Debt

A garden of paper flowers had bloomed on the table by the time Haruto had finished recounting the events of Toshio's visit. He mindlessly folded a kusudama flower and planted it at the end of a row, balancing it on the table's edge. It fell off and landed by Hana's feet.

Hana picked up the flower and handed it back to Haruto. "Did it work? Were you able to make paper out of the bones and fold time?"

Haruto crumpled the flower in his fist.

"Haruto?" Hana prodded.

He began to fold another sheet of paper. "It worked perfectly."

Hana clutched his wrist, stopping him in the middle of a crease. "Haruto, please. Tell me what my father saw."

He set the paper down. "I cannot."

"Why? Because my father made you promise to keep his secret? What use is a promise if he is dead? We need to find him before it's too late."

"I cannot tell you because I do not know what your father saw. Your father took the time I had folded and left."

"No." Hana's voice frayed. "There has to be more. Something. Anything."

"My only other memory of that day is the look on your

father's face when I put the folded day in his hands. And all I saw in his eyes was regret. Whatever that day revealed must have something to do with his disappearance. It cannot be a coincidence. But as to where he has gone or why, there is nothing more I can tell you. I'm sorry. I wish I could have been of more help."

"You can be," Keishin said. "Do it again."

"What?" Haruto shot him a sharp glance.

"Fold time again."

"Didn't you hear anything I said? Folding time from our world is forbidden. Folding time taken from the stolen bones of a Shiikuin is a thousand times worse. To this day, I wake up at night wondering if this is the hour that I will find the Shiikuin at my door."

"You took the risk for Toshio," Keishin said.

"I did. Is that not enough?"

"Not if you truly want to help Hana as you say you do. If you cared about Hana at all—"

"It is not your place to presume to tell me how I should feel about Hana or what I should or should not do. Who do you think you are? You don't even belong here."

Keishin stood up, his jaw tight. Hana gripped his arm and pulled him away from Haruto. "Haruto is right."

"But—"

"What he did for my father is more than enough." Hana let go of Keishin and turned to Haruto. "I cannot and will not ask you for more than you have already done. Keishin and I will find another way to find my father." She looked at Keishin. "We should go."

Keishin nodded and reached for her hand.

"Wait." The word tumbled from Haruto's mouth before Keishin's fingers found Hana's. "I will do it."

Hana gasped. "But the Shiikuin—"

"Can try and stop me."

Hana moved closer to him. "You don't have to do this . . ."

"I will not be able to forgive myself if something happens to you because I was a coward," Haruto said.

"You're not a coward." Hana touched his arm.

"I only have one bone fragment left. I used the other two for your father and saved one in case something went wrong. I will make the paper and fold time as best I can, but I cannot guarantee that you will be able to see everything that your father did."

"Whatever the paper holds, it will be more than I know now," Hana said.

"Every single person in our world owes your family a great debt. I owe your father even more. I will never be able to repay what he did for me and my mother, but I will try," Haruto said. "But first I need to collect the bone from the place I hid it. I did not dare to keep it here. Retrieving it may take some time. You will be more comfortable if you spend the night at the guest house in town and return tomorrow morning. I should have everything ready for you by then." He pulled a blank sheet of paper from his sleeve and handed it to Hana. "Take this. I will use it to get in touch with you in case something goes wrong."

"Nothing will go wrong." Hana took the paper from him.

Haruto turned to Keishin. "Keep her safe."

"I will," Keishin said.

"Thank you for doing this, Haruto." A tear escaped Hana's lashes.

"There is no need to thank me. This is a debt that I owe to your father." Haruto tilted Hana's face up and wiped away the tear with his thumb. "And my duty to you, as my wife."

CHAPTER TWENTY-EIGHT

Safe. Far. Secret.

As a scientist, Keishin thought the concept of folding time by trapping it in paper was the most exciting thing he had ever heard in his life. The possibilities of such technology were boundless. Space exploration. Time travel. Research. But no matter how hard Keishin tried, he could not bring himself to care. A single question occupied his mind, following him from Haruto's home to a rented room at the nearby town's only minshuku, a room that he and Hana had to share.

The room was enclosed by paper walls and boasted a view of a mountain that Keishin could not see in the dark. Two futons that Keishin guessed would take up most of the floor when unrolled leaned against a corner by the room's only window. Hana took one of the futons and spread it over the tatami. She reached for the second.

"Don't," Keishin said. "I . . . I mean thanks, but I'll do it myself."

Hana nodded and lay down. She turned away from Keishin. "You should try to get some sleep. We will head back to Haruto's home first thing in the morning."

"Haruto," Keishin said, not realizing he had said the name out loud. "Your husband."

"He's not my husband," Hana said without looking at Keishin. "Yet."

"Oh." There were probably more than a hundred better responses, but it was the best Keishin could do without betraying the rock in his gut that he knew had no right being there.

"That bothers you," Hana said.

"What? No. Of course not. Why would it bother me?"

"It bothers you because I kissed you and you kissed me back."

"That's not—"

"I should have told you. I am sorry. Haruto and I were matched by the Horishi when we were children. His name is written on my skin." Hana traced an invisible name over the inside of her arm.

"You don't have to explain."

"I want to." Hana sat up. "Most people in my world do not meet their spouse until the day of their wedding, but my father wanted something different for me. He told me that what happened to my mother might have been prevented if he had understood her better. That is why Haruto and I were made to meet as children.

"I did not make it easy for him to be my friend. As a little girl, I hated being told what to do, and Haruto liked to tease me that when he became my husband, I would have to follow whatever he said. We ended most of our visits with me trying to grab Haruto's hair and my father trying to pull us apart."

"That sounds like the foundation of a perfect marriage," Keishin said in a tone that he had meant to sound funny but came out stiff.

"Haruto and I are very different from each other, but we have learned to be friends. We have felt nothing for each other beyond that. My father used to tell me that we already had a better start than most people had, and that love or something close enough to it would come later."

"Are you sure about that?"

"About what?"

"About how Haruto feels about you. He's risking his life to help you."

"As are you."

"That's different."

"Is it?"

A cold wind blew through the room, snuffing out its only lamp. Hana gasped and scrambled to stand. "We need to leave," she said, gathering her things. "They have found us."

Keishin climbed over the minshuku's window and landed on the grass next to Hana. A rock stabbed his palm. Keishin bit down a yelp and swiftly scanned the town's dark streets. "I remember passing by a well on our way here. I think it was in that direction." He pointed to the left of the house. "Can we use it to get away?"

"Yes," Hana said. "Now, run."

The second to worst part about traveling through a well was falling into it. The worst was trying not to scream.

Nothing in Keishin's lifetime of experiences could offer him any assurance that he had not just jumped to his death. He crashed into the icy water feetfirst but was too busy being terrified to feel cold. He sank into the darkness, repeating Hana's instructions like a prayer. She had asked him to think of a place where they could hide, a refuge only he would know. It would be harder for the Shiikuin to find them if he led the way.

Safe. Far. Secret.

Safe. Far. Secret.

Safe. Far. Secret.

Lights shimmered above him. The surface of the water was close. Keishin glanced over his shoulder. Hana was nowhere in sight.

あわせもの、はなれもの

PART THREE

What has been joined may be separated.

CHAPTER TWENTY-NINE

Spicy Pork or Chicken?

College. Marriage. Kids. These were the big decisions that people believed mattered. They were wrong, of course. In reality, it was the choices that people didn't even realize they were making that set the course of their lives. The shifts were small, even minute, but, by the tiniest of angles, they pointed one in the direction of what was going to happen next.

In Keishin's case, everything that was going to define the rest of his life was decided the second his eyes shifted from the instant spicy pork ramen to the chicken-flavored one, then back to the pork. He reached for the bright red pack and dropped it into a green plastic basket. This was not the time to experiment with new flavors. His long-haul flight to Tokyo was the next day, and the last thing he needed was an upset stomach during his trip.

He wrinkled his nose at his instant ramen dinner and swore to get himself some real ramen as soon as he landed in Japan. He took a step back from the ramen shelf, planting the thick heel of his boot squarely on top of something that was clearly too soft to be the convenience store's tiled floor. A sharp yelp shattered any hope that he'd wronged a wayward pastry instead of a stranger's foot. He twisted around, an apology tumbling from his tongue ahead of him. "Oh my god. I'm so sorry."

"Where are we?" the woman said in Japanese.

"Oh . . . hello . . ." he said, shifting to Japanese. He scoured her small, heart-shaped face, searching for anything that might tell him who she was. He had never been good at names, but he doubted that he would have forgotten hers. "I'm sorry. Do I know you?"

Hana frowned. "It's me. Hana."

"Were you in one of my classes?"

"What? No. Don't you remember? We jumped into a well and I asked you to find a safe place for us to hide."

"Right . . ." He backed away from her. "I'm sorry, but I need to go," he said, heading to the cashier.

"Wait." Hana grabbed his arm. "I know you and you know me. Your name is Keishin. You are a physicist, and you have accepted a job at the Super-Kamiokande detector. You are trying to find neutrinos."

"Everyone at the university knows why I'm moving to Japan."

"You were abandoned by your mother, and all your life, every achievement and discovery you have chased after has been about trying to find something that will make you feel worthy of her love."

Keishin's basket slipped from his hand, scattering his dinner over the floor. "Who told you that?"

"You did. You told me about how your mother left you when you were a young boy. The rest . . . I saw for myself."

"Who put you up to this? Is this some kind of prank? Because if it is, I'm not laughing."

"Keishin . . . Kei . . ." Hana approached him slowly. "You need to listen to me very carefully. You did as I asked. You found a safe place for us to hide. We are in a moment in your mind so insignificant and small that no one would think to look for you in it. But you have hidden yourself too well, you have gone too deep."

"This is insane." He marched to the exit.

"Where will you go? To your apartment? To sit on a leather couch while listening to a song that will take you to a little boat floating on a quiet lake beneath the ground? Your beautiful trap?"

"How did you . . ."

"You took me there. We were on the boat at the Super-Kamiokande."

"But that's just a—"

"A memory you borrowed from someone else." Hana looked around the convenience store. "But this memory is your own, a fragment from a time before you stepped through a pawnshop's door."

"The pawnshop . . ." Keishin squeezed his eyes shut. "It . . . it was ransacked."

"Yes."

"And you were there. Your foot was bleeding."

"I had stepped on—"

"Glass." Keishin blinked and stared at Hana. "I . . . I remember."

Hana exhaled, throwing her arms around him.

Keishin held her tight. "Are we safe?" he whispered into her hair.

"For now. We are still falling."

"Falling?"

"Through the well." Hana drew away. "This is a detour. We could not go directly to any of the places I knew. Those places would have been easier for the Shiikuin to find. I am hoping that they will lose our trail if we stay here for a while."

"How long?"

"Until morning," Hana said. "And then we will need to go to Haruto."

"Hana . . ." Keishin hesitated.

"What is it?"

"If the Shiikuin were able to find us at the minshuku, don't you think that they could have found out about Haruto too?"

"No."

"But—"

"No." Her voice caught in her throat. "He's safe. He has to be."

Keishin watched her draw short, ragged breaths through pale lips. He nodded, allowing Hana to believe the lie she told herself. When running for your life, honesty was a luxury. Courage, even the false kind, was not.

Keishin and Hana sat at one of the convenience store's counters, waiting for their instant ramen to be ready. Other customers walked past them without casting a sideward glance.

Keishin lifted the ramen bowl's foil lid. "It's ready. Just give it a stir."

Hana stirred the noodles with a plastic fork. "It does not look like ramen."

Keishin smiled. "Go on. Try it."

Hana cautiously brought a forkful of noodles to her mouth. "It is . . . not bad. But it is not ramen either."

"Definitely not like any ramen you'd find in your world." Keishin laughed. "And that's a good thing."

"Why?"

"Because nothing in that bowl is remotely good for you."

Hana swallowed another forkful. "It is fortunate that none of this is real then."

"I should probably eat every single thing here while I don't have to worry about making myself sick." Keishin scanned the shelves.

"That looks interesting," Hana said, pointing to a frozen-drink machine. "Why is it colored blue?"

Keishin wrinkled his nose. "I wouldn't recommend trying that even if it isn't real."

Hana laughed.

Keishin laughed too. A small chuckle that tickled his belly and did a little happy dance over his tongue. It grew, rolling around his stomach and expanding in his chest, uncontrollable and relentless. Keishin chortled and gasped for air. A fit of giggling burst from Hana's lips. Laughter exploded between them, knocking both of them to the floor. Keishin rolled to his side and clutched his belly, tears welling in his eyes.

Hana sat up and leaned against a snack shelf, bringing her laughter to a stop with slow, deliberate breaths.

Keishin sat next to her, his long legs stretched across the aisle. "Damn, that felt good."

Hana smiled. "It did."

"I don't even know what we were laughing about."

"At nothing." Hana panted. "And everything."

Keishin's eyes wandered around the store. "It feels strange being back here."

"Because it isn't real?"

"I don't think it would feel real even if I was actually here. This memory is only from a few days ago, but I no longer feel like the same person that was in it."

"That will change." Hana fiddled with a pack of chips she had plucked from a shelf. "When all of this is over, your old life will feel like the only one you've ever lived."

"Because I won't remember you," he said quietly.

Hana rested her head on his shoulder. "You said that you were okay with not remembering my world."

"I was."

"And now?" She closed her eyes.

"It's . . ." He held her hand, weaving his fingers through hers as though it would keep her from slipping away. "Different."

Keishin had lived all his life believing that time wasn't something you could hold, but tonight it fit perfectly into the paper cup warming his hands. Fifteen minutes looked and smelled exactly like a steaming latte. At the end of this time, when he had sipped the last of his dark-roasted seconds, he was going to wake Hana, as she had requested, from the nap she was taking on his shoulder. She had said that they needed to be on their way before the sun was up, back to chasing clues. And being chased.

But for now Keishin's cup was full, and he had time to watch Hana sleep. He brushed a stray lock of hair from her face. Hana slept surprisingly peacefully for someone sitting on a convenience store's questionably clean floor. Keishin felt calm too, partly because it felt good not to have to constantly look over his shoulder, but mostly because he had finally found an answer to a question that involved a broken elevator, a pregnant woman, and a battered box of free old books.

CHAPTER THIRTY

Ina May's Guide to Childbirth

❀ *One year ago*

Keishin's apartment building cast a welcome shadow over the street. He quickened his pace. His mind reached home ahead of him, hurriedly peeling off sweaty clothes and tossing them onto the floor. It hopped into the shower and stood beneath the stream of cool water, waiting for the rest of Keishin to join it. It was used to leaving him behind. His body was always trying to catch up with his thoughts. Later, when they were reunited, Keishin would pour himself a cold glass of white wine, put a record on, and fall asleep on the couch listening to his favorite song, his hair still wet from his shower.

Keishin rushed inside his building, his shirt clinging to his chest. Sunscreen and sweat stung his eyes. Luckily, Keishin didn't have to see where he was going to find his way to the elevator. The tapping of his footsteps over the black-and-white marble tiles was enough. Next to the gurgle of his coffee machine, the little taps were his favorite sound in the world. There were exactly twenty-two of them. Each ferried him closer to a small metal box that whisked him from the noise of the day. He didn't like sharing it.

A pregnant woman, vigorously fanning herself with a Chinese take-out menu by the elevator's doors, crushed his hopes of solitude. The elevator doors slid open. Keishin threw a glance at the stairs and dismissed climbing up the ten flights to his apartment almost as soon as he considered it. The elevator dinged. Keishin met the woman's eyes. She looked away, sending her thick ponytail swinging like a pendulum against her nape. She shuffled inside the elevator, stuffing the take-out menu into an oversized shoulder bag while cradling a box of jelly donuts. Keishin followed her in and pushed the button for his floor.

"Eight, please," the pregnant woman said. "Thanks."

Keishin pressed the button for her.

The cab jolted. The woman stumbled forward, sending her donuts flying and knocking Keishin into the elevator door. Metal slammed against his cheek. The lights went out, plunging the cab into darkness. An emergency light flickered to life.

Pain radiated through Keishin's jaw. "Are you okay?" he said, trying to rub the pain away.

The woman clutched her stomach. "I . . . I think so."

"Okay. Good. I'll call for help." He pressed the elevator's emergency call button. "Hello?"

The speaker crackled to life.

"Hello?" Keishin said. "Can you hear me? The elevator's stuck."

"I can hear you. Is everyone okay in there?"

"We're fine."

"We're calling the repair crew right now. They should be here soon."

Keishin took a deep breath, telling himself that things could be worse. He could have gotten stuck in the elevator with Trisha, the neighbor he had made the mistake of sleeping with after a bad movie, a forgettable dinner, and too many bottles of wine.

"I'm Liz," the woman said. "Eighth floor."

"I know."

"Right. I asked you to push the button for me. Sorry. Pregnancy brain."

"I'm Kei. Tenth," he said, not because it was necessary, but because it was polite. He expected their situation to be rectified soon and didn't think that waiting for the elevator required conversation.

Liz lowered herself onto the floor and fanned herself with the Chinese take-out menu. "I hope they get us out of here soon."

"They will." Keishin sat opposite her.

Liz winced and rubbed her belly. "Oh god . . ."

"What is it? What's wrong?"

Liz groaned, doubling over. Sweat beaded on her brow. "I . . . I think the baby's coming."

"What?" Keishin scrambled to her.

Liz clenched her teeth and grabbed his sleeve. "I don't suppose that I was lucky enough to be trapped in an elevator with a doctor?"

"Er . . . yes, but the useless kind."

Liz's face crumpled in pain. She squeezed his arm and groaned. "I don't want to have the baby in an elevator," she said, breaking into a sob.

"We'll get out of here. Soon. I promise."

"No, not 'soon.' Now. We need to get out now." Liz drew rapid breaths. Sweat dripped down her face and over her pale lips. "I can't breathe. We're running out of air. I'm going to die. My baby . . ."

Keishin clasped her hand. He didn't know much about childbirth but was well acquainted with anxiety attacks. In the early months after his mother had left, Keishin found his father curled up into a ball, believing that he was dying, at least once every other week. Like Liz's, his hands were cold and clammy, and they trembled against Keishin's palms. He had held his father's hand until his breathing slowed, trying to soothe him the only way he knew how. He lay next to his father and recounted, like a story, an inventory of things his young mind knew to be true. *The sun is a star. The brain cannot feel pain. An elephant's pregnancy lasts almost two years.* Facts had always comforted Keishin. His mother's love had once been at the top of his list, before any trivia about the earth or the moon. When she left, he collected as many truths as he could, having convinced himself that one day, he was going to have enough to fill a hole in his chest that had once been filled with certainty. He shared his collection of the unquestionable and the unchanging with his father, giving him something to hold on to whenever a current of doubt threatened to sweep him away.

Keishin squeezed Liz's hand. "'Remember this, for it is as true as true gets: Your body is not a lemon. You are not a machine. The Creator is not a careless mechanic. Human female bodies have the same potential to give birth well as aardvarks, lions, rhinoceroses, elephants, moose, and water buffalo,'" he said.

"*What?*" Liz panted.

"It's a quote from the book *Ina May's Guide to Childbirth,*" Keishin said. "And a fact."

"And you know that because?" Liz said, her breathing slowing down.

"Do you want the long or short story?"

"Short." Liz blew out air in measured breaths. "Definitely short."

"My father's favorite price was free."

"And?"

"That's it. You asked for the short version."

"Okay. I get it." Liz wiped the sweat from her brow. "You're trying to distract me from my impending doom."

"Is it working?"

"Yes. Go on. Tell me the long story, or maybe the medium version."

"Okay, but you need to promise me one thing first."

"What?"

"You need to keep your baby inside you for a little longer, okay? I think this situation calls for a professional with a greater understanding of childbirth than someone who found Ina May's dusty midwifery book in a box his father picked up from the side of a street."

"Deal."

Liz broke her promise.

Keishin clung to Ina May's words as though they were the very cable that kept the elevator from crashing to the ground. Liz, he repeated to himself, was not a lemon, and with Ina May's time-tested guidance, she was going to give birth as smoothly as any aardvark. "You're doing great, Liz," he said, looking over her bent legs. "Just give me one more big push, okay?"

Liz groaned, her brows meeting.

"We're almost there. Deep breaths, Liz. This is it. I can see the head." Keishin positioned his hands between Liz's legs, cradling the baby as it emerged. "I got her!"

"Is . . . is she okay?" Liz sobbed.

Keishin gently ran his hand over the baby's nose and mouth

as Ina May had instructed, clearing them of fluid. A lusty cry escaped the baby's lips. Keishin laid her in Liz's arms.

"She's beautiful." Liz alternately laughed and cried. "Thank you."

Keishin wiped his forehead with his sleeve. "Thank Ina May."

The elevator doors slid open. A man in a dark blue-gray jumpsuit stood outside, his jaw on the floor. "Holy shit . . . are you guys okay?"

Keishin glanced back at Liz. Her smile seemed out of place in a steaming elevator reeking of blood, sweat, and birth fluids. It was a smile that could belong only to someone who was utterly content to be stranded where she was. This, Keishin thought, was what happiness looked like: an exhausted woman sitting in a puddle of amniotic goo and smashed jelly donuts, a crumpled Chinese take-out menu at her side. Liz's eyes saw only her daughter, and no one and nothing else mattered beyond the bundle in her arms. Keishin wiped the blood from his hands on his pants and walked out of the elevator, wondering if he was ever going to be happy enough to sit perfectly and quietly still.

CHAPTER THIRTY-ONE

The Message

Hana leaned against Keishin's shoulder, hoping that if her eyes were closed, her last fifteen minutes inside a convenience store that wasn't real would feel longer. She refused to spend any of it imagining what was going to happen when it was over. She needed every second of it to rewrite a memory of her own. Here, in the instant-noodle aisle of a store with too many colors and bright lights, was where she should have met Keishin for the first time, not in a pawnshop littered with broken glass. Here, they might have had the chance to be more than just two strangers clinging to each other for safety and warmth. It made her think of her father's story about how the pawned birds could reset time if they escaped. This, she thought, would be the moment she would fly straight back to if, like the birds, she could break free.

Paper rustled by her ear. Hana jolted up, nearly knocking Keishin's coffee cup from his hand.

"Whoa," Keishin said. "Careful. This is hot. Even if it isn't real."

"Did you hear that?" Hana said.

"Hear what?"

The sound of rustling paper grew louder. Hana grabbed her bag and stuck her hand inside. She pulled out the piece of paper

Haruto had given her. It wriggled in her hand. "It's Haruto." She set the paper on the floor. "He is sending us a message."

Hana and Keishin watched the paper move in a flurry and crease on its own, folded by an expert invisible hand. When it reached its final, angular shape, it grew still.

Hana stared at the origami creation. "You were right about the Shiikuin finding out about Haruto helping us. We cannot go back to his home."

"How do you know that?"

"Because Haruto just told us where to go instead."

Keishin picked up the folded paper. "A star?"

CHAPTER THIRTY-TWO

The Valley of Stars

Blue slushies, as it turned out, had a purpose other than giving you a brain freeze. Keishin watched Hana pour one out over the floor. He jumped and sank into the blue puddle, pleasantly surprised that he didn't feel cold.

The trip was quick, over before Keishin could even begin trying to understand what it meant to travel to a star. Foxes made of sand and living scrolls had forced him to redefine what "fantastic" meant, and a star, he was certain, was going to test the new definition's limits. It was therefore quite understandable that Keishin had a difficult time hiding his disappointment when he reached their destination.

"This is not what you expected," Hana said, surveying a small village at the bottom of a gently sloping hill.

"I think that I must have misheard you. I thought you said we were going to a star."

Hana smiled. "You heard correctly. But we will not be seeing one star. We will be seeing many. That village has one responsibility. Each night, it creates the sky."

The energy throughout the village's cobbled streets buzzed in the air and tingled against Keishin's skin. No matter where you looked, you could not find a single person standing still. Everyone, including the smallest child, had a task. Baskets flowed in an endless stream down both sides of the street, ferried on backs and shoulders. Small groups hunched over worktables cutting washi paper or splitting bamboo into thin spars, barely pausing to speak or look up from their work. The children were charged with carrying around trays of food and drink. A little girl with chubby hands stopped and offered Keishin and Hana savory rice crackers.

"Thank you," Keishin said, taking a round, golden-brown cracker from her.

She bowed and smiled in a way that puffed up her cheeks. She carried her tray down the street, searching for the next person to share her crackers with.

"Every person in this town is working toward the singular goal of getting the night sky ready. Some prepare the stars. Some clean. Some make sure the others do not go thirsty or hungry while working. At the end of the day, they put up the sky and go to bed. The next morning, they do everything all over again."

"I think that out of everything I have seen and heard since stepping into your world, what you just told me makes the least sense. What do you mean they're getting the night sky ready? How do you prepare the stars?"

"It is better if you see it for yourself," Hana said. "Come."

They stopped at the end of the street across from a two-story wooden house. A cart, being unloaded by two men, was parked in front of it. The men handed baskets of small, silk-wrapped packages to two women who carried the baskets inside the house.

"This is where the whole process begins," Hana said. "Think of this entire village as a workshop. Each street is assigned a specific task, and each house along that street is responsible for fulfilling the various elements of that task. This house is in charge of collecting and sorting hope."

"Hope?" Keishin arched a brow.

"Even in a world like ours, where our entire life is mapped out for us, we still need to hope, or at least have the illusion of it. On our birthdays, we are allowed to send our hopes to this village. We write them down a few weeks before our birthday and send them here. It is the village's duty to send them up to the sky," Hana said. "That is what those baskets contain. Hope. Every household on this street is charged with collecting and sorting them.

"But not all hopes are the same. Some require more work than others. The homes that are in charge of preparing the hopes people have about love have the most difficult duty."

Keishin and Hana were warmly welcomed into a home along the next street as though they were longtime friends of the family. Suzuki Fumiko, a stooped elderly woman who had a harder time seeing than chattering away, led them to a room where a small group of people were gathered around a table, painting on thin sheets of paper.

"It is not often that we have visitors come to our village." Fumiko squinted at Keishin. "I am always happy to see the faces of those who send their hopes here."

"Thank you for allowing us to see your work, Suzuki-san," Hana said.

"It is my children who paint now. My eyes gave up on me before my mind and hands did. But oh, what beauty I used to paint. Everyone said that my work was the prettiest in the village. Even better than my sister's. Faces were my specialty.

Lips. Eyes. Noses. I painted all of them with the greatest care," she said, barely taking a breath. "Oh. I apologize," she said with a chuckle. "Here I go again. It is an old woman's vice to ramble and take advantage of people who are too polite to tell her to be quiet."

Keishin smiled, finding her chattering soothing. It gave him something to think about other than being chased by the Shiikuin. It also made the day with Hana feel like one wherein they were simply two tourists with nothing on their minds except wondering where they were going to have lunch and buy souvenirs. In a way, it was like a date—their second, if he counted the imaginary one they had while riding his song. It even came with all the tiny bubbles that fizzed and popped in your stomach as you stood next to each other, hands close enough to touch. "We are happy to listen to whatever you wish to tell us."

Fumiko beamed. "I like you. You remind me of my father. He stopped whatever he was doing, no matter how busy he was, to listen to my stories about insects I had found or a rock that I thought was pretty. He made me feel that they were the most interesting things in the world. His face and the other old treasures I keep in here are the only things I see clearly now." She tapped the side of her head with a crooked finger. "But I do not have any cause to complain. My family has had the privilege of painting every hope our world has ever had about love. They say that hopes about children are the most colorful, hopes about health the brightest, hopes about happiness the prettiest, and hopes about love the most difficult to paint. And they are right. It is very challenging to capture all the shades love has with pigment. But we do our best, and I have enough memories of all the hope I have painted in my lifetime to fill the largest museum. There is nothing more I need to see. I trust my children to carry on our family's duty." She pointed to the farthest side of the table. "Mikio is my eldest son and a gifted illustrator."

A slightly built man with a sparse head of hair glanced up from a hexagonal sheet of washi paper and greeted Keishin and Hana with a polite smile. He returned to his work, painting over the sheet with black ink, using a combination of thick and thin brushstrokes. The image on the paper was less than half done, but Keishin was able to make out the features of a striking face.

"And that is Emiko." Fumiko gestured to a woman with a face that reminded Keishin of a peach. "She brings Mikio's drawings to life."

Emiko looked up from her corner of the table and nodded shyly. She dipped her brush into a small clay pot, tapped it lightly on the pot's rim, and colored in the delicate blush on a woman's face. From where he stood, Keishin could almost feel the warmth radiating from the painted cheek.

"Will you be staying to see the stars tonight?" Fumiko said. "It will be quite a sight. I have lived in this village all my life, and yet every night feels new."

"We do not know what our plans are yet," Hana said. "But thank you for sharing your work with us. Everything is so beautiful."

"Every hope deserves to sparkle in the sky." Fumiko smiled, deepening the lines around her eyes. She patted Hana's hand. "Even for just one night."

A question was wedged between Keishin's brows when they left Fumiko's home. "Were the paintings they were making supposed to be stars?"

"They will be. They are not finished yet. Once they dry, they will be sent to those houses over there." Hana pointed to an intersecting street. "Those families are responsible for attaching the painted washi to a bamboo frame. The households across from them are in charge of inserting the string and bending the bamboo to make sure that everything is firmly stuck together."

Keishin narrowed his eyes, imagining the assembly. "They're making kites?"

"One kite for every hope that is sent to the village. Tonight, they will float in the sky as stars. This is the one place that the Shiikuin are forbidden to go, a place where we can pretend that we are free."

"So that's why Haruto told us to meet him here," Keishin said. "Because the Shiikuin can't follow us."

"That, and because the person he trusts most in this world lives in this village."

"Who?"

A tall woman with white-blond hair whose face bore a striking resemblance to Haruto's walked up behind Hana. "His mother."

Hana twisted around and bowed to her. "Masuda-san."

"Hana," Masuda Masako said without smiling.

"Is Haruto here?"

Masako raised her hand, silencing her.

Hana nodded, glancing around to check if anyone had overheard them.

Masako narrowed her eyes at Keishin. "*Outsider,*" she hissed beneath her breath.

Masako said the word so sharply that it sliced through the air and nicked Keishin's left cheek. Keishin flinched. The word was all too familiar. It was how he felt about himself no matter where he was. It may as well have been his name.

"Keishin is a friend, Masuda-san," Hana said, looking her directly in the eye.

"You have no idea what kind of danger you have put all of us in, Hana."

"I know. I am truly sorry. We will leave as soon as—"

"As soon as," Masako cut Hana off, her face dark, "you see what they have done to my son. Because of you."

Masako's home sat in the shade of a large tree. Gampi bushes, mitsumata shrubs, and kozo bushes grew as they pleased over its front garden, nearly covering the path to the house.

"Take care not to step on them." Masako stepped over one of the overgrown shrubs. "I need them to make my paper."

"We saw the washi you made in the village," Hana said quietly. "They were very beautiful."

"It keeps me busy. It is what sensible people do when they retire. They do sensible things. They do not chase after ghosts and put the people around them in danger." She stopped and faced Hana. "This is all your father's fault. Why couldn't he have left the past alone? I don't care what my family owes him. He has gone too far and asked too much of Haruto, of everyone. The Shiikuin would not have . . ." She clenched her fists at her sides, tears in her eyes. She looked away to hide them. "Come. Haruto is waiting for you inside."

Masako led them through sliding doors to a room at the back of her home. A lean figure lay on a futon in the corner, his body facing the wall, his long white-blond hair disheveled.

"Haruto?" Masako said quietly.

Haruto stirred.

"They're here," Masako said. "I will wait outside while you talk." She stepped out of the room, sliding the paper doors shut behind her.

Haruto slowly pushed himself up from the futon, letting out a small groan as he did.

"Are you all right?" Hana hurried to him. "What happened?"

Haruto turned toward her, his face damp with cold sweat. His hair lay plastered over his forehead and the sides of his cheeks. "I'm fine," he said, forcing a smile that betrayed his pain.

Hana reached out to brush the hair from his face.

"Don't." Haruto's arm flew up to block her. A bloodied bandage covered his hand from fingertips to wrist.

Hana's eyes filled with horror. "No . . ."

Keishin gaped at Haruto's hands. Both were wrapped in bandages stained with blood. "Did the Shiikuin do this?" he said, his throat closing around his words.

"Someone told them that they had seen you and Hana at the museum. The Shiikuin came to my house and questioned me. They demanded to know why the two of you came to see me and where you were. When I refused to answer them . . ."

"They could have killed you." Hana choked on her tears.

"No, they could not," Haruto said. "My mother is too old to do my work, and I do not yet have any sons or daughters to pass on my trade. No one else can do my duty."

Hana cradled his hands. "And so they did worse."

"I wanted them to. It was the only way."

"What are you talking about? It was the only way to do what?"

"If the Shiikuin did not hurt me, if they did not do something terrible to force me to talk, they would not have believed the lie I told them."

"What lie?" Hana said.

"That you believed your father had found a way to cross over safely into the other world, and that you were trying to find a way to follow him. I told them that you were looking for something from the museum exhibits that could help you cross. I confessed that I had assisted you by taking some of the hours from the exhibit and giving them to you so that you would have more time to search for your father before fading away. I told them that I had sent you to the Lotus Lake to collect the materials I needed to make the paper to hold the hours."

"And they believed you?" Keishin said.

"After they broke my second hand and I repeated the same story, they did."

Hana wept. "You did not have to do this, Haruto."

"My hands will heal. Besides, if I had told them the truth, then all the trouble I had gone through to retrieve the bones would have been for nothing."

"You . . . mean . . ." Hana's voice quivered.

"I did it. It worked. I folded time. But . . ."

"But what?" Keishin said.

"I cannot give it to you."

"Why not?" Keishin asked.

"Because I had to swallow it to hide it from the Shiikuin."

"I . . . I understand. That was the right thing to do," Hana said.

"I cannot give it to you," Haruto said. "But I can tell you

everything I saw. I know that it was not my place to look, but after I had folded time, I could not stop myself. I am sorry."

"Thank you." Hana threw her arms around him. "Thank you."

"But Hana . . ." Haruto said.

"Yes?"

"The story I will tell you will not be easy to hear."

CHAPTER THIRTY-THREE

The Trial and Sentencing of Ishikawa Chiyo

❀ *Twenty-one years ago*

The morning at the pawnshop began as it always did, with the bubbling of a kettle and the brewing of green tea. Beyond that, nothing was the same. A heaviness filled the room, making it difficult to breathe.

"Say something," Chiyo said, her thin hands wringing her skirt over her lap. "Anything. Please."

Toshio looked up at her from across the table. "Nothing I can say will change the fate you have doomed all of us to live."

"What I did," Chiyo said, "I did for us."

"You did it for yourself."

"Perhaps." Chiyo lowered her eyes. "And I would do it again."

"But you cannot." Toshio slammed his fist on the table and stood up. "You cannot do it again. You will not be able to do anything ever again because, after today, you will be dead."

Chiyo walked toward him. "I am still here now."

Toshio took a step back, breathing hard. "Don't."

Chiyo circled her arms around him and pressed her cheek against his chest. "Tell her stories about me so that she won't forget about her mother."

"I will tell Hana one story about you." Toshio pushed her away. "I will tell her about this day so that she will know never to be as foolish as her mother."

"Will you really let these be the last words we exchange, Toshio? You loved me once . . ."

"I . . ." Tears eroded the edges of Toshio's voice. "I still do."

"But you wish that you did not."

Toshio clenched his jaw. "I wish I could hate you for what you have done to us. It would be easier to forget you when you are gone."

"And I wish that I did not have to steal that choice, but it was the only way."

"There was another way." Toshio's voice broke. "You could have been content with what you had. You could have just been happy. You . . . you were always enough for me."

"Then have me now," Chiyo said. "While we still have time."

Toshio crushed her to him, claiming her lips. Chiyo kissed him back, hard and long, not caring for air.

The pawnshop, Toshio thought, had never been so silent. Not even the leaves of the tree in their courtyard seemed to make a sound. Or maybe all the screaming he had done inside his head since he had learned about Chiyo's crime had made him deaf. He watched the Shiikuin slowly climb out from the pawnshop's pond, their masks stripped of emotion. Hana slept in his arms the way only babies could, soundly and deeply, without the shadow of worry to follow them into their dreams.

His daughter's life was going to change forever after today, and she was not even going to remember a single second of the life she had before it. And perhaps this was for the better. It was easier to chew on misery if you did not know what happiness tasted like. Though the Shiikuin had come to punish Chiyo for her crime, it was Hana who was going to be tainted by it. Losing a mother under the best of circumstances, when she was old and gray and longing for rest, cut to the heart. Losing a mother to the Shiikuin cut deeper.

Two Shiikuin moved gracefully toward him, their arms folded across their chests, their talons hidden in the sleeves of their kimonos. The sight might have been beautiful if one did not know their real intent. They had discovered Chiyo's crime months ago, on the day they had come to collect the birds from the vault. They would have exiled her then if not for her pregnancy. The child she carried was no different from any other child in their world; it belonged to them. Chiyo had robbed them once. The Shiikuin had no intentions of allowing her to steal from them again. Her punishment, they decided, would be handed down once their property had been delivered. There was, after all, nowhere Chiyo could run. Today, their wait was over.

"Where is the criminal?" the Shiikuin asked in unison, their voices a choir of at least a hundred more.

Hana stirred in Toshio's arms. He rocked her gently, lulling her back to sleep. "My wife is waiting for you inside."

The Shiikuin nodded and walked past him. Toshio followed them, his mind racing back to all the minuscule seconds that had led them to this day. Each point looked exactly like the rest, small and unnoticed, making it impossible to tell where he and Chiyo had veered horribly and irreversibly off course.

Chiyo met the Shiikuin in the middle of the pawnshop with her shoulders drawn back and her spine pulled straight. Though she came up only to his ear, in this moment, Toshio thought, Chiyo stood a hundred feet tall. She looked directly into the Shiikuin's dark eyes as though it were she who was about to sentence them.

"Ishikawa Chiyo," the pair of Shiikuin spoke. "You have been accused of the gravest of crimes. You took that which did not belong to you, a choice claimed by the Shiikuin on behalf of the dutiful citizens of this world. How do you plead?"

"To dream . . ." Chiyo lifted her chin. "To desire . . . to aspire for more than what is written on my skin is not a crime."

"To steal it is. Your solemn duty was to collect these choices and keep them safe. By taking a choice as your own, you broke your husband's trust and the trust placed in you by our world. Do you deny this?" the Shiikuin said in unison.

The rims of Chiyo's eyes quivered. "I do not."

The Shiikuin turned to Toshio. "Is there anything you wish to say in your wife's defense?"

"Yes. I . . ." Hana wriggled against Toshio's chest and began to cry. Toshio cradled her, feeling her grow heavy in his arms. He broke into a sweat, struggling to bear the weight of a life that was now fully dependent on him. He looked at Chiyo. She met his eyes, silently pleading with him to keep the promise she had forced him to make. She had begged him to remain silent for their daughter's sake, to not anger or defy the Shiikuin further. Hana could not lose her father too.

"Speak," the Shiikuin said.

"I have nothing to say." Toshio lowered his eyes, trying to look at nothing beyond his daughter's face. Chiyo was lost to him the instant she took the choice from the vault. Hana was all that mattered now.

"Ishikawa Chiyo," the two Shiikuin said. "You have been found guilty in the eyes of this court. We sentence you to exile."

"I accept my punishment." Chiyo bowed her head. "May I hold my daughter one last time?"

The Shiikuin turned to each other, conferring without saying a word. "No, you may not."

"I beg you." Chiyo dropped to her knees. "I just want to say goodbye."

"No."

"Please. Hana will not have a mother to hold her after today. Kill me for my crime, but do not punish my daughter. She is innocent."

The Shiikuin tilted their heads as though considering her words. "Very well. You may say goodbye."

Toshio laid Hana in Chiyo's arms. Chiyo nuzzled her cheek and hair. She kissed Hana's forehead and handed her back to Toshio. She caressed Toshio's cheek. "Take care of each other."

Toshio kissed her through his tears. "I love you."

"I love you too." Chiyo walked back to the Shiikuin. "I am ready."

The two Shiikuin took their places on either side of Chiyo and gripped her arms. They looked at Toshio. "Leave us."

"No. I want to be here," Toshio said, holding Hana tightly.

"What you want is of no importance," the Shiikuin said, digging their talons deeper into Chiyo's wrist. "Leave."

"Do as they say, Toshio," Chiyo said. "You do not need to see this. I do not want you or Hana to be here. This is not a memory that I wish either of you to keep."

The two Shiikuin led Chiyo to the pawnshop's door, gripping her arms tight. Chiyo wondered if fading away was going to be quick or painful. She didn't imagine that it could hurt more than letting her daughter go. The Shiikuin on her right closed its talons around the doorknob and pulled the door open, then it stopped suddenly and pushed the door shut. Both Shiikuin closed their eyes and bowed their heads, tilting them slightly as though trying to listen to something faint or far away.

"It will be done," they said, responding to someone Chiyo couldn't see or hear. They lifted their heads and looked at Chiyo.

"What's going on?" Chiyo said.

"We have changed our mind."

"What?" Chiyo gasped.

"We have decided that you require a punishment more fitting of your crime." The two Shiikuin angled their heads, allowing shadows to morph their unmoving plaster lips into a sneer. "Death is more than you deserve."

CHAPTER THIRTY-FOUR

Family

Haruto leaned against the wall, his lips pale. Sweat trickled down the side of his face. He closed his eyes, drawing tired breaths. "I wish I could tell you more, Hana," he said, his voice frail, "but that was all that fragment of bone would reveal. If I had the amount I used when I folded time for your father, I might have been able to see where they had taken your mother. I'm sorry."

"You have nothing to apologize for. You have already done so much for me. Too much." Hana eased him back onto the futon. "I do not know how I can ever repay you."

Haruto smiled up at her and stroked her cheek with his bandaged hand. "There is nothing that needs to be repaid."

Hana stiffened at Haruto's touch and glanced at Keishin. He looked away.

Haruto drew his hand back, his smile erased. "There is nothing to be repaid because we are no closer to finding your father than we were before I folded time. We still do not know where your parents are. The paper told us nothing."

"No," Hana said. "It told us the most important thing. The Shiikuin kept my mother alive. She was not erased."

"What do you think the Shiikuin meant by 'a punishment more fitting' of her crime?" Keishin asked.

Hana shook her head. "I don't know."

The paper door slid open. Masako stepped through it. "It is time for you to leave. You have what you came for. Do not put my son in any more danger."

Haruto pushed himself up from the futon, wincing as he sat. "They should stay. This village is the safest place for them to be while we try to figure out what the Shiikuin meant."

"*We?*" Masako said. "This is their problem, Haruto, not yours. You should never have involved yourself in any of this."

"I owe Ishikawa-san my life."

"You owe him nothing. He would not have needed to save you if Chiyo had not—" Masako cast a sharp glare at Hana. "You owe *her* nothing."

"Hana is family," Haruto said.

"Not yet," Masako said. "She is not yet your wife."

"She will be. Her name is written on my skin as clearly as my father's name was written on yours. Do you wish me to stray further from my path and anger the Shiikuin more?"

Masako shook her head and sighed. "Of course not. That's not what I meant."

"Then it is settled. Hana and her friend will stay with us while we try to find out where the Shiikuin took Hana's mother," Haruto said.

Hana gently touched his shoulder. "It is not right to put you in any more danger. We should leave."

"And where do you intend to go, Hana?" Haruto said. "If you leave without a plan, you will only be giving the Shiikuin a better chance of catching you."

"Haruto is right," Keishin said. "Running blindly from the Shiikuin is not going to help us find your parents."

"This is my house, and I will decide who can stay and who cannot," Masako said. "Hana may stay, but I will not have an outsider sleep under my roof. He will be just as safe in the inn as he will be in this house."

"I will go with him," Hana said.

"No," Keishin said. "You should stay here. Haruto needs you. If any of us comes up with any ideas about what the Shiikuin meant about your mother's punishment, we can regroup."

"Kei . . ."

"It's all right, Hana," Keishin said. "It's for the best. I need some time alone to think."

"About what?"

Keishin glanced from Haruto to Hana. "Everything."

The bowl of okayu warmed Hana's hands, stirring memories of the days when her father made the watery rice porridge for her when she was sick. He liked to serve it with eggs and sweet potatoes. Masako topped the dinner she had made for Haruto with a pickled plum. Hana scooped a spoonful of the porridge for Haruto. He waved it away.

"You need to eat something to get your strength back," Hana said.

"I'm not hungry."

"Just one spoonful?" Hana said. "Please?"

Haruto sighed. "Just one."

Hana fed him the porridge.

"You do not need to take care of me, Hana."

"I want to." Hana dabbed his lips with a soft cloth.

"Do you?"

"Of course I do."

"You did not even want to be here." Haruto lay down. "You wanted to be with Keishin."

"Because he's a stranger here. I was worried about him staying at the inn by himself."

Haruto stared up at the ceiling. "Is that the only reason?"

"What other reason would I have?"

"You care for him."

"Yes," Hana said. "As a friend."

"Just as you care for me," Haruto said. "As a friend."

Hana gently placed her hands over his. "My dearest and oldest friend."

"We will be married in one month, Hana."

"I . . . know." Hana had pushed the date into the back of her mind. Since Keishin had arrived, she'd found herself shoving it deeper.

"And you do not love me yet."

"I do love you."

"Not in the way a wife loves her husband."

"I know that is what my father wanted for us, but we already have more than anyone in our world does when they wed. My father saw my mother for the first time on their wedding day. As did your parents. We have a friendship deeper than most people will ever know in their lifetime. Is that not enough?"

"I know that it should be," Haruto said. "But it isn't."

"My mother learned to love my father. Whatever we do not have now, it can come later."

"Will it? We have known each other all our lives. If you have not learned to love me yet, do you think that a ceremony at a temple will change anything? I just wish that . . ."

"What is it? Tell me."

"It doesn't matter." He looked out the window at the darkening sky. "The only place for hopes and wishes is in the sky."

CHAPTER THIRTY-FIVE

Among the Stars

Keishin followed the procession out of the village, not knowing where it would lead him. Putting one step in front of another felt better than lying in bed at the inn and waiting for the sun to rise. He did not like the thoughts that kept him company. He had tried putting them to the task of solving the puzzle that Haruto had left him and Hana with, but they slipped from his grasp and cared only to paint Hana's face behind his eyelids. Before he could retreat into any dream, he would have to endure restless hours staring at a smile that was never meant for him.

Masako, Keishin thought, had been right to shun him. He was an outsider in his world and in this one. He had intruded into Hana's life, inserting himself into a script that had no part for him to play. Seeing Hana with Haruto had made that very clear. Haruto had made a sacrifice that only a person who had committed his life to someone else could make. Haruto had given Hana his heart a long time ago. And now he had given her his hands. His life's purpose. His ikigai.

Keishin should have admired him, but he could not feel anything beyond his shame. He wanted a woman he barely knew, knowing full well that he was not capable of the same sacrifice the man who truly loved her had given. But still, he wanted her.

As much as he wanted to know the stars and all their secrets. Maybe more.

This, he thought, was the basest of instincts that drove people to steal. Hana's mother had felt it too. Keishin did not know what Chiyo had stolen. He didn't have to. Thieves understood thieves. They all desired the water moon. Keishin imagined Chiyo sitting inside the pawnshop's vault, surrounded by all the things she couldn't have. His mother, he had no doubt, felt the same way whenever she used to hold him in her arms. The life she desperately wanted waited for her just outside her door, and all she had to do was empty her hands to pull the door open and step through it.

"It is you again," an elderly voice said from behind him. "Hello."

"Suzuki-san." Keishin bowed. "Good evening."

"Where is your friend? Have you decided to stay and watch the stars?"

"She's somewhere up ahead," Keishin lied. "And yes, we decided that we didn't want to miss seeing the village's hard work."

"You will not regret it," Fumiko said with a smile that showcased two missing teeth. "I promise that it is a sight you will not soon forget. But we'd better hurry. It is almost dark, and the stars will not wait."

The villagers gathered in a grassy field beneath a starless sky. Those at the front carried large baskets on their backs and at the sound of a distant gong unhooked the baskets from their shoulders. They each reached inside their basket and pulled out a kite, passing the basket along to the person standing behind them. This went on until the baskets reached the very back of the crowd. A smiling woman turned around and handed an empty basket to Keishin. Keishin smiled back, trying not to look disappointed.

"It's all right." Fumiko patted Keishin's arm. "You cannot look up and run at the same time. Tonight's show is not on the ground."

The wind picked up and whipped at Fumiko's kimono. Keishin lifted his eyes to the sky, expecting to see rain clouds. "I'm sorry," he said without thinking, compelled to apologize for his bad luck with the weather.

Fumiko tilted her head. "For what?"

"The weather. I think it's about to rain. The kites won't be able to fly tonight."

Fumiko chuckled. "Why should anyone apologize about the weather? Besides, the rain knows that it is forbidden here. All the water we need is provided by the river and dew. Nothing keeps the stars from finding their place in the sky. Neither rain nor any Shiikuin can stop them from taking flight."

"You are very lucky to be free of those monsters here," Keishin said.

"Monsters?"

"The Shiikuin."

Fumiko patted Keishin's hand. "The Shiikuin are not monsters. They are necessary. They are playing their part just as you and I do. There is an order to our world because they cull those who would disturb it."

"Do you really believe that?"

"Of course. The cranes at the Kyoiku Hakubutsukan have shown us the follies of the world beyond the door. A village such as ours could never exist in such chaos. The blinding lights of that world have hidden all their stars. The Shiikuin may not come here, but every villager is grateful for their service. Who else would collect and keep the birds?"

Another gong sounded, more thunderous than the first, charging the air with an energy Keishin could feel in his bones. The villagers raised their kites over their shoulders, and row after row they ran into the field, trying to catch the wind. Keishin watched them coax their kites higher. The kites glowed as they climbed, and for a moment, Keishin thought that they had caught fire. One by one, they rose into the sky, flying higher than any conceivable string could let them. More than a hundred kites twinkled against the canvas of night, diving and swirling, forming constellations Keishin longed to name. And when every kite had found its place, the villagers cut their strings, leaving Keishin to stand beneath a sparkling canopy of an entire world's hopes. "This is the most beautiful thing I have ever seen," Keishin said, craning his neck to take it all in.

"Ah." Fumiko smiled. "You do not have children?"

"No, I don't. Why do you ask?"

"Because if you had children, then this sky would only be the second most beautiful thing you would have seen," Fumiko said. "This is something that you and Hana will understand when you become parents."

"Hana isn't . . . I mean we aren't . . . uh . . ."

"I'm sorry. Please forgive this old woman for her foolish tongue. I did not realize that there were no children written over your and your wife's skin. But we must trust the map the Horishi has given us."

"Uh . . . yes." Keishin nodded. "We must."

"Some people are simply not fated to have children. Like me."

Keishin frowned. "But you have children. We met them at your home."

"They are my sister's. When she died, I raised them and loved them as my own. And they have loved me," Fumiko said. "As much as they could. There were many nights when they lay next to me and cried for their real mother until they fell asleep. Even though the stars lit up the village's sky, those were the darkest nights I ever had. And yet, I could not help but feel that I deserved it."

"Deserved it?"

"I had sent up a hope that had no place among the stars. I hoped for children even if there was no trace of a single child's name on my skin. When my sister's children were placed in my care, I could not help but feel that somehow, I had stolen her fate." Fumiko looked up at the sky. "There is no greater misery than holding in your arms something that you know is not truly yours. In the worst of times, I thought that I would have preferred to have traded places with my sister."

"Why?"

"Because death is kind and swift. Longing is a life sentence. But of course, things are better now and I—"

" 'A life sentence.' " Keishin repeated Fumiko's words, not realizing he had said them out loud.

"Did you say something?" Fumiko asked.

"I . . . I'm sorry. I need to go."

CHAPTER THIRTY-SIX

Tuna Casserole, a Blue Tie, and a Stranger in a Box

If he had passed away in Japan, he would have been dressed in white. But Keishin's father had died thousands of miles from his old home, and in this place, the dead wore suits that made them look as though they were dressed for a job interview.

Keishin's father had never worn a suit in his life, and his stepmother had spent hours at the sales rack trying to choose between a gray suit with a black tie or a pinstripe suit with a blue one. If she had asked for Keishin's opinion, he would have told her that it didn't matter. The man in the coffin was going to look like a stranger either way. Cancer had made a feast of his father, gnawing at him until all that was left was skin and bones. His stepmother finally selected the pinstripe and blue tie option when the sales clerk told her that it was an additional 20 percent off. The other thing that appeared to be on sale that week was tuna. After the fourth tuna casserole from one of their neighbors had been squeezed into the refrigerator, Keishin was almost certain that by the end of the week, he was going to sprout gills.

Keishin picked at his third tuna casserole dinner in a row, counting down the forkfuls until he could dive into the latest book he had borrowed from the library, a yellowing copy of Stephen Hawking's *A Brief History of Time.*

"You don't have to finish it," his stepmother said without looking up from her own untouched plate.

Keishin stared at her, trying to process what he had just heard. Those words had never been uttered in their home when his father was alive. Hearing them might have killed him faster than his cancer had. His father loved many things about his new homeland, but the amount of food that he saw thrown away each day at the restaurant he worked in made him gnash his teeth.

"I'll finish it." Keishin shoved a forkful of the tasteless casserole into his mouth.

"Things don't have to stay the same," his stepmother said. "If you don't want them to."

Keishin swallowed without chewing. "What do you mean?"

"You don't have to pretend anymore," she said. "I know that you have tried your best to accept me as your new mother when your father and I got married. I appreciated that. Truly. But your father is gone now. You don't have to pretend for his sake or mine. I would rather that we be honest with each other than polite. Perhaps, that way, we can even learn to be friends."

Keishin set his fork down and looked at his stepmother as though seeing her for the first time. He had never heard her speak more openly or plainly. A part of him felt relieved to have her say those words to him. It wasn't that he didn't care for her. He did. And he knew that she cared for him. But being his father's wife did not magically transform her into his mother, and neither did him calling her "okaa-san" make him her son. Calling anything by a false name only made it feel less true. And yet, there was another part of Keishin that felt sad to hear his stepmother speak this way. Their lie, like most lies, had been a balm to a truth that chafed. Without it, all he was left with was the relentless awareness of having the perfect likeness of a mother going through the motions good mothers were supposed to do.

And this is how Keishin knew, upon hearing Fumiko's words that night beneath the stars, that he needed to run, as fast as he could, to Hana. He had realized what Chiyo's real punishment was because, just like Fumiko, he had been sentenced to it too.

CHAPTER THIRTY-SEVEN

A Punishment to Fit the Crime

Hana lay next to Haruto and watched him sleep. He drew uneven breaths, a furrow etched between his brows. Hana got up from the futon and walked over to the window. The village's work twinkled in the sky.

"Hana?" Haruto rubbed his eyes with the back of his bandaged hand.

"You crossed the bridge early. It isn't morning yet."

"I didn't have any dreams to keep me." He sat up. "Why are you still here?"

"I wanted to be here in case you needed anything."

"I told you. I can take care of myself."

"All right. I'll go." Hana headed to the room Masako had prepared for her.

"Wait. I'm sorry. Stay . . . if you want to."

Hana sat on the futon next to him. "When did you know?"

"When did I know what?"

"When did you know that what you felt about me was more than just friendship?"

He shook his head. "There is no need to talk about this. I know that you don't feel the same way about me."

"I want to know," Hana said. "I need to."

"I don't think that I have an answer to your question. It was not a specific day or an exact moment. I did not wake up and suddenly feel that I loved you. The only answer I can give you is that it happened gradually. Slowly, and unnoticed, the way the ocean turns rocks into sand. And you are an ocean, Hana. Gentle and quiet, yet powerful enough to sweep away any man or ship. I drowned in you a long time ago and I did not even know it."

"What if . . . what if it is the same with me? What if I loved you and did not realize it?"

"I can help you find an answer to that, but I must ask you a question first." Haruto leaned closer, his eyes asking his question before his lips did. They could never hide anything from Hana. They gave away the subtlest shifts inside him, telling her exactly when he was feeling awkward, shy, fearful, sad, happy, or surprised. Tonight, in no uncertain terms, they told her that he wanted to kiss her.

"Yes," Hana said.

"Yes?"

"You are going to ask me if you can kiss me. My answer is yes."

"Are you sure that this is what you want?"

Hana looked into his eyes and saw the boy who enjoyed nothing more than to fold paper into flowers for her and the man who had sacrificed his hands to keep her safe. She closed her eyes and waited to feel Haruto's lips on hers, to finally know if she could be the wife that he deserved. "I am."

"I hope you find what you are looking for, Hana." Haruto's lips teased her mouth open.

Hana's heart pounded against her ribs, growing so loud that she was sure that Haruto could hear it too. A loud rapping on the door thundered over her heartbeat. Hana jolted back. "Shiikuin," she said, scrambling to her feet.

"Hana?" a man called from behind the door. "Haruto?"

"Keishin?" Hana hurried to the door.

Keishin clutched his sides, breathing hard. "Fumiko . . ." he said, trying to catch his breath. "She . . . knows . . ."

"What does she know?" Hana asked.

"She knows what it's like to have something that you desperately want." Keishin wiped the sweat dripping into his eyes. "Knowing full well that it's not what it seems."

"What are you going on about?" Haruto said.

"I think I know what kind of punishment the Shiikuin had in mind for Hana's mother, what torture would be worse than death. The Shiikuin don't care about justice." Keishin's eyes fell on Haruto's broken hands. "They care about causing the most amount of pain. And what greater pain is there than being so excruciatingly close to something you long for," he said, shifting his gaze to Hana, "but that you know isn't really yours?"

"I don't understand," Hana said.

"The Shiikuin saw how desperately your mother wanted to hold you. They knew how much she loved you," Keishin said. "Death would have torn you from her, but that punishment wasn't enough. The Shiikuin wanted her to suffer."

"How?" Haruto said.

"By giving her a life sentence," Keishin said. "By letting her live out her days in a place where she would be constantly reminded of the daughter she left behind."

Haruto shook his head. "Even if you are right, where exactly are we supposed to look for her? Are you planning on searching every prison in our world?"

"You may not have to." Masako walked into the room.

Haruto turned to his mother. "What do you mean?"

"I believe the outsider is right. Exiling Chiyo to the other world would have erased her and her pain. But exiling her to a place where she would be surrounded by something she wanted but could never have would be crueler than death. What better punishment for someone who took something that wasn't hers? As a mother, I can think of only one prison that would inflict such torture."

"What prison is this?" Haruto said. "Where is it?"

"I do not know where it is, but I have heard whispers of it at the Night Market. They say that it is a place where children who are not really children dwell. Children who spend endless days and nights crying for a mother."

Keishin frowned. "What do you mean by 'children who are not really children'?"

"If you need more answers, you will have to get them for yourself," Masako said.

"Then we should go to the Night Market as soon as possible," Haruto said.

"Keishin and I will go to the Night Market," Hana said. "You need to stay here."

"Hana is right," Masako said. "You are not well enough to travel. You would only slow them down. If you are truly concerned about Hana's safety, the best thing that you can do for her is to stay here."

Haruto hung his head, heaving a sigh.

"We need to make one stop before we go to the Night Market," Hana said.

"Where?" Haruto asked.

"It is better if you do not know."

"I agree," Masako said.

Hana turned to her. "I know that I have already asked for too much, but there is one last thing I will need to ask of you before we go."

"If it will make you leave sooner, then I am happy to provide you with whatever assistance you require."

CHAPTER THIRTY-EIGHT

The Lights in the Lake

The lights from the village grew smaller as Keishin and Hana paddled down the river. Fireflies swarmed around trees in animated constellations rivaling those shining down on them from the sky. Even the water was alive. Tiny glowing creatures, smaller than grains of sand, swirled around Keishin's oar and trailed behind their small boat, filling the river with stars. Keishin peeked over the boat to get a better look. The creatures circled and swarmed, shifting in shape until they created the mirror image of his face. Keishin jolted back from his living reflection.

"We call them hansha," Hana said. "They like to copy whatever they see."

Keishin extended his arm over the water. The hansha twisted and swirled, mimicking the exact shape of his arm and hand. Then they dimmed, changing from a shimmering reflection to a solid form that looked as though it were made from flesh. Keishin wriggled his fingers. The hansha wriggled too.

"Incredible . . ." Keishin said, pulling his hand back.

"They are quite remarkable," Hana said, her voice tired.

"I can row by myself the rest of the way," Keishin said from behind her.

"I am not tired." Hana kept her eyes in front of the boat.

"We will get to the waterfall faster if we both row. The lake is just through it."

"Why didn't you want to tell Haruto where we were going?" Keishin asked.

"Because he would have only tried to stop us."

"Why?"

"Because the Lotus Lake is exactly where he told the Shiikuin we would be."

"What? Then why are we going there?"

"They broke Haruto's hands to get him to tell the truth. Imagine what they would do to him if they found out that he lied. We need to go to the lake so that the Shiikuin will not think that he misled them."

"Am I missing the part of the plan where you explain how exactly we're supposed to avoid getting caught by the Shiikuin when we get there?" Keishin stopped rowing.

Hana twisted around, rocking the boat. "Why did you stop?"

"I understand that you want to protect Haruto, but walking into a trap isn't going to help anyone."

"We will not walk into any trap."

"How can you be so sure?"

"Because we will be swimming into it."

Fog and darkness hid the top of the waterfall cascading down the steep rock face. The thunderous way it crashed into the river made Keishin believe that it was falling from the sky. He gripped his oars, struggling to keep their little boat steady as they approached it.

Hana groaned as she rowed, fighting for every inch between them and the waterfall. "Just . . . a . . . little . . . more."

The waterfall parted like a curtain, revealing the gaping mouth of a large cavern. Keishin felt the boat grow steady, gently steering itself without the need for oars. The waterfall closed behind them and fell silent, leaving them with nothing but the sound of their boat drifting over the water. Hansha teemed in the pool and made the entire cavern glow with a soft, warm light. Four caves branched out from the cavern, the light of the hansha fading into their dark mouths. Their boat stopped in the middle of the pool as though allowing Keishin and Hana to decide which way they wanted to go.

Hana pointed to the leftmost cave. "That one leads to the Mourning Mountains. The one next to it brings you to the Singing Forest. The cave beside it leads to where we need to go."

"The Lotus Lake."

"Yes."

"And the last cave? Where does it lead?"

"Tokyo Station."

"That's . . . er . . . convenient."

"So, are you clear with the plan?" Hana said.

Keishin nodded.

"And remember, try not to scare them. Do not make any sudden movements when you are in the water." Hana turned her back to Keishin and began to undress.

Keishin averted his eyes and pulled off his clothes. "No sudden movements. Got it."

Hana lowered herself into the water. Hansha swarmed around her, illuminating her skin. "If they like you, they will keep your shape longer."

"I'll be my charming best." Keishin followed her into the pool, bracing himself for the cold. Warm water, just the way he liked his bath, embraced him instead.

"Be careful." Hana drew a deep breath and submerged, disappearing beneath a swirling layer of liquid light.

Keishin dove in after her. Glowing galaxies revolved around his body, slowly exploring every inch of his limbs. They paused and then moved as one, shifting and turning until Keishin found himself staring his exact twin in the eye. Keishin blinked. His twin blinked too. Keishin waved. His twin waved back.

Hana swam to Keishin and motioned for him to surface. Keishin swam next to her, struggling to keep his gaze from wandering over Hana's soft curves. She moved as gracefully as the hansha, their light twinkling like fairy lights over every inch of her skin.

Hana broke through the pool's surface, inhaling deeply. "We did it."

Keishin treaded water across from her. "Now if only the rest of your plan was just as easy."

The only light inside the cave's tunnel came from the two schools of hansha that had taken Keishin's and Hana's forms. They swam on either side of the boat, glancing up occasionally to smile at Keishin and Hana and wave.

"At least two of us don't seem to be nervous," Keishin said.

"I am just grateful that they decided to follow us."

"Hana . . ."

"Yes?"

"If the plan doesn't work . . ."

"It will work."

"But in case it doesn't, in case something goes wrong, you need to think about yourself. Not your father. Not your mother. Not Haruto. You need to run. Promise me that you'll run and not look back."

"I will, but only if you promise me one thing too."

"What?"

"That when I run . . ." She took Keishin's hand. "You won't let go."

Keishin reviewed Hana's plan in his head as he tied the boat to a rock jutting out next to the end of the tunnel. The plan involved being in two places at the same time, a notion that less than a week ago would have made Keishin laugh out loud or roll his eyes. Now he did neither. He had lost track of how many laws of science he had broken since stepping into Hana's world. Adding one more to his list was not going to make a difference.

"I was not sure if Haruto's mother was going to agree to do this for us. I am glad that she did." Hana rummaged through her bag and pulled out two origami fish. "This plan would not work without them."

Keishin took one of the fish from Hana and stared at the waterfall covering the cave's mouth. Though it was not as wide as the waterfall at the entrance to the cavern, it was just as powerful. Keishin had not yet gotten used to how something so mighty did not make a sound. He wished that it did. It could have drowned out the pounding of his heart and made pretending to be brave a lot easier. He pressed his back against the cave wall and inched along the narrow ledge that led out of it. The waterfall parted to let him and Hana through.

Keishin and Hana crouched behind a cascading stream of water, huddling as close together as the ledge allowed. Keishin looked out through a gap in the stream. A field of lotus stretched into the horizon, giving the appearance of a sprawling flower garden rather than a lake. Unlike the lotus in his world, which awoke only for the sun, the lake's large white flowers smiled lovingly up at the moon. Dark figures glided over the lake, the edges of their robes barely grazing the water. Each wielded a sickle and cut down the flowers in its path.

"Shiikuin," Keishin whispered to Hana.

"How many are there?"

"At least ten. They are clearing the lotus."

"They think we are hiding in the water."

"As you said they would."

"And now we will give them something to find." Hana released one of the origami fish Masako had made into the water and watched it dart away.

"Your turn," Keishin whispered to his fish before setting it free. It swam after its mate as soon as it touched the water.

Keishin's hansha twin emerged from the waterfall and chased after the paper fish. Hana's twin followed close behind. The lotus in their path trembled over the water. The Shiikuin twisted in the direction of the disturbance and broke into a chorus of curdling shrieks.

Ice ran up from Keishin's ankles to his spine. He crouched lower, his breath racing in and out of his chest. "Remember your promise, Hana."

Hana clutched his hand. Her fingers trembled around his. "Remember yours."

The Shiikuin fell silent and lowered their sickles. They stood as still as statues, with only their heads tilting to follow the movement in the water. They looked at one another, nodded, and gave chase.

"I don't believe it," Keishin said. "It actually worked."

Hana exhaled.

"What happens now?" Keishin asked.

"The hansha will have their fun for a while. When they get bored, they'll disperse and return to the cavern, but not before giving the Shiikuin a glimpse of our faces. They are mischievous that way."

"Giving the Shiikuin no cause to doubt Haruto," Keishin said.

Hana nodded. "And us a head start to the Night Market."

CHAPTER THIRTY-NINE

An Infestation of Ticks

Keishin's shoulders and arms burned from rowing. The subterranean river that led to the Singing Forest was twice as long as the one that had led them to the lake. The sky lightened behind the waterfall at the end of the cave. Keishin kept his eyes on the light and pulled on the oars, ignoring the pain shooting up his raw palms. A tinkling melody drifted through the water falling over the exit. "Do you hear that?"

"The forest is close," Hana said. "This is its song."

"How far is the Night Market from the forest?" Keishin said.

Hana continued to row as though she had not heard his question.

"Hana?"

"I am sorry." Hana sighed. "I know that you are exhausted, but I am afraid that it will take more than half a day's walk to get through the forest. Once we reach the clearing, a puddle will take us to a village near the market."

"No need to apologize." Keishin glanced back at Hana with a smirk. "After sitting in this boat the whole night, I could use a long walk."

Hana smiled. "Of course."

Multicolored glass wind chimes in the shape of leaves grew from the branches of the towering trees and sang in the wind.

Sunlight filtered through the shimmering canopy, painting a rainbow over the forest floor. Keishin marveled at the sight, unable to tear his eyes from the chimes. Their haunting song shifted from cheerful to melancholy, changing at the wind's whim.

Hana grabbed his elbow. "Watch your step."

"Whoa." Keishin glanced down and stopped before tripping over a rotting log. "I definitely do not need to add a sprained ankle to the list of our problems."

"The chimes can be distracting," Hana said, stepping over the log. "I have fallen and scraped my knees in this forest more than once."

"Distracting is an understatement." Keishin forced himself to focus on the winding path. "I think I could easily spend my entire life in your world and still find something to be amazed about every single day."

"That's how I feel about your world," Hana said.

"Really?"

"The glimpses I caught of it always fascinated me. Our clients' clothes. Their things. Their stories. They lived in my mind long after the clients left and the Shiikuin came to collect their choices."

Keishin frowned, tilting his head.

"What's wrong?"

"We've been so busy running from the Shiikuin that it just occurred to me that I don't even know what the Shiikuin want my world's choices for."

"Perhaps we should keep it that way." Hana walked on.

Keishin caught up with her. "After everything we've been through, don't you think I deserve to know the truth? And what did Haruto mean by your entire world owing a debt to the pawnshop and your father?"

"It is not about deserving the truth."

"Then what is it about?"

"It is about being protected from it."

"You don't need to protect me, Hana."

"Not you." Hana stopped walking. "Me. If you knew the truth about what my father and I really took from your world and what we did with it, you would never be able to look at me the same way."

"Nothing you could tell me would change how I feel about—" Keishin caught himself. "How I think about you."

Hana met his eyes. "Maybe you're right. Maybe you should know. Maybe then you'll realize that coming here was a mistake and that you should go back home before it's too late."

"Home . . . it's a mapmaker's ultimate challenge, don't you think?" Keishin kicked away a rock. "A cartographer can craft the most detailed map, include every landmark, and draw the clearest roads. His map can help you get to almost anywhere you wish. Bridges. Parks. Libraries. But not home. You won't find it labeled on a single map in the entire world. You can live in the same place for years and memorize every bus, bike, and walking route back to it and never really know your way home. Maybe that's why you can't find it on any map. Because it doesn't exist." Keishin looked at Hana with a sad smile. "Or because it's changeable."

"What are you saying?"

"I'm saying . . ." Keishin said. "What if I don't want to go back?"

"We take souls," Hana said.

Keishin stared at her, his jaw slack.

"The birds we keep in our vault . . . those aren't just choices." Hana's voice shook. "They are pieces of our clients' souls. Our clients think that they are trading an old regret for contentment, but they are wrong. My father tricks them. I trick them.

"My father told me that the piece of their souls that we took was so small that they would not miss it, but I never believed him. What we take may be small, but it is the best part of you, the part that made a decision to go left instead of right. It does not matter what the outcome of the choice is. It could be terrible, and they could regret it, but when clients leave their choice at the pawnshop, they give up a chance to make their own peace with the life that they did choose. It will be a journey they will never be able to complete, a lesson they will never be able to learn. How can you be at peace if a part of you is missing? It will be a hole that you will try to fill all your life without ever knowing why that hole exists in the first place."

Keishin drew a long breath and exhaled it just as slowly. "And what do the Shiikuin do with the pieces you give them?"

"Do you remember the empty cages you saw at the Horishi's home?"

Keishin nodded, dreading the answer Hana was about to give him.

"You asked me where all the birds were." Hana pushed back her sleeve and held out her arm. "They're here. In our skin, in the Horishi's ink. We take your souls because we don't have our own. This is the 'debt' this world owes my father for the duty he performs. Without the pawnshop, this parasite world that you think is so fascinating would not exist. This cannot be your home, Keishin. It is nothing but an infestation of ticks gorging on a dog's back."

* * *

Keishin and Hana sat in the grass, leaning on opposite sides of a tree's thick trunk. Branches swayed in the breeze above them, conducting an orchestra of glass and wind. Keishin looked up at the cloudless sky through the wind chimes and found himself missing the rain that usually followed him everywhere. The weather had chosen an inconvenient time to decide that it liked him. Or perhaps, chasing away the clouds was its way of being even more unkind. A storm would have been quite useful in hiding tears that threatened to fall as soon as Keishin blinked. He wasn't sure if they were angry tears or sad ones, only that they were going to sting.

"When we get to the clearing, you can use the puddle there to take you back to the pawnshop. Once you get there, you just need to walk through the front door to get home," Hana said. "You will forget everything that happened here and move on with your life. You will find your neutrinos and answer all the questions you have about your universe."

"And I'll be happy."

"Yes."

"If only I could believe you."

"You do not trust me."

"How can I?" Keishin got up and marched over to Hana. "You just told me that you've spent your entire life being taught how to lie and manipulate people into giving up part of their souls. How do I know that what you're telling me now isn't a trick? What if I get back home and remember everything? How am I supposed to go on with my life and pretend that everything I've seen in this world doesn't exist? How do you even know what happens to your clients once they leave your pawnshop? All you know is what your father told you, your father who abandoned you to chase after his dead wife." Keishin regretted his words as soon as they tumbled out of his mouth. "I . . . I'm sorry."

Hana stood up. "Why should you be sorry? It's the truth. My one real skill and duty in this world is to lie, and my father did abandon me. And you're also right that I don't know what will happen to you when you go back. All I know is . . ." Tears watered her voice. "You will be safe."

Keishin fought the urge to gather her to him. "Please don't cry."

Hana dried her eyes with the back of her hand. "You are right. Parasites do not deserve to cry."

"Don't say that. You are not a parasite."

"I am." Fresh tears filled Hana's eyes.

"No, you are not." Keishin circled his arms around her. "I don't know why your world works the way it does or why it needs mine to exist, but I know this. You have given me more than you've taken. You've shown me things beyond my imagination and . . ." He tilted her chin up. "And made me feel things I never thought I could."

"Things that you shouldn't."

"Because Haruto is your fate." Keishin lowered his eyes.

"Haruto has nothing to do with this."

"He loves you."

"Yes."

"And one day, you'll love him too."

"I won't."

"You don't know that."

"I do. I kissed him," Hana said. "And it was different."

"From what?"

"From when I kissed you." Hana pulled away from him.

"But whatever we feel for each other has no place in this world or yours."

"It doesn't have to belong to either of our worlds, Hana. It just needs to belong to us."

Hana leaned her head against his chest, letting her tears fall.

CHAPTER FORTY

Ghosts

The small village had slipped out of time's hands and tumbled to the wayside of life's road a long time ago. It stood, a shell of its former self, waiting to crumble in the late-afternoon sun. Once it had longed for visitors, but now it was too tired and it had too much dust in its eyes to notice the two people that had climbed out of the puddle next to a footbridge that might have once been bright red. A bed of round, dusty rocks ran beneath the bridge, their edges smoothened by a vanished river.

Hana tightened her ponytail and surveyed their surroundings. She and Keishin had barely spoken during their hike out of the forest, and even after traveling through the puddle, she still did not possess any words that were worth the air and effort to speak.

"The chimes made it easier," Keishin said.

"To do what?" Hana asked.

"To not talk to each other. The chimes filled the void." Keishin looked around the empty town. "But the silence in this place makes the air feel stale. It's hard to breathe. I'm sorry, but if you don't say anything, I'm afraid I'm going to have to bore you with a lecture about quantum physics and other extremely tedious things just so we don't suffocate."

"Welcome!" A man waved at them from across the footbridge. "Welcome!"

"Oh . . . hello." Hana bowed. "I did not realize that anyone still lived here."

The man walked over to them with a wide smile. "I'm Uchida Tomo. Are you looking for a place to stay? My family owns a ryokan here."

"Oh . . . uh . . . thank you, Uchida-san, but we are headed to the Night Market," Hana said.

"The market won't open until midnight and both of you look like you have not had much sleep. Why don't you stay at the ryokan while waiting? My wife can cook you a warm meal."

"We could use some sleep," Keishin whispered to Hana. "And food."

Hana pulled her mother's glasses from her bag and turned to Tomo. She raised a brow and just as quickly yanked it down. She nodded at Tomo and smiled. "Where is your ryokan, Uchida-san?"

The simple, well-kept ryokan stood at the foot of the mountain. Compared to its dilapidated neighbors in the village, it looked like a palace.

"Not many people come around to the village anymore," Tomo said, leading them across a small garden. "My wife will be thrilled to have guests."

"I have passed by this village a few times on the way to the Night Market. I did not realize that anyone still lived here. I thought that it was abandoned."

"It is just me and my wife now," Tomo said. "When the river dried up, everyone else moved on. But this is our home, and we do not wish to live anywhere else."

A slender woman with a kind face greeted them at the door. "Welcome."

"This is my wife, Yui," Tomo said, introducing Hana and Keishin.

"Please, come in." Yui smiled. "I will show you to your room."

A small plate of daifuku, mochi balls filled with mashed azuki beans mixed with honey, and a bowl of karintō, sweet, deep-fried twiglike snacks coated in brown sugar, were arranged next to a freshly brewed pot of green tea on a low table in the middle of the room.

Keishin shot a look at Hana, showing his surprise at finding their refreshments waiting for them.

"The onsen is through here." Yui walked over to a set of sliding doors across the room and opened them. A steaming outdoor bath, fed by a hot spring and bordered by smooth rocks, was cocooned by an ornamental garden. "We do not have any other guests, and so you have the onsen to yourselves."

"Thank you," Hana said. "It looks lovely."

"Your meal will be served in the dining room after you have enjoyed your bath. I will leave you now so that you can rest, but please do not hesitate to let me know if there is anything else you need." Yui bowed with a smile as she left, sliding the door behind her.

"For a ryokan in an abandoned town, they seem quite prepared to receive guests. It almost seems like they knew we were coming," Keishin said, lowering his voice. "Do you think it's a trap by the Shiikuin?"

"It is not a trap."

"But don't you think it's strange that—"

"They're ghosts."

"*What?*"

"Tomo and his wife are ghosts." Hana took off her mother's glasses. "I saw who they really were through these. They have been dead for a very long time."

"Then what are we still doing here?" Keishin's eyes flashed.

"You said it yourself. We need rest and a meal."

"But—"

"They are harmless."

Keishin looked around the room. "Is any of this even real?"

"It is real because Tomo and Yui believe that it is."

"They don't know that they're dead?"

Hana shook her head. "And it is not our place to tell them otherwise."

Keishin kneaded his nape. "I never believed in ghosts."

"Oh? But isn't that why you moved to Japan? To find them?"

"Neutrinos aren't ghosts."

"You told me that they are remnants of the past. Wisps of nothing that you cannot see or touch. Echoes that carry stories of dead stars. How are they not ghosts?"

"I . . . I don't know," Keishin said. "I don't think I know anything anymore."

"There's nothing wrong with not knowing things."

"There is, when your whole career is about finding answers."

"Have any of the answers you've found made you happy?"

"Science isn't about finding happiness."

"I thought that finding happiness was what life in your world was all about. That is why it has always been so easy to convince our clients to give up their choices. All any of them wanted was to smile. If happiness were as simple to obtain in this world, I would have given up part of my soul for it too."

"What do you want me to say, Hana? That nothing I did in my world truly made me happy? That I've spent my life trying to fill a void carved out by my mother? That when I came here, pretending to be all noble and saying that I wanted to help you, all I was really thinking about was finally discovering something that would make me worthy of being loved? You weren't the only one who hid the truth."

"I suppose that we are more alike than I thought."

"I suppose we are."

Hana and Keishin rested their chins on their folded arms on opposite ends of the onsen, their gazes wandering over the surroundings. The newly risen moon bathed the garden in an otherworldly glow, revealing its truth. It was more than just a picturesque landscape. It was its creators' unique point of view about the world and their place in it. The garden was nature in miniature, an idealized version where rocks were mountains, and koi ponds were seas. It was a pleasure that was not meant to be indulged in all at once, but rather slowly explored, with delights hidden by little hills or trees. Uneven stepping stones forced you to watch your step, keeping you in the present and fully aware of the unfolding path.

"This is Tomo and Yui's heaven, isn't it?" Keishin said.

"I want to believe that it is."

"I wonder if everyone is free to create their own afterlife."

"What kind of heaven would you create for yourself?" Hana asked.

Keishin turned to face her, brushing a damp lock of silver-white hair away from his eyes. Hana had never met a man more unaware of how he filled the space around him, charging the air. The streak of lightning in his hair made her believe that if the moon disappeared and darkness swallowed them, he alone would remain lit. He strode toward her, moonlight gleaming on his wet shoulders.

"It would look exactly like this place and everything in it. I wouldn't change a thing," he said, locking onto Hana's eyes. "How about you?"

The steaming water rippled between them, caressing Hana's breasts. "I am not sure."

"Try. Close your eyes and try to imagine what would make you happy for eternity."

"I don't think I know what eternity is. It is too big."

"Then go smaller. Imagine now. Something you can hold in your hands."

Hana kept her eyes closed and let the heat of Keishin's body guide her fingers to his face. She let them wander over the angles of his jaw and brush over the bow of his lips. "Like this?"

"Hana . . ." He groaned her name, circling her waist and pulling her into his chest.

Heat licked Hana's breasts and writhed like a flame between her legs. "I should push you away."

"You should." Keishin left a trail of kisses from behind her ear to her shoulder.

Hana moaned. Keishin lifted her from the water and took her breast in his mouth. Hana knotted her fingers in Keishin's hair, clutching him to her. His tongue erased almost every argument she had summoned to run from him, drawing a list of reasons to stay in little circles around her nipple. "Kei . . ." she said, forcing the last of her clarity into something she hoped resembled words. "We have no future."

Keishin pulled away, breathing hard. "You're right."

Hana's throat tightened. A part of her had hoped that he

would argue with her, that he would scoff and insist that some scientific law in his world made what she said completely unsound.

"No one is promised tomorrow," Keishin said. "No contract, vow, or even magical tattoo can guarantee forever with someone, regardless of whether you share a world. But what we do have is what you and I have been fighting to deny almost from the second we met. There is a connection between us, Hana, a knot without any measurable form or weight, a knot that only gets tighter the more we struggle to pull away."

"Then that knot is a trap. A beautiful one like the watery cage for your ghosts from the stars."

Thunder rumbled over the ryokan.

"It's going to rain," Hana said, surprised that it had taken the rain so long to find her. It was, it seemed, the one constant in her life, always at the ready to remind her of her duty. "We should go inside."

"Or what?" Keishin said. "We'll get wet?"

A laugh rose from Hana's belly and burst out of her, taking with it all the pain she had been swallowing back. Keishin laughed with her, their tears falling into the bath, cleansing them, and turning to wisps of steam. Rain fell over their cheeks and trailed down their shoulders. Hana's skin glowed with the Horishi's blue ink. Her hand flew up to cover herself.

Keishin caught her arm by the wrist and gently drew her hand away. "I told you, Hana. I see you. Only you." Raindrops splattered over Keishin's wrist. A name, tattooed in blue ink, glowed on his skin.

Hana.

Hana gasped. "What . . . how . . ."

Keishin let go of her arm. He ran his thumb over Hana's name. "The Horishi told me that she had never tattooed a grown man's fate. I had already lived so much of my life, and she thought that the best way to start my story was at its end. Your name. It was all she had managed to write when you showed up and told her to stop."

"Why . . . why didn't you tell me?"

"Because telling you wouldn't have changed anything. It's done, Hana. My fate, like yours, is written."

"But what does it mean?"

"I think you know what it means as well as I do. This journey with you is where my story ends."

"No. Do not say that. You will go back to your world. You will find your way home."

"It's okay, Hana. This was my choice. I told you, no one is promised tomorrow. I'm grateful for the time I have now. Seeing ghosts. Listening to wind chimes. Holding you, no matter how brief. For the first time in my life, my head is filled with something other than questions. I have my answer. It's written on my skin."

Hana pressed her lips to Keishin's mouth and drank him in. Hours, weeks, or years could have passed and Hana would not have noticed. The breadth between her skin and Keishin's left no room for time. Urgency took up every available space. Everything beyond Keishin's mouth vanished, leaving only the tremble that passed from his lips and into hers. She tasted his longing and could tell from the way Keishin devoured her that he tasted hers too. But there was something else that laced their tongues, an unspoken fear that made their kiss taste bittersweet. Last times almost always came in disguise, never revealing who they were until they were gone and all you could do was miss them.

But Hana had known that the day she met Keishin was the beginning of a long goodbye. On their first and possibly last night together, Hana made sure to remember every detail. To each other, they were already ghosts.

CHAPTER FORTY-ONE

Endings

Keishin could not recall how they had gotten from the onsen and onto the floor of their room at the ryokan. He had lived lifetimes inside Hana, and when exhaustion overwhelmed desire, he dissolved, happily, in her embrace. He closed his eyes, enjoying the weight of Hana's head on his chest.

"Will you ever tell me the end of Taro's story?" he asked, stroking her arm.

"Why do you want to know?" Hana said, her voice sounding like it came from somewhere more than halfway down the path to sleep.

"Do I need a reason?"

"Yes. The right one." Hana sat up, pulling her robe around her. "Because if you want to know the end because you think you will die here, then—"

"I want to know the end because from now on, I don't want to leave anything unspoken between us. No more secrets."

Hana searched his eyes. "All right," she said, settling back onto his chest. She took his hand and kissed the spot where the Horishi had written her name. "Old age."

"Old age?"

"That's what was in Taro's box. Time had passed differently in his world than in the ocean. When he returned to his village and opened the box the princess had given him, all his years caught up with him and he grew old."

Keishin stared up at the ceiling. "I think that's what would happen to me too if I ever went back. I'd turn into an old man. What I've experienced here feels like it would overflow from just one lifetime. I feel stretched, struggling, every second that I'm here, to fit everything into a tiny room that used to be my whole world. There are times when I feel that if I breathe too deeply, speak too loud, or move too fast, I'll crack wide open."

"Even now?" Hana whispered into his heart.

"No, not now." Keishin kissed the top of her head. "For the first time since I got here, there aren't any walls around me to break."

Tomo and Yui bowed and waved goodbye as Keishin and Hana left the ryokan. In the moonlight, Keishin could almost see through them. He waved back and smiled, feeling his feet grow heavier with every step. In an abandoned town, in a ryokan haunted by ghosts, he had found a small patch of heaven. And now he was leaving it all behind.

"The Night Market is not that far from here," Hana said.

"Is it wrong to say that I wish it was?"

Hana looked up at him with a sad smile. "I wish that we did not have to leave the ryokan too."

Keishin weaved his fingers through hers. Her palm was warm and soft, a welcome shelter from the cold. Keishin found himself wanting to take smaller, slower steps. "Can I ask you a question?"

"Of course."

"But you don't need to answer it. It's just something that I can't get off my mind. I know that my story ends with you, but I don't know how . . ."

"My story ends?"

"I hate that the question has been rolling around in my head for so long, but it feels even worse saying it out loud. I feel terrible for asking it. I'm sorry."

"Don't be. My name is on your wrist and your life is tied to mine," Hana said. "But I'm afraid I can't give you an answer."

"Oh. That's . . . um . . . okay. I understand."

"I don't know how my story ends."

"But I thought that your whole life was mapped out?"

"It was, but I've strayed so far from my path that I don't recognize anything on my map anymore. Nothing about it has changed, but it feels like someone else's story now, a stranger whose path ends in . . ." Hana touched the invisible mark on her wrist. "A moon in the water."

"What does it mean?"

"I don't know. It used to bother me that I didn't understand what the image meant when other people's paths were so clear. But now it doesn't matter."

The sound of vendors setting up their stalls drifted over Hana's voice.

"The market was closer than I thought." Keishin sighed. "But I suppose the sooner we get to it, the sooner we'll get answers."

"It may take some time to find the people who can help us. The Night Market is a big place."

"I'm glad it's big. If the Shiikuin track us to the market, we'll have somewhere to hide."

"Running from the Shiikuin might be difficult at the Night Market."

"Why?"

"We might fall through the clouds."

CHAPTER FORTY-TWO

The Night Market

Four anchors, as large as houses, hooked into the ground, one in each corner of the grassy field. The ropes attached to them disappeared into the night sky. Muffled voices and the clinking and clanking that came with a market coming to life seeped through the starless sky. Keishin looked up, straining to see through the thick soup of clouds. "How do we get up there? And notice how I did not bother to question how it was even possible for a market to be set up in the sky. I expect that I wouldn't understand any explanation you gave me anyway."

"We get up by climbing ladders. And the answer to the question you didn't ask but, deep inside, really want to know the answer to is 'crows.' "

"Crows," Keishin said. "Of course."

Colorful ladders unfurled from the sky and landed on the ground at different points across the field. The little bells hanging from the ladders tinkled in the breeze, announcing to the crowd milling below them that the Night Market was open. Keishin and Hana headed to the closest ladder and fell in line.

Keishin looked up at the swaying ladder, cold sweat forming on his palms. He wiped his hands on his coat. "I don't think that I ever mentioned to you that I'm afraid of heights."

"I hate heights too," Hana said. "My father used to tell me to keep my eyes on the ladder and to never look down."

"Did it help?"

"Not at all."

"Wonderful. Thank you for the advice."

Keishin reached the front of the line. He drew a deep breath, gripped the sides of the ladder, and climbed. His hands, still raw from a night of rowing, burned. The wind grew stronger the higher he climbed, making the ladder swing in wide arcs. Keishin stopped climbing and glanced down to check on Hana.

"Keep climbing," she called up to him.

Keishin nodded back, his hands trembling and damp. The relief that came from seeing Hana securely on the ladder was swiftly replaced by the horror of seeing the ground. Keishin raised his leg to climb onto the next rung. His foot slipped, sending half of his body through the ladder to dangle in midair.

"Kei!" Hana screamed below him.

Keishin hooked his arm around a rung and pulled himself up. "I . . . I'm fine," he said, doubling his pace up the ladder before he lost his nerve.

A rough hand gripped his fingers when he reached the top. A man with a leathery face pulled him up from the ladder and onto a stepping stone floating over a cloud. "Welcome to the market," he said, creasing every inch of his face with a wide smile.

The stone wobbled beneath Keishin's foot. "Uh . . . thank you," he said, not quite succeeding in finding his voice.

Hana climbed up after him. "This place seems even bigger than when I was last here."

Keishin looked around. Brightly lit stalls selling wares he didn't recognize stretched out in rows over the clouds. Narrow boats ferried the market's customers between them. Clouds churned in the wake of the boats, parting occasionally to give a glimpse of the ground.

"This way." Hana skipped onto a stepping stone. "We will need to hire a boat to get around."

A tall woman stood at the rear of the boat, clutching a long paddle. She used the paddle to push away from the dock, sending the boat drifting into a river of clouds. She steered the boat so gracefully and effortlessly between the market stalls that had her movements been set to music, it would have been a dance.

Keishin turned from their boat's pilot and let his eyes wander over the market's stalls. Glowing balls of light were piled high on one stall's table like mounds of fruit. The stall next to it sold bottles filled with stars. The last stall they had passed appeared to sell absolutely nothing, but boatloads of customers seemed all too eager to buy. "I don't even understand what I'm seeing," he said, whispering to Hana. "What does this market sell anyway?"

"Lost things. Found things. Things crafted by hearts or hands." Hana pointed to a stall on their left. Conch shells of varying sizes were arranged in neat rows on tiered shelves. "That was one of my favorites to visit as a child."

"Let me guess," Keishin said. "You enjoyed listening to the ocean."

Hana tilted her head. "Ocean?"

"The sound of waves in the shells."

"Oh. Is that what the shells in your world sound like?"

"Don't yours?"

"They tell jokes." She pointed to the stall's top shelf. "Those tell the best ones. I once laughed so hard I almost fell through the cloud."

Keishin chuckled. "I would give anything to see that."

Hana smirked and arched her brow. "You want to see me fall?"

"I want to see you so happy, you laugh your heart out."

"I . . . wish the same for you."

He stroked her cheek. "Then your wish has already come true."

"Good evening." A man in a silver-gray kimono greeted them from a nearby stall. "We have a fine collection tonight. Would you like to take a look?" He gestured to an elegant display of necklaces and bracelets made from strands of what looked like shimmering blue pearls.

"What are those?" Keishin whispered to Hana.

"That stall sells memories. Those are kioku pearls."

Keishin leaned over the side of the boat to get a closer look. The pearls turned out to be little crystal orbs filled with miniature oceans, complete with a horizon of sunrises, sunsets, and clouds. The vendor held a necklace to Keishin's ear. Waves crashed against the crystal as loud as though he were walking along a shore.

"Thank you." Hana bowed to the vendor as their boat drifted past his stall. She turned to Keishin. "People keep memories inside them to pass on to their children like heirlooms. But some people sell their memories. That vendor turns them into jewelry."

"Why?"

"In a world where your path is set, other people's memories are sometimes your only way to see lives that could never be yours." Hana pointed to a stall that no boats stopped at. "That stall sells healing salves and potions."

"Like a pharmacy?" Keishin said.

"Something like that."

"It doesn't seem to be very popular."

"Most people cannot afford what they sell."

"How does it manage to stay open?"

"All it needs is a single person desperate enough to pay its price. If it managed to sell to one customer in a year, that would be enough."

"Are you interested in visiting any place in particular?" the boat's pilot said.

"We need to go to the porters," Hana said.

The pilot tilted her head. "The porters?"

"There is a rumor that we want to learn more about. We were told that it began here at the market."

"All rumors begin here," the pilot said. "And you would be right in seeking out the porters. They know everything that is whispered."

"Good," Hana said.

"But I must warn you about the porters," the pilot said. "They are greedier than any of the vendors here and they like to play games."

Porters packed their baskets with their customers' items and strapped them onto their backs. They checked one another's loads, making sure that each was tied securely. Those who were ready lined up at a well, climbed into a large bucket, and lowered themselves through a hole in the clouds.

"They have been contracted to deliver those items directly to their customers' homes so that their customers do not need to worry about carrying their purchases down the ladder," Hana said.

"I can see the value of their service. Climbing the ladder without carrying anything was hard enough," Keishin said.

Hana approached a group of porters playing a game of dice on a floating wooden dock. "Good evening," she said, bowing.

They looked up from their game, stood up, and bowed back. "Good evening," the porter standing closest to Hana said. One hundred oceans shimmered in the moonlight from two strands of blue pearls dangling from her neck. "Do you need assistance with your purchases? I am Nakajima Natsuki, the head porter here."

"We were hoping that you could help us with another matter, Nakajima-san," Hana said.

"Oh?" Natsuki tilted her head. "What sort of matter?"

"We heard a rumor that—"

"Ah. A rumor." Natsuki smirked. "Our other service."

The group laughed.

"Which rumor have you heard?" Natsuki planted her hands on her hips. "There are many."

"The one about the children who aren't children," Keishin said. "Have you heard of it?"

"Of course," Natsuki said, looking offended. "We hear everything."

"What can you tell us about it?" Hana asked.

"We can tell you a lot of things," Natsuki said, "about many things."

"But you need compensation," Hana said.

"No, not at all." Natsuki shook her head. "All information we provide is free. We only ask that you play a game with us in return."

"A game with a wager, I presume," Keishin said.

More porters gathered around Keishin and Hana, an excited murmur buzzing among them.

Natsuki smiled. "A game without anything at stake isn't worth playing."

"What game do we need to play, and what kind of wager must we make?" Keishin asked.

"The game is simple. Dice. It is what we will be betting that will make it interesting. Here, we play for memories."

"Memories?" Keishin said.

"Do not worry. We have no interest in recollections of anyone's painful past. We have enough of our own. All we ask for is a chance to share in your joys. We were born in this market and we will die here. We know of no other life. The glimpses we catch of the world beneath the clouds when we deliver our clients' purchases only make returning to the market harder. Naturally, you will keep the original memory, but the copy will be ours to do with as we please."

"You want a happy memory," Hana said.

"The last time your entire body smiled. As you know, extracting a kioku pearl can be . . . messy. We do not want you to have to dig deeper than necessary. Healing is expensive, and this, after all, is simply a bit of fun to keep my men entertained." Natsuki twirled her necklace around her finger. "Shall we play?"

Entertained. The word gnawed at Keishin's gut. His last memory of happiness was in Hana's arms, and he suspected that Hana's last memory was just as intimate. It didn't matter which one of them played against the porters. The idea of Hana being anyone's entertainment, on display for all to see, made vomit and rage rise up his throat. He clenched his fists at his sides. "No."

"As you wish." Natsuki returned to her dice game.

"Kei." Hana gripped his arm. "We do not have a choice. We have to play."

"If we lose . . ."

Hana strode up to Natsuki. "We will do it. We will play."

Natsuki smiled and waved at a stocky porter standing next to stacks of empty baskets. "Daichi! Fetch the box."

The porter nodded and ducked behind the baskets. He retrieved a small wooden box and hurried to Natsuki with it tucked under his arm.

"Thank you." Natsuki took the box from him. She turned to Hana and Keishin and opened the box, revealing a marbled clay wine jug and a black-handled deba knife, a blade used for filleting fish. Beside the knife were a fishhook and a spool of fishing twine. "Have you decided which one of you will play and which one of you will carve out the player's stone? We need to have all wagers up front."

Keishin shot Hana a glance. *"Carve out?"*

Hana drew Keishin away from the assembled porters and lowered her voice. "The wine will form the pearl inside whoever drinks it. The pearl can form in different parts of the body, depending on where the memory is kept. Some memories live in the stomach, some just beneath the skin. Some memories are rooted deeper. I have heard of pearls growing inside bones. But do not concern yourself with this. I will play against the porters."

"No," Keishin said. "I will."

"Kei—"

"This isn't up for argument, Hana. If there is anyone who needs to be cut open or whose bone needs to be carved out, it should be me."

"Why?"

"Because there is no scenario where I could ever bring myself to cause you more pain than you are already suffering. I can't. I won't. Now, please hand me the wine so we can be done with this."

* * *

The wine warmed Keishin's throat and belly. Natsuki had said that he needed only one swig, but Keishin took two. His first swig was to make the memory stone. His second was to numb the pain of being sliced open with a fish knife. While he trusted Hana, he did not trust himself not to scream.

Keishin set the wine jug aside and lay down on a woven mat a porter had laid over a cloud. Another porter brought over two lanterns for extra light. Keishin stared into one of the lanterns' flames, wondering if he would feel the pearl form inside him. A warmth stirred and grew on his wrist over a vein that led to his heart, in the exact spot the Horishi had tattooed Hana's name. Keishin rubbed the spot and looked up at Hana. "It's here. I can feel it."

Hana poured wine over the deba's blade. "Don't worry. I will be quick."

Keishin positioned a broken basket handle between his teeth and closed his eyes.

Hana moved a lantern closer to Keishin's arm. She drew a deep breath and ran the blade over Keishin's skin.

Keishin flinched.

"I see the pearl," Hana said. "But I will have to cut a little deeper to free it."

Keishin bit down on the basket handle, refusing to provide the porters with additional entertainment. Sweat dripped from his brow.

"I have it," Hana said, pulling out the pearl.

Keishin spat out the handle and exhaled.

"Kei?"

"Yes?"

Hana threaded the fishing twine through a small hook. "I

think you should keep that handle in your mouth for a little while longer."

Keishin clenched his teeth over the handle and squeezed his eyes shut, retreating into the warmth and shadows of his favorite Indonesian restaurant and an Almost Smile waiting for him at his usual table.

"What can I help you with this time?" Ramesh sipped his Bintang beer. "Are you still pretending not to be the least bit interested in that woman you met at the pawnshop?"

Keishin pulled out a chair and sat down. "I lost that battle."

"You don't seem too upset about it." Ramesh set his beer on the table.

"I'm not." Keishin smiled and took a bite of his satay.

"So why am I here? It looks like you've got everything under control."

"*Control?* I wish. I am presently being sewn up with a fishing hook and twine."

"Ah, I see. Should I order us more beers?" Ramesh asked. "Or maybe we should get something stronger?"

Keishin shook his head. "I just need a distraction."

"From your Frankenstein surgery?"

"From the dice game I am about to lose." He sighed. "I have the worst luck. I never win at that sort of thing. Any tips?"

"Are you planning on cheating?"

"No."

Ramesh shrugged. "Then I don't have any advice for you."

"Ah, Ramesh. What would I do without you?"

"Right now? Probably be screaming in pain." Ramesh scooped a spoonful of nasi goreng.

"I wish you could see Hana's world. I can't even begin to

wrap my head around it. It's beautiful and . . ." Keishin ran his thumb over the droplets that had condensed over his beer.

"And what?"

"Frightening at the same time."

"The best mysteries are," Ramesh said. "And how about Hana? Does she scare you too?"

"More than anything ever has."

Ramesh's brows shot up. "Well, that was honest. I wasn't expecting that from you."

"If I can't be honest with my oldest and dearest imaginary friend, who can I be honest with?"

"I have good news for you then."

"Oh?"

"You will win the dice game."

"I just told you that I've never been able to win at that sort of thing."

Ramesh rolled his eyes. "What kind of physicist are you? Haven't you heard of Ramesh Kashyap's Second Law of the Universe and Dice Games?"

"I must have skipped class that day."

"It states that the probability of winning a dice game is directly proportional to what the player has at stake." Ramesh lifted his beer bottle in a toast. "And for the first time in your life, Kei, there is something every atom in your body is completely and utterly terrified of losing."

Keishin held the blue pearl between his forefinger and thumb, watching the sun set over the little ocean inside it. It was difficult to imagine how the hours he and Hana had spent discovering each other's bodies fit inside something so small.

Natsuki held out her palm. "I will keep the pearl safe until the game is over."

Keishin reluctantly handed the stone over to her.

Natsuki admired the stone against a lantern's light. She glanced from Keishin to Hana with a knowing smirk. "Definitely a prize worth winning."

"What now?" Keishin said.

Natsuki tucked the stone into a small purse slung across her chest. "Now we play. The rules of our little game are simple. You will wager whether the sum of the dice rolled is even or odd. Win two out of three times, and the information you seek is yours. Lose, and you will leave here without answers or your pearl. Daichi will be our dealer."

The small crowd of porters that had gathered in a circle around Keishin and Hana cheered. Daichi stepped out of the crowd. He shed his jacket and top and walked into the middle of the circle. He raised his arms and turned slowly, displaying his bare, muscular chest.

"Are you satisfied that our dealer is not concealing anything?" Natsuki asked.

"Yes," Hana said.

Natsuki offered Keishin and Hana two six-sided dice and a bamboo cup for inspection. "We would like you to be assured that there will be no cheating that will take place here."

Keishin nodded and handed the cup and dice back to Natsuki.

"Let us begin." Natsuki gave the dice and cup to Daichi.

Daichi dropped the dice into the cup and shook it. He overturned the cup onto a small table and looked at Keishin.

"Even," Keishin said, keeping his eyes on the cup.

Daichi removed the cup, displaying the dice. Five and four.

The crowd cheered. Daichi collected the dice and returned them to the cup.

Keishin cursed.

"We still have two more chances," Hana said.

Dice rattled inside the cup. Daichi flipped the cup over.

Keishin drew a breath and squared his shoulders. "Even."

Six and two.

Hana squeezed Keishin's hand.

Daichi shook the cup.

Probabilities, combinations, and permutations tumbled inside Keishin's head, rattling louder than the dice inside the cup.

Daichi turned the cup over. He rested his palm on the bottom of the cup and waited for Keishin's choice.

"Even," Keishin said, for no reason other than that he liked the feel of the word in his mouth. His instincts roamed freer in Hana's world, refusing to be reined in by calculations or logic. Here, pouring oceans into orbs was possible, and probability carried as much weight as a market floating on the clouds. Ramesh Kashyap's Second Law of the Universe and Dice Games was on his side. It had to be. Keishin held his breath.

Daichi lifted the cup from the table.

Three.

Keishin's eyes darted to the second die.

One.

"Yes!" Keishin lifted Hana by the waist and kissed her.

Hana kissed him back as the crowd dispersed.

"Well done." Natsuki plucked Keishin's pearl from her purse. "Congratulations."

Keishin set Hana down. He took the pearl from Natsuki and

stuffed it into his pocket. "We would like to have the answers you owe us now, please."

"And you shall have them," Natsuki said. "You want to know more about the children who are not children."

"What are they, and where can we find them?"

"We cannot speak of such things here." Natsuki gestured to a small boat. "Come with me."

Natsuki steered their boat to the edge of the cloud, away from the bustle of the market. She pulled her paddle into the boat and sat down.

"My necklace was much shorter when the rumor first weaved its way through the market," Natsuki said. "Many of the vendors who worked here at that time have since retired. This rumor traveled faster than most, not because it was thrilling, but because once they had heard it, people could not bear keeping such misery to themselves. They passed it on quickly, hoping that if they shared it, they would have less of it living in their minds. I can tell you from my own experience that it did not work."

"What did you hear?" Hana said.

Natsuki stared at the market's bright lights. "Our world exists because there is an order to things. Everyone knows their duty and their place. The vendors sell their wares. Porters carry them. Sweepers go over every inch of the market at the end of each evening, cleaning and making sure that everything is ready for business the next night. We wake up to days that look exactly the same and find ways to amuse ourselves to make the hours go faster, only to sleep, wake up, and do it all over again until our voices are too hoarse to hawk our wares or our backs are too brittle to carry our baskets. But we do not complain. Why? Because we know that there is something worse than drudgery. And even death."

"What does any of this have to do with the rumor about the children?" Keishin said.

"As everyone is taught from when we are children, in the hierarchy of our world, there are two kinds of people whose duties hold the most importance. The pawnshop owner who collects souls and the Horishi who infuses them into us as maps." Natsuki nervously looked over her shoulder, scanning the clouds. She lowered her voice to a whisper. "The Shiikuin do not wish us to know this, but sometimes, they fail."

"What do you mean they fail?" Hana stiffened.

"The pawnshop owner is not always able to collect enough souls for all the children born in our world. When such children are brought to the Horishi, they are unable to receive any soul or fate. They are husks. Soulless shells."

"Soulless . . ." Hana pressed a hand over her trembling lips.

Keishin put his arm around Hana's shoulders and drew her closer. "What happens to those children?"

"They are not children," Natsuki said. "They are monsters."

"But why have I not seen such children . . ." Hana caught herself. "Such creatures? Do the Shiikuin kill them?"

"That would be the kind thing to do, but the Shiikuin are not kind. According to the whispers . . . they are buried alive."

"Alive?" Ice ran up Keishin's ankles.

"Where are they buried?" Hana asked.

"That is something that you will need to ask the source of the rumor."

"Who?"

"The owner of market stall number five hundred and ten."

CHAPTER FORTY-THREE

Stall Five Hundred and Ten

Baskets, glass jars, and wooden crates were displayed on tiered shelves in front of market stall five hundred and ten, each containing a different item for sale. Ballpoint pens, sorted by color, bloomed from jars like plastic bouquets. The biggest collection was the color blue. Next to the pens, a row of smaller jars held an assortment of the knickknacks that one would find collecting lint in the bowels of a purse. Tubes of lipstick. Receipts. Loose change. Baskets overflowing with mountains of eyeglasses and keys were arranged beneath them. Crates occupied the last shelf closest to the clouds, each filled with an impressive collection of mismatched socks.

"I hate to admit it," Keishin said, "but except for the lipstick, this stall kind of reminds me of my old college dorm room during finals week. The only difference was that my junk wasn't arranged in baskets. It was an obstacle course over my floor."

"I am not surprised," Hana said. "Everything this stall sells is from your world. The door shared by the pawnshop and the ramen restaurant is not the only way into your world. Sometimes, cracks appear. The things that are lost or forgotten in your world's dusty corners fall through them." She picked up a gold-colored credit card from a short stack. "I used to collect these. Your world has such pretty bookmarks."

"Er, yes. Very pretty." Keishin bit down a laugh. "Forget finding neutrinos. Life's greatest mystery is finally solved. I always wondered where the socks that vanished from my washing machine went." Keishin plucked a coin from a jar and rolled it across his knuckles.

A man bundled in a multicolored patchwork coat appeared from behind the stall. Keishin spotted the bottom half of a gray-and-red-striped necktie stitched to a sleeve from a theme park's souvenir T-shirt near the coat's waist. The vendor greeted them with a deep bow and a smile that was as cheerful as his coat. He glanced at the coin in Keishin's hand. "Are you interested in that item? It's called a coin. The people in the other world use it to pay for things. And coins that have holes in them like the one you are holding are supposed to bring good luck."

"How . . . uh . . . interesting." Keishin returned the coin to the jar.

"I just received a new delivery of wallets," the vendor said. "I have not had a chance to display them yet, but I can fetch them for you if you would like to take a look."

"Thank you, but we are not here to purchase anything. Nakajima-san told us that you could provide us with answers to some questions we have," Keishin said.

"Nakajima Natsuki? The porter?"

"Yes," Keishin said.

"If Natsuki sent you my way, then I assume that your questions are not the sort that would be wise to say out loud." The vendor fetched a notebook from the back of the stall and plucked a blue pen from one of the store's jars. "Here," he said, handing them to Keishin. "Write your question down and I will see what I can do."

Keishin closed his hand around the pen, struck by how its

weight and shape felt familiar and odd at the same time. He could not recall a day that he had not grabbed a pen to scribble down a reminder or an idea as he darted off to a class or worked at the university's lab. He kept two pens in a chipped mug on his nightstand for the all too frequent nights when one of the resident questions in his head decided that it couldn't wait until morning to chatter away in his ear. But Keishin had not held a pen since he had arrived in Hana's world, and tonight it felt more like an exotic artifact than a commonplace tool. He opened the vendor's notebook and wrote a question down on a blank page. He steered the pen over the paper, mindful of every stroke. Control was a luxury in a world where he had done nothing but chase one strange question after another while running for his life. He savored every second of it.

The vendor ran his eyes over the notebook. He ripped the page out and burned it in the flame of one of the lanterns in his stall. He blew out the lantern and scattered the page's ashes over the cloud.

"I will need to have words with Natsuki for sending you here," the vendor said after making sure that every bit of ash had been swallowed by the cloud. "I am not inclined to give her any business for a while."

"Will you help us?" Hana said. "My father . . ."

The vendor held up his hand. "I do not want to know your reasons. The less I know, the better. I will help you only because I know that Natsuki has already made you pay a hefty price for an answer she could not give." The vendor pulled out a stool and sat down. He hunched over the notebook and wrote so feverishly that Keishin worried he was going to rip the paper. The vendor tore out two pages, folded them in half, and gave them to Hana. "This is everything I know."

"We owe you a great debt," Hana said.

"You can pay it by leaving the Night Market and never coming back. I do not even wish to know your names. But you may have mine. It is Nakano Yasuhiro. Tell my mother that I sent you." The vendor reached into a jar and tossed a coin to Keishin. "And take this for luck. You will need it."

CHAPTER FORTY-FOUR

The Library of the Lost

Hana stood in the shadows of a bamboo grove, clutching the pages Yasuhiro had given her. She crumpled them in her fist. "He was right about the rumor being unspeakable. Those poor children."

"They weren't children, Hana," Keishin said.

"It wasn't their fault they didn't have souls. It was my fault and my father's."

"It happened long before you were born, even before the pawnshop was your father's responsibility."

"It doesn't matter. It is still my family's shame."

"We don't know the whole story."

"We know enough. We know that the vendor's grandfather was a porter and that the Shiikuin ordered him to collect a package from the Horishi's home and to bury it. And now we know what the package turned out to be." Her voice broke. "A soulless child."

"It's a terrible story, but don't you see, Hana? Now we have a real trail to follow. Yasuhiro's mother knows where her father took the child, the field where he heard the voices and wailing of children beneath the ground. This has to be the same place the Shiikuin imprisoned your mother. What could be a crueler punishment for a mother desperately missing her own child?"

* * *

The sun glowed behind the clouds as Hana and Keishin trekked up the narrow steps chiseled into the side of a mountain's gray face. The snaking path, slippery from wear, was the only way to and from a village that did not seem to want to be found. Only the wooden doors dotting the slope gave Yasuhiro's mother's hometown away. Hana held on to a guide rope that ran the length of the steps and tried to keep her eyes from the ground.

"I never thought I'd say this," Keishin said, "but I prefer the Night Market's ladders to this. Whoever had the idea of carving homes into a mountain must have needed a lot of excitement in his life."

"It could be worse."

"How?"

"We could be climbing up these steps at night or in the rain."

"Don't give the weather any ideas." Keishin gripped the rope tighter. "I told you, it hates me."

Hana rolled her eyes. "And I told you that the rain that has been following us around is because of me."

"Fine. I won't argue with you. At least not until we've found Yasuhiro's mother and are safely behind one of these doors."

Two children skipped down the path toward Hana, not noticing or caring about how narrow or slippery the steps were. They grinned at Hana and bowed.

A vision of monstrous, soulless children took the place of the two who stood in front of her. Hana froze. Keishin gave her shoulder a comforting squeeze as though reading her mind. Hana blinked the image away. "Oh . . . uh . . . hello. Do you know where a woman named Nakano Hiroko lives?"

The shorter of the children looked up at a door directly above them.

"But she is never home," the older child said. "She spends her day at the library."

"Where is the library?" Keishin asked.

The children pointed to a door at the very top of the steps. "Over there."

The door of the library was taller and wider than any of the wind-worn doors along the mountain's face. It was as shiny and black as a piano key and, with the exception of its brass door knocker, showed little signs of wear. A blackened dragon held a ring in its mouth, waiting for visitors to come its way. Hana gripped the brass ring and rapped it against the door twice. Shuffling footsteps echoed behind the door.

"Hello?" a woman's voice answered through the door.

"Hello," Hana said. "We are looking for Nakano Hiroko."

The door opened inward with a loud creak.

"I am she," the woman standing in the doorway said. Her hair was as gray as the rock the library was carved into, her smile as warm as the sun shining on Hana's nape.

"Nakano-san." Hana bowed. "My name is Ishikawa Hana, and this is my friend Minatozaki Keishin. Your son, Yasuhiro, told us that you could help us find . . ." Hana hesitated, reluctant to mention the soulless children out in the open. "Something."

"I do not know what you are searching for, but if you have misplaced 'something,'" Hiroko said with a smile, "the Library of the Lost is a good place to start looking for it."

Towering stone shelves, sculpted from the mountain, fanned out from the large circular reading room like the rays of the sun. Fireflies, in far larger swarms than in the teahouse of

Hana's grandmother, swirled above the shelves and illuminated the library's aisles with dancing light. Hana ran her hand over the chisel marks on the shelves, trying to imagine the time and will it took to carve out a library that looked more like a fortress than a place that stored dusty books and scrolls.

"I can see that you have the same question written on your face as everyone who visits this library for the first time," Hiroko said. "You want to know what treasure requires the safety of such a formidable sanctuary. I wanted to know the answer to that question too ever since I first set foot here as a child, but the map on my skin told me that my duty was at my husband's side at the Night Market. My question had to wait until I had retired."

"And have you found your answer?" Hana asked.

"I have. The library guards everything and nothing at all. Books do not find value when they are written. They find value when they are read. Every book here is both worthless and priceless at the same time. It depends on who you ask. As I have not yet had the pleasure of reading half of the library's collection, I can say that only the books that I have taken from the shelves and stored in my heart are truly precious." Hiroko gestured to a shelf across the room. "That section of the library is my favorite. It is where all possible endings live. When a writer changes his mind about the fate of a character, his story's alternate path finds its way here. It's quiet now, but when the books wake up, all the endings like to argue which one is best."

"I think I could live in this place," Keishin said.

"I share your sentiment." Hiroko chuckled. "I am as much of a fixture here as these shelves."

"Why is it called the Library of the Lost?" Keishin scanned the shelves.

"It is named after its prized collection," Hiroko said. "The library houses a little trove that my family's stall at the Night Market has contributed to over the years. Sometimes, things that are far more precious than pens and coins fall through the cracks. We bring those items here. Unsent love letters. Abandoned stories. Childhood diaries. Yellowing postcards. Borrowed books that were forgotten beneath a bed and never returned. Were you interested in anything in particular? The other world's books are quite strange, but are worth browsing."

"We aren't looking for a book, Nakano-san," Hana said. "We were hoping that you could help us find a place."

"A place?"

"The place where your father heard children cry beneath the ground."

Hiroko clamped her hand over Hana's mouth, her eyes darting around her. "Do not say another word."

Hiroko led them to a dark corner of the library whose shelves were covered by cobwebs and a thick layer of dust. "This section houses all the stories with happy endings. As you can see, it is not very popular. Even the fireflies avoid this place."

"Why?" Keishin said.

"People come here to escape, not to envy." Hiroko glanced down the empty aisle. "We can talk here."

"I wish we did not need to ask you about the children," Hana said. "But lives depend on it."

"I did not know that words I had spoken as a child would follow me into my old age. I suppose that this is my punishment for spreading a secret that was not mine to share. All I could think about then was that I did not want to be like those letters I had found." Hiroko's eyes glossed over with tears.

"Letters?" Keishin asked.

"Lost, unsent letters from the other world. I found them rotting inside a damp, crumbling box. They smelled foul and were covered with mold and dirt, all their words and sentiments decayed. That is what happens when words are left unsaid. It does not matter how beautiful they are. In time, everything rots. That is how I knew that my father's secret rotted inside me too. I could smell its stench. I had to tell someone. Anyone. I told a friend, a porter's son, and made him swear not to tell anyone. Before the day was over, everyone in the market knew my crime. And now you have carried my shame to the one place I thought it would never find me again."

"We are sorry," Hana said. "We did not realize that this would cause you so much distress."

"It is not your fault. It is mine. My father did not know I had followed him to the field. He always said that I was too curious for my own good. He was right. There is not a day that I do not regret hiding in the ruins of that temple and seeing the 'package' the Shiikuin had ordered my father to bury among the wildflowers." Hiroko covered her ears with her hands and squeezed her eyes shut. "The children . . . their voices . . . I can still hear them rising from the ground, louder than the gurgle of the stream."

"Where is this field, Hiroko-san?" Hana said.

Hiroko dropped her hands to her sides. "Please believe me when I tell you that this is not a place you wish to find."

"I have no choice. I need to find it."

"The only choice we have in this world is to be content," Hiroko said. "But I was a willful and greedy child who wanted to see more than the world outside my window. I disobeyed my father. It is a mistake that I will have to live with for the rest of my life. The cries in my head will never let me forget. I will take them with me to my grave, no matter how much their secret rots inside me."

Keishin sat on the steps of the mountain, his eyes not daring to wander past his feet. He did not want to look at Hana. Their search for her mother and father had come to an end, becoming the latest addition to the library's dusty collection of lost and unfinished things. "I'm sorry, Hana. We tried."

Hana stared out into the valley.

Keishin reached for her hand then changed his mind. Holding her was only going to make him feel more helpless. There was nothing he could say to comfort her, no way to hold her tight enough to make her feel that everything was going to be okay. He dug his hands into his pockets. Something hard and cold brushed his fingertips. He pulled out the coin Yasuhiro had given him. It had failed to bring them any luck, and Keishin had half a mind to hurl it off the mountain. He gripped the coin, raised it over his shoulder, and stopped, remembering a way to put it to better use. He set the coin on the step and spun it, following a script from another life. The coin twirled dangerously close to the mountain's edge, slowing Keishin's thoughts and muffling the noise inside him enough to hear the advice of an old friend.

Keishin hurriedly weaved through the packed Indonesian restaurant and nearly ran into a server. He pulled out a chair across from Ramesh and sat down, panting. "I need to find a field."

"A field?" Ramesh set his fork down. "Now that's a first. What kind of field?"

"The kind you bury secrets in."

Ramesh rubbed his chin. "Interesting. Go on."

"The only person who knows where to find it refuses to tell me where it is. I've reached a dead end."

Ramesh folded his arms over his chest. "What did that person say exactly?"

"Hiroko said a lot of things. Just not anything useful."

"Good." Ramesh spooned vegetable curry and rice into his mouth and chewed slowly.

"How is that a good thing?"

"She could have just said no when you asked her about the location of the place and that would be the end of this conversation. It would be a shame to waste all of this food. 'A lot of things' gives us something to work with."

"I wish that were true. But Hiroko just went on and on about how much she regretted secretly following her father to the field."

Ramesh smiled. "Now we're getting somewhere."

"We are?"

"If Hiroko followed her father without him knowing it, then I'm guessing that she found a good place to hide."

"She did. She hid in a—" Keishin's brows shot up. He jumped from his seat, knocking over his beer. "Thanks, Ramesh. I can take it from here."

"You're welcome." Ramesh sighed, looking longingly at the food they had barely touched. "Good luck."

The spinning coin fell from the side of the mountain, taking Hiroko's deafening refusal to reveal the field's location with it. In the silence, Keishin heard all the words she did say. "She hid in a ruined temple . . . that's it."

"What are you talking about?" Hana said.

"I know how to find the field."

"You do? How?"

"Hiroko may not have told us its exact location, but whether intentionally or not, she gave us a chance to find it. I think that a part of her did want to set the secret free. She told us three things about the field that we didn't know before. First, there are ruins of a temple near the place her father buried the creature. Second, the field is covered in wildflowers. Third, there is a stream close by. Temple ruins. Wildflowers. Stream. That should narrow our search considerably."

Hana jumped to her feet. "We need a map."

It looked more like a campsite than a train station. An assortment of colorful tents ran alongside the tracks, some as large as decent-sized homes. People cooked over bonfires on the platform while others hung their laundry from ropes strung along the station's posts. Some had even managed to plant vegetable gardens. Children chased one another between tents, giggling as they ran. No one, Keishin thought, seemed to be concerned that the sign meant to announce the arrival times of the trains was blank.

Hana walked back to Keishin with a handful of maps. "This is everything I could find."

Keishin stared at the makeshift village on the platform. "Why are they camped out here?"

"They are waiting for their trains."

Keishin raised his brows. "How long have they been waiting?"

"A while."

"How often do the trains come by?"

"This is not like Tokyo Station. The trains here do not have a schedule. They arrive when they arrive. Some of the passengers were born waiting here, and some will die without even getting a glimpse of their train."

"And they're okay with that?"

"They do not have a choice. The railways do not always stay in one place, especially the ones that travel over oceans. Currents change. The train tracks can drift and send the trains on very long detours," Hana said. "Come. We need to find a place where we can take a look at these maps."

They walked over to a less crowded part of the station. "Do you want to hear something weird?" Keishin said.

"Stranger than trains that get lost at sea?" Hana knelt on the floor and set down the maps.

"Not that strange." Keishin smirked. "I don't like maps."

"Why not?"

"They remind me of all the things people pretend to know, all the things we make up to make us feel like we understand everything and are in control. Maps are more of an art form than a science. They're designed at the discretion of their makers. Some things are shrunk, others are enlarged, some places are kept, and some are left out. We draw thick red lines around spaces we claim as our own as if we could actually see where one space ended and another began. But borders are simply constructs. They exist only in our minds."

Hana kept quiet, unsure how to completely yet politely disagree. Borders were real, and the ones that were the most difficult to cross were not the invisible lines between towns, but the walls people built around themselves. Borders were necessary. They kept secrets safe. "Then you will be happy to know that our maps are a bit different from the maps you are familiar with." She spread out a map over the floor and revealed a blank page.

"I can see that." Keishin crouched next to it. "How do we find anything on it?"

"We do not. The maps will find the place for us. If we ask nicely enough."

"Given that I've never had a conversation with a map before, you should probably do the talking."

Hana smoothed down the map's edges. "Excuse me, but can you help us find a field?"

The map shivered on the floor. A crescent-shaped mountain range formed over its surface, creasing the page. The map rippled and carved a field into the range's inner curve. It shook, as though asking Hana if this was the field she was searching for.

"A field with wildflowers and a temple," Hana said. "And a stream."

The mountains over the map receded, leaving the paper as smooth as it was before they had appeared. The map folded itself back into a rectangle.

"Maybe the next map will know where it is," Keishin said.

Hana spread out a second map and asked it the same question.

The map refolded itself.

Keishin chewed the nail on his thumb.

Hana unfolded the third map and asked it about the field. She spoke slowly to make sure that the map understood every word.

The map lay flat and still.

Hana reached for the fourth map.

The third map trembled. Two mountains rose over opposite corners of the blank sheet, leaving a valley between them. The valley creased and formed a temple. A strip ripped across the middle of the valley, exposing the floor beneath it.

"Kei . . ." Hana stared at the rip, transfixed. "I think that's a . . ."

"Stream." He squeezed her hand.

A train rumbled over his voice. Cheers erupted through the camp. A fourth of the people on the platform scurried around, stuffing their belongings into bags and balancing things that couldn't fit in their arms. A man made his young daughter ride on his shoulders as he ran toward the train with two bulging bags in each hand. His daughter bobbed as he ran, hugging a small potted plant to her chest. The small group they had shared a tent with chased after them to wave goodbye.

Keishin ignored the commotion, focusing his attention on the long strip of paper hovering over the map. It twisted in the air, shredding itself into tiny petallike pieces. The shreds turned the palest blue before falling like rain over the map and scattering over the paper valley. "Wildflowers . . ."

The map grew still. Its shreds re-formed, and in less time than it took to blink, the map was pristine and whole. Brushstrokes slowly appeared over the page where the valley had been, revealing the field's location one carefully painted word at a time.

"We did it!" Keishin threw his arms around Hana as the train pulled away from the station.

More words formed on the map. Hana's eyes darted over the completed directions. She stiffened in Keishin's embrace.

Keishin released her. "What's wrong?"

"I know where the field is." She stared at the empty tracks. "And we just missed the train the map told us to catch to get there."

* * *

A blanket of quiet settled over the tent village as its residents retreated into their makeshift homes and went to bed. A few pockets of hushed conversation remained, exchanged between groups huddled around bonfires. They had talked about the same thing for hours, none of them growing tired of reliving the excitement of the train's arrival earlier that day.

Hana sat among a small group gathered in a circle around a fire, warming her hands by the flames. "What if the train never comes?"

Keishin put his arm around her. "It will. It has to. We've come too far to give up now."

"You're new here, aren't you?" said an elderly man sitting next to Keishin.

"We are," Hana replied.

"Welcome. I am Ono Aritomo. I can always tell who the new arrivals are." The man flashed a nearly toothless grin. "They are the ones in a rush. I was that way too when I arrived here with my mother."

"Your mother?" Keishin tried and failed to hide the surprise in his voice.

Aritomo smiled. "I was a young boy then, barely twelve. I wed and raised a family here. My wife's train arrived ten years ago. Our son went with her."

"I am sorry to hear that, Ono-san," Hana said.

"Why?" Aritomo scratched his chin. "My wife was on her own journey and I am on mine. When her train arrived, she had to get on it. There is nothing to feel sorry for. I have lived a good life. I have been a son, a husband, and a father. To many of the people here, I am a friend. I have grown a garden and fed the hungry, and built a tent where strangers have found rest.

What more can a man ask for? Arriving at one's destination is never promised. Only the journey is. Waiting is part of that journey."

Keishin nodded slowly. "You are a wise man, Ono-san."

Aritomo shook his head. "Not wiser than any of those who wait here. We have been blessed with the time to think. It has allowed us to realize that life is about finding joy in the space between where you came from and where you are going. I may never get to where I want to go, but I can look back on my life and say that I did not waste a second of it being bitter that I was not someplace else. Happiness does not exist in a place. It lives in every breath we take. You need to choose to take it in, over and over again."

Aritomo's words warmed Keishin more than the bonfire did, finding and filling empty spaces he didn't know he had. "I am grateful that I met you."

"There is no need to thank me. I have met all sorts of people over my years at this train station. Some pass through quickly, some stay for a while. Everyone I have ever encountered, no matter how brief, has either taken something or left something behind. Rude people can rip the smile from your face. Kind ones can give it back. I have learned that there is nothing to be gained from stealing other people's happiness. No matter how much you have stolen, it is not something that you can ever use for yourself."

Hana lay curled against Keishin, molded into his chest. "Could you be happy here? Could a vegetable garden on a train station's platform make you as happy as your neutrinos and stars?"

Keishin rubbed her shoulder with his thumb. "As much as I

would like to pretend to be as wise as Aritomo, I know that I couldn't be content here."

"Why?" Hana turned to face him.

"Because I refuse to break my promise to you, Hana. We will find your parents one way or another. I don't care how far away the field is, how difficult it is to get there, or how many Shiikuin chase after us. We will find them."

"I'm sorry," a woman sharing the tent with them whispered to Hana. She pulled her dark hair from her tanned face and coiled it into a loose bun. "I didn't mean to overhear your conversation."

"I . . . I apologize for waking you," Keishin stammered.

"You said that you are looking for your parents?" the woman said. "And that the Shiikuin are looking for you?"

Hana paled.

"Don't worry. I can keep your secret. My name is Keiko. I am no friend of the Shiikuin. I know how cruel they can be. I lost my father to them. He was sick and had fallen asleep at his stall at the Night Market, and the Shiikuin chased him into the river for it."

"I'm sorry," Keishin said, remembering the story that Hana had told him.

"There is another way than by train to get to where you are going," Keiko said.

"There is?" Hana said. "But the map told us that—"

"No map would suggest this manner of travel," Keiko said. "It is spoken of only in the darkest corners of the Night Market, and only by the most desperate."

"Why?" Keishin said.

"Because people believe it to be shameful and dishonorable," Keiko said. "But if the lives of those I loved depended on it, I do not think that I would care about honor."

"Neither would I," Hana said. "It is only a matter of time before the Shiikuin find us here. We do not have the luxury of waiting for our train."

Keiko nodded. "The Forbidden Way will take you wherever you need to go, but it will not be easy."

"We will do it," Hana said. "When can we leave?"

"Soon. There is something that both of you must do first."

"What must we do?" Keishin said.

"Drink."

CHAPTER FORTY-FIVE

The Third Bottle of Sake

一杯目人を酒飲む二杯目は酒酒を飲み三杯は酒人を飲む

Ippai-me wa hito sake o nomi, nihai-me wa sake sake o nomi, sanbai-me wa sake hito o nomu.

It is the man who drinks the first bottle of sake, then the second bottle drinks the first, and finally, it is the sake that drinks the man. Hana realized that she had not fully understood this old saying until this evening at the train station. She emptied her cup and wiped the sake dribbling from her chin with the back of her hand. The platform and all the tents on it swam around her. She waved a fourth bottle of sake away when Keiko tried to refill her cup.

"I am sorry." Keiko poured out the last of the sake into Hana's cup. "But this is necessary."

"Cheers." Keishin tossed his head back and swallowed his drink in one gulp. A shadow play, cast by the bonfire, danced over his face.

Hana squinted, watching the shadow story unfold through the haze in her head. Keishin was a hero on a quest with no idea how close the monsters really were. She drained her cup and slammed it down on the train station's floor.

Keiko nodded. "Now you can go."

"You still haven't told us how we're supposed to leave," Keishin said.

"This next part is simpler," Keiko said. "All you have to do is talk, and all I have to do is listen. The sake inside you should make it easy to speak your mind and select which words to whisper."

Hana massaged her temples, unsure if it was the sake or the exhaustion in her bones that made Keiko's words difficult to grasp.

"There is nothing that travels faster than a rumor," Keiko said. "And rumors that bear the most truth are the swiftest of them all. Tonight, you will choose a rumor to spread and ride it until you reach your destination."

Keishin rubbed his eyes. "I'm sorry, but I don't think I'm drunk enough to comprehend how we're supposed to hitch a ride on a rumor."

"You do not need to understand it for it to work," Keiko said. "But you do need to trust me. My family's stall at the Night Market sold more than just trinkets. We offered a way out. Before my father died, he taught me how to do it."

"Tell us what we need to do," Hana said.

"Hana." Keishin drew her away from the fire. "Are you sure you want to do this? This could be a trick. Keiko could betray us to the Shiikuin."

"You were a complete stranger just a few days ago," Hana said. "And you have not broken your word yet."

Keiko approached them. "Are you having second thoughts?"

"No," Hana said.

"Then choose your truth and be on your way."

The choice was obvious. Hana would have never agreed to sharing it had she been sober. But the sake inside her made a convincing argument. There was no rumor that would travel faster than Keishin's secret. Keishin gripped her hand as he whispered it into Keiko's ear.

I am not from your world.

Hana watched herself fade. Her feet were the first to vanish. Her legs were next, disappearing in small increments from her ankles. The last to go were her eyes, and when they were gone, only darkness remained.

CHAPTER FORTY-SIX

The Rumor About a Man Named Minatozaki Keishin

I am not from your world. Keishin unraveled with every word. The truth he had whispered into Keiko's ear turned him back into the stardust from which all things were made and cast him into the air and darkness. The particles of his mind could grasp only one thought. Even as dust, he held on to Hana, and what remained of her clung to him.

Keishin drifted until he began to gather in the spot that used to be his stomach. He couldn't be sure. He had no eyes to see. He felt himself being stitched together one atom at a time, and when he had eyelids, he opened them and watched Hana take shape.

"Where are we?" Hana said as soon as she had lips to form words.

"Wherever we are . . ." Keishin glanced around. A tent surrounded them, crammed with all manner of things. Blankets. Baskets. Pots. Books. They balanced in stacks, filling every available space. "I don't think we got far. It looks like we're still at the station."

Hana walked over to the tent's flap and pulled on it. It refused to move. She tugged harder. "It won't open."

Keishin tried to lift one of the tent's fabric walls but could not find a gap between the tent and the floor. He pushed against it. It pushed back, sending him to the ground. He got up, took as many steps back as the clutter allowed, and rammed the tent with his shoulder. He collided with something as hard as bone. Pain exploded in his arm. Keishin staggered back, clutching his throbbing shoulder. He cursed and pounded the wall with his fist. "Keiko! Keiko! Let us out."

Hana pulled Keishin away from the wall. "It's no use. We are trapped. You were right. Keiko betrayed us."

"We got in here." Keishin shoved away a stack of baskets. "That means there is a way out."

The tent shook violently, tossing Keishin and Hana to the floor. Hana tried to get to her feet. Keishin grabbed her hand. "Stay down."

The rumbling stopped. Bright light poured into the tent. Hana peeked over the clutter and squinted. She gasped and pushed herself off the floor. "The flap's open!"

Keishin stood up. "Run!"

They scrambled to the opening, knocking over teetering piles of books and jumping over an obstacle course of blankets and clothes. They burst out of the tent, shielding their eyes from the light. Keishin pulled his hand from his face just in time to watch Hana fade away.

Collecting the scattered pieces of himself went faster the second time around. Or maybe it only felt that way. It was difficult to get a sense of time without a body. Keishin opened his eyes. Hana stood in front of him, her limbs molding themselves from thin air.

Hana stared at her newly formed hands and flexed her fingers. "What's happening to us?"

Keishin's eyes flew around him. They stood beneath a hexagonal gazebo that was surrounded by a shimmering lake. A full moon floated in the water. Keishin extended his arm, but an invisible wall kept his fingers from reaching beyond the gazebo's wooden frame. "Another trap."

Hana looked out at the calm lake. "It does not feel like a trap."

"What else do you call a place you can't leave?"

The ground shifted beneath them, sending waves across the lake. They grabbed on to the gazebo's posts. Light washed over them as though an invisible door had opened and let the sun in.

"It's happening again." Hana squinted at the glare.

Keishin took a tentative step toward the light.

"Kei, wait." Hana grabbed his arm. "We might fade away again."

Keishin narrowed his eyes at the light. "Maybe that's what's supposed to happen."

"What?"

"Maybe you're right. Maybe this isn't a trap."

"Then what is it?"

"What if this is what Keiko meant by traveling inside a rumor?"

"You think that we're inside someone's mind?"

"Until they pass the rumor on to someone else." Keishin held out his hand to Hana. "But there's only one way to know for sure."

People's minds, Keishin discovered, came in many different sizes and shapes. Some were no larger than cupboards, while others were the length of the train. A few rooms had barely anything inside them, and quite a few overflowed with an assortment of odds and ends. The strangest so far had been a room perched on top of a tree, with every inch of its floor covered by a carpet of steaming cups of green tea.

Keishin stood inside a curved room made of glass and waited for Hana to become whole. The time they spent in each room grew shorter with each leap into the light. This, he thought, was the nature of a rumor. As it grew, it gathered speed. Keishin took in his latest surroundings, hoping to linger in them a little longer. He liked this mind. It was shaped like an orb and floated among the stars.

"This is beautiful." Hana admired the constellations.

"Yes." Keishin watched the stars twinkle in her eyes. "It is."

"I wonder what kind of person has a mind like this?" Hana pressed her palm against the clear wall.

"The kind of person I would envy very much," Keishin said.

"Envy? Why? I imagine that your mind would be filled with nothing but stars too."

"I wish it was. But sadly, it's probably just a gray room with poor lighting littered with numbers and charts. And maybe a chair. And an empty bag of Funyuns. Or two."

"Funyuns? Do I want to know what that is?"

"You don't. It's a horrible addiction. I can't work without them. I packed a suitcase full of them because I was afraid that I wasn't going to be able to find them in Japan. And now that I've said it out loud, it sounds like the silliest thing in the world to worry about." Keishin stared up at the stars. "It's funny how the mind finds ways to fill itself up with worthless things as though it was afraid of being empty."

"Or quiet," Hana said.

The orb shook. Light broke through its crystal.

Keishin clasped Hana's hand. "Let's go," he said, stepping into the light.

* * *

It was impossible to tell where the wildflowers ended and the sky began. The blue of the petals matched the cloudless horizon perfectly. Keishin did not question how the flowers bloomed in autumn. He was just grateful that they did.

The rumor had dropped them off on a dirt road along the valley of wildflowers when a farmer could find no one to share it with but his cart horse. The horse had neighed and swished its tail, brushing the rumor off like a fly. It cared little about a man named Minatozaki Keishin and less about the world he came from. All it cared about was getting home to its warm stall on its master's farm, away from a sprawling blue field that made it sneeze. The rumor hung in the air between the farmer and his horse, swirled for a moment, and drifted away with the wind.

Hana's mouth fell open when she had formed a jaw to drop. "We're here."

"We should start walking if we're going to find the temple and the stream," Keishin said. "We have a lot of ground to cover."

"This place is a lot bigger than I imagined. Where do we even start?"

A strong wind blew in their direction, sending ripples through the wildflowers.

Hana cocked her head. "Did you hear that?"

"Hear what?"

The wind whipped Hana's hair. Hana gathered the loose strands back into her ponytail. "Nothing. It was just the wind."

A breeze kissed Keishin's cheek and carried the sound of children's laughter past his ears. He froze mid-step. "Hana . . ."

Hana locked eyes with him. "I heard it too."

CHAPTER FORTY-SEVEN

Beneath the Wildflowers

Only the temple's torii, stone gates that marked the border between the secular and the sacred, remained. To step through them was to enter the world of the spirits. But as Hana passed through the gates and crossed a stream that cut through the ruins of the temple, she did not feel like she was in the company of any god she knew. The beauty of the field was equal only to how oppressively desolate and cold it felt beyond the threshold of the temple.

"I do not like it here." Hana hugged her arms to her chest.

"That makes two of us," Keishin said.

"I cannot hear them anymore. Do you think we are in the wrong place?"

"This place matches Hiroko's description. It has to be it."

A muffled giggle rose from the ground.

Hana jumped.

"It's coming from over there." Keishin pointed to a patch of wildflowers that were paler but grew thicker than the rest of the field.

Hana crouched by the patch and laid her ear against the ground.

"Do you hear anything?" Keishin asked.

Hana pressed her finger to her lips and closed her eyes. Footsteps scampered beneath the flowers. "It sounds like they are running around. Playing. Hiroko told us that they were crying when she heard them. I wonder what changed?"

"We won't find any answers up here," Keishin said, his eyes fixed on the wildflower patch. "I hope you packed a couple of shovels in your bag."

"I did not." Hana stuck her arm into her bag all the way to her elbows and rummaged around. "But my father keeps two in our garden in a little shed near the pond."

The children's laughter grew louder the deeper they dug. Hana battled the urge to dig slower. The field was their last lead, and if they didn't find her father or mother here, she had no idea what she was going to do next. She tried to picture them somewhere safe, but her mind could not imagine a world beneath the ground that didn't make her want to clamber up from the hole she and Keishin were digging.

The laughter fell silent.

Hana squeezed the handle of her shovel. "Why did they stop?"

Keishin leaned his shovel against the wall of the hole and pressed his cheek to the ground. "I can hear some movement. They're still there, but I think they're quiet because . . . they're listening to us too."

Hana could no longer see the field from where she stood at the bottom of the hole. The sky glowed purple and orange above them. Soon, the hole was going to be too deep to climb out of and the field too dark for them to find their way back to the road. Fleeing was no longer an option no matter what was waiting for them beneath the ground.

Hana wiped the sweat from her forehead and left a streak of

mud on her face. Every muscle was on fire, but it was her raw palms that hurt the most. The makeshift gloves she had fashioned from the strip of cloth she had ripped from the bottom of her blouse hung loosely from her hands, threatening to unravel at any moment.

"You should take a break," Keishin said.

"I'm fine." She pushed away the pain and dug.

"Wait." Keishin planted his shovel on the ground. He took her torn hands in his and gently rewrapped the cloth around her palms. "That should hold for a while."

"Thank you," Hana said.

Keishin wiped the dirt from Hana's face. Blood seeped through the cloth wrapped around his hand.

"You're bleeding."

"It's nothing," Keishin said.

"It is strange how 'nothing' looks exactly like blood."

"It's just a small wound. Nothing worse than the cut you got on your foot at the pawnshop."

Hana looked up at the darkening sky. "That day feels like a lifetime ago."

"For me, it *was* a lifetime ago. I'm not the same person who showed up at your door. I've seen, heard, and"—Keishin's eyes lingered on Hana—"felt so many things I never imagined were possible. I don't know what we're going to find down there or what's going to happen next. I need you to know that I care about—"

"Don't."

"Don't what?"

"Don't say that you think that you care about me. That night at the ryokan was a mistake. Whatever we feel about each other is an illusion, no matter how real it feels. I told you when you first came to my world that nothing here is as it seems. Not the sky. Not this field. Not me. I'm grateful for everything you've done, really, I am. But somewhere along the way, we both let ourselves believe that you and I were a possibility. We are not. We can never be."

Talons burst from the ground and clawed at Keishin's legs. Hana screamed.

"Run, Hana!" Keishin's face crumpled as mud-crusted nails dug into his skin. "Run!"

Hana grabbed her shovel and struck at the clawlike hands. They clung to Keishin tighter, pulling him deeper into the ground. Hana hooked her arms around Keishin's shoulders and anchored her feet against the hole's crumbling walls. The muddy hands pulled harder, tugging Keishin from her grasp. "No!"

Keishin choked on mud. "Go."

Hana clung to his wounded hand. His skin grew slick with blood, unraveling the cloth around it. "Hold on."

Keishin looked into her eyes. "I'm sorry," he said and let her go.

A flurry of hands grabbed his head and pulled him into the ground, retreating into the soil after him.

"Kei!" Hana threw herself onto the spot Keishin had vanished from and clawed at the soil. "Kei!"

She slumped back, sobbing, her hands caked with mud. The stretch of sky above the hole grew blurry with her tears. She let her tears fall, roll off her cheeks, and water the ground. Her shovel disappeared into the mud. Hana gasped and sat up. Gnarled hands grabbed her waist. More hands burst from the earth around her. They locked their fingers onto Hana's legs and arms and dragged her into the ground as she screamed.

CHAPTER FORTY-EIGHT

They Looked like Children

The soft giggling of children echoed around him. Keishin crawled blindly on his hands and knees, coughing out mud. He rubbed the dirt from his eyes and blinked. The most he could make out from the shadows was that he was in some kind of tunnel or cave. Dark figures came into focus as he pushed himself to his feet. "Where am I?" He squinted at the blurry shapes. "Who are you?"

The echo of his voice answered him back. Laughter followed it.

"What do you want with me?" Keishin said.

"Play with us," a chorus of children's voices replied. "We want to play."

"Play?" Keishin's sight cleared. A group of young children circled him, the light from their faintly glowing lanterns swallowed by their completely black, sunken eyes. Long wisps of thinning dark hair that barely covered their scalps clung to their ashen cheeks. Keishin staggered back.

The children raised their lanterns higher, illuminating their mud-covered, clawlike nails. "We want to play."

A scream pierced the dark.

"Hana!" Keishin twisted around.

"Kei?" Hana's voice rang through the tunnel.

Keishin rushed to follow her voice. The children dug into

Keishin's arm with their nails and held him back, their icy fingers draining the warmth from his own. Keishin flinched. The only time he had ever touched a corpse was when he'd held his father's hand to say goodbye. These children felt colder, stripped of the smallest residue of life. They tugged at his arm. "Play with us."

"I . . . I will," Keishin said, trying to ignore the chill seeping into his bones. "But I need to find my friend first. Both of us will play with you. We'll have more fun."

The children looked at one another and then back at Keishin. "We'll have more fun," they said, mimicking Keishin's tone.

"We will. I promise. Just take me to Hana."

"Hana! Hana!" The children laughed as they said her name in unison.

"Hana!" Other children giggled in the tunnel's shadows. "Hana!"

A group of children emerged from the dark, dragging Hana between them.

Keishin wrestled free from the children, slicing his arm on their sharp nails, and nearly reopening his stitched wound. He ran to Hana. "Are you okay? Did they hurt you?"

"I . . . I'm just a little dizzy." She rubbed her forehead. "I hit my head when I fell."

"Play with us," the children said. "You promised."

"We will," Keishin said. "But Hana can't play now. She needs to rest. And water. She needs water."

"Water!" The children giggled. "We will play in the water. Come. You promised. Come."

"No," Keishin said. "Hana's hurt. She—"

"We should go with them," Hana said, her left heel sinking into the mud. "Any place has to be better than here."

Keishin lost track of how long they walked through the tunnel, but he felt their continuous descent in his ears. He swallowed hard to clear them.

Hana walked alongside him. "You should not have let go of my hand."

"And you should have run when you had the chance," Keishin said. "I think we've established by now that we're both too stubborn for our own good. Can we agree that arguing about this is pointless?"

"I was not going to argue with you. I was going to thank you for looking out for me," Hana said. "But you need to stop. I told you. Nothing here is as it seems. Not even me."

"You keep saying that like I'm supposed to understand what you mean. If you're not who you say you are, then please, for god's sake, tell me the truth. You owe me that much. I'm a scientist, Hana. I believe what I can see and what I can prove. All you've shown me is a woman who is selfless, strong, brave, and devoted to the people she loves. Until you show me evidence to the contrary, what you're saying remains a hypothesis. A bad one."

Light, where there should have been darkness, poured through the end of the tunnel.

Hana shielded her eyes. "Is that the sun?"

The children ran out of the tunnel and into a seemingly endless rock garden. Pruned trees, sculpted bushes, and water fountains dotted the pebbled landscape. A wide, fast-moving stream snaked through the garden, rushing under arched bridges and gurgling over rocks. Above the garden, the sun lit a clear blue sky.

"How is this possible?" Keishin gaped at the sky. "We were descending the whole time. How did we get to the surface?"

Hana watched clouds drift over them. "We did not," she said, pointing to a cloud. "Look."

The cloud moved, revealing a patch where the sky thinned. The cavern's rock ceiling showed through it.

"We are still underground," Hana said.

"We're still trapped," Keishin said, his voice hollow.

"Or we are exactly where we should be. We were searching for the children, and now we found them. My parents have to be here."

"Play with us." A child tugged on Keishin's arm, squeezing his wrist with its talons. "In the water. You promised."

"Yes, I did." Keishin walked over to a tree and plucked a leaf from it. "We will have a boat race."

"A race!" the chorus of children chimed.

"A race with rules. You may each choose only one leaf as your boat," Keishin said. "And you must run after it as it flows down the stream. It must never, ever leave your sight. If it does, you lose the race. Do you understand?"

"Rules. Leaves." The children scattered through the garden gathering leaves from trees.

"I think I know what you have in mind," Hana said, lowering her voice.

"I hope it works."

The children returned with their leaves. Keishin crouched by the stream and set his leaf boat on the water. He held on to it, waiting for all the children to take their places along the stream. "Ready?"

The children nodded.

"Go!" Keishin dropped his leaf into the water.

The children let go of their leaves and chased after them as the stream carried them away.

"Now, Hana," Keishin whispered. "Run."

CHAPTER FORTY-NINE

Hide and Seek

Pebbles flew in their wake as Keishin and Hana sprinted across the rock garden. They had not thought of any plan beyond fleeing from the creatures that looked like children, and every stride they took thrust them deeper into the unknown. They ran toward the fake sun because, in a garden beneath the earth, it was the only thing that felt familiar. Hana dropped to her knees, gasping for air.

Keishin clutched his burning sides. "You need to get up. Just a little farther, okay?"

Hana pushed herself to her feet. She ran and stumbled.

Keishin rushed to her side. "Are you all right?"

"I just need to catch my breath." Sweat beaded on her brow.

Keishin scanned the area. "We can't stay out here in the open. We can rest over there," he said, pointing to a grouping of rocks arranged to look like a mountain range.

Hana nodded and stood up.

"Hold on tight," Keishin said.

"To what?"

Keishin scooped her up in his arms. "Me."

Hana leaned against the rocks, breathing hard. "I thought I knew what to expect when Yasuhiro told us about the children."

"Monsters," Keishin said, staring at the cuts they had left on his arms. "They were monsters, Hana."

"Monsters," Hana said as though she had eaten something foul.

"No matter what they looked like, they weren't children. You felt their touch. They were . . . hollow. Dead."

"I know," Hana said. "But I don't think they meant us any harm."

"That giant bump on your head might disagree with you."

"That was an accident."

"Clawing at us and dragging us into that tunnel wasn't."

"If they are monsters it is because my family failed in our duty."

Keishin shook his head. "I'm not going to pretend that I know what these creatures are, why they exist, and why they do what they do. I just know that if we're going to find your parents, we need to stay as far away from them as possible."

Hana nodded. "We should wait here until—"

Footsteps crunched over pebbles.

Keishin clamped his hand over Hana's mouth.

The footsteps grew closer.

Keishin's muscles tensed, waiting for instructions: Fight or flee.

The footsteps stopped, scampered in the opposite direction, and grew faint.

"They're gone." Keishin exhaled, relaxing his shoulders. "You should try to get some rest. You'll need to keep up your strength for tonight. This garden is huge. We have a lot of ground to cover." Keishin fought a yawn. Whatever adrenaline had fueled his sprint was nearly exhausted, and what little remained he used to keep his eyes open. "I'll keep watch."

"I think you need sleep more than I do," Hana said. "Go ahead. Rest. I couldn't close my eyes even if I wanted to."

"Why not?"

"It's not important."

"Is it that time of the day again when I need to remind you how stubborn I am and that I won't accept no for an answer?"

"There is no need to remind me. It is not something you have allowed me to forget."

"Then go on." Keishin folded his arms. "I'm listening."

Hana tucked her knees into her chest. "I can't stop thinking about what it would be like to finally see my mother. Everything I know about her is from what my father and grandmother have told me. I used to have this perfect version of her that lived in my head."

"And now?"

"I find myself blaming her for everything that's happened. To my father. To Haruto. To you. We're trapped beneath the ground and surrounded by these . . . *things* because she was selfish and took something that didn't belong to her." Hana picked up a stone and rolled it around in her hand. "There. I said it. Is that enough evidence for you? Is that enough proof that I am not the person you think I am? You think that I am this dutiful daughter on this brave quest to save her parents, but all I can think about doing when I finally see my mother is push her away. If being hollow and cold makes the children here monsters, then I am a monster too."

"If you're looking for someone to judge you for what you feel about your mother, I'm afraid you're hiding behind rocks with the wrong person," Keishin said. "You just described exactly how I feel about my own mother. I've spent my entire life trying to find ways to make me feel worthy of her love, but the truth is, all I want is to be able to look her in the eye and shove everything I've ever achieved without her in her face to prove to her that choosing another life over her son was a mistake. I'm a man pretending to care about discovering the origins of the universe when all I really care about is finding a way to hurt the woman who gave birth to me."

"What a match we make," Hana said. "Two monsters hiding behind rocks."

"Feeling things for each other that, as you claim, aren't real."

"They aren't."

"At least tell me what these fake feelings you have for me are."

"If they aren't real, why does it matter?"

"I told you when we first met that I was a curious person. I want to know. I need to." Keishin leaned in close enough to feel the heat radiating from her skin. "And maybe because something that feels real when you're running for your life is close enough."

Hana pulled Keishin to her lips. Keishin melted into her mouth, understanding that this was Hana's answer. The heat between them burned through the time they had left, making Keishin keenly aware of their unique tragedy. The hours that strengthened bonds between lovers pulled them apart. Every passing moment dragged them back to worlds where the other could not follow. Including this kiss. There was no room for air between their lips, but Hana was already a thousand miles away.

Stay, Keishin screamed in his head. *Stay with me.*

"Hana?" a man's voice called from behind the rocks.

Hana broke away from Keishin's mouth.

"Hana?" the voice repeated with more urgency.

Hana attempted to stand.

Keishin grabbed her wrist. "Stay down," he whispered. "It's a trap."

"No." Hana pulled her hand away and stood up. "It's my father."

Keishin jumped to his feet. An older man with Hana's cheekbones and the same quiet strength behind his eyes stared back at him. A girl no older than seven gripped the man's hand with her talons. Unlike the other children, the dark wisps on her head were neatly combed into the smallest bun, more flowers and ribbon than hair.

"Otou-san . . ." Hana said.

Toshio gasped. "Hana."

The girl tugged on Toshio's hand and smiled up at him. "I told you, Otou-san." She giggled. "I told you that our sister was hiding here."

CHAPTER FIFTY

A Good Daughter

Every detail was as Hana remembered. The pawnshop looked exactly the same. The only difference was that this pawnshop built in the middle of a sprawling rock garden was pristine. There was no trace of the chaos she had awoken to the day her father had vanished.

"Please, have a seat," Toshio said, offering Keishin a place at their dining room table.

"Thank you, Ishikawa-san," Keishin said, shock and confusion still lingering on his face.

Hana wondered if she looked the same. Sitting for tea with her father in the middle of a building that looked exactly like their home was the last thing she had expected to find beneath the ground.

"I know that you have a lot of questions, Hana," Toshio said. "But first let me ask you one of my own. Why are you here?"

"Why am I here?" Hana's voice came out in a tone she had never used to speak with her father. "What do you mean, 'why am I here'?"

"I mean exactly the words I asked. What are you doing here?" Toshio said. "You shouldn't have come. I thought that you would have understood the message I left you."

"What message?" Hana said.

"The same message that apparently led you here."

"You had vanished, the pawnshop had been ransacked, and a choice had been taken from the vault. What did you expect me to do?"

"I expected you to be smarter."

"*Smarter?*" Keishin said. "Do you have any idea what your daughter's been through just to be able to find you?"

"Kei." Hana placed her hand on his arm. "Don't."

Toshio turned to Keishin. "I have devoted my life to teaching Hana to be better than this, training her to take over the pawnshop one day. And yet now she is here because she forgot one of the most important lessons I ever taught her."

Hana stared into the reflection in her teacup. "Nothing is as it seems . . ."

"I ransacked the pawnshop and stole the choice so that the Shiikuin would have a story to believe about my disappearance," Toshio said.

"Because you wanted them to think that you chased after a thief," Keishin said.

"Yes." Toshio turned to Hana. "But I also left another message, a message that I couldn't risk putting into words."

"Mother's glasses by the door and the tea," Hana said.

Toshio nodded. "I wanted you to know where I had really gone in case . . ."

Hana lowered her eyes. "In case you never came back."

"I never meant to put you in any danger. Finding your mother was my duty, not yours. I taught you that appraising the choices brought to the pawnshop required detaching your emotions from your actions and thoughts. I had hoped that you could do the same when it came to examining your own decisions. You should not have tried to find me, Hana. You should have just let me go." His voice filled with tears. "But you were always better at being a good and selfless daughter than a heartless thief who stole pieces of people's souls."

"Otou-san . . ." Hana wept.

"I'm sorry." Toshio embraced her tightly and sobbed into her hair. "For everything."

Her tea had gone cold when Hana ran out of tears. Still, she cupped it in her hands, trying to borrow some warmth. She could not think about her reunion with her mother without her insides turning to ice. "Where is she?"

"Your mother is taking care of the children," Toshio said, his eyes swollen from the tears he had shed. "She will return at sunset."

"The creature . . ." Hana said. "It called me its sister."

"The *children,*" Toshio said, emphasizing the word, "know all about you. Your mother speaks of you to them often. She hasn't forgotten you, Hana. But . . ."

"But what?" Hana said.

"She has forgotten other things. The years here have changed her."

"Changed her? How?"

"She created this copy of the pawnshop from memory, but she does not remember much else. She remembers our family, but she cannot recall the circumstances that led her here. She does not know that she stole a choice, or anything about the day the Shiikuin came to the pawnshop and changed her sentence from a swift, merciful death to exile here." Toshio looked at Hana. "But I am guessing that you do. You followed the same clues I did to get here. Haruto must have folded time for you too."

Hana flinched at the mention of Haruto's name. She had

come all this way to find someone who did not want to be found, and it was Haruto who had paid the price for her foolishness.

"What's wrong?" Toshio said. "Did something happen to Haruto?"

Hana squeezed her teacup. "His hands . . ."

Toshio paled and clenched his fists. "Tell me what happened, Hana."

"The Shiikuin broke them when they found out that Haruto was helping me."

Toshio's hands trembled on the table. "This is all my fault. I should have never gone to him. Haruto is too good and generous of a man, and I took advantage of his kindness."

"It was his choice," Keishin said. "He said that he owed you a great debt."

Toshio swallowed back tears. "He owes me nothing. What I did for him was only to try to right a wrong that would never have happened if . . ."

"If what?" Hana said.

Toshio's chest caved in as though he were shriveling from the inside. He walked away from the table looking more feeble and older than Hana had ever seen him.

"Otou-san?" Hana stood up and followed him.

"I failed him, Hana."

"How?"

"One choice. One soul. It is a simple duty and I failed it. The choice your mother stole . . . it was meant for Haruto."

CHAPTER FIFTY-ONE

Souls and Skin

Twenty-one years ago

The infant boy's cry filled the Horishi's home just as Toshio's month-old daughter's wail had done earlier that day. When Toshio laid Hana over the Horishi's table, he had not given a single thought to how she would feel when her fate was carved into her small body. His blinding focus from the moment she was born had been to give her a soul. But when the first of countless needles pierced his little girl's skin and made her cry, Hana's pain became his own. That's how he knew that the mother of the crying boy was suffering too. But he also knew that her pain far exceeded his. And that it was all his fault.

Toshio knelt on the ground with his head touching the floor, prostrating himself at Masako's feet. The weight of his failure crushed him, pushing him deeper into the Horishi's mat. He stayed silent. There were no words that could ever atone for the choice he had lost, the choice that was meant to be Masako's son's soul.

"Stand up," Masako said, cradling her wailing baby. "I want you to look at my son and tell him how you have cursed him. Stand up!"

Toshio slowly pushed himself to his feet. "I . . . I am deeply sorry. My wife did not mean to—"

"Your wife has already paid for her crime. She is dead. You

are not. Tell me, what is your punishment for failing to keep Haruto's soul safe? Who must I see for my revenge?" Masako wept, her tears falling on Haruto's face. "You and your daughter will go on with your lives as though nothing has happened, but I will have to live the rest of my life knowing that you killed my son. You have taken everything from me." She hurled herself at Toshio and pounded her fist against his chest.

Toshio braced himself, accepting every blow. Though it was Chiyo who had stolen the choice, it had been his responsibility to keep it safe. He deserved worse than Masako's fists.

"It is time." The Horishi approached them. "Give me the creature."

Masako staggered back, clutching Haruto. "I won't let you take him. He isn't a monster. He is my son. His father is dead. Haruto is all I have left."

"It does not belong to you." The Horishi moved closer to Masako.

"No." Masako backed into a wall. "Stay away."

Toshio blocked the Horishi's path. "Stop. Do not make yourself a liar."

The Horishi paused. "I never lie."

"You will, if you take Haruto," Toshio said. "It rained when I brought Hana home from here. I saw the name you wrote on her skin. Haruto is Hana's fate."

Masako gasped. "Is this true, Horishi-san?"

"I do not control what the ink writes. Neither do I know the reasons behind the direction it chooses to steer my hand. I merely hold the needle through which it flows." The Horishi turned to Haruto. "And collect that which has no soul."

"I will find another soul for Haruto," Toshio said. "I just need more time."

"Every choice is promised as soon as it is pawned," the Horishi said. "You cannot steal from one child to give to another."

Thoughts swirled inside Toshio's head. "What if I did not have to steal it?"

"What do you mean?" Masako held a crying Haruto tight. "Where would you get the soul?"

"From me."

Toshio lay on his back on the Horishi's table and bit down on the piece of wood the Horishi had given him.

"Are you certain that you want to do this?" the Horishi said.

Toshio nodded. If he spoke, he was afraid he was going to change his mind.

"I can give you something for the pain. This will not be swift." The Horishi sharpened a blade.

Toshio shook his head. He wanted to feel every slice the Horishi made into him. This, he convinced himself, was the reason Haruto's name was on Hana's skin. Haruto was his daughter's fate. And the sentence for his crime. Giving up his soul to ensure that Hana did not stray from her inked path seemed more than a fitting punishment for his failures.

"Masuda-sama does not wish me to take all of it," the Horishi said.

Toshio spat out the bit and sat up. "What? Why? You will need every drop of ink that you can get from my skin to map Haruto's fate."

"She is a mother." The Horishi heated the knife over a candle. "Her rage has not blinded her to your daughter's wellbeing. Hana has already lost her mother. Masuda-sama does not wish to take her father from her too."

"But . . ."

"I will take enough from you to give Haruto a good life, and you will have enough left to raise Hana until she is ready to take over the pawnshop when you retire."

"How much time will Haruto have?"

"His fate is tied to yours. Unless his life is cut short by illness or mishap, he will have one year with Hana."

"Hana will not be alone after I'm gone . . ."

"Masuda-sama will have her son, and Hana will have her husband," the Horishi said. "And her father. For a while."

Toshio gripped the edge of the table.

"Do you wish to proceed?" the Horishi asked.

Toshio placed the bit in his mouth and lay down. He squeezed his eyes shut, not wanting to scream when the Horishi took his skin.

CHAPTER FIFTY-TWO

A Reunion

The Horishi's cuts outlined the scar like the frayed edges of an old map. It covered Toshio's entire back. Hana stared at the scar, unable to speak. Haruto and her father each had one year to live because her mother had not cared about anyone but herself.

Toshio refastened his robe around his waist. "Haruto owes me no debt. It is I who owe him. He has but a fraction of the life he was meant to live. My failure stole the years he was supposed to have with you."

"It was not your fault, Otou-san," Hana said, her voice hard. "It was my mother's. She was the one who was selfish. She did not just steal Haruto's life. She stole yours."

"That was never her intention."

"I do not care what her intentions were. Why did you even want to find her, Otou-san? A monster belongs with monsters."

"Toshio?" a woman's voice called from behind Hana.

Hana turned. The woman she had known only from one faded photograph stood in front of her. Hana staggered into Keishin. He clasped her by the shoulders, keeping her steady. "Okaa-san . . ."

"Toshio?" Chiyo's eyes flew from Hana to Keishin. "What's going on? Who are these people?"

Toshio led Chiyo to a seat. "You must be tired. You should sit down."

Chiyo lowered herself onto a floor cushion and smiled up at Toshio. "Are they clients? The pawnshop has not had any clients in so long. But you are here now. That is why business is better."

"They are not clients, Chiyo," Toshio said. "This is Keishin."

Keishin bowed.

"And this is Hana," Toshio said gently.

Chiyo tilted her chin. "Hana?"

Hana pulled her shoulders back, refusing to bow. "Yes."

Chiyo smiled. "You have the same name as our daughter. May I offer you some tea?"

"Chiyo . . ." Toshio took a seat next to her and clasped her hand. "She *is* our daughter."

Chiyo laughed. "Forgive my husband. He is confused. Our daughter is still a baby."

Toshio took her hand. "No, Chiyo. Hana is not a child anymore. She has grown up."

"That is not possible. I remember Hana. I know who my daughter is. I have told all her brothers and sisters about her. I was holding her in my arms when—" Chiyo yanked her hand away from Toshio. She wrapped her arms around herself, rocking in her seat. "Hana is a baby. You are wrong. Hana is a baby." She pointed at Hana. "And you are a liar. Liar! Get out of my house! Get out!"

Toshio hurried over to Hana. "She is just in shock. I will explain everything to her."

Hana shook her head. "I should just leave. You were right. Coming here was a mistake."

"No. Don't go. She doesn't recognize you, but she will. I

promise. Wait in your room. I will talk to her. I will make her understand. Please, Hana. She is still your mother."

It was strange being in her old room again, surrounded by things that were supposed to be familiar but were not. It was like looking at her mother's face. The mother she found was both the woman in the picture in her head and a stranger. In this version of the pawnshop, her room was still the space where everything that did not have a place to live anywhere else in the pawnshop found a home. She ran her fingers over stacks of books and overflowing boxes of odds and ends, feeling an affinity with things that didn't belong anywhere.

"Are you all right?" Keishin asked. "I'm sorry that she didn't recognize you."

"I did not recognize her either. She is like those creatures outside. She looks like my mother, but she isn't. I will never forgive her for what she did to Haruto and my father. I wish I never came here. I was a fool."

"Loving your parents and wanting them to be safe doesn't make you a fool."

"It does when all this time, I should have been caring for only one of them. My father never hid my mother's crime from me. I knew that she was a thief, and yet I didn't care. I justified her actions. I told myself that she did not deserve to be punished for what she did and that the Shiikuin were cruel. They were not. They were too kind. My mother has a life here. A family. A home. Haruto will have none of that. And my father, he is too blind to see that she is stealing the little time that he has left."

Toshio burst into the room, his face pale. "Hana . . ."

"What's wrong?" Hana stood up.

"The girl who found you . . ."

Hana frowned. "What about her?"

"She is back."

"Are we in danger?" Keishin said. "I thought that you could control them."

"She is not here to harm you. She came to warn us. The Shiikuin are in the tunnels."

Keishin and Hana flew down the steps of the pawnshop. The young girl who had led Toshio to them in the garden sobbed against Chiyo's breast. But something about her was different. She had aged.

"Is that the same girl?" Hana stared at her face. "She looks like she's ten years old now."

"Time goes by differently for the children here," Toshio said.

"Hush." Chiyo stroked the girl's cheek and gently re-tucked a loose pink flower into her hair bun. "Hush. Don't cry. Your brothers did not mean to scare you. Thank you for coming here to tell me that they have arrived. They hardly ever visit. I will make some tea for all of us."

"Brothers? Tea?" Hana said. "What is she talking about?"

"There is no time for this now," Toshio said. "You need to leave before they get here."

"Enough. I'm done with lies and secrets. I am not going anywhere until you tell me what's going on."

"It is difficult to explain," Toshio said.

"The Shiikuin are my children." Chiyo held the girl's hand.

Hana froze. "What did you say?"

"The children have no souls, Hana," Toshio said. "They grow up but can never die. In time, parts of their bodies will wear out and they will have to . . . replace them."

"With metal parts . . ." Keishin said.

"Chiyo revealed the truth she had learned about the Shiikuin when I found her," Toshio said. "But the Shiikuin are different from the children. They have forgotten everything about being human. They must not find you here. You must go."

"What about you?" Hana said.

Toshio put his arm around his wife. "I will stay here."

"Otou-san, please listen to me. This woman . . . she is not my mother. She is not your wife. She's a monster. Leave her."

"You do not understand, Hana."

"I understand that the Shiikuin will kill you if you stay."

"I am dead either way. Let me at least die saving you. There is no life for me to return to. I stole a choice just as your mother did. The Shiikuin will hunt me down until the end of my days."

"They won't. Not if . . ." Hana swallowed hard. "You give them back what they are really after."

"What are you talking about?" Toshio said.

"They would forgive you if you returned the choice you stole."

"I cannot return it. I set it free."

"That is why . . ." Tears quivered in the rims of Hana's eyes. "I brought it with me."

"What do you mean, 'you brought it with you'?" Keishin's throat constricted.

"I told you, Kei . . ." Hana pulled out her mother's glasses and a small mirror from her bag and offered them to Keishin with her head bowed.

This was not how she had planned to tell Keishin the truth. She had thought about what this day would be like since he showed up at the pawnshop, and nothing she had imagined came close to the reality unraveling in front of her. She had hoped that she would be more composed, that she would have the right words to explain exactly why she had done what she did. The only image she had gotten right was what Keishin's face would look like when she told him. All warmth had fled his eyes, replaced by sadness and rage. "Nothing here is as it seems."

CHAPTER FIFTY-THREE

A Bird and a Bus

A few days prior

Toshio could have chosen any of the birds from the vault, but it was the brightest one that caught his eye. He unhooked its cage from the chain dangling from the ceiling, opened it, and carefully took the bird out. Takeda Izumi's glowing choice tilted its head as though asking where it was going. Toshio set it on his shoulder. It looked around nervously, refusing to join the other birds in song.

"Do not worry." Toshio stroked the bird's head. "Everything will be okay."

Toshio threw the empty cage on the floor. The birds fell silent. Takeda Izumi's choice trembled on Toshio's shoulder. Toshio raised his foot over the cage and smashed it to pieces.

Toshio gripped the front door's knob and looked over his shoulder. Shards of glass glinted among the chaos he had left for Hana to find. He had given Hana a story to tell the Shiikuin, a story that would free her from any blame when they discovered that he was missing. He drew a deep breath, twisted the doorknob, and pulled the door open. A dark Tokyo street slept on the other side. Toshio took the bird from his shoulder and let it perch on his finger. He extended his hand outside the door and set the choice free. It flew into the autumn sky without looking back.

❀ *Twenty-eight years before. Or after.*

A seventeen-year-old Izumi stood at a bus stop, waiting for the bus that would take her to the ramen shop where Junichiro worked. There were still a few more minutes before the bus arrived, enough time to buy her favorite sweets from the store across the street. The store owner's son was a pleasant boy with a kind face who always put an extra treat in her bag whenever she dropped by. It was probably one of the last few times she was going to be able to go to the store while hiding her growing belly. Soon, she was no longer going to have clothes that were large enough to keep her secret. She had not yet told Junichiro that he was going to be a father, but she did not doubt that he was going to do the honorable thing. He loved her, and she loved him. He was going to take care of their little family as well as an apprentice cook at a ramen restaurant could.

Izumi held her stomach, thinking of everything she would have to let go of to hold a baby in her arms instead. She had hoped to open a flower shop one day and never have to worry about having enough money for bus fare or sweets. A friend in school had told her that there was one way to keep her dreams. All that was needed was a wire coat hanger.

Izumi glanced down the empty street. The single straight road to the ramen restaurant forked in her mind. Down one path, she watched the bus drive away, leaving her with a life without the boy she loved or the baby in her womb. Down the second, she got on the bus and paid the driver to take her to a life that had an equal chance of being happy as hard. Tears welled in her eyes. She turned on her heel and ran from the bus stop.

A blindingly bright blue bird flew past her. Izumi nearly tripped over her feet. The bird darted back and circled around her. Izumi shielded her eyes. Metal clattered over the pavement. Izumi peeked out from half-open lids and looked around. The bird was gone, and on the ground, glittering in the sun, was the exact amount of coins she needed to take the bus to meet Junichiro. She glanced back at the bus stop. She picked up the coins and stuffed them into her pocket. She walked back to the bus stop, the coins jingling with every step. Their tinkling reminded her of a song that was both happy and sad. The bus came to a stop in front of her. Izumi stared at the open door.

"Are you getting on?" the driver asked.

"Yes, yes. Sorry," she said, hurrying on board.

Izumi sat at the back of the bus and looked out the window. She rubbed her belly and thought about the choice she had just made, the flower shop she was never going to open, and the secret that she and Junichiro were now going to share. She tucked a loose silver lock of hair behind her ear and wondered if their child would take after her or him.

CHAPTER FIFTY-FOUR

The Reflection in the Mirror

The mirror shattered on the pawnshop's floor, scattering jagged pieces of the truth in every direction. Keishin stared at the shards. It was almost funny how his strange adventure with Hana began and ended with broken glass. When they met, Hana had cut her foot on one of the broken pieces littered across the pawnshop. Now she had stabbed him with the sharpest of them in his back. He looked down, expecting to see it poking out of his chest, but it had lodged in his heart, shredding him from the inside with every breath he took.

He finally understood why the weather had never liked him. He had always lived in a world that didn't want him there. He pulled Chiyo's glasses from his face. "When did you know?" he said, unable to look at Hana.

"The second I opened the pawnshop's front door and saw you," Hana said. "My mother's glasses revealed who you were: the brightest choice I had ever seen."

"You knew who I was all this time and you didn't say anything?" Keishin balled his hands into fists.

"I told you when we met that the only answers I could ever give were lies. But I gave you every chance to walk away. I . . . pushed you away."

"So you've been planning to hand me over to the Shiikuin all this time? Why didn't you just do it when they first showed up at the pawnshop? Why run? Why go through all of the trouble of keeping up this charade?"

"Because I did not know what had happened to my father. You were the only thing that I could use to bargain with the Shiikuin. I could not deliver you to them if I did not know what I was even negotiating for."

"And now you do."

Hana dropped her eyes.

"Is this really what you want, Hana?" Toshio said. "This is not who you are."

"Isn't this what you always wanted me to be? Someone who could lock away her emotions and close a deal without the slightest remorse? You taught me not to make my mother's mistake, to never allow my heart to drive me to take what was never meant to be mine."

"But are your emotions truly locked away?" Toshio said. "Today I saw something in your eyes that I had never seen before. I watched you grow up with Haruto and not once did you look at him the same way you look at this man you are about to betray."

"What I feel and who I care about does not matter. That is what you have told me all my life. Duty comes first. Always."

"Look around you, Hana," Toshio said. "You are not in the pawnshop anymore. We are in an illusion we conjured. We built the bars of this prison and created our own jailers. Have you thought about what would happen if we stopped?"

"Stopped?" Hana said.

"This cycle. What if we stopped giving the Horishi's ink and the Shiikuin power over our lives? What if we stopped collecting souls? That baby in Masako's arms was no different from you, and yet we believed that it did not . . . *could not* have a soul because the Horishi had no ink to dictate its life. Our world buries babies like Haruto alive because we are afraid that we cannot control them. We bury them because they are different and then wonder why they become monsters. And then when the monsters—*our fears*—grow up . . ."

"They come back to control us," Hana said.

"And the cycle goes on," Toshio said. "And so I am going to ask you again. Is this really what you want to do?"

A loud banging on the door thundered over Toshio's voice.

Chiyo fell to her knees and clasped her hands over her ears. "They're here. They've come to sentence me. They're here to take me away. Toshio, I don't want to leave you. I don't want to leave . . ." Chiyo stared at Hana and blinked as though trying to see clearly through a fog. "Hana. It's you. You're here. You're really here."

"Okaa-san . . ." Hana trembled as a dam broke open inside her. A lifetime of loneliness burst out in a flood of hot tears.

The banging on the door grew louder.

Toshio ran to the door and pressed his back against it. "Choose, Hana."

"Wait." Chiyo grabbed a knife from the counter and sliced her arm. "Hana must know the truth."

"Stop!" Hana screamed.

Chiyo dug into the wound with her fingers and pulled out a small blue orb. A tiny ocean glowed inside it. Chiyo pressed the pearl into Hana's hand. "Take this."

The door shook violently.

"Choose, Hana." Toshio pushed his back against the door.

"Otou-san . . ." Hana wept. "I won't leave you."

"This is not about me, Hana. Don't you see? I am already dead. I knew where this path would end when I decided that even just one day with your mother was better than another year of not knowing where she was."

"We made our choice, Hana." Chiyo held Hana in her arms. "Now it is time to make yours."

"No," Keishin said, "it isn't."

Hana turned to him, her eyes brimming. "I—"

"This is *my* choice." Keishin strode toward the door.

Hana grabbed his arm. "What are you doing?"

"I was never meant to be here. I'm a regret. A mistake someone wished to forget." He pulled away from her and looked at Toshio and Chiyo. "But I can make things right."

A talon broke through the pawnshop's door and ripped Toshio's shoulder. Toshio crumpled forward and groaned, clutching the wound. Chiyo screamed.

"Do it now, Hana," Keishin said. "Make your trade."

Hana sprinted to the door, half-blind from tears.

CHAPTER FIFTY-FIVE

Hana's Choice

There is a river that runs between knowing and understanding. Tonight, inside an illusion of her home, Hana crossed it. Though she had long known about how the Shiikuin experienced time differently, it wasn't until she stood between Keishin and the door the Shiikuin were battering down that she glimpsed a fraction of its meaning. Her mother's screams and the Shiikuin's shrieks evaporated the seconds around her, but within the walls of her mind, time slowed to a stop. Hana wondered if this reprieve was a kindness given to those who hovered close to danger or death, a moment to sift clarity from chaos or make peace with their end. In this brief eternity, Hana found herself standing in a place that was as familiar as it was not. The pawnshop she had grown up in looked different from the opposite side of the counter.

"Thank you for choosing to visit us today." A woman who was Hana's mirror image smiled. "I am certain that you will find that we make very fair, if not generous, offers at this pawnshop. What choice would you like to pawn?"

Hana inhaled sharply, taking a step back. Her father had trained her to handle every possible scenario as the pawnshop's new owner but neglected to provide any instruction on how to be her own client. "No. This is a mistake. I . . . I have nothing."

"You would not be here if you had no need of our services."

Hana shook her head. "I do not have any regrets."

The woman with Hana's face leaned forward and looked into her eyes as though reading the pages of a book. "Ah. I was mistaken." She bowed. "You have nothing to exchange. Please forgive me."

"You do not have to apologize. I understand. This is your first day." Had the woman behind the counter been real, Hana might have bothered to tell her that a choice worth more than all the pawnshop's silk-wrapped boxes of green tea waited to be made at the end of this imagined respite. Collecting a choice this rare would have made the woman's father beyond proud. There was nothing more valuable than a choice that honored one's duty. But as this conversation was nothing more than wisps of fancy, Hana settled on being polite. "Perhaps I will return when I have something for you."

"You won't," her other self said with a well-rehearsed smile.

Hana wrinkled her brow. "Why not?"

"Because a decision worth trading," the woman said, "requires being able to tell the difference between a real choice and cowardice in a clever disguise."

"Hana!" a ragged voice ruptured Hana's thoughts.

Hana jolted. Time resumed its course, sweeping everything in its current.

"Trade me now," Keishin pleaded. "Before it's too late."

"You are right, Kei. You are your mother's regret." The Shiikuin shrieked over her words, but Hana did not hear them. She dried her tears and pulled her shoulders back as she had been trained to do in front of clients. The view from the other side of the counter had reminded her of who she was. She was the pawnshop's new owner and her job was to collect regrets, not make them. She glanced at her father, her bleary eyes passing a message she was confident that he would understand. Silence had always been their language, and Hana had never needed words less. Toshio nodded back, a tear finding his small smile. She grabbed Keishin's hand. "But you will not be mine."

The young girl who had warned them about the Shiikuin led Hana and Keishin through the garden to a shortcut into the tunnels. Hana sprinted, trying to outrun her thoughts. They gave chase faster than the Shiikuin did, trying to drag her back to the pawnshop and her parents. Her mother's last words to her echoed louder, screaming for her to run.

The girl pushed a bush aside, revealing a small hole in the cavern's wall. "The tunnels are through here."

"Thank you." Hana hugged her. "I never got to ask you your name."

"Hana." The child smiled up at her. "Okaa-san calls all of us by your name."

Hana and Keishin felt their way through the dark, through a tunnel that was narrow and barely high enough to stand in. Hana was grateful that the darkness hid his face. She couldn't bear to look him in the eye. "Kei . . ." she said when she found the courage to speak.

"Don't, Hana. Just don't."

"There were so many times that I wanted to tell you the truth."

"But you didn't. Our entire time together was a lie."

"My feelings for you were real. I know that now. It is true that in the beginning, I had every intention of handing you to the Shiikuin. When I first saw you through my mother's glasses, all I saw was a chance to end the nightmare I had woken up to. By some incredible miracle, Takeda Izumi's missing choice had walked through my front door. Every lesson my father had instilled in me about dealing with our clients . . . manipulating them . . . making them feel at ease . . . making them feel like the decisions they were making at the pawnshop were entirely their own . . . they came alive like instinct."

"That's bullshit, Hana." Keishin twisted around, his voice quivering with tears. "That's bullshit and you know it. It wasn't instinct. It was a choice. You keep saying that the map on your skin keeps you from making decisions of your own, but that's exactly what you did when you chose to lie to me. You strung me along, letting me care for you, letting me believe that you cared for me too."

Keishin's words struck Hana harder than any fist, hitting a spot north of her diaphragm just below her lungs, in the exact square inch where the softest part of her soul lived. Tears boiled behind her eyelids. "I do care for you, Kei. More than I planned and more than I wanted. Despite convincing myself that I had to turn you over to the Shiikuin, I could not bring myself to do it because . . ."

"Because what, Hana? Because you realized that I wasn't a good enough bargaining chip to get your family back into the good graces of the Shiikuin? Because you got cold feet? I'm all ears. I'm looking forward to hearing something out of your mouth that isn't a lie."

"I deserve your anger. Your hate. I know that there is nothing that I can say that will ever make you want to forgive me, but I want you to know that I chose you over bargaining for the safety of my father, my mother, and myself not because I was scared I was going to fail, but because I was certain that I was going to succeed."

"What are you talking about?"

"The Shiikuin would have spared my life for the same reason that they had spared Haruto's. No one else can run the pawnshop. No one else can collect souls for our world. The Shiikuin would have made me suffer to make an example out of me, but they would let me live."

"If you knew this, then why didn't you hand me over to them?"

"Because in a vault full of choices, you were blinding. You are meant to do great things, Kei. Not for your mother. Not for revenge. For yourself. You will find answers to all of your questions, and those answers will change your world. You have no reason to trust me, but I swear to you that I will do whatever it takes to get you safely back home."

The empty Indonesian restaurant was as dark as the tunnel he and Hana were groping their way through. Keishin had never seen it this way. He blindly shoved away tables and chairs, searching for his old friend. "Ramesh? Are you in here? Ramesh?"

The echo of Keishin's own voice answered him. He slumped on the floor next to a toppled chair and screamed at the ceiling. "Where are you?"

A firm hand squeezed Kei's shoulder. "Get up."

"Ramesh!" Keishin jumped to his feet and threw his arms around him. "You're still here."

"Where else would I be? I live here, remember?"

"Here." Keishin spat the word out. "What does that even mean? In my head? My memories? I just found out that up until a few days ago, I was a glowing bird in a cage."

Ramesh frowned, leaning heavily on his walking stick. "Nonsense. Nothing has changed. You're still you. This is still your mind. And for god's sake, please switch the lights on. I nearly walked into a wall."

"You don't understand—"

"Understand what? What's real and what isn't? I think that more than anyone, I know the difference between the two. I am imaginary. You are not. I cannot exist outside of you. You, meanwhile, are in a tunnel, running for your life."

"Hana lied to me, Ramesh. Everything was a lie."

"If that were the case, then you wouldn't have come rushing in here, overturning tables and chairs, shouting for me like some kind of madman," Ramesh said. "You turned off all the lights because you didn't want to see the truth."

"What truth?"

"Switch the lights on and see for yourself."

Moonlight washed over the wildflowers, making them almost seem to glow. Keishin and Hana climbed out of the tunnel and collapsed onto the field. Hana rubbed the bruise on her head.

"How's your head?" Keishin asked softly.

"You do not need to be polite or talk to me," Hana said. "You can pretend that I am not here."

"I think that's going to be rather difficult to do considering that there are only two of us here. Running for our lives might be more efficient if we coordinate. That's just a theory, of course. I could be wrong."

"I cannot tell if you have forgiven me or if you just hate me even more."

Keishin pretended to scan the field. He had reluctantly done as Ramesh had asked and faced what he had hidden in the dark.

At the edges of the familiar dining room's warm lights, giant steel bars surrounded him. What he had thought had been a refuge was a cage no different from those that hung inside Hana's vault. Keishin stood next to Ramesh, his mouth agape. "Has . . . it always been this way?"

A sad smile settled on Ramesh's lips. "You've spent your life observing the world from a distance. Always objective, always detached. Science was the cage you chose to live in when your mother abandoned you, a place where nothing could hurt you like she did. Within the confines of its laws, you felt safe."

He pointed to a gap in the bars where the cage's door was wide open. Across from it, Hana stood at a pawnshop's doorway. "But now you are not bound by its rules. You are free, Kei. To forgive. To hate. To love a woman who betrayed you . . . and sacrificed her family to save your life."

A knot formed in Keishin's throat. Freedom, at its most absolute, was more terrifying than the Shiikuin.

"What you felt for Hana was not a lie," Ramesh said. "And now, like Hana, you have a choice to make."

"Kei?" Hana's voice found its way into Keishin's thoughts. "Did you hear what I said?"

"No, sorry," he lied. "I was just trying to figure out how to get back. I don't think that we'll be able to hitch a ride on any rumors from here unless wildflowers like to gossip."

A Shiikuin's shriek tore through the field.

Keishin and Hana scrambled to their feet, their backs pressed against each other. A chorus of shrieks echoed around them.

Keishin's eyes darted around the field. "Where are they?"

"Everywhere."

七転び八起き

PART FOUR

Fall seven times,
stand up eight.

CHAPTER FIFTY-SIX

A Gathering of Cranes

Soft tapping noises, like raindrops hitting the ground, filled the air. The rain, Keishin thought, had finally decided to show up. He applauded its timing. It could wash away the blood from the field when the Shiikuin were done with him. He waited to get drenched. A small paper crane hit him on the nose. Another struck him on the left shoulder. Keishin glanced up. Origami cranes of every color circled above him like a storm cloud and fell like rain over the field. "What in the world . . ."

The shrieks of the Shiikuin grew louder.

Hana picked up a crane from the ground. "This is Haruto's work."

"What are the cranes doing here? Why did he send them?"

The carpet of cranes stirred over the wildflowers. They flapped their wings and lifted off the ground. They swarmed Hana and Keishin, whipping up the wind. Keishin could see nothing through the blur of paper wings. He took comfort in knowing that the thick curtain of cranes worked both ways. The Shiikuin could not hunt what they could not see.

Hana pointed to the ground. "Look."

Keishin looked down. His feet hovered an inch over the tallest wildflower. The siege of cranes thickened, sweeping Hana and Keishin up to the sky.

* * *

It took a while for Keishin to get used to drifting through the night on a cloud of paper cranes. The cranes bobbed and shifted beneath him, taking turns carrying his and Hana's weight. He imagined that flying beneath Hana was more difficult. Her burden was heavier than his. He had not left his parents at the mercy of the Shiikuin. "I'm sorry about your parents."

"They were together in the end. Like they wanted."

"They could still be alive."

Hana shook her head. "I need to believe that they are not. It is easier to put grief on hold than to sit still. If I allowed myself to think that they were still alive, I would jump off these cranes, run back through the tunnels, and try to save them. Believing that they are gone allows me to tell myself that I will grieve them when you are safe."

"Hana . . ."

"My parents made their choice, and I made mine. They chose each other, and I chose to finally do the right thing."

A paper house built on a sharp cliff came into view as the cranes descended. The moon cast a pale glow over its crisp white paper roof and walls. "Why are they bringing us to Haruto's home?" Keishin said. "Isn't Haruto supposed to be hiding at his mother's house?"

"Maybe he thinks that the Shiikuin believe that we would never dare to come back here."

The cranes hovered over the ground, allowing Keishin and Hana to hop off their backs. They took flight and scattered over the cliff.

"I wonder how Haruto made all of those cranes," Keishin said. "His hands couldn't have healed that fast."

"There is only one way that could have restored his hands that quickly, but I am hoping that he was not foolish enough to try it."

"What way?"

"The healing stall at the Night Market. Their prices . . . are too high."

Haruto stood outside his home and waved at Hana with perfectly healed hands. "How was the ride?"

Hana stared at his hands. "Please tell me that you did not go to the—"

"I did and it is done," Haruto said.

"You fool." Hana gritted her teeth. "What payment did they ask for?"

Haruto folded his arms over his chest. "I imagined this reunion was going to begin with you saying, 'Thank you for saving our lives,' and me responding, 'You're welcome.' "

"Thank you for rescuing us, Haruto," Keishin said. "I mean it."

"You are welcome, Keishin." Haruto turned to Hana. "See? Was that not a lot more pleasant?"

"Tell me what you paid for your hands," Hana demanded.

"Whatever I paid for them is my business, not yours." He plucked a piece of paper from his sleeve and threw it in the air. He flicked his hand its way. The paper folded into a butterfly in midair. "I was even able to negotiate for a few improvements."

"Haruto—"

"Enough, Hana. We should go inside." A crane flew over and perched on his shoulder. "The cranes have told me that the Shiikuin are still hunting you down."

* * *

Haruto sat with steepled fingers as Keishin and Hana filled him in on what had happened at the tunnels. "And your father?" he said, struggling to keep his voice even. "What happened to him?"

Hana swallowed back tears. "He's—"

"He held back the Shiikuin so that we could escape," Keishin said. "We don't know what happened after we left."

"Then he could still be alive." Haruto looked at Hana hopefully.

Hana lowered her eyes.

"That is a possibility," Keishin said.

"We have answered your questions," Hana said. "Now you must answer mine."

"I told you, what I paid for my hands is not your concern."

"Then tell me how you knew where to find us."

Haruto set his palms on the table. "I heard the oddest thing when I went to the Night Market to heal my hands . . . whispers about a man from the other world."

"You followed the rumor," Keishin said.

"My cranes did. The rumor was too fast for me, and I gave up any hope of catching a train. I sent my cranes to track you down. I had a feeling that the rumor you rode was only a one-way trip."

"You saved our lives," Hana said. "Thank you."

"Finally. Some gratitude."

Hana managed a hint of a smile. "Enjoy it."

"What do you plan to do next?" Haruto said.

"I am going to make sure that Keishin returns home."

"And after that? The Shiikuin will not let your crimes go unpunished."

"I have not thought that far yet." Hana dug her hands in her pockets. Her fingers brushed against a cold orb. Hana pulled it out and wiped her mother's blood off of it with her sleeve.

"A kioku pearl." Haruto eyed the ocean inside the gem. "Freshly picked. Whose is it?"

"My mother's. She gave it to me before we escaped. She said that it would show me the truth."

"The truth?" Haruto leaned forward. "About what?"

Hana set the pearl in the middle of the table. It began to spin and grow bright, churning the ocean inside it. Rising waves cast shadows over the room's paper walls. The shadows morphed, weaving a story from darkness and light.

CHAPTER FIFTY-SEVEN

The Choice Ishikawa Chiyo Stole

❀ *Twenty-one years ago*

The map on Chiyo's skin glowed in the rain and came to life over her reflection in the pawnshop's pond. She traced the map with her eyes, knowing fully where every single road tattooed on her body led. She ran into the garden behind the pawnshop each time the sky grew dark, nursing the tiniest hope that one day, if she stood in the rain long enough, a storm was going to reveal a path she had missed.

"Chiyo." Toshio walked up from behind her and held a coat over her head. "You're soaked. Come inside."

"Just a little longer." Chiyo held out her hands to catch the rain.

"Come. I will make you some tea."

Chiyo looked at her husband and watched his fate glow on his skin. She stroked his wet cheek, running her thumb over the path that led to her name. "How do you do it?"

"Do what?"

"Be content. How do you keep yourself from wanting more than what the Horishi has written?"

"I am sorry." The rain streaked over Toshio's face and made it impossible for Chiyo to tell if he was crying.

"For what?"

"For not making you as happy as you make me."

"You do make me happy, Toshio."

"Just not enough," Toshio said, leading her back inside.

Chiyo waited for Toshio to fall asleep before she slid out of bed and crept downstairs. She took great care to avoid the stairway's last step. The storm howling outside would have kept her husband from hearing the creak the step made, but she did not want to take any risks. Toshio was not going to understand why she needed to open the pawnshop's vault in the middle of the night.

Chiyo could not get the choice that had been pawned that day out of her mind. It was the brightest one she had ever seen. Toshio had told her that if that choice had been made, it could have changed the world. Chiyo had lain in bed, listening to Toshio's breath, counting down the minutes until she could see the choice again.

Her fingers swiftly found the notch on the side of the bookcase in the dark. She pushed it and let the bookcase swing open. The birds in the vault greeted her with a song. Chiyo hurried inside the vault, forgetting to shut the door. A bird perched in a cage to her right glowed brighter than all the rest. Chiyo unhooked its cage with no other plan than to get a closer look. The bird frantically flew around the cage and slammed into its bars. "I won't hurt you," Chiyo said, trying to calm the bird down. "I promise."

The bird crashed into the top of the cage and set the other birds in the vault into a chirping frenzy.

"No . . . no . . . please be quiet. You'll wake Toshio." Chiyo glanced at the vault's wide-open door. She hugged the birdcage to her chest and ran out.

* * *

The bird grew quiet on her desk. Chiyo gently lifted the silk tea box wrapping she had thrown over its cage. The bird calmly preened its glowing blue feathers. When Chiyo took off her glasses and set them on top of the month's record book, a bottle of sake took the bird's place.

Chiyo reached inside the cage and carefully pulled it out. This bottle contained all the sake its former owner never drank, on all the nights that she had refused invitations to have a life outside her gray work cubicle. She had a plan and schedule for herself and refused to be distracted. In time, her gray workspace grew larger. Eventually, it turned into a corner office on the building's top floor. The invitations grew fewer and farther between the closer she got to the top. One day, they stopped coming. The woman sat in her office every night after everyone had gone home, wondering what kind of life she might have had if she had believed that she was worthy of rest. She imagined the conversations she would have shared, the people she might have met, the man she could have fallen in love with, and the family they might have had. She liked to think about the names she would have given her children. She was especially fond of the name she had picked for her daughter.

Chiyo stared at the bottle of sake, envying her client. Regret was a luxury no one in her world had. Chiyo wondered what it tasted like. She raised the bottle to her lips, telling herself that no one would ever know if she took just one sip.

"Chiyo?" Toshio walked over to her desk. "What are you doing down here?"

Chiyo yawned and stretched her arms over her head. Glass glinted in the corner of her vision. Chiyo rubbed her eyes and blinked. An empty bottle of sake lay on its side. "No . . ." Chiyo gasped, remembering, in a flurry of images, how a sip of sake had turned into many, the last sip the longest of all.

"What is this?" Toshio picked up the bottle and set his glasses on his nose. Toshio's hand shook and dropped the bottle as though it were on fire. It shattered on the floor.

"Forgive me . . ." Chiyo said.

"Chiyo, what have you done?"

"I . . . I took something that wasn't mine." She pressed her hand over her belly and felt, in a way beyond what any words could ever explain, the path she had been denied growing inside her. "And her name is Hana."

CHAPTER FIFTY-EIGHT

A Choice Named Hana

The waves of the tiny ocean inside the pearl grew still. The orb dimmed but continued to hold the three people seated around it in its grasp. Keishin was the first to break away. "Hana . . ." he stammered, trying to remember how to speak.

Hana's eyes flooded with tears. "This can't be true."

Keishin clasped her hand. Hana clung to him just as tightly.

"I understand now," Haruto said quietly.

"Understand what?" Hana lifted her head.

"Why you chose *him*."

Hana let go of Keishin's hand. "Haruto . . ."

"I think that this is a conversation that the two of you should have on your own." Keishin stood up. "I'll be outside if you need me," he said, gently touching Hana's shoulder before he left the room.

"You and he are the same, Hana." Haruto's fingers flitted over the spot where the Horishi had tattooed Hana's name on his arm. "Your name is on my skin, but greater gods have carved your fates into your bones. You and I were never meant to be. In truth, I did not require your mother's memory to know this. I needed it only to help me find the will to admit it to myself. I did not make a mistake when I agreed to pay the price for healing my hands."

"What did you pay them, Haruto?"

"Nothing. Yet. I negotiated for the payment to be collected after the cranes brought you back. I needed to see you one last time."

"Last time?" Hana gripped Haruto's sleeve. "What are you talking about? What have you done?"

"I did what I needed to do. My hands were shattered. Without them, I was less than nothing. I had no purpose or duty. I had no life. The vendor at the healing stall told me that he could fix my hands, but at great expense. I possessed only one thing that precious. My memories of you. After you leave, I will return to the Night Market and surrender all of them."

The color drained from Hana's face. "I cannot let you do this."

"Why not? The ink the Horishi took from your father was not enough to write a full life for me. Your father told you that I only have one year left. Let me live what remains of it without longing for something I cannot have. If you cannot give me your love, then at least allow me to find peace."

Piercing shrieks cut through the paper walls of Haruto's home.

Haruto jumped to his feet. "Shiikuin."

Keishin ran through the door. "They're here."

"How many are there?" Hana said.

"Too many." Keishin bolted the paper door. "We need to get out of here. They'll rip through these walls."

"My paper is stronger than you think," Haruto said. "And they will not have to rip through any walls if you let them in. Open the door, Keishin."

"Open the door? Have you lost your mind?" Keishin said.

"When I give you the signal, run through that door," Haruto said.

"What door?" Keishin said.

Haruto waved his hand at the wall facing the cliff. The paper ripped and folded into a door. "That one."

"There's a hundred-foot drop behind that door," Keishin said.

"Trust me," Haruto said. "You won't fall."

"*You?*" Hana said. "Aren't you coming with us?"

Haruto took her in his arms and kissed the top of her head. "Neither of you belongs in this world. You should not have to die here."

"What are you saying?" Hana pulled away from him.

"I'm saying that I changed my mind. Dying while I remember you is better than living a day without knowing your name." Haruto pulled the front door open.

Seven Shiikuin burst into his home.

"Now, Hana!" Haruto flicked his wrist at the door facing the cliff. It folded open, revealing a sheer drop.

"No!" Hana screamed as the Shiikuin closed in.

Keishin tackled her by the waist, hurling them through the door and into thin air.

A sea of cranes broke their fall. They carried Keishin and Hana on their backs past the cliff's edge and up to the sky. Hana scrambled to the edge of the cranes, scanning the ground for Haruto's home. The paper house shook and began to fold itself. The Shiikuin shrieked from inside it.

"No!" Hana screamed as the house shrank with every fold. "What is he doing?"

Keishin pulled her back from the edge. "Keeping you safe."

Hana trembled as she watched the house fold, over and over again, until all that remained was an empty cliff and the memory of the paper home and the man who used to live in it.

CHAPTER FIFTY-NINE

A Thousand Water Moons

One crane lingered, pecking at a pebble by Hana's feet. Hana crouched to pick it up, but it flew away before she could catch it. It flapped its paper wings and climbed up to the sky, joining the other cranes as they disappeared behind the clouds.

"They're gone." Hana stared down the road Haruto's cranes had delivered them to. The pawnshop was a few steps away, but she could not find the strength nor the will to move her feet. "He's gone. I have no one left."

"Come with me," Keishin said.

"What?"

"Come with me to my world . . . *our* world."

"I don't belong there."

"You don't belong here either. There's nothing left for you here, Hana. Do you really want to spend the rest of your life running from the Shiikuin?"

"I don't have a choice."

"You have more choices than you've ever had in your life. Left. Right. Up. Down. You can go anywhere. Be anyone. All you have to do is walk through a door. With me."

"It is not that simple."

"Why not?"

"Because we will never let you go." A chorus of shrill voices spilled out of the mouths of the two Shiikuin standing at the end of the road.

Hana and Keishin raced through the pawnshop as the Shiikuin's shrieks grew louder behind them. Hana yanked the front door open. Blinding rain blew through the doorway, soaking the pawnshop's floor.

"Go!" Hana yelled over the storm.

Rain lashed at Keishin. He held out his hand to her. "Come with me."

A Shiikuin's talons closed around Hana's arm. Keishin threw himself at the Shiikuin and wrestled it to the floor. The Shiikuin slashed at his face, slicing his cheek open.

"Kei!" Hana ran to him.

A door slammed over her voice. A lock clicked shut.

Hana twisted around. The second Shiikuin turned from the locked door, an illusion of a sneer curling over its mask.

The other Shiikuin broke away from Keishin and stood next to the Shiikuin blocking the door. "There is no way out," they chorused.

"But there is a way down." Hana grabbed Keishin by the hand and dove into the rain puddle on the pawnshop's floor.

Golden moons shimmered above the water. Hana and Keishin swam up to them. They broke through the surface and found a rubber raft floating close by. Keishin clambered onto the raft and helped Hana climb on board. They lay back, completely dry. Keishin stared up at the sky of golden moons. The light detectors were much closer to the water's surface than in the memory he had borrowed from his colleague. The Super-

Kamiokande's water tank was nearly full, and if he stood on his toes, he could touch the glass bulbs.

"How did we get here? I thought that puddles could only take you to places in your—" Keishin caught himself. "In the other world."

"The puddle we dove into was not from that world. It was from this one. I was not sure that it was going to work. I just prayed that it would understand me when I told it to take us to someplace safe."

Panic flashed in Keishin's eyes. "Does this mean the Shiikuin can use the puddle too?"

"I'm counting on it."

"You *want* the Shiikuin to follow us? Why?"

"Because I am tired of running. I told you when you first took me here that this was a beautiful trap." Hana grabbed an oar and handed it to Keishin. "Now we get to use it."

Talons broke through the water on both sides of the boat. Hana shoved a Shiikuin with the oar, keeping it from surfacing. Keishin slammed his oar into the Shiikuin on his side. The Shiikuin shrieked, their voices garbled by the water. Each time they clawed at the surface, Keishin and Hana beat them down.

"How long can they keep this up?" Keishin panted, striking the Shiikuin on the head. Its mask cracked, revealing the face decaying beneath it. Scraps of metal covered a hole where a nose should have been. "Why haven't they drowned yet?"

"Because they can't."

"The Shiikuin can't die . . ." Keishin said, remembering what Toshio had told them. "They just change parts when they wear down."

"Metal parts." Hana struck the Shiikuin's shoulder.

"If you're hoping that the water will dissolve them like that wrench I told you about, it's not going to happen." Keishin shoved the Shiikuin from the raft. "At least not before our arms give out."

The water grew still. Keishin held the oar above his head, waiting for the Shiikuin to surface.

Hana settled back into the boat, resting her oar at her side. "They're gone."

"Gone? How?" Keishin scanned the quiet water.

"Time passes differently for the Shiikuin. A lifetime should be more than enough time for the water to consume every piece of metal and skin."

Keishin paddled the raft to an opening at the top of the tank. Hana leaned back, watching the ripples they left in the water.

"Hana." Keishin said her name so softly that Hana wondered if he had spoken or sighed.

"Did you say something?" Hana said, looking up.

"I was just testing something out."

"Testing what?"

"If I still remembered your name. I was worried that I would forget you now that I'm back here. I haven't." Keishin smiled. "I remember everything."

"Maybe it's because you are from both worlds."

"Like you."

"Like me . . ." Hana ran her hand over her arm. "I am still here."

"I suppose this means that we were both right about the weather hating us."

Hana stared at her reflection in the water.

"Hana? Are you okay?"

She drew a heavy breath. "The Shiikuin will never stop hunting us, Kei. It is their duty. They do not know anything else."

"We're almost at the hatch. We're safe."

Hana gripped the sides of the raft. "It's too quiet."

"We're underneath a mountain. It's supposed to be quiet. I would be worried if it wasn't."

"Maybe if I can find a way back, they will leave you alone."

"Hana, stop. Don't even think about that."

"Not thinking about it will not make it less true. I do not care what they do to me. They can have my eyes. My hands. My life. But I would never forgive myself if they found you."

"Look around you, Hana. We've escaped. We're free."

"I can still feel them, Kei. I can still hear their shrieks. They are close. I know it."

Keishin stopped rowing. "Come here," he said, taking Hana in his arms. He kissed the top of her head. "Hana—"

Talons burst from the water and dug into Keishin's arm. Keishin screamed in pain. Blood poured out from his wound. The Shiikuin pulled itself onto the raft, clutching Keishin's bleeding arm. "You do not belong here," it shrieked.

"Neither do you." Hana leapt at the Shiikuin, throwing herself and the creature into the water. The rippling reflection of a thousand golden moons swallowed them whole before Keishin could scream.

CHAPTER SIXTY

One Year Later

All love stories began with one word and ended with another. "Hello, goodbye." "Stay, leave." "Yes, no." When Keishin had met Jackie during his sophomore year in college, they started their relationship with an unremarkable "please" and ended it four months later with a polite "thank you."

A year after Hana had vanished from Super-Kamiokande's water tank, Keishin still struggled to figure out what their words were. He was inclined to settle on "sorry" as their first. It was his safest bet. They had wronged each other and sought forgiveness so many times that, statistically, one of their apologies had a high probability of standing at the border between where their friendship had ended and something harder to describe began. Determining their last word was more difficult. His last memory of Hana was made up of screams.

Keishin waited outside the ramen restaurant, burrowing his hands deep into his coat pockets to keep warm. Two people shivered in line ahead of him. He wished there were more. Hope kept him company while he waited and abandoned him as soon as he was ushered through the door. A year of disappointment had made him lose his taste for ramen but did not stop him from returning to the restaurant whenever he could. Still, there were days when making the trip from Gifu to Tokyo felt as futile as reaching out and trying to grab the moon.

Those were the same days that Keishin wondered if the real Keishin had been left behind in Hana's world and a Shiikuin had taken his place. He sat on the train, soulless and cold, an empty shell.

Despite what Keishin had learned in biology, purpose was more important for keeping someone alive than the blood in their veins. Having lost his, he was surprised that he was still breathing. It was, he thought, one of the strange things about being human. Even when you had nothing to live for, there was always going to be a part of you that refused to die.

A party of three people walked out of the restaurant, their bellies full and their faces content. The bearded man managing the queue waved the next three people in line inside. Keishin sucked in a breath and closed his eyes. He stepped through the doorway, repeating a fervent, frayed prayer. *Please, please be there.*

The clinking of bowls and cups gave Keishin an answer he did not wish to hear. He turned on his heel and fled, apologizing to the server who had let him in.

The sky broke open and emptied over Keishin, soaking into his shoes and socks. He had expected it. Every weather report that day had told him that it was going to rain. That's why he had left his umbrella in Gifu. He wanted to have the best chance of getting drenched. He took the longest route back to the train station and pushed up his sleeves. Maybe, this time, he was going to find the tattoo of Hana's name on his wrist and have proof that meeting her had been more than just a dream. Without it, all he had was a year's worth of train tickets and ramen receipts.

"I told you to bring an umbrella." Ramesh walked alongside

him, sheltering beneath a large black umbrella. "I'd offer to share mine with you, but I'm not really here."

Rain plastered the silver streak in Keishin's hair to his face. "I liked it better when we met at the restaurant."

"You chose to walk out of that cage. You can't go back."

"I chose Hana." Keishin stared at the empty spot on his wet wrist. "And she's not here."

"I'm sorry, Kei," Ramesh said. "But this is one problem that I cannot help you solve."

Keishin shoved his hands into his pockets and trudged to the station, holding his breath as he stepped into every puddle he could find. "I know."

His father had once told him that there was only one measure of how well a person spent his day. It depended on how much of the day you spent pining for the future or regretting your past. By that scale, Keishin was undoubtedly having a terrible one. He blew his nose and regretted, with every hacking cough, his decision to drown in the rain. He curled up beneath his covers, shivering. A knock on the door distracted him from his misery. "Come in," he said, his voice hoarse from a night of nonstop coughing.

"Dinner is served." Hana carried a bowl of soup on a tray into the room and set it on his bedside table. Pieces of tofu and shredded seaweed bobbed in a clear broth. "How is my patient?"

Keishin propped himself up against the headboard. "Better."

"You don't look any better. Let me check your temperature." She slipped a digital thermometer under his arm.

"Thanks for the soup."

"You're welcome. I made it from scratch," Hana said. "I opened the packet and poured boiling water over it all by myself."

Keishin chuckled then choked on a raspy cough.

A high-pitched beep interrupted him. Hana retrieved the thermometer and checked its small screen. She held it in front of him. "You're burning up."

Keishin waved the thermometer away and coughed. "I'm fine."

Hana rolled her eyes and pressed two paracetamol tablets into his hand. "Take this and try to get some sleep."

"No." Keishin clasped Hana's hand, dropping the tablets on the floor. "I don't want to."

"Why not?" She dabbed his forehead with a damp towel.

"Because when I wake up, you'll be gone. I know that you're just a dream. The only thing worse than losing you is losing you over and over again."

"You've dreamt about me before?"

"Many times. Different dreams, but they all end the same way." Keishin wept. "You leave me."

"Maybe this time it will be different." She climbed into bed next to him. "Maybe I'll stay."

Keishin put his arm around her. "No more lies, remember?"

"It's not a lie. It's a wish. I wish I were real."

Keishin tried to dry his tears, but more fell. He would have asked them to stop, but even in a dream, the only law they followed was gravity. "Do you know what I wish? I wish that I could grieve you. Grieving ends. But I can't grieve. You're not dead. You're just . . . *gone.* And I can't do one damn thing about it."

"I'm sorry." Hana laid her head on his chest.

"God, I miss you, Hana."

"I miss you too."

"Can you tell me a story?" Keishin closed his eyes. "Just until I fall asleep?"

"What story would you like to hear?"

"The one about the fisherman and the turtle that became a princess." Keishin pulled Hana close. "But this time, don't let him leave her in the sea."

"All right, but only if you do something for me too."

"Anything."

"Stop looking for me, Kei. I live in your past. You can line up at the restaurant all you want, but yesterday has no door."

CHAPTER SIXTY-ONE

The Last Bowl of Ramen

It looked exactly like the first bowl of ramen he'd ever had at the restaurant, but it tasted nothing like it. Two years of visiting the restaurant and finding nothing but a crowded dining room behind its door had soured the soup. Keishin gagged, struggling not to spit it out.

A woman wearing a strand of cheap plastic pearls took the empty seat next to him at the counter. The bun that held her silver hair threatened to come undone. She wore a faded shirt printed with the logo of a small flower shop chain.

People, Keishin thought, were a lot like neutrinos. Countless numbers passed right through you, unnoticed and invisible. The only time you noticed a neutrino was when it collided with a water molecule. In the silver-haired woman's case, Keishin would not have noticed her if her pink name tag had not fallen from her shirt and clattered on the floor by his foot. He picked up the tag and handed it back to her.

"Thank you." The woman dropped the tag into an overstuffed purse and smiled. "You look very familiar. Do you come here often?"

"No." He pushed back a silver lock of hair from his face. "I live in Gifu."

"Gifu? That's quite a long way to come for ramen. But I understand. It is the best in the city. May I ask what you do in Gifu?"

Keishin set his chopsticks down. "I watch the stars from beneath a mountain."

The woman raised her brows. "Wouldn't it be easier to watch the stars from the top of the mountain instead of under it?"

"I will pass your suggestion on to my boss. And how about you? What do you do? No. Wait. Let me guess. You work at a flower shop."

"How did you . . ." The woman glanced down at her shirt and chuckled. "Oh."

"Do you like working there?"

"On most days. I like flowers. People are always happy when they buy flowers." The woman narrowed her eyes at Keishin. "Are you sure that we haven't met before?"

"No, I don't think so."

"The mind plays tricks on you when you get older. Or perhaps it is simply wishful thinking."

"Wishful thinking?"

"My son would be your age now. But . . . I . . . we . . . lost touch a long time ago."

"I'm sorry to hear that. A son shouldn't abandon his mother."

The woman stared at her feet. "He didn't."

"Oh," Keishin said quietly. "I see."

"Leaving him was the worst mistake of my life," the woman said as though the entire restaurant had disappeared and she was talking to no one but herself.

"Why did you do it?"

"For the same reason all fools give up good things. We look at our hands and wonder what we could hold if they were empty." She hastily wiped the tears from her eyes. "I'm sorry. I don't know why I'm telling you all of this. You just seem so familiar. I feel like I know you. Please forgive me. I will leave you to your lunch."

"Do you ever think about your son?"

"All the time. I wonder if we've passed each other in the street or sat next to each other in a restaurant just like this one. Sometimes, I manage to convince myself that I've spotted him in a crowd even though I don't know what he looks like. Loneliness and regret have a way of making you see things that aren't really there."

Keishin stared into his bowl of ramen. He had intended it to be the last bowl he would have at this restaurant. Two years was a long time to stand in line for a bowl of disappointment. He had told himself that if he did not find Hana that day, he was going to let her go. Hoping for nothing cut deeper than the Shiikuin's talons. He touched the faint scar across his cheek. "Yes, they do."

"I apologize," the woman said. "Your ramen has grown cold."

"It's all right," Keishin said. "I don't mind."

"I'm sorry that it was your misfortune to sit next to a silly woman who has no one else to talk to. My boss scolds me whenever I chat too long with our customers. He told me that I should get a cat so that I could have someone to talk to when I get home. You are a very patient man to put up with me." She smiled at him. "Any mother would be lucky to have a son like you."

"Even you?"

"Of course. Very lucky. A mother's joy is raising a son who is considerate and kind even to people he doesn't know. It is a happiness that I gave up my right to know, and so I am grateful for the rare times I catch a glimpse of it."

Keishin checked his watch and stood up. "I'm sorry. I need to go. I have to catch a train. But please, allow me to pay for your meal."

She shook her head. "No. I couldn't impose."

"I insist. My mother would scold me if I didn't."

"Thank you." The woman smiled. "Have a safe trip."

Keishin bowed to her. "Have a good day, Takeda-san," he said, repeating the name he had read on her name tag. He had expected his mother's name to taste bitter, but it did not. Maybe in time, he thought, it might even taste sweet. "I hope that we meet again someday."

CHAPTER SIXTY-TWO

Five Years Later

College. Marriage. Kids. These were the big decisions that people believed mattered. They were wrong, of course. In reality, it was the choices that people didn't even realize they were making that set the course of their lives. The shifts were small, even minute, but, by the tiniest of angles, they pointed one in the direction of what was going to happen next.

In Keishin's case, everything that was going to define the rest of his life was decided the second his eyes shifted from the instant spicy pork ramen to the chicken-flavored one, then back to the pork. He reached for the bright red pack and dropped it into a green plastic basket. This was not the time to experiment with new flavors. His flight to Switzerland was at six the next morning, and the last thing he needed was a bad stomach. In less than twenty-four hours, he was going to stand in front of an auditorium filled with scientists and press and announce the greatest scientific discovery of the last five decades. He rehearsed his speech in his head. His phone rang over his thoughts. "Okaa-san?" he answered.

"Keishin, make sure that you do not eat anything spicy before your flight," Takeda Izumi said from the other end of the line. "You do not want to have a bad stomach before your speech."

"Don't worry." Keishin smiled. "I won't."

"I think I am more nervous than you are."

"As someone with some authority on the matter, I can tell you that that is scientifically not possible."

"I am so proud of you, Keishin. I love you."

"I love you too. I'll see you when I get back." Keishin stuffed his phone in his pocket. He took a step back from the ramen shelf, planting the thick heel of his boot squarely on top of something that was clearly too soft to be the convenience store's tiled floor. A sharp yelp shattered any hope that he'd wronged a wayward pastry instead of a stranger's foot. He twisted around, an apology tumbling from his tongue ahead of him. "Oh my god. I'm so sorry."

"It's all right." A woman with a ponytail that pulled her hair back from her heart-shaped face smiled at him. "I'm used to it."

"Hana . . ." Keishin dropped his basket. He scooped her up and broke down in sobs.

"I'm sorry I'm late." Hana wept into his shoulder.

Keishin set her down, refusing to blink, worried that if he did, she was going to disappear. "I went back to the restaurant so many times, but the pawnshop never appeared. I began to think that everything that had happened in your world was just a dream."

"You could not find the pawnshop because I tore it down."

"What? Why?"

"My world was broken, and someone had to fix it. The children in the tunnels made me realize that we never needed the choices the pawnshop acquired. We had told ourselves a lie for so long that we made it real. We trapped ourselves in a myth that we forgot we created. Learning to live with freedom is almost as difficult as learning to live without it. But the work has started. There is still a long way to go, but there are many who are now paving a new way. They do not need me anymore."

"Does that mean . . ."

"I'm staying," Hana said. "With you."

Keishin pulled her into an embrace. "I can't believe you're here. If you destroyed the pawnshop, how did you get here?"

"Collecting rainwater is always a good idea. You never know when you are going to need it." She pulled a little amber bottle from her bag. "A little bit goes a long way." She tucked the bottle back into the bag and extended her hand to him. "Hello. My name is Hana. What's yours?"

Keishin arched a brow. "What are you doing?"

"Starting over. It should be interesting trying to get to know each other when we are not running for our lives, don't you think?"

Keishin laughed and realized that he was crying at the same time. His chest lightened as his tears fell. It was remarkable, he thought, how much tears weighed. "Starting over without any lies." Keishin smiled through his tears and shook her hand. "My name's Keishin. I'm a doctor. The useless kind."

"It's nice to meet—"

"Hana, wait. On second thought, I think we may want to reserve the right to have a few lies now and then."

"Oh?"

"Small ones, you know, for the times when you might ask me if an outfit makes you look fat or if I ask you what you think of my cooking."

Hana laughed and clasped her hands around Keishin's nape. "So . . ." She smiled up at him. "Have you changed the world yet?"

"Not yet, but I will." Keishin checked his watch. "In about twenty-four hours, the world will finally discover what a bag is really for. And I don't want to spend another second of it standing in this store."

"It's raining."

"What's new?" Keishin led Hana outside and ran into the downpour. "It's just the weather telling us that we don't belong here."

"Or maybe, all this time, it's been trying to tell us something else." Hana held his rain-streaked face.

"Like what?" Keishin brought his lips next to hers.

"That we belong to each other."

ACKNOWLEDGMENTS

This book is in your hands because I was lucky enough to have met people in this lifetime who, for reasons that will forever be beyond my understanding, persist in believing that the words that wake me up at three in the morning are worth printing on a page.

To my parents, grandma, and family, who have loved everything I have written since before I could spell.

To my kids, whom I trust to groan and roll their eyes at the slightest hint of cringey-ness or clichés.

To "The Gang," who has not tired of luring me out of my writing cave with evenings of wine, food, talk, and did I say wine?

To Aueeie and Mina, who gamely strapped themselves in on this roller-coaster ride with me.

To Tricia and Frankie, whose vision, wisdom, and guidance have helped make this book the best version of itself.

To Amy, whose contagious passion and belief in this story gave me a new lease to do what I love.

To the amazing Team Water Moon at Penguin Random House and my international publishers, who have given their hearts, time, and talents to bring this book to life.

To Regina Flath and Fritz Metsch, whose creativity led to this wonderfully designed book.

To Haylee Morice, whose magical cover art profoundly captured the spirit of this story.

To Sachiko Suzuki, whose careful review and thoughtful insights have ensured that the beautiful culture that inspired this book was treated with utmost respect and sensitivity.

To Tennant, Alfie, and Westley, who are doggos that cannot read this book but who have, throughout their successful career of eating things they should not, taught me everything about living without regrets.

And finally, to the man I have shared half my life with, the choice I will make over and over again.

Thank you. Thank you. Thank you.

ABOUT THE AUTHOR

SAMANTHA SOTTO YAMBAO is a professional daydreamer, aspiring time traveler, and speculative fiction writer based in Manila. She is the author of *Before Ever After, Love and Gravity, A Dream of Trees,* and *The Beginning of Always. Water Moon* is her fifth novel.

samanthasotto.com

Facebook.com/samanthasotto

X: @samanthasotto

1
WATER MOON
2
WATER MOON
3
4
5
6
4-6
7
8
9
10
11
12
13